SHADOW MAN

ALAN DREW

CORVUS

Coventry City Council	
STO	
3 8002 02400 752 0	
Askews & Holts	Nov-2018
THR	£7.99

First published in the United States in 2017 by Random House, an imprint and division of Penguin Random House LLC, New York.

This paperback edition published in Great Britain in 2018 by Corvus, an imprint of Atlantic Books Ltd.

10 9 8 7 6 5 4 3 2 1

A CIP catalogue record for this book is available from the British Library.

Paperback ISBN: 978 1 78649 333 0
E-book ISBN: 978 1 78649 332 3

Printed and bound by CPI Group (UK) Ltd, Croydon, CR0 4YY

Corvus
An imprint of Atlantic Books Ltd
Ormond House
26–27 Boswell Street
London
WC1N 3JZ

www.corvus-books.co.uk

SHADOW MAN

By Alan Drew

Gardens of Water
Shadow Man

For Miriam, Nathaniel, and Adeline

Free yourself, like a gazelle from the hand of the hunter,
like a bird from the snare of the fowler.
—PROVERBS 6:5

Find a little strip, find a little stranger
Yeah you're gonna feel my hand
I got a livin' angel, want a little danger
Honey you're gonna feel my hand
—IGGY AND THE STOOGES

Part
One

THE THINGS THAT KEEP YOU SAFE

Electrical currents pulsed in the tip of each of his fingers. When he had keyed open the trunk of the car fifteen minutes earlier to find the gloves and the X-Acto knife, a spark had leapt off the keyhole. Now the wind was up, just as the man on the radio had said, ripping leaves from the eucalyptus trees and scattering them into the playground. There, beneath the bruised late-evening sky, a couple swayed on a swing, the teenage girl draped across her boyfriend's lap.

He leaned against a tree trunk for a moment and watched them—their tangled bodies swaying in a half circle, her small hand pressed against the boy's cheek, her kisses wide-mouthed and devouring. He peeled strips of bark from the tree until the green skin was exposed to the desert air. The two kids were aware of nothing except each other's body—not the wind, not the deepening darkness, not the screech of the swinging S-hook, not the man standing fifteen yards away in the night shadow of the bowing eucalyptus trees.

The streetlamps flickered to life, and suddenly the dark path of the greenbelt was illuminated, a cement walkway snaking the grass behind fenced backyards. The girl glanced up at the light, but her mind was focused on the boy, on the inner storm heating her body. She might have felt him there, he wasn't sure. People felt things; he'd learned that in the last few months—the heat of his eyes on the backs of their necks, his electric body radiating beneath the windowsill, the hint of his footsteps on their patio steps. It excited him, his presence pricking their awareness. He stood still in the darkness, just as he did now, watching their momentary pause as though hearing some primal echo of people once hunted. Yes, you were prey once.

The girl blinked blindly and then slid down her boyfriend's thighs, her hand moving toward his belt. He could see what her hand was doing, and a memory gripped him—a door thrown open to bursting light, fingers like giant spider legs prickling his skin, his childhood name whispered among the earwigs and beetle bugs and white curlicue worms of the basement. And his childhood voice spoke something, not in his head, not in the memory, but out loud into the present world.

"Who's there?" the girl said, and he was jolted back to himself. Dusk. Santa Ana winds. Greenbelt running through the center of a housing tract.

"Who the hell's there?" the boy spoke now, his voice pitched low to hide his sudden fear.

He liked the boy, liked his fear.

Awake to himself, he spun around the tree trunk and walked behind the grove of eucalyptus.

"Creeper," he heard the girl say.

"Rent a goddamned movie," the boy yelled after him.

His head throbbed now. The electricity buzzed in his teeth and the row of trees bowed over him, their limbs shaking in the wind. He could feel his left eye fluttering and closing, his mind spinning into vertigo until his adult self chastised his childhood self and everything found its place again in the world. The lights illuminating the path were like bright white moons stabbed into the ground. He was drawn into the warm pools of light and then into the cool darkness and back into light until he found himself in the half darkness of a flickering bulb. He stood for a moment beneath the staccato filament until finally it sparked and popped.

Another light caught his attention then. Beyond the pathway was a window. It glowed orange in the night and cast its mirror image on the mowed lawn beneath it. In that window stood a woman, her head enveloped in steam, her features smudged as though an eraser had been rubbed across her face. He watched the woman now, from the greenbelt, music from her stereo floating into the hot evening. Some sort of jazz, his fingers tingling with the beat, a cigarette-scorched singing voice turned loud to keep her company. She was alone, he could feel it. There was an opening in her fence — no locked gate, just a garden of stunted cactus twisting out of white rock.

He didn't always know what he was looking for. Sometimes he just went for walks in the neighborhoods — watching the boys in the street popping ollies on their skateboards, sniffing the dampness of pesticide sprayed on the grass, peering into windows where women slipped blouses over their heads. These neighborhoods with their privacy fences and dwarf palms, their greenbelt walks and rows of eucalyptus, their leaves spicing the air with oily mint. Here, in these neighborhoods, people left garage doors open, left backyard sliding glass doors unhinged. They slept with their windows cracked, the ocean breeze on their necks in the early morning. He might go three or four nights without the feeling. A week, maybe. Sometimes he got lucky and felt what he was looking for two nights in a row. Tonight, standing in the pool of darkness beneath a shorted-out bulb, he felt it, and he stepped over the cactus spines into her backyard.

He came up along the side of the house. There she was, bent over a cutting board, slicing tomatoes. She was cooking pasta, the starchy thickness of the noodles steaming out the screened side window, knotting his stomach. It had been a while since he'd eaten. The window beaded with steam, turning the glass into a mirror, and for a moment he could see half of his face. He'd caught only glimpses of it in the last few months — a shard of it in the rearview mirror, a cheek and an eye in the side-view, a nose and a forehead while bent over a sink, scouring his hands. His face was soft and boyish, and he was forced to look at it now, that baby face, until the woman slicked her hand across the pane and glanced through the window. He froze and stared back at her, feeling the charged current pass between them. If she saw him, he would run, but if she didn't . . . It was dark outside her window and he knew it was a mirror for her, too. When she tried to look through the glass, all she saw were her own eyes staring back, as though what had frightened her was imagined. No, he said to himself. What you're afraid of is real.

Then she turned to the sink and washed a bowl, her back to him, her shoulders sloped, her flowery housedress tangled around her waist. The music blared into the kitchen—trumpets, bass, drums rat-a-tat-tatting a beat, notes plinking through the screened window like pieces of candied metal. When she was finished she sat on a stool, facing the boiling pasta, and sipped a glass of wine. There was no ring on her finger, no one coming home to her tonight. He liked her, liked her loneliness; her aloneness would make things easier; people who had someone else, he had discovered, fought harder.

He found the sliding door. The glass was pulled back, the house opened to the hot wind. Just a screen separated him from the carpeted living room. He tugged on the handle. Locked. He felt his blood rush then, a brief fluttering of his left eye. The door to the basement had had a lock on it, an iron hinge clamped shut from the outside. When the door closed, when he was his childhood self, he had been like a bird with a hood pulled over his eyes, blinking in the darkness of his own brain until the voice in his head strung made-up syllables together and a space opened up in his mind where the voice lived and the voice kept him from being afraid.

Locked. The screen was locked. He watched the woman in the kitchen, her back bowed with heavy shoulders, the steam swirling above her head, the music a chaos of metal clinks. It's just aluminum and mesh, he wanted to say to her. Mesh and aluminum. The stupid things that make you feel safe. Doors and walls, screens and lights. He put on the gloves first, like slipping into new skin, and slit a line along the aluminum frame with the X-Acto knife—the plinking of each thread drowned by the squeal of trumpets. When it was cut, he peeled back the screen, and the mesh yawned open to let him inside.

1

E MMA WAS ALREADY UP IN THE SADDLE. SHE SIDESTEPPED GUS across the gravel driveway, the horse's hooves kicking up dust that blew across the yard.

"C'mon, Dad," Emma said. "It's getting late."

Detective Benjamin Wade was hammering the latch back onto the barn door. When they came up the driveway in his cruiser fifteen minutes earlier, the door was slung wide open, the latch ripped out of the wood by the gusting Santa Ana winds. The winds had burst into the coastal basin midmorning, dry gusts billowing off the desert in the east that electrified the air. The morning had been heavy with gritty smog, the taste of leaded gas on the tongue. By early afternoon, though, the basin was cleared out, the smog pushed out over the Pacific. A brown haze camouflaged Catalina Island, but here the sky was topaz, the needle grass in the hills undulating green from early-fall storms.

"I'll meet you up there," Emma said, spinning Gus around and cantering him up the trail.

"Hold on," Ben said. But she was already gone. He dropped the hammer, the latch swinging loose on a single nail. He pulled himself up onto Tin Man, raced the horse after her, and finally caught up to her on Bommer Ridge.

"You're getting slow, old man," Emma said, turning to smile at him.

"You're getting impatient."

"You want to be here as much as I do," she said.

That was true. This was exactly where he wanted to be—in the hills, riding a horse, with his daughter. They rode side by side now, Emma rocking back and forth on Gus's swayback. Tin Man snorted a protest, shaking his head to rattle the reins; the horse was getting too old for that kind of running, his cattle-rustling days well behind him. Gus and Tin Man were the last of the cutters. Four years ago, in 1982, when the cattle ranch officially shuttered the Hereford operations, they were set to be shipped off as dog-food canners. Ben wasn't having any of that, so he bought them for the price of their meat and taught his daughter to ride.

The horses guided themselves along the fading cow path past the old cowboy camp, hooves flushing jackrabbits out of sagebrush clumps. He smiled and watched Emma, her thin back and wiry legs in perfect control of Gus. He wished his father could have met her; she was a natural on a horse, a cowboy in a place that didn't need them anymore. They rode through a tangle of manzanita, the branches scratching their calves, and sidled through the shade of gasoline trees until they were in the open again, trailing the backbone of Quail Hill. A slope of poppies spread beneath them, blossoming orange into El Moro Canyon and down to the blue crescent of Crystal Cove.

One of the advantages of being a detective was the flexible hours, and when things were slow, as they mostly were in Rancho Santa Elena, Ben could pick up his daughter from school. He had done this for four years now, a reliable pleasure that continued even after the divorce was finalized a year and six days ago and he and his wife—his "ex-wife"—negotiated joint custody. Picking up was not a part of the settlement, but Rachel had stacks of papers to grade and when he proposed it to her she was thankful for the extra time. The added benefit of the gesture, too, was that sometimes Rachel gave him an extra night with Emma or let him take their daughter for horseback rides on weekday afternoons that weren't supposed to be his. He savored every moment with Emma; he figured he had another year or two of these afternoons together, and then it would be all boys and cruising South Coast Plaza mall with her girlfriends.

"How was the algebra test?" he said, taking advantage of the moment.

"Irrational."

He smiled.

"Shoot anyone today?" she said.

"Was in a gunfight over at Alta Plaza shopping center," he said. "You didn't hear about it?"

"I missed the breaking news."

It was her daily joke; in the four years since Ben had left the LAPD and moved south to join the Rancho Santa Elena police force, he hadn't discharged his weapon, except into the hearts of paper bad guys on the firing range out by the Marine base.

"How are you and Mrs. Ross getting along?" he said, hoping Emma hadn't gotten in another argument with her ninth-grade English teacher.

"Equitably," she said, another witty evasion. "Arrest anyone today?"

"Nope," he said. "But there's always tomorrow." He'd driven down to the Wedge in Newport Beach at sunrise, bodysurfed a few windblown waves, and rolled back into town by 8:00 A.M. for his shift. He'd awoken a man sleeping in his car on a new construction site in El Cazador, checked his tags, given the man his fresh coffee, and sent him on his way. He'd run IDs on a psychologist he suspected of selling psychotropics on the side. He'd been called to a skateboard shop off Via Rancho Parkway to hunt down two eleven-year-old boys who'd absconded with new Santa Cruz boards. "Just borrowing them, dude," one of the kids said, when he found them kick-flipping the boards at the local skate park. In master-planned Rancho Santa Elena, he was mostly a glorified security guard, paid to make residents feel safer in a place already numbingly safe—and both he and Emma knew it.

"How's your mother?" he asked, hoping for a tidbit.

"Domineering."

And there she went, standing in the stirrups, cantering Gus down the hill ahead of him. Rachel said it was normal, this pulling away from them—she was fourteen, after all—and he guessed it was, but it didn't make him feel any better about it.

"Take it easy," Ben called out to her. "It's steep here."

"Geez, Mr. Overprotective," she said, reining the horse in and plopping back in the saddle.

He could feel her rolling her eyes at him, a condition that had worsened in the last year.

Emma kept her distance now, trotting Gus along the ridgeline, the two of them disappearing behind an escarpment of rock before coming back into view. Down into Laguna Canyon, Ben could see the stitching of pink surveying flags waving in the wind—the "cut here" line for the new toll road, if the environmentalists couldn't fend it off. The flags followed an old cattle trail that led to the beach. On full moons, Ben and his father would ride the trail together in the shadows of the canyon, the hillsides rising milky white above them. This was the 1960s, before the developers had started bulldozing the hills, and the land was silently alive with owl and raccoon, with the illuminated eyes of bobcat. It was so wild back then that when a grizzly bear escaped a local wild-animal park, it took game wardens two weeks to hunt the animal down and shoot it in the darkness of a limestone cave. For thirteen days it was the last wild grizzly in California, making an honest symbol out of the state's flag.

After two hours of riding one moonlit night, Ben and his father had reached Route 1, recently renamed the Pacific Coast Highway, a four-lane expressway zipping cars up and down the coast. They had to sit perched on their horses for five minutes, waiting for the blur of headlights to pass. "In ten years," his father had said, bitterness in his voice, "everything will be goddamned concrete." His father had lived out here since the Dust Bowl days, he and his family escaping a bone-dry Kansas in '34, stepping off a coast-to-coast Greyhound into irrigated fields of orange groves. When he was ten, this was ranchland all the way down to the frothing surf, and he had spent his life watching it be slowly devoured. When there was finally a break in traffic, Ben and his father had nudged the horses across the cement until sand silenced the clipping hooves. They tied the horses to a gnarl of cactus and sat watching the bioluminescent waves crash the beach. It was the red tide, his father said—blooms of algae that sucked the oxygen from the water and flopped dead fish onto the beach. During the day the ocean was stained rust with it, but at night the foam of crashing waves glowed phosphorescent blue, swelling and ebbing bursts of light arcing down the coastline.

Ben and Emma reached the top of the hill now, the fledgling city of Rancho Santa Elena spreading beneath them in a patchwork of unfinished grids. Even when Ben was a kid, the basin had been mostly empty—a dusty street with a single Esso gas station, the crisscrossing runways of the Marine air base, a brand-new housing tract out by the new university, a few outlying buildings for ranchers and strawberry pickers. Now Rancho Santa Elena spread in an irregular geometry from the ocean to the base of the eastern hills of the Santa Ana Mountains, where newly paved roads cut swaths through orange groves. The center of town, the part of the master plan that was finished, looked vaguely Spanish—peaks of red-tiled rooftops organized in neat rows, man-made lakes with imported ducks, greenbelts cutting pathways for joggers and bicyclists. It was like watching a virus consume the soft tissue of land, spreading to join Los Angeles to the north.

A sudden screech, and an F-4 fighter jet roared above Emma's head. Tin Man leapt backward, and Gus startled and bucked, losing his purchase on the rocky trail.

"Heels in," he called out to Emma, as one of her hands lost grip on the reins.

Ben dug his boot heels into Tin Man's flanks and the horse steadied, but Gus stumbled down the hill and Emma flipped backward, thumping solidly on her back in the dirt. Ben was off Tin Man, rushing to her, and by the time he was there she was already sitting up, cursing the plane and its pilot.

"Asshole," she said, slapping dust from her jeans.

"You all right?" Ben said, his hand on her back.

"No." She slapped the ground, her brown eyes lit with fury. "I want to kill that guy."

"Anything broken?"

"No," she said, standing now. "Where's Gus?"

"Don't worry about the horse." She had fallen before, of course, but his panic never changed about it. "Just sit. Make sure your ribs are in the right place."

He touched the side of her back, pressed a little. She elbowed his hands away.

"I'm fine, Dad."

She went to Gus, who was shaking in a clump of cactus, a few thorns stabbing his flank. She hugged the horse's chest as Ben yanked the thorns out, points of blood bubbling out of the skin. The jet swerved around the eastern hills, dropped its landing gear, and glided to the tarmac.

"Asshole," Ben said.

"Yeah," Emma said, smiling. "Took the words right out of my mouth."

IT WAS NEARLY DARK WHEN they got back to the house, the western sky a propane blue. Emma walked the horses past his unmarked police cruiser and into the barn, and Ben retrieved a Ziploc bag of ice from the house and tried to hold it to Emma's back.

"Thanks, Dad," she said, hoisting the saddle off Gus, "but I'm fine."

He let her be and they worked their tacks alone, the rushing sound of the 405 Freeway in the distance.

Ben's house was in the flats on the edge of the city, down a dirt road that ended at a cattle fence that closed off Laguna Canyon and the coastal hills, a patch of wilderness, and the last of the old ranch. The place was a low-slung adobe, set in a carved-out square of orange grove—his father's house, a cowboy's joint, the house Ben had lived in until he was eleven. Emma had dubbed it "Casa de la Wade" three years before and the name stuck; they'd even fashioned a sign out of acetylene-torched wood and nailed it above the front door. When he and Rachel had moved back here from L.A. four years ago, they spent the first year in a rented apartment near the new university. He would drive out every once in a while to look in on the old place—the windows boarded up, the barn roof sagging. He had asked around at the corporate offices of the new "Rancho," out by John Wayne Airport. Some of the suits remembered his dad from back when it was a working ranch, not a corporation with valuable real estate to sell, and out of respect to his father's memory they let him have it for a moderately inflated price. The house and its acre of land hadn't then been part of the town's master plan; it was in the flight path of the military jets, and the Marines had wanted at least a quarter-mile perimeter of open land surrounding the runways in case an F-4 bit it on approach. The feds, though, had recently decided to close the base, and suddenly the Rancho Santa Elena Corporation zeroed in on the surrounding land. Letters from the Rancho's lawyers had already offered him 10 *percent over market value* for the place. He had written back and simply said, *Not interested*, though he knew they wouldn't give up so easily. The Rancho had already declared eminent domain to bulldoze artist cottages in Laguna Canyon. It had its sights set on the old cowboy camp at Bommer Canyon, too, just up the hill from Ben's place.

It took a year of evenings and weekends, one hammered broken finger, and a nail through the arch of his right foot to get the place in shape, though mostly it remained a cowboy flophouse, stinking of leather and coffee grounds, and he liked it that way.

Ben forked hay into the barn stalls now, while Emma cotton-balled Betadine onto the cactus cuts on Gus's flanks.

"You ready for softball?" he asked.

"I'm not going to play this year."

"You love softball." She had an arm; she could whip it around in a blur and pop the ball into the catcher's mitt.

"*You* love softball," she said.

"Why not?"

"You look at those girls in high school and they're all, I don't know, manly."

"Manly?" he said. His tomboy little girl had a sudden need to be "pretty." She'd started spending hours in the bathroom, rimming her eyes with eyeliner, thickening her lips with lipstick. "There's nothing wrong with those girls."

"I just don't wanna play anymore, all right?"

"I gotta talk with your mother about that," he said, glancing at her. Her face was tanned, her dark hair sun streaked. "And, by the way, you're perfect, if you ask me."

"Yeah, well, you're my dad, so it counts like forty-five percent."

Emma finished with the Betadine and closed Gus up in his stall. They had a big dinner planned—carne asada tacos, fresh avocado from the farmers' market, corn tortillas he'd picked up that morning from the tortilleria in Costa Mesa. *Back to the Future* had just come out on VHS, and he'd already slipped the cassette into the VCR.

The Motorola rang in the cruiser. He stepped over to the car and leaned through the open window to grab the receiver. "Yeah, it's Wade."

"Been trying to get you on the horn." It was Stephanie Martin, the evening dispatch.

"It's my night off."

"Hope you enjoyed it," she said. "Got a call from a Jonas Rafferty down in Mission Viejo. They got a DB down there that's still warm. He's asking for you."

A dead body. It had been a long time since he'd been on a murder scene.

"Gotta get you to your mother," Ben said to Emma.

"What about Fiesta Night?"

"Friday," he said, latching up the barn door. "We'll do it Friday. I'm sorry."

"You need a nine-to-five, Dad," Emma said.

Seven minutes later, he parked the cruiser in front of his ex-wife's new condominium in the center of town. Rachel opened the door a crack to let Emma in, but Ben still saw the man sitting on the couch, legs crossed at the knees, a glass of white wine resting in his palm as though cupping a breast.

"A professor?" Ben said, looking over Rachel's shoulder as Emma waved a hello to the man and walked to the kitchen. "Drives a Datsun four-banger?"

She smiled, the dimple in her left cheek killing him a little.

"C'mon, Ben," she said quietly. "You think I'm going to give you that?" She had used the shampoo he liked, cherry blossom or something like that, and for a moment in his mind her wet hair lay across her pillow next to him in the bed they used to share. "You've got a crime to solve, remember?"

"It's a DB," Ben said. "Barring a miracle, it's not going anywhere."

"Here?" she said. "In Santa Elena?"

"No," he said. "Mission Viejo."

"Thank God," she said. "Is Emma's homework done?"

He shook his head and Rachel sighed. "Out riding again?"

"She fell," Ben said.

"Jesus, Ben."

"One of those F-4s snuck up on us," he said. "Spooked Gus."

"She all right?"

"She says so," he said. "But check on her anyway."

"If she'll let me."

Apple in hand, Emma snuck behind Rachel and started up the steps to the second floor of the condo.

"Forgetting something?" Ben called through the cracked door. "Where's my kiss?"

"Geez, Dad," Emma said, pushing her way between her mother and the door. She leaned forward and deigned to present him her cheek, and Ben took advantage of the wide-open door to once-over the professor sitting on the couch. "Hey," Ben said, nodding once.

"How are you this evening?" the man said, not even bothering to uncross his legs.

Pompous ass. "Got any outstanding parking tickets?" Ben said in a serious voice.

The man shifted his weight on the couch.

"Ben," Rachel said, pushing him back from the door.

"A joke," Ben said, holding up his hands. "Just a little police humor."

"Go do your job, Ben," Rachel said, and then she closed the door.

A body was growing cold seven miles away, but he walked to the carport anyway, trying his hunch on the vehicles, looking for a University of California faculty parking tag, a MEAT IS MURDER bumper sticker, anything that would give the man away as an elitist wimp. And on the fifteen-minute drive down to Mission Viejo, riding the shoulder past a red sea of taillights, all he could think about was that man's soft hands on his ex-wife's skin in the bedroom next to where their daughter slept.

THE HOUSE WAS ON MAR Vista, off Alicia Parkway, .46 miles from the 5 Freeway, according to his odometer. The street was already a carnival, with neighbors straining the yellow tape and half of the Mission Viejo police force parked on the road, cruiser lights spinning blue and red circles. When Ben pulled up, Rafferty was standing on the porch, giving directions to a uniform. It was 7:47; Ben wrote it down on a yellow legal pad sitting on the passenger seat. Rafferty saw Ben's cruiser and waved him in.

Rafferty had been a vice detective in L.A., and he took the job in Mission Viejo for the same reasons Ben had taken the job in Santa Elena—safe neighborhoods, great schools for his two kids, little smog, good benefits and retirement plan, and an easier caseload, which allowed him to put his feet up at night with a beer and watch his sons swim in the backyard pool. Mission Viejo was another in a chain of master-planned communities in southern Orange County that set out to create an idyll that never existed—lakes where there had been rock, grass where there had been dust, shade where there had been sunlight. It survived on being the opposite of L.A.—clean, organized, boring. In L.A., people were used to crime scenes, used to the fact that there were bad people and they did bad things. Here, the neighbors crowding the crime-scene tape already carried the look of communal shock.

"Got a DB on the kitchen floor," Rafferty said, his voice pitched high with adrenaline. He placed his hand on Ben's shoulder; his palm was hot. "I'm glad you're here."

Since moving south, he and Rafferty had worked a couple of cases together—an illegal-immigrant smuggling operation with tentacles in both Mission Viejo and Santa Elena, a medical-insurance fraud case.

"Homicide's not vice, is it?" Ben said.

"At least no drugged-out chick is screaming at me," Rafferty said without any humor.

Ben could feel his blood pressure rise when they walked into the house. It was brutally hot, the heat of the day still trapped by the walls of the house. The foyer was lined with pictures of children or grandchildren, their smiling faces pinned behind glass. The living room was tidy—the carpet recently vacuumed, magazines stacked on a coffee table. Glass figurines—panda bears, cows, miniature unicorns, a seagull with wings outstretched—sparkled in a lighted cabinet against the far wall. A cheap oil painting of a wave catching the light of sunset, probably purchased at a convention-center art sale, hung askew. It wasn't until he saw what was in the kitchen that he understood what had knocked it off-kilter.

Scuff marks blackened the yellow wall, the sole of one of her shoes ripped apart at the toe. She had kicked and kicked the common wall that separated the living room from the kitchen and nearly knocked the picture off the hook. The woman's legs were pale in the kitchen light, her dress pushed above her knees. Her torso and face were hidden behind the kitchen island. On top of that island was a cutting board, a tomato sliced into thirds, and a knife slicked with pulp and seed. A fan motor rattled above the oven. A pot of pasta sat on the stove top, the smell of starch thickening the heat in the room. The screen to the sliding back door had been peeled open.

"Anyone touch that door?" Ben said to Rafferty.

"No," he said. "First on scene said it was like that when he got here."

She had been at the cutting board, he guessed, her back to the door. Between the fan and the boiling water, and the carpet on the floor to soften the intruder's footsteps, she wouldn't have heard anyone sneaking up behind her.

"Get someone to print that," Ben said, pointing to the stove.

There was another smell, too. When he came around the corner of the island, he saw the puddle glistening beneath her dress, the orange flowers deepening red where it was soaked with her urine. He could tell she had been strangled before he saw the bruises on her neck and the fingernail crescents cutting blood out of her skin, before he saw the scratches crisscrossing her chin, before he discovered the petechiae around her eyes like little pinhole blisters.

"Medical examiner on the way?" Ben asked.

"Don't have one." Rafferty shook his head. "It's me."

"The perks of living in paradise, huh?"

"I can do it," he said. "I just don't want to fuck it up. That's why I called you. I mean, this is the guy, right?"

"Let's not get ahead of ourselves," Ben said.

In recent months, there had been a series of killings in L.A. and northern Orange County, mostly manual strangulations. No one yet had said there was a serial on the loose, but cops had started to whisper exactly that to one another. The last body, six days ago, had turned up in Seal Beach, thirty-five miles away.

Ben knelt down next to the body. One eye was open, the sclera red with broken blood vessels.

"She fought," Ben said. "Hard."

The woman was in her late forties, at least. Barefoot, a reddening burn on her left thigh—from splashed pasta water, he guessed. Jesus. Ben could understand the shootings in L.A. It was business, a twisted ethic among the gangs, a harsh world with harsh laws, and the kids bought into it. But not even a Crip or Blood, not even a Loco, would strangle the life out of someone. It was too much work, too personal, too brutal. You had to be out of your head angry to do such a thing, psychotic angry, or else you had to enjoy it, had to find pleasure in the power of your hands.

"Who found her?"

"Anonymous tip," Rafferty said.

"The killer?"

"That's my guess," Rafferty said. "Doesn't seem to have much faith in us."

"Look what I've done," Ben muttered, looking at the bruises on the woman's neck.

"What?" Rafferty said.

"This guy wants an audience."

"Sick dick."

"Get a call in to the Orange County ME," Ben said. "We need some science down here."

NATASHA BETENCOURT WAS IN THE MIDDLE OF TEACHING A class on weighing organs. Liver, 1,560 grams. Lungs, 621 grams. And the heart: 315. That always surprised the UC students, the lightness of the heart. When the call came in, she was placing a kidney (276 grams) on the scale. Some of the students had tissue paper stuffed up their nostrils—a bad idea, she told them, since you tasted the stink then; tamp down one sense and another compensates. Vicks was the way to go, but everyone dealt with the smell the way they dealt with it. She'd already lost two students to the toilets. The first one with the Y cut and the second when she unraveled the lungs. Those were the sentimental ones. She had a soft spot for those students; they still attached a person to a body, still sympathized with the cadaver. An admirable sentiment, but misplaced and ultimately ineffective in this line of work. "The soul flew away a long time ago," she liked to say in the examination room. "Just tissue and bone here."

"Detective Wade on the line," Mendenhall said, his head poking through the half-open examination room door. "Needs you down in Mission Viejo."

"You wanna take over?"

Mendenhall, the lieutenant medical examiner, never taught classes. He felt it was beneath him to walk the UC students around, much less show them how to use a Stryker saw, so it was left to Natasha, his deputy. Charging her to teach the classes was Mendenhall's way of reminding her that a woman didn't belong in the medical examiner's office, though he was more than happy to let her do most of the work. Worse than his disdain for teaching, though, was Mendenhall's distaste for fieldwork. Too messy. He was all clinical, liked to keep his shoes clean.

"School's out early," he announced to her students.

Natasha was in Mission Viejo in thirty-five minutes, smoking cigarettes on the way to kill the stench of the examination room. The smell: It didn't bother her in the lab, but out in the world it did, when she felt it was tangled in her hair, trapped in the fibers of her clothes. That was the problem with being an ME: balancing the examination room and the outside world. Everything was clear in the medical examiner's office but not out here, not at all.

She ducked under the yellow tape in front of the house, stepped through the foyer into the kitchen, and came around the corner of the island to take in the scene.

"I thought this kind of thing didn't happen down here," she said to Ben, who was down on his haunches, taking notes on a yellow legal pad.

"It didn't," Ben said. "Until it did."

She set her kit down on the floor and knelt across from Ben. One of the deceased woman's blue eyes stared at her. She understood why Mendenhall didn't like the field. The examination room was impersonal, but kneeling next to a body on the floor of her own kitchen was a different thing. The woman had been alive just minutes before; the color was still in her cheeks. Alive was alive, dead was dead. Where the two met was the difficult part. In your mercy, she thought, turn the darkness of death into the dawn of new life. She hadn't been to Mass in years, but being on scene always brought out the Catholic schoolgirl in her.

"Strangled," Ben said.

"I see that." She opened the kit and slipped on gloves. Petechiae. A necklace of bruises around the throat. "You been out riding?"

"How'd you know?"

"You smell like horse."

Fractured hyoid bone. The larynx caved in.

"You need anything, sweetheart?"

Natasha turned to find a detective standing over her, his badge dangling from his leather belt, his face full of condescension. "Yeah, *honey,*" she said. Crime scenes were generally a boys' club, full of testosterone-driven machismo. "I need you and all these other idiots out of my crime scene."

Ben looked at the floor and smiled. The detective, without another word, cleared the kitchen. Cops. These entitled little boys.

"How's Emma?" Natasha asked. She had shared an In-N-Out burger with Ben and Emma a week ago—his invitation—but he hadn't called her since. A little over par for the course for him.

"She's a teenager." He shrugged.

"Ah, you're not her knight in shining armor anymore."

Ben flashed her an ironic look and then got back to business. "Seems like it's manual," Ben said, pointing to the woman's neck. "No ligature."

"Is that so?" Natasha said. "Go do your job, Ben, and let me do mine."

"Right," he said, slapping his thighs before standing up.

"One more thing," Natasha said. "What's her name?"

"Hold on. I got it written down."

Ben flipped pages on the legal pad while Natasha got down on her elbows, Dictaphone in hand, and examined the woman's neck. She would have passed out quickly, but the killer would have had to stare into her face for two to three minutes—a quiet face, a nice one—crushing the trachea, snuffing her out with his hands before the brain shut down.

"Emily," Ben said finally. "Emily Thomas."

"All right, Emily," Natasha said quietly, so only Emily could hear. *Cardinal sin*, she'd tell her students. *Don't personalize the body.* But on scene was different; on scene there was disturbed energy in the air. "Show me what he did to you."

IN THE THIRTY-FIVE MINUTES THEY had waited for Natasha, Ben had studied the sliced-open door screen: a clean cut, with a scalpel-like instrument, probably an X-Acto knife. The chrome appliances shone in the kitchen track lighting, none of them smudged—at least to the naked eye—by an intruder's fingertips. Ben had stuck his nose down near the dead woman's neck, to see if he could smell it. There it was, the petroleum-and-baby-powder scent: The killer had worn latex gloves. Ben had sent a uniform out to interview the neighbors, too, asking them if they saw anything unusual—a car parked on the street, a man climbing a fence or slipping behind the shrubbery. Nothing.

Natasha was on her knees photographing the body, a bright flash and then everything back into focus. A junior detective finally finger-printed the stove, and Ben turned off the fan so he could hear himself think.

"Broken hyoid bone," Natasha said into her Dictaphone. Then whispering, not into the Dictaphone but almost as if she were sharing secrets with the woman. He'd seen her do it before—when a boy drowned in a backyard pool, when a woman was hit by an Amtrak train. He almost asked her about it one night when they were out having drinks but decided against it. Another camera flash, everything overexposed, then all the colors and shapes in the right place again. "Dead sixty to ninety minutes."

"What's with her?" Rafferty said.

"Natasha?" Ben said, smiling. "She's not the 'sweetheart' type."

"What a bitch."

Ben bristled a bit. "Jonas, how about calling her 'Dr. Beten-court'?"

Rafferty had gridded the house. Officers were searching each section for evidence. It was still horrifically hot inside, humid with pasta steam, stinking of death and onions. In the time since he'd last been on a murder scene, whatever immunity Ben had built up to it had been lost. Homicide was not like riding a bike. He watched Natasha, stretched across the kitchen floor, side by side with the DB — flash — then stepped outside for some fresh air.

The street was a circus. Reporters pushing against the yellow tape, kids on BMX bikes gawking at the scene, a neighbor crying. He saw, between two houses, a couple walking a golden retriever on a path beyond the backyard, beneath a burned-out streetlight.

"Jesus Christ," he mumbled. "Suburban cops." He climbed the front lawn and walked back into the house and found Rafferty bent over an investigator dusting the screen door for prints.

"Raff," Ben said. "We need a perimeter back here."

Rafferty called out to a couple of uniforms and Ben squeezed through the torn opening of the screen door, following a line of matted grass with a flashlight to a cactus garden at the edge of the backyard. There he saw the prints — Vans skateboard shoes; he could tell by the hexagonal pattern outlined in the pale soil. Eights or nines, he guessed. A uniform was rolling out tape that cut off the backyard from the greenbelt.

"Go inside," Ben told the cop, "and tell Rafferty to get someone out here to take pictures of these."

Then Ben was up on the greenbelt sidewalk, standing beneath the blown-out bulb and the eucalyptus bowing in the wind. Every hundred feet down the path stood a brightly lit streetlamp, except here, except right here. The house to the left had a six-foot privacy fence and a locked gate. The house on the right had a line of juniper trees, maybe ten feet tall, cutting the backyard off from this one. It wasn't difficult to see why the killer chose this house. There were no clear lines of sight from the neighbors'; the only place where you could see inside was right here. He stood in the dark and watched a house full of men combing the first floor. He could see Natasha on her knees now, snapping more photos of the body, the warm light framed by the windows like an invitation.

NATASHA ACCOMPANIED THE BODY UP to the county ME's office in Orange nearing midnight. Ben left the scene to Rafferty and was back at the station in Santa Elena by 12:52 A.M. The night-shift cops were hauling in the drunks, lawyers, and businessmen, one VP for Security Pacific Bank threatening to sue. He typed up his report and left it on Lieutenant Hernandez's desk. It was Rafferty's case, Mission Viejo being out of his jurisdiction, but Ben made it official anyway. He liked to dot his i's and cross his t's. Every deadbeat he'd known, every crooked cop, had cut corners, used loopholes, exploited vulnerability. *Follow the rules*, he liked to tell Emma; *it'll make you a good person.*

He left the station at 1:42 and drove the mile over to Rachel's condominium, idling the cruiser in the complex parking lot. The rush of the freeway echoed hollow, as though the sound carried all the way from Los Angeles and beyond. If the killer had driven the Santa Ana down to Mission Viejo earlier tonight, he'd passed the off-ramp that led straight to this condo. Ben could tell the kitchen window was wide open. He knew, too, that Rachel liked to leave the sliding glass door to the backyard open, the ocean breeze cooling the rooms. That's why they'd moved back here. It was safe; you could leave your doors unlocked. Hell, you could leave them flung wide open.

A blue light flashed from Rachel's window, and he knew she had fallen asleep with the television on. A wave of satisfaction washed over him; the professor hadn't stayed over. If things hadn't fallen apart between them, he would sneak into the room right now to find her clasping two pillows to her chest. He'd click off the screen and slip into bed with her in the beautiful silence of the early morning, everything he gave a damn about breathing the same air he did.

The move here was supposed to save their marriage. The last

straw, the thing that finally made them pack up their Marina del Rey apartment and drive the thirty-eight miles south in a rented U-Haul, was the shooting. Emma had been nine then, and Ben had been popped in the left arm six months before in East Hollywood by a twelve-year-old gangbanger who had been forced into a blood-in initiation ritual by his older brother, a heavy in the La Mirada Locos. Shoot the 5-0 and you're in; don't shoot the cop and you're out and we won't protect you. That was the kind of choice kids in the worst L.A. neighborhoods had to make. Ben didn't even see the kid; heard the shot and then felt the burn in his arm, just like that, the bullet streaking through his unmarked Ford's open window. There was a shitload of blood, slicked over the armrest and splattered across the steering wheel. He called it in but didn't wait around to bleed to death; he gunned the car to St. Vincent and walked himself in, his head like helium by the time the nurses got the gurney.

Later, at the court hearing, the kid had apologized, dressed in a suit too big for his underfed body, a sewing-needle tattoo etching the side of his neck. Not even shaving yet, his voice still singing soprano, and already owned by the street. He was sent to juvie and then released to the custody of his grandparents, and two weeks later the kid ended up facedown in a vacant lot, shot in the back of the head by his cousin, a smog-stunted palm tree waving above him. And that was it for Ben; what the hell were you supposed to do with that? He investigated the murders, sure—the drive-bys, the drug deals gone bad—but he tried to work with the kids, too, tried to show them a way out. He had naïvely thought he could bring some order to their lives. But once it went Cain and Abel over gang allegiance, what could you do? That was something permanent, something rotten in the culture.

At the time, he didn't tell Rachel it was a kid who shot him. What was he going to say? A prepubescent child nearly sent him toes up? Jesus, it rattled him enough, not to mention how it would scramble her. The hole in his arm was all she needed to know. They had to get themselves out of L.A. Rachel was too unhappy, too confused. She couldn't take it anymore—the constant worry, her exhausting teaching position at the underfunded high school in North Hollywood. At first the job felt like an admirable mission to a third-world country, but it quickly grew into an exhausting exercise in futility. L.A. had worn them out—Rachel trying to save the kids with education and Ben trying to save them with the law, and their marriage going down the toilet. Not to mention Emma's own educational future. L.A. public? No way. They had a child to raise and Rachel wasn't going to do it alone, and he was damn well not going to make her. Rachel wanted to go home, back to Santa Elena, where they both grew up, back to where things didn't seem to be spinning out of control.

The Santa Elena assistant police lieutenant, Ramon Hernandez, had been fishing partners with Ben's late father, and the police department was expanding. Ben got an interview, and the job offer came two weeks later. Rachel found a good job at the high school in El Toro, the next town over, and all the dimly lit stars aligned. Now here they were, nearly five years gone, in the gorgeous other side of L.A., and everything had finally gone to hell.

Sometimes he thought if he had stayed on the force in L.A., they would still be together. During the day, he and Rachel would be bound by their fear, and in the evening they'd share the relief that someone hadn't popped a hollow-tipped bullet into his chest. It was too good in Santa Elena, too easy to get bored, to be sucked into the vortex of complacency. You started to believe you deserved more than you had, deserved what your neighbor had—and they always had more—and once you started thinking like that there was an anxiousness that set in on you, a rotting dissatisfaction. Maybe that's what happened to them after they moved here. When you had it bad, you were glad for the good, any good. When you had it good, you wanted it better.

Emma's window was dark, glowing only with a string of white Christmas lights she kept hung from the ceiling year-round. He got out of the car and walked the sprinkler-dampened grass to the back of the condo. As he suspected, the sliding glass door was pulled open, just the screen separating outside from in. He tugged on the plastic handle, but the lock was engaged. He found the penknife in his coat pocket, jimmied the lock free, and slid the door open. Click locks were nothing; door locks could be picked with a paper clip. Only deadbolts were worth a damn. He stood there for a moment in the dark, waiting to hear Rachel moving upstairs. Silence. It was too easy to get in; thirty seconds and the killer could be standing in the family room. He closed the screen and the sliding glass door, engaging both locks. He walked the edge of the room, jumping around the creaky spots on the floor—he'd visited enough to know such things—and slid closed and locked the window in the kitchen. A pad of paper was sitting near the phone and he wrote Rachel a note.

You're going to be pissed off, he wrote, *but ask me about it later.*

He checked the coffeemaker. The timer wasn't set, no coffee in the filter. Ben had always taken care of the coffee, a full pot at 5:30 A.M. every day. He found the tin in the cupboard and scooped a few spoonfuls into the filter. He set the timer, pressed start, and left the note propped up against a clean coffee mug.

He snuck through the hallway into the foyer and stood gazing up at the weak light emanating from Emma's cracked bedroom door. He wanted to go up there, wanted to kiss his daughter, wanted to crawl into bed with Rachel. He wanted to rewind the last five years of their lives together, pinpoint the places he'd screwed up, and fix them all. But of all the useless thoughts in the world, this was the most useless. All you could do was say you were sorry and hope they believed it.

He opened the front door by millimeters, turned the door-handle lock—man, they needed a deadbolt—and stepped out into the night, pulling the door closed behind him and checking it twice to make sure the lock was engaged.

AFTER THE AMBULANCE DELIVERED THE body to the medical examiner's office, Natasha was alone in the examination room. The body lay on a stainless-steel gurney, covered to the toes by a blue sheet. She found a tag, wrote down the woman's name—*Emily*—and tied it to the big toe on her right foot. The toenails were painted with chipping teal enamel.

She liked it like this, the silence, particularly after being on scene. On scene, the body seemed demeaned to her, all those people milling around, standing over it, the chaos of an investigation. Here, the bleached-white tile of the examination room felt appropriately serious to the disrespectful task of opening up a body. Here, her job was clear: Determine the cause of death. Not: Who caused the death? Not: Why did they kill? Just: What? Straightforward, objective. It was like a puzzle with clear rules, like the ones her father, an immunologist, used to play with her as a child. "If this cell kills this bacteria," he would say, "why does it not kill this one?"

An autopsy couldn't be performed until next of kin were notified, a job that got left to the detectives. But she would wash the body tonight, dignify it by making it clean. She wheeled the gurney over to the floor drain near the sink, soaked a cloth, pulled back the sheet, and pressed the cloth between Emily's toes. She swabbed the arch of her right foot and then her left. She then moved up the woman's calves, washing away the indignity of having lost her bowels, the blood starting to pool purple in the fat of her thighs.

Natasha couldn't help it; it always disturbed her, the bodies of women killed violently. Men who had been shot or stabbed, men who had OD'd, men's bodies in general, didn't bother her; for the most part they were killed by some stupid business they'd gotten themselves into. But not the women. Women, most often, were killed by the men who got themselves into stupid business. She tried to remind herself that death was death, equal in its permanence, but the moments before death were not equal in their terror, and Natasha couldn't convince herself not to be bothered by this.

She moved up Emily's torso, washing away the sweat of the day, then wiped clean the more-intimate places, tossing one cloth out and starting again with a fresh one.

She remembered the night on Signal Hill; it sometimes came to her when she was here alone with a female body. "Let's go watch the submarine races," the boy had said, leaning into her in the doorway. She had been at a frat party. A stupid nineteen-year-old girl. She wasn't a little sister, but her roommate at the time, Kris, had been. It was a cheap night out—a backyard keg, jugs of wine, boys, most of them clean-cut and drunk. She had known this boy, the one with the plastic cup of beer dangling from his fingers, the one with the blue eyes and the easy smile. He had been in her psych class and she had watched him from afar, flirted with him over coffee in the university courtyard. Submarine races? The joke was so obscure she couldn't register its meaning. She was a little drunk herself and enjoying the loose feeling of her muscles, her sudden lack of anxiety, the boy's blue eyes on her. "Sure," she'd said, laughing.

The boy—well, he was a sophomore in college, twenty—had parked the car, a nice car, a Camaro, on the edge of a ravine, the orange port lights of Long Beach spread beneath them like shattered glass, the mechanical hum of oil derricks pumping behind them. There was one other car parked on the edge of the hill, thirty yards away, and she remembered seeing the glowing point of a lit cigarette behind the darkened glass. And when the boy started pressing himself against her, she'd said no—at least, that's what she remembered saying. And when he'd gotten his hands up her shirt, she had said no again, but he was drunk and moving quickly, and her back was pushed up against the door handle, and he was six foot four—something she'd admired about him, his lanky limbs, his butterflied back—and it was over quickly. Afterward he'd kissed her on the neck, tenderly, as though what had just happened held great meaning for him. And his passion, his belated tenderness, confused her.

Natasha washed around the woman's breasts now, cleaning away dried sweat, and then moved to her neck, where the killer's hands had clamped down, and dabbed the cloth on the crescent-shaped cuts surrounding her esophagus.

She didn't think about that night often; it didn't obsess her. It simply floated into her mind occasionally, when the deceased had been sexually assaulted, strangled. The submarine races. She had been drunk, and he had been speaking in code, a code she later discovered other girls spoke. She'd gone out on a date with him a week later, the boy using his fake ID to buy them a bottle of Blue Nun at a little Italian place strung with white Christmas lights. She'd even let him kiss her at her dorm room door. Let him place his fingers on the curve of her left breast, all of her insides cramping into knots. He called her again two days later, and she told him he was nice but that she wasn't interested in dating someone right now. She could hear the disappointment in his voice, hear him saying, "But I thought—" and "What the hell, Natasha." She hadn't been a virgin, they'd both been drunk, he was mostly a nice boy, and she let it go, burying herself in her studies after that. Getting straight A's the rest of the year, grades she'd never gotten before, grades that prompted her parents to take her out for a lobster dinner at Nieuport 17. "We're so proud of you," her father had said. "I knew you could do it."

She pulled back the sheet to expose the woman's face, Emily's face. She washed the dried vomit from the woman's lips. Then she washed the hair, too, combing out the tangles with her gloved fingers.

"You did nothing wrong," she told Emily, while she strung out her wet hair on the stainless-steel table. "You did not deserve this."

It was nearly 3:00 A.M., the coffee had worn off, and she could use herself as a cautionary tale in her classes. *Don't get attached; keep the heart for the outside world. Draw lines between work and home. Don't lose your husband to an aerobic-dancing account executive.* "It freaks me out," he'd said to her once. "Spending all your time with dead people. It's like you bring them home with you."

She pulled the sheet over Emily's face and was presented with only the body. She looked at the neck again and noticed something. After finding a tape measure, Natasha counted the span of the fingernail cuts. From bloodied crescent to bloodied crescent: 172 mm. She set the tape down and spread her hand across the body's neck, her fingers shadowing the marks left by the killer.

She peeled off her gloves and found the phone on her desk.

"Wade," Ben said when he picked up.

"You sleeping?" she said.

"You kidding?"

"Out in the barn?" she said.

"Can't think at the station."

"You should come over here," she said. "It's dead quiet."

He chuckled, but she could tell he was troubled by the night, too, and sometimes black humor didn't work no matter how much you needed it to.

"Small hands," she said.

"What?"

"Whoever killed this woman has small hands," she said. "No bigger than mine."

"The killer's a woman?"

"That's your job," she said. "But they're woman-sized hands."

BEN GOT OFF THE PHONE with Natasha and put a call in to Rafferty to tell him what Natasha had discovered about the killer's hands. He got the detective's station voicemail. Probably at home asleep in bed with his wife. Rafferty was one of the few cops he knew who was still married, despite his taking liberties while working vice in L.A. Delia, his wife, had found out; that's what prompted the move south, though Ben knew once a man started craving anonymous sex, no clean streets or nice parks or evenings by the pool with the kids would satiate that urge. The boredom of it all most likely fed the impulse. He left a message telling Rafferty to call him in the morning and turned on the scanner.

Soon after he and Rachel had moved into the house from L.A., Ben had rigged up a den for himself in one of the unused stables in the barn. Desk, police scanner, boom-box stereo, a mouse nest in the corner behind the old empty feed trough. He had fastened a combo-locker to the wall where he kept his .40 caliber, empty of bullets, safety on. There was a 12 gauge, too, and his father's Browning bolt-action, all of them under lock and key. He didn't like bringing the ugly side of the job into the house—the gun, the handcuffs, the pho-tographs; he wanted the illusion for his daughter and his wife that nothing ugly happened here. It was the illusion that all happy child-hoods were built upon. To be happy in this world, you had to ignore some things.

It was the usual stuff on the L.A. County scanner tonight—drive-by on Whittier Boulevard in East L.A.; robbery in progress at Las Palmas gas station, both suspects "black and short," according to the dispatch; DUI in West Hollywood, Ferrari, "a person of note," the uniform said over the radio with a bit of glee: an actor, of course.

Ben had left the barn door open, the dry air blowing through the gabled rooftop. He watched the eucalyptus bow in the Santa Anas; gusts to sixty tonight, the forecast said, maybe seventy—a dry hurri-cane. The barn frame creaked; blasts of dry air puffed through gaps in the wooden slats.

Ben had a topo map of the basin, from Oxnard to Oceanside, hanging on the wall—the bowl of land terraced downward toward the beach, the shoved-together cities like detritus washed down the ravines of the San Gabriel Mountains. He found the Mission Viejo scene on the map and penciled a mark on the street: 1431 Mar Vista, just off the 5 Freeway.

The scanner went quiet, a white hush of static in the room, and he switched it over to the Orange County wire. He pushed a file on his desk aside—surveillance photos of a suspected cocaine dealer in Santa Elena. The man ran an RV dealership he'd taken over from his father in the seventies. He had three kids, a wife—a very thin, young, Mercedes-driving wife, who often suffered nosebleeds at the gym, according to one of the detectives. Ben had an informant, a fright-ened ad executive picked up for possession in the bathroom of a Ben-nigan's out by the airport. *Tell us your supplier and there'll be no*

charges. Simple stuff. He'd been out to interview the dealer at Travel-
and, tailed him going in and out of restaurants, but had nothing yet
to hang a search warrant on. He could ignore the guy, honestly, just
let him keep snorting the stuff and selling the stuff to be snorted by
his buddies. No one was fighting for market share, for territory; these
weren't people terrorizing a neighborhood to build an empire. They
were wealthy and bored and wanted to get high. Polite criminals, the
type Santa Elena could tolerate.

The scanner squawked: a woman on the number 54 bus in Orange threatening to shoot the driver for not pulling over at her stop.

A wash of static again, electricity humming the wires.

He ran his index finger up the Santa Ana Freeway and rode the
interchange to the 405 up to the Seal Beach crime scene, the last
place the serial killer hit.

Fullerton clicked in. 242. Frat-party fight.

A gust shook the rafters of the barn, and Annie Oakley—Rachel's
horse—kicked the boards next door. "Shh," he said. "It's all right,
girl. Just the wind."

He slid his finger back onto the 405, traced the freeway past the
industrial stench of Carson and the civil war that was Compton. A
murder felt like a disruption in the atmosphere, but it wasn't. You got
used to it, mostly. Most of the time the killings made twisted sense—
a dealer crowding in on another's territory, revenge for stolen money,
a man losing his mind when he discovers his wife's lover. A serial
killer, though, that was something different. The serial killed for the
sole purpose of killing; that was like a hole opening up in the sky and
letting out the oxygen.

He pushed his finger south onto the 110 toward the harbor, until
he came to the estates of Palos Verdes. The third house the killer hit
was right there, a few blocks off the highway. He'd already pinned it
with a red wall tack.

The box squawked again. 503. Stolen car. Huntington Beach.

He ran the basin with his finger, cruising the freeways, trying to
find a thread, a connection, a symbol etched into the map between

red pins—La Cañada, Santa Monica, Palos Verdes, Seal Beach, Diamond Bar, Yorba Linda, and now Mission Viejo. Nothing. Just freeways, off-ramps, seven houses and seven murders spread over 1,200
square miles.

The scanner was quiet, the static hum of the early-morning calm.
Even killers sleep. He switched it off, clicked a cassette tape of Marvin Gaye, and stared at the map.

"Ah, things ain't what they used to be, no no . . ."

He pictured the woman on the floor of her kitchen tonight, contorted with stiffened muscles, and that memory collided with the
memory of Emma falling off Gus. The way she went down—
backward, headfirst—was just the way it had happened to his father.
Sitting there on Tin Man, he was terrified Emma was going to break
her neck. He was sure of it, and he couldn't shake the feeling of that
knowledge; for a moment, in his heart, she had died. Talk about an
atmospheric disruption.

"Poison is the wind that blows from the north and south and
east . . ." Marvin crooned.

The afternoon of the day his father was killed, they had been
pushing the cattle into Bommer Canyon, where the grass was still
knee-high. His father, up on the ridge, herded the cows toward Ben,
down in the flats. A heifer was bawling at a clump of manzanita, her
cries echoing off the limestone wall of the hillside. It was early summer, just a few months after birthing season, and when Ben came
up along the side of the cow he saw her calf in the bushes, its head
flopping up and down. Camouflaged in the brush, a mountain lion
had its nose buried in the calf's stomach, devouring the still-living
animal's intestines. The lion was ten feet away, just ten feet. Ben
could have taken a shot, could have blasted open the lion's skull,
but his stomach upended and he dry-heaved into the bushes. By
the time Ben got his stomach back, his father was racing down the
hill, popping off shots at the lion. All three shots missed, and the
lion bolted up the rocks, all claws and sinew, into the deep brush
beyond.

"Put that animal out of his misery," Ben's father said to him, before he heeled his horse into pursuit down the finger canyon.

Ben stood there, his .22 in hand, watching the dying calf. Behind him, the heifer bawled, a sound he never imagined an animal could make—something almost human about it. Ben heard the clap of his father's rifle echo down the canyon, and he cocked his own rifle. But Ben couldn't make his finger work; he was eleven and his mind wouldn't send the necessary impulse to his finger. He watched the calf's head go rigid in the underbrush before he sighted the space between its eyes and pulled the trigger. A useless cover for his cowardice.

"Wipe those tears," his father had said when he got back. Two important lessons: Kill when necessary, and don't cry about it. *You're almost twelve, for Christ's sake, not a little kid anymore.*

They hunted the lion up Moro Ridge, rode a deer trail along the cleft of the hill, the evening sun cutting geometry out of the ridges, the grass in the valley below bruising purple in the approaching fog. They rode for three hours, down into splinter canyons, both their rifles cocked, picking along the edge of limestone outcroppings as the fog blanketed the sage and manzanita, the gray sky swallowing the gray hillsides, the clouds erasing the landscape.

It was nearly dark when they left, fogged in and sunless, and the paved road was so new on the landscape that Ben forgot it was there until he heard the clip-clop of his father's horse's hooves. Ben's horse, Comet, balked at the cement, and Ben steadied him just in time to see a streak of green metal flash in front of the horse's nose. A Chevelle, a '66, he was sure of it. It never stopped, just appeared out of the darkness and clipped the hindquarters of his father's horse. In the headlights, the horse spun, and in the taillights, Ben watched his father and the horse flop into the ditch.

His father's neck was snapped against an aluminum irrigation pipe, his body horribly still. His father's horse stood, miraculously, at the bottom of the ditch, a two-inch gash bleeding on his hindquarter. Ben stumbled into the ditch, tried his father's pulse, held his hand to his father's open mouth, hoping for a breath, but necks weren't meant to turn that way. Crying, Ben tried three times to run the horse out of the irrigation ditch, the dry ground giving beneath their weight, until he found a purchase on the cement and led the horse out. He walked both horses home to the barn, cleaned the cuts with Betadine, combed the sweat out of each, and put them in their stables for the night. He must have been out there for forty-five minutes, the wires gone crazy in his head.

And three hours later, after Ben had told his mother, after the sheriff had pulled his father's body out of the ditch and inspected the horse's wound, after he'd taken a statement and declared to Ben and his mother that the police would find the car, Ben's mother eyed him across the kitchen table.

"You put the horses away," she said, swollen pillows of skin beneath her eyes. "Why didn't you come get me immediately?"

"I don't know," he said.

Shock, Ben knew now, but then he didn't know why, had no way to explain it.

"You left him there and cleaned the horses?" She narrowed her eyes as if she identified something new in him that she didn't like, and she looked at it hard. "Maybe he could have been—"

He burst out sobbing. His mother's eyes softened then and she held out her arms and he tried to curl his eleven-year-old body, all lanky legs and knobby joints, into her lap.

Now he sat on the metal folding chair and listened to the freeway rush, the white noise of millions of cars speeding on pavement, Marvin singing, the boards and slats moaning in the wind. One shot, and none of it would have happened. If he'd made that one shot and killed the mountain lion, his father might still be alive. He thought about that a lot—when he was a kid, after his mother remarried, when he went off to the police academy, even now: the necessary things left undone.

The wind was picking up again, and through the open barn door he watched the trees bend, their thin bodies outlined by the orange glow of the distant city. There was a killer out there somewhere, a woman's body growing cold on a stainless-steel table at the county medical examiner's office. A gust scuttled sand across the floor of the barn. Ben pulled a red pin from a bowl and stabbed it into the map at the Mission Viejo address. He shut off the lights and sat in the dark, the trees arcing and swaying, arcing and swaying.

3

A T 6:07 THE NEXT MORNING, HE GOT THE CALL. HE STUMBLED, half asleep still, from the couch to the kitchen to grab the phone off the hook.

"Sleeping in today, huh, Ben?" It was Ken Brady, the overnight desk sergeant.

"Yeah, Ken," he said, rubbing his eyes. "Beauty sleep."

He had finally crawled into bed at 4:12 and tossed until 4:53 before retiring to the couch, listening to the house beams buckle and moan in the wind, before nodding off into a half sleep.

"Shame I have to bother you, then," Ken said. "Must be a blue moon. Got a body out in the strawberry fields. Serrano Canyon and Junipero."

On a legal pad, he scribbled the time of notification, then called it in to Lieutenant Hernandez and Natasha. He ran his head under the kitchen faucet to jolt himself awake and grabbed an apple from the fridge. In the barn, he snatched the .40 caliber out of the locker, and he was on the road in three minutes.

There were three black-and-whites on scene—two parked on the south edge of the field, near an irrigation ditch, and another patrol car pulling a perimeter on the west. He radioed dispatch to get more

units out to cover the corners, parked his car on the south side, near
the two patrol cars, and surveyed the scene from a distance. The body
lay a hundred to a hundred twenty yards away, on the western third
of the field; he couldn't see it from here, but he saw that a uniform
was standing over it. On the eastern edge of the field stood tenement
camps but no squad cars.

The uniform next to him nodded. "Detective." He was leaning
against his cruiser door, smoking.

"Officer," Ben said. "Put that cigarette out. I need you over at that
camp. No one in or out."

The officer flicked the butt into the dirt and slid into the squad
car, muttering something before driving the black-and-white down
the dirt service road bordering the field.

Ben took latex gloves out of the trunk of his cruiser and scrambled into the irrigation ditch, hopping the trickle of water dripping
into the metal drain. He held his breath as he made it across the
field, counting the beats of his heart. Calm, man. Calm down.

It was a kid, just a kid, not much older than Emma. A boy. Ben
leaned on his haunches to take it in. It was the worst when it was a
kid. Something twisted up inside you with the waste of it.

"You first on scene?" he asked the beat cop standing a few feet
away. The cop had a notebook in hand and flipped to the previous
page to look at his notes.

"Five fifty-seven." His voice shook; his face was bleached white.
He couldn't have been more than twenty-five.

"First DB?" Ben said.

The cop—Chang was his name—nodded. "I threw up," he said,
as though at a confessional.

"No shame in that." Ben stood and rested his hand on Chang's
shoulder. Ben's first DB was a drive-by, a nineteen-year-old shot-
gunned on his low-rider bicycle. He was alive when Ben arrived on
scene, twisted in the spokes of his bike. Ben held his hand while he
bled out into the gutter. "I'd like to say it gets easier," Ben said, "but I
hope it doesn't. If it does, means you've seen too much of it."

"He's a teenager."

"Yep," Ben said. Two of the old-timers had taken him for drinks that night and let him cry it out. A sort of rite of passage: one first DB and one public-crying jag. "Should I get someone else?"

"No, sir. I'm okay."

Ben flipped the notebook page in Chang's shaking hand and glanced at his watch.

"Six twenty-one," he said, pointing to a line on the paper. "Detective Wade on scene."

The officer wrote it down.

"You don't have to look at him," Ben said. "Just write what I tell you. When the ME gets here, you do the same with her."

"Right."

Chang turned his back to the body, staring out toward the mountains in the east, his hand pinching down the blowing pages.

Ben noted the revolver clenched in the boy's hand, an old Colt .45, the handle dented, the chamber popped open. Shot close range, no doubt, near the back of the skull; he could see the burn marks at point of entry. Thank God for the wind; it kept the flies away but not the ants, not the beetles. Natasha would need to collect them to help determine time of death. It was early—no bloating tissue, no decomposition. Natasha would know, but he guessed four to five hours. Suspect could be three hundred miles away by now, out of state, in Mexico even, sipping Coronas in Ensenada.

"You touch anything?" Ben said to Chang. Ben watched the lights of black-and-whites on the edge of the field, responding to the scene. Just lights, no sirens. No need to wake anybody up.

"No, sir."

He walked through the scene with Chang, his adrenaline cooling off with the business of the investigation. Chang had gotten the call from dispatch at 5:53. Dispatch said it sounded like a Hispanic male who made the call.

"Name?"

"No," Chang said. "Anonymous tip."

Generally speaking, serials took a break after a killing, their anger, desire, whatever it was, briefly satiated. It was barely ten hours since the woman's body had turned up in Mission Viejo. Was it possible he hit twice in one night?

"Anybody here when you arrived?"

"Some Hispanic workers on the edge of the field." He pointed toward the camp. "But they took off when they saw me."

"You stayed with the body?"

"Yeah."

"Good," Ben said. "You done good."

Ben circled the body, widening the arc as he stepped over clumps of strawberries. Footsteps running left to right and crossed over one another. Knee impressions in the dirt. A bucket tipped over with strawberries spilling out. Coyote or dog prints. A Dulces Vero candy wrapper crushed into the dirt.

Natasha arrived on scene ten minutes later, carrying the tackle-box forensics kit in her left hand and a cigarette in her right.

"Never thought I'd be so lucky," she said, "to see you this early in the morning."

"Play the lottery today."

"I'll meet you over at 7-Eleven as soon as we're done here."

Natasha was short, with a wiry gymnast body that looked good slipped into jeans and a T-shirt. She had a difficult time stepping over the strawberry bushes, and Chang offered her a hand, which she took with the cigarette clasped in her teeth. "Ah, a gentleman," she said. "You're a dying breed.

"Shit," she said when she saw the body. She dropped the kit in the dirt and knelt near the boy's vacant face, the bone structure misshapen, its architecture knocked off-kilter by the gunshot. "A kid?" She took a drag of the cigarette, closing her left eye to keep the smoke out of it.

"Yeah," Ben said. He began to share his observations with her, but she cut him off. "I know," he said, holding up his palm. "I'll go do my job."

The migrant camp was on the eastern edge of the field, two dozen low-slung plywood shacks squeezed between the strawberry field and an orange grove. He'd been here once before, when he was investigating the theft of a professional racing bike snatched from an open garage. A landscaping team had recently mowed a couple of lawns in the neighborhood; the owner of the bike thought a "beaner" had taken it, and this was the obvious place to look. Ben knew immediately that nobody from this camp had taken the bike. There was no place to ride out here, and any Mexican trying to sell it risked deportation. Turned out to be a neighbor, a white kid living two doors down. Generally speaking, the illegals were among the most law-abiding citizens, in Ben's experience. If we were all threatened with deportation, Ben sometimes thought, this would be the most strait-laced country on the planet.

There were two rows of tenements—card houses, basically, the walls leaning against one another. All the doors were closed. A couple of pieces of cardboard lay in the street, ripped loose by the wind. A rooster picked at discarded sunflower-seed shells. He could smell the burn of beans and coffee, and the fecal stench of an open toilet. Immigration harassed the camp every few months, sending a few people back over the border. A cynical game, really, since the owners of the fields didn't want their people deported, but local immigration needed to look as if they were doing their job. So, a compromise: Haul a few away, get it in the newspapers to appease a certain type of voter, and then let more come in to replace the ones sent home. Ben had been asked to assist in a raid when he first started with the department four years ago. He helped drag a few out of camp and pack them into vans, but he felt like an A-grade asshole doing it.

Someone was crying, faint sobs audible in the silences between wind gusts. He stopped in the middle of the street, trying to get a direction on it, but the freight-train howl of wind confused the sounds. He knocked at the first house, the mildewed wooden door tied shut with yellow packing twine. A dark hand reached through the space between door and wall, the fingertips raw with fruit-picking scabs, and unwound the twine. A tiny woman stood in the half dark, holding a sleeping baby in her arms.

"*Buenos días,*" he said.

The woman's eyes were deep brown, almost black, her face wide and flat like a plate. Mayan, he thought. Not Mestizo. Behind her, a boy lay asleep on a cot.

"I would like to speak to you," Ben said in his awkward Spanish, "about the body in the field."

"*No entiendo.*"

He tried again, taking care with his accent, articulating every syllable like a child.

"Please," she said. "Speak more slowly. *Habla más despacio.*"

The baby woke and cried, and she pulled up her shirt to feed him. Ben pointed beyond the walls of the house, toward the field.

"*Muerto,*" he said, as simply as possible. "*En el campo. Sabes?*"

"No," she said, shaking her head. "No."

He knocked on three more doors and got the same answer. "No," they said. "We know nothing." But no one asked what happened, no one looked shocked to hear the news. He tried to get names, tried to get any kind of statement, but people just shook their heads and closed cardboard doors in his face.

At the second-to-last house, a man, in his forties maybe, stood stooped in the doorway. Beyond him, a woman sat on a stool in the corner of a makeshift kitchen. Mottled patches of morning light splattered through holes in the wall, making it difficult to see, but he thought her face had the ashen pallor of someone who had been crying. Another woman, a younger one, knelt at the woman's feet and clasped her hand, lightly running her fingers over the knuckles.

"Do you know anything about the body in the field?"

"No," the stooped man said. He glanced at the ground when he said it. "Sorry, no."

"Does she?" Ben said, nodding toward the woman in the back.

"No."

Two little girls sat quietly on a blanket in the corner of the room.

"I'm not immigration," Ben said.

One of the girls flashed her eyes at him when she heard the word, then she looked away.

"I know."

"I could get them, though," Ben said. "I could call them from my cruiser."

The man lifted his chin, his eyes narrowing. "Please," he said, his voice sharp with anger. "The devil wind was up. No one got any sleep."

Ben gave the man his card. "Call me, please. A boy is dead."

"Murdered?" the man asked.

"I don't know yet. You got reason to believe he was murdered?"

"No." The man took the card and slipped it into the chest pocket of his shirt. "Please go now."

Ben glanced at the woman in the corner; his eyes had adjusted to the darkness and he could see her black eyes watching him as the man quietly closed the door in his face. She was the boy's mother, Ben was sure of it.

"ANYTHING TO GIVE US AN ID?" Ben asked when he got back to the body.

Natasha ignored him as she snapped pictures of the boy's hands, his fingers curled stiff. "How old are you?" she whispered to the boy. "Sixteen? Seventeen? Seventeen's a tough year for a boy."

"Mexican," she said to Ben finally, her eye pressed to the viewfinder.

"I knew forensics was a precise science."

"You're in my light," she said.

Ben moved, and the crisp sun shone brightly on the boy. He had been trying to grow a mustache, but the skin along his jawline was wax-paper smooth. "Sixteen, seventeen," Natasha repeated. Just six thousand or so days. A waste. Some poor mother out there remembered the day he was born, this boy slicked with life, crying the pain of first air filling his lungs.

"Make yourself useful," she said to Ben, "and gather up some of these beetles."

Ben grabbed a plastic vial and a pair of tweezers from her tackle box and started pinching the bugs into the vial.

"High school age," she said, keeping the camera close to her face.

Ben could see the lights of the high school football stadium towering above the rooftops of the El Paraiso housing complex. He dropped another beetle into the vial, then one more, before placing the cap back on, carrying them to the tackle box, and filing them inside.

"He was a good-looking kid," Natasha said.

Ben stopped and looked at the boy's face. The symmetry of it had been knocked out of line, but, yeah, if you could push everything back into place he was handsome — had been handsome.

"Could be self-inflicted," Natasha said. "Burn marks at point of entry, no signs of struggle."

Ben looked out over the field, the red fruit dotting the rows, the swirling lights of the police cars cutting the field off from the orange groves and the hills beyond. On the western edge of the field, nearest the closest housing tract, stood a small crowd — reporters, curious morning joggers, a television van topped with a satellite dish. Beyond the crowd stood the brand-new homes, their red-tiled roofs staggered in the sun. Through the wrought-iron gate to the backyard of the nearest home, Ben watched a woman dive into a swimming pool, her body arcing above the blue water like a falling arrow.

"Something's off about it, though," she said.

He knew enough not to ask; she'd tell him when she was ready. He watched the body while he waited — the limbs still and stiffening, the bottoms of his bare arms purpled with settling blood. Natasha maneuvered around the body and took pictures of his shoes, the soles thick with mud. Sixteen, seventeen: born in 1969 or '70. The wind blew his hair, and his T-shirt fluttered at the waist, exposing the boy's stomach—the muscles still rippled there, a little hair poking up to his belly button.

"See those calluses on the fingers of his right hand?" Natasha said.

Ben bent down and saw the reddened skin. "Right-handed," he said. Out here picking strawberries. Two, maybe three years older than Emma, his whole life ahead of him, though what kind of life was it? Living in this camp. Bent at the waist all day in the sun, picking fruit. Why not take your own life, if this was what life is? There was a certain bravery in it, a clear-eyed pragmatism about the options before him.

"Yes."

"But the .45 was in his left," Ben said.

"You do pay attention, Detective Wade." She pointed to the back of the boy's head. "A suicide, you shoot yourself at the temple or through the soft palate, not back here."

"Anything to link it to Rafferty's DB?"

"Be patient," she said. "I'm just getting started."

Ben hoped it was murder. People did bad shit; you nailed them to the wall for it. A suicide just left things wide-open, forever unanswered.

"Been a busy twenty-four hours," he said.

"Santa Ana winds," Natasha said, her camera pointed at the back of the boy's head.

When the Santa Anas blasted into the basin, it was a bad time to be a cop—or a good time, depending on your way of seeing things. There wasn't any scientific evidence for this, but every cop knew something went haywire in people when the winds hit; there was a charge in the air, literally, the air full of spark. Electricity zapped between blankets, little lightning strikes popped off skin-to-skin contact. When he was in L.A. and the winds were up, the captain packed the night shift with uniformed officers. Husbands beat wives, Crips slaughtered Bloods, drunks bashed other drunks over spilled beer, crazies let out of institutions for lack of funding heard voices telling them to attack blondes in apartments down the hall: spores of violence floating on the wind. Ben could feel this edge in himself, too, an extra pulse in the body, a humming in the teeth.

"No one's talking at the camp," he said.

"Illegal?" Natasha said.

"I suspect so."

"Good produce deals at Safeway, though."

"Yep," Ben said. "My guess, we're not going to get an ID."

"Just another Juan Nadie," she said.

Juan Nadies facedown in the desert. Juan Nadies drowned in rivers. Juan Nadies shot on street corners. Dying of old age in falling-down neighborhoods.

"You check the pockets yet?" Ben said.

"No."

"May I?" he said, trying to sound as gentlemanly as possible.

"Be my guest, Detective Wade." She smirked. "But don't you dare disturb his position."

Lying down in the row, Ben slipped his hand into one of the boy's front pockets—feeling the arch of his hip bone, the muscles of his leg, the unnerving intimacy of death—and fingered three pennies and a candy wrapper. He dropped the items in a plastic evidence bag and slipped his hand into the next pocket. Down at the bottom, tangled with lint and bits of thread, he found a paper clip and an erasable pen and slipped those into the evidence bag, too.

Natasha shuffled down the row of strawberries, snapping photos of shoe prints. Ben moved to the back pockets, getting down in the dirt to edge his hand in without disturbing the twist in the boy's torso. The ground stank of pesticide and loam, and he thought he smelled something else, too—chlorine? In the right pocket, he found a slip of paper. It was ripped and folded into a small square. Still lying on the ground, he unfolded the paper. Something jumped in him and he lay there for a moment looking at the handwriting, his heart beating double time. He glanced over his shoulder. Natasha was still down the row, her back to him, snapping pictures. Quickly, he folded the note up, stuffed it into his jeans pocket, and stood.

"Anything?" Natasha called out.

"A pen and paper clip." He zipped closed the evidence bag.

"A studious one, then."

NATASHA WAS WRAPPING THINGS UP, the body bagged, and Ben sat in the cruiser trying to write notes on the legal pad through his shaking hands. *On scene @ 6:21*, he wrote. *Teenage boy. Mexican.* He knew he should slip the piece of paper back into the evidence bag, but it was too late; the bags were closed up in the forensics kit in the back of Natasha's van. He took a few deep breaths, counting out a slowing rhythm, and steadied his hands on the steering wheel. He'd have to get it back with the other evidence later. It was 8:07.

He dialed Rachel's number on the Motorola.

"What are you doing sneaking into my apartment?" she said.

"I knew you'd be pissed off."

"Of course I'm pissed off," Rachel said. "You know the law, Ben. You get to come inside my house when I invite you inside."

"The scene rattled me last night," he said. "I just needed to know the bottom floor was locked. I was worried. For Emma—and for you."

She let out a frustrated sigh, but he could feel her soften.

"Ben," she said. "We're trying to get out the door. We have to get to school."

"Em all right?"

"A bit sore," she said.

"She can breathe okay?" he said. "Turn her neck all right?"

"She's a little stiff," Rachel said, "but nothing bad."

The coroner assistants were trying to wheel a gurney up the row of strawberries. The wheels got stuck in the dirt, and the assistants tried rattling them loose.

"I mean, the way she fell yesterday," he said. "It scared the h—"

"I know," she said. "I know. You want to talk to her?"

"No," he said, hesitating. Not now, not when he was rattled. "Tell her 'I love you' for me."

Silence.

"You don't sound good, Ben." There was almost a question in her voice, a note of worry.

"Bad morning."

The assistants gave up on the gurney and finally lifted the boy's bagged body and started laboring it across the field. The bag sagged in the middle and scraped the leaves of the plants.

"Hungover?" she said.

"No," he said. *Jesus, Rachel,* he wanted to say. *People do change.* "Not that kind of bad. Not for a long time."

The assistants hoisted the boy's body into the back of the wagon and closed the door. It would be cold in the back, antiseptic and cold.

"Listen, Ben. We've got to go." He pictured her at the door, dressed for school, her hand on the door handle, her bag of papers dangling from her shoulder. Off to do the clean work of teaching.

"Yeah," he said. "I know." She didn't even mention the coffee he had made. "Didn't mean to hold you up."

He held the Motorola for a minute, listening to the drone of the empty line, and watched the ambulance silently speed away. Phone call. Anonymous tip. Hispanic. There weren't any phones in the camp, unless someone had run an illegal line. The ambulance passed a shopping center and a lit-up Texaco station on the edge of the field, a phone booth standing on the corner.

"Natasha," he said when she was back at her van. "Don't pack up yet."

A SWELL LIFTED BEN TEN feet into the air, the water sucking at his torso, dragging his body up the face of the wave. He was bodysurfing at the Wedge down in Newport Beach, a south swell pumping hard. For a moment there was no horizon, the water cutting into the sky, the land pitching sideways. The swell crested, the wind blowing spray off the lip. He turned in to the wave and it shot him toward the beach.

His palm carved the glass in front of him, his body rocketing across the face. Then suddenly the wave jacked up against the jetty. He was airborne briefly, before his torso spun back into the water. He cut his hand into the face of the wave and shot the pipe, and just before it closed him off, a second before the slam and grind of the ocean floor, he flipped out the backside into the ebb of the receding churn.

Three hours earlier, he'd followed the body to the medical examiner's office. He usually stayed away from autopsies. When he was a recruit, his class had been required to attend autopsies to learn what kind of evidence was important to a case, so they didn't destroy forensic particulars on scene. The day he witnessed, the body was a young woman. He'd kept his stomach through external examination and even through the Y cut from shoulder blades to pubic bone, but when the examiner laid the blade of the electric saw against her ribs, he couldn't take it. He barely made it to the toilets. Ever since, he avoided it: the smell of the rooms, the dun-colored stains on the floors, the whole stainless-steel cool of the place. But he couldn't leave this boy; he felt some kind of responsibility toward him.

So he smeared Vicks above his top lip and stood in the corner while Natasha and Dr. Mendenhall removed the body from the bag. He watched as they swabbed the boy's mouth and cut his nails and placed the clippings in a plastic bag. He watched as they combed his hair around the wound, untangling strands from the comb to keep for testing. He imagined the boy standing in front of a mirror, combing his own hair in the minutes before school, slicking it back into a thick black streak.

Now, in the ocean, three swells were stacked up ahead of him. Out of breath, he freestyled against the tide, pulling himself through rope kelp and sea froth. He dove beneath a breaking wave. The churn rolled over him, a muted rumble on the surface of the water, until he burst out into oxygen, filling his burning lungs with it as another wave crested above him. He turned and caught the wave, carving the swell, feeling its tug and pull, but riding the beautiful clean glass just in front of the break.

He had stayed through the Y cut, though his stomach roiled and he had to hold the Vicks to his nose. Mendenhall unceremoniously carved through the body, intoning medical terms into the microphone. Natasha, though, held the boy's arm as if comforting him. Ben watched her hands—her fingertips pressed lightly to the boy's skin, as though afraid to bruise him—as the doctor worked on the ribs. That kept him calm, her soft touch on the body. He watched her hands, too, when she assisted Mendenhall with the first of the boy's organs, but that was all he could take; he stood in the corner of the examination room, his hands in his pockets, staring at the graying grout that held the tile together.

"We can call you when we're finished," Natasha said.

"No. I'll stay."

He stared at the wall and listened to Mendenhall call out numbers, medical minutiae, and thought of the boy's mother sitting in a small, dark room while her son lay here on a stainless-steel table. He would stay until it was done; he would.

The wave closed out and broke all at once, grinding him into the sand, dragging him head over feet across the ocean floor. His body was the ocean's for a few moments, and he let himself be raked across the pebbles and broken shells, his rag-doll limbs useless against the churn. Then he was up into the air, his lungs expanding with oxygen, the sun glancing off the water.

He dove beneath the kelp bed, into the dark below. He swam the bubbling silence, his shoulders aching as he tugged himself against the tide. The weight of the water pressured his ears, but his body felt weightless now, and for nearly a minute he forgot about everything except the rush of water slipping down his limbs.

When the medical examiner finished, Natasha placed her palm on his back.

"Waiting for this?" she said, the disinfected bullet in her hand.

He didn't know what he was waiting for, but, yeah, he guessed that was it. Evidence. His job. "Yeah," he said, taking it in his hand. She gave him a plastic bag and he slipped the slug inside.

"You okay?" she said.

"Yep," he said. "Just fine."

He had run the revolver and the bullet over to ballistics and spent an hour at his desk, typing up the death investigation form on one of the new Macintosh computers. *Case number: 12-00443-UI. Decedent name: _____. Decedent DOB: _____. Decedent address: _____. Location of body: Strawberry field, Junipero and Serrano Canyon Roads. Cause of death: Homicide.* He got three more lines down the form before he realized which box he'd marked. He returned to the cause-of-death line and let his hand hover over the erase key, the green cursor flashing at him. It didn't look like the work of a serial killer, but maybe he was wrong, maybe he was missing something. He stared at the X in the box for at least a minute, his finger hovering midair, before Lieutenant Hernandez leaned over his desk, the air around him spiced with aftershave.

"What's the deal with this?" he said. "Bad fucking timing to have a body turn up."

Ben gave him the lowdown while Hernandez bent over the monitor, reading glasses on the tip of his nose, and scanned the screen.

"Mayor's got investors in today," Hernandez said. "They want to build a 'campus' with upscale houses for employees. Some computer-software crap. Want the city to have a 'family feel.'"

"And we all know nothing bad happens in families," Ben said.

"Homicide?" Hernandez said. "Unless you got something not listed here, you're getting ahead of yourself, Wade."

"Things don't line up for self-inflicted," Ben said.

"They line up for murder?" Hernandez said, standing up now. He wasn't a tall man, but he had the broad shoulders of a wrestler. A couple of years back, Ben had seen him pin a six-foot-five perp freaking on PCP against a bus-stop bench, until Ben and two other officers could handcuff him to the bolted-down legs.

"Not yet," Ben said.

"When they do, you can check that box."

When the lieutenant was gone, Ben stared at the flashing cursor.

Something about this was all wrong, suicide or murder. This one was going to be shit; he could feel it. Finally he pressed the erase key and marked the box that read *Unknown*.

Now the surfers were out, boys with arrow-like Plexiglas boards. They straddled the boards between their legs while they waited for the swells and talked about getting laid or getting loaded or about new punk bands who threw keggers in garages in Huntington Beach. These losers were taking over the whole South Coast. They swooped down on you, ran you over, cursed you for getting in the way of their "shredding." Surfing was a lesser sport, as far as Ben was concerned, like riding waves with a life raft. Another set came in, and even though the second wave was bigger than the first, Ben caught the smaller and rode it to shore, the world coming back to him as his feet touched sand.

A Juan Nadie, a pistol, and handwriting on a small slip of paper.

4

E MMA WASN'T LOOKING FOR HIM THIS AFTERNOON. USUALLY she stood on the steps and waited for his cruiser, but he was early. Her back was to him, her hand resting on the chest of a boy he'd never seen before. The boy's arm was looped around his daughter's waist, his hand sunk into the back pocket of her jeans. She was fourteen, barely six weeks into ninth grade, the last year of junior high. He remembered dinner and a candle in a pink cupcake just last spring. He sat in the cruiser, the engine idling, the radio scratching out 10-codes—non-injury traffic accident, missing elderly, check for record—and watched, trying to tell from her body language how far this had already gone. She kept her hand on the boy's chest and she didn't turn around to look for him, not a glance, even when he got out and slammed the door, climbed the cement steps, let the lapel of his coat hook on the butt of his .40 caliber, and stuck his hand out for the boy to shake.

"Emma's dad," Ben said.

"God, Dad," Emma said, her hand on her sternum now. "You scared me."

"Emma's friend," the boy said, pushing the sun-bleached hair out of his eyes and shaking Ben's hand. No muscle in it. Not trying to impress. Trouble.

"Lance," Emma said, her face flushed. "Dad, this is Lance."

He was older, maybe sixteen or seventeen. The high school was adjacent to the junior high school, a mistake in master planning if you asked him.

"You surf?" Ben said. "Newport? Thirty-second Street?"

"Yeah," the boy said. The kid's pupils were dilated, black saucers yawned open to the emptiness of his cranium. Stoner. He didn't recognize the kid, but he knew the type.

"Break's better down at the Wedge."

"Dad likes to bodysurf," Emma explained.

"You work the parking meters?" the kid said.

Ben smiled. "Robbery, assault, homicide." Punk kid. "Drugs."

"Radical, man," the kid said, squinting into the sun.

Then another kid, dragging a skateboard behind him, slapped Lance's hand. Emma blew the punk a kiss goodbye, and finally she was sitting in the passenger seat next to him.

"Geez, Detective," she said. "What's with the interrogation?"

She was wearing a hoodie, not one of hers. It held the faint sweetness of marijuana. He didn't like that one bit. That was ownership, the boy marking territory.

"I haven't heard about this kid."

"Mom knows."

Of course she does. What else was Rachel keeping from him? Em must have understood his silence, because she shape-shifted back into herself, the girl who used to allow him to tuck her into bed at night.

"Shoot anyone today?" she joked.

He watched Lance on the steps: his hair falling in his face, his corduroy pants and Vans two-toned shoes, his surfer cool and the goofy hand gestures he and his friends signed at one another, the secret language of all teenage groups, guns or surfboards.

"Not yet," he said.

* * *

"I'M NOT CRAZY ABOUT THE looks of this kid," Ben said to Emma.

They were up on Moro Ridge, the horses dipping their noses in an old cattle trough, a cut-open oil drum filled with rainwater from last week's storms. Rachel had a faculty meeting today, so Ben got an extra ride in with Emma. The two of them sat in the shadow of a scarred black oak, its limbs twisted east from the coastal breeze. Below them, Crystal Cove cut a crescent out of the hillside, and beyond that the Pacific curved blue all the way to Asia.

"You don't even know him," she said.

"I've been around enough kids to know the good from the bad."

"Well, who would you like, Dad?"

She had a point. He couldn't think of any type of hormone-addled teenager he'd like zeroing in on his daughter. A serious problem considering she was a year and a half into puberty and seemed to enjoy making herself a target. *Button that blouse. No way you're walking out that door in those shorts.*

"How long've you been seeing this boy?"

Now she leaned on her bare arms—thankfully she'd left the kid's sweatshirt back at the house—her elbows hyperextended and fragile-looking. She wouldn't look at him, just stared at the swells stacked and rolling in.

"Not long."

"A week, month?"

"God, Dad, you make me feel like a criminal."

"And you make me feel like a cop."

In third grade, Emma had been identified as "gifted," a genetic blessing Ben was certain had been passed down from Rachel. He was proud of Emma's intelligence and the accelerated classes she took, but he wasn't crazy about what the school psychologist called a "propensity for precociousness in the gifted student." Precociousness, as far as Ben was concerned, was simply a "propensity" to let curiosity get you into hot messes. When she was five, inspired by a painting she'd seen on a school trip to the L.A. County Museum of Art, Emma painted the wall opposite her twin bed full of acrylic sunflowers. After they'd moved here, she got it into her head to perform an "experiment" with matches and gunpowder extracted—unbeknownst to him or Rachel—from old shotgun shells she'd found in the barn. "Curiosity killed the gifted student," Ben had said after they put out the small brush fire with the garden hose. Her precociousness now had mellowed into a general artistic pretentiousness concerning "post-punk" and "New Wave" British bands, a mostly benign affront to Ben's ears. But "boys" and "precociousness" were two words he didn't want used in the same sentence.

"It's only been a few weeks," she said.

"As in three?"

"Five or six."

Jesus.

"He's nice."

"Guys aren't nice until they're thirty."

She leveled the lay-off look—her chin lowered and her eyes, rimmed in black eyeliner her mother had started letting her wear, two stabbing darts.

"He buys me lunch, made a mixtape for me . . ." She counted them off with her fingers. "He's got good taste—the Clash, Social Distortion, Minutemen. Good taste matters."

Mixtapes? Buying lunch? A high school boy's tickets to admission. Next he'll be telling her some sob story about how he's ignored by his father.

"You meet him at the record store?" Ben asked. Emma and her friends hung out at Viral Records, and sometimes he did drive-bys just to check up.

"Strike one," she said. "He lives over in El Camino Real. Hangs out at the skate park near Alta Square."

"School, then?"

"You *are* a detective," she said, wagging her finger at him. "Gray!" she said suddenly, sitting up and pointing out to sea.

The plume, maybe a half mile out in the ocean, fanned in the wind, and then the heavy arch of the whale's back broke the surface.

"Must be one of the first," she said. Emma was standing now, her hand shadowing her eyes, an excited little girl again. His daughter's childhood was measured by the same topography that had measured Ben's, and sometimes he had the strange feeling that they were living their childhoods simultaneously, as though the hills were some fold in time where their youths intersected. Ben and his father would catch their breath here on long rides, when his father was still running cattle for the ranch. The land was being gnawed away even then, and his father knew it—Leisure World terraced into Cherry Canyon, UC Med School cantilevered above San Joaquin Wash— and they stopped here often, his father staring at the ocean as though developers would fill it in with gravel and pave a parking lot over it. Ben's father never lost his wonder for the Pacific, from the moment he first saw it, azure and sun-starred, out the window of the coast-to-coast Greyhound, until the afternoon of the day he died. The man never swam in the ocean, not even a toe dip in it, but he walked the edge of it, pressed his boots into the damp sand to snatch seashells from the salt; he watched it, too, from his perch on his horse, talked about the swells coming all the way from Korea, where his brother, Everett, had been killed a decade earlier trying to take Pork Chop Hill. He pointed out plumes of whale breath as the animals lumbered the shallow coastal waters in the fall, shielded his eyes to watch pelicans swoop the ocean's surface. He knew where to find tide pools when the ocean ebbed, knew the names of the animals clasping tidal rocks—the rockweed and gooseneck barnacles, the wavy-top turban and dead man's fingers.

It was only a single plume, and Emma sat back down.

"Mom's talked to you, right?" he said.

"We talk all the time," she said.

"I mean . . ." He hoped to God Rachel had taken care of this. *"Talked* to you."

"About sex?"

"Yeah," he said, clearing his throat.

"Geez, Dad." Her cheeks reddened a bit. "Yeah, she's talked to me."

"I hope she said something like, *Don't do it or I'll kill you.*"

She laughed. "I think she mentioned bamboo sticks under my fingernails."

"Good," he said. "You know, no one talked to me about it. It made things confusing."

"You can stop now."

A gust of wind rained oak leaves down around them.

"How old is this kid?" Ben said.

"Sixteen," she said. "But he's only a freshman. They held him back a year."

Great. Fucking great.

"Why?" He tried to take the detective out of his voice, tried to soften it.

"He's got an abusive relationship with math," she said. "He's an artist."

Jesus. An artist! A pot-smoking, surfing artist. Graffiti probably.

"It's not what you're thinking," she said.

"What am I thinking, Miss ESP?"

She leaned back onto her elbows, splayed her fingers in the clump grass. She had painted her nails a neon red. He remembered, for a moment, the dead boy in the field this morning. It just burst out of his memory, an image imposed upon this lovely picture of his daughter.

"Graffiti, airbrush, something lame like that."

He laughed. Her face was in profile to him, her sun-freckled nose, her long dark eyelashes. Her mother's jaw.

"Comics," she said.

"What? Like Superman?"

"Superman's lame," she said. "More like a novel with pictures. He's working on this one where the hero rides a tidal wave as it crushes Los Angeles. It's like this updated Armageddon story."

"Well, I don't like him."

"Bro-ken rec-ord," she said.

Ben glanced at his watch: 5:03, and it'd take fifteen minutes to get back. "Let's get you to your mother," Ben said.

On the ride back, they passed the old cowboy camp in Bommer Canyon. A decade ago, if you were running a winter herd, you could escape a rainstorm here or put in for the night. Now a yellow front-loader sat idle beneath the oak tree. The Santa Elena Historical Society had petitioned to save the place, but it was Rancho Santa Elena Corporation's property, and as soon as the ink dried on the few hundred signatures, one of which was his, the heavy equipment had moved in. Up until a few years ago, he had thought the hills would be safe from development, but he had been naïve. The toll road would run through here, and the Rancho had a vested stake in the expressway being built. Inside, he knew, the camp stank of piss and animal shit; there were broken beer bottles in the corners, graffiti scrawled across the walls. When the ranch was a working endeavor — clean cots pushed up against the walls, a small stove in the corner to make coffee — he'd spent the night out here once with his father, the hills outside a moonless inky black. Ben lay awake that night listening to the whoops and screeches, his father whispering to him in his cigarette voice, "There's nothing out there'll hurt you; there's nothing out there . . ." until his father fell to snoring and Ben stared at the shapeless sky outside the window, nodding off when dawn outlined the twists of oak-tree branches.

"They're going to knock the camp down," he said to Emma as they passed.

"It's falling down anyway," she said.

"You said five," Rachel called from the front steps of his house when she saw them coming up the drive. It's where she used to sit when they were still married, face turned to the sun, watching the hills and road as though perpetually waiting for something. Her knees were pushed together, and she was grading a paper on her lap. She wore acid-washed jeans that fell just above her ankles. Her socks, he noticed, mismatched blue to black. She was always the geek who didn't give a damn about fashion, but a beautiful geek, a geek who turned heads.

Emma walked Gus to the barn and poured out a bucket of oats for the horse. Ben rode Tin Man over to Rachel, looking down at her from the saddle while she squinted into the sun.

"How's the professor?"

"He's in computers," Rachel said. "Software."

"Floppy-disk guy? Sits at a desk all day?"

"A lab." She huffed a bitter laugh. "What, you haven't investigated this?"

He gritted his teeth.

"You're growing up, Ben." She smiled, rubbing the pencil lead from the edge of her hand onto the thigh of her jeans. "Did she do her homework?"

Rachel knew the answer, just wanted to make it official. He shook his head.

She let out an exasperated breath. "I spend all day making kids do their schoolwork. I don't have horses to entertain her with."

"You gave that up."

"They've always been *your* horses." She stuffed the paper into a manila folder and stood up. "I just got to rent them in exchange for good behavior."

Emma was out of the barn, walking toward them. "Hi, honey," Rachel said, giving Emma a kiss on the part in her hair. It softened him, her lips on their daughter's hair. It was all he could hope for, to witness that every day. "Go get your stuff and let's eat," she said.

Emma went into the house and Rachel stared up at him, leaning on her left hip in a pose he knew well. He swung himself off Tin Man and stood holding the reins.

"When were you going to tell me about this kid she's seeing?" he said.

"Isn't that hers to tell?" Rachel said, raising an eyebrow.

"I thought we had joint custody for a reason."

A military jet flew high above them and they both glanced at it, a silver spark in the sky.

"I'm sorry," she said. "I should have filled you in. Been a lot on my plate at school. This thing with the boy is new."

"She says six weeks."

"Get used to it, Ben," Rachel said, shooting him an annoyed glance. "She's going to have boyfriends."

"What if he's a jerk?" he said. "What if she's getting into trouble?"

"We don't need to make trouble where there's none yet."

"I'd like to avoid the other side of 'yet.'"

"So would I."

"Dad," Emma called from the kitchen window. "Where's the sweatshirt I was wearing?"

"Look in the hall closet," he said. "So the professor?"

"Programmer."

"You like him?" Shut your mouth, Ben. Just shut up. "Play Ms. Pac-Man together and stuff like that?"

"Jesus, Ben," she said. "He's a friend, and I don't have to explain myself to you. Not that you'd listen."

She hoisted her school bag to her shoulder, disorganized edges of lined paper poking out.

"Besides, how's Natasha?" Rachel said. "That's her name, right?"

She and Emma had been talking. "Yeah," he said. "That's her name. Just work friends."

"Work friends." Rachel smiled wryly. "Emma Eunice," she yelled at the house. "Let's go!"

"I need the sweatshirt."

"If I find it," Ben called to the window, where he saw his daughter tossing throw pillows into the air, "I'll bring it to you in the morning."

Emma stomped out of the house, full of teenage fury.

"What, do we have a train to catch?"

"Don't talk to me like that," Rachel said. Ben simultaneously echoed the sentiment, and Emma stared at the two of them as though they were a team conspiring against her. For a moment, Ben was tricked into feeling married again.

"Geez."

Rachel tugged Emma toward her Buick.

Oh," she said, pulling a thin box from her bag. "Here." See's Candies. "For Margaret when you see her."

Margaret, Ben's mother, had been diagnosed with early-onset dementia soon after his stepfather died six years ago. Sixty-four years old and her memory was slowly being erased. She was at Leisure World— Seizure World, as the EMTs called it—a home down in Laguna Niguel.

"Nice of you. Thanks."

A quick smile.

"He pushes your buttons, then?" Ben said, unable to leave it alone. "The professor?"

"Cute," Rachel said, walking away from him.

He watched them go, a cloud of dust following them down the road. Alone. He was alone, and no doubt he deserved it.

HE BRUSHED OUT THE HORSES, a little too roughly, and put them in for the night. In the house, he straightened the decorative carnage wrought by Emma and called in to the station to check his messages: missing elderly found telling jokes in the produce section of Safeway; Rafferty thanking him for the tip on the killer's small hands; a problem with his articulation on an affidavit for a search warrant on a suspected burglar of hi-fi stereos. Pain in the ass. Nothing from ballistics, nothing from Natasha.

In his bedroom, he opened the sock drawer of his dresser and yanked out the boy's sweatshirt. No chance Emma would check there. Inside the hoodie he found the boy's last name scrawled in Sharpie on the tag: *Arnold*. The fabric stank of sweat and the faint sticky-sweet of weed. He checked the pockets for any plastic bags or shake, any papers. Nothing. According to the white pages, there were two Arnolds in the El Camino Real area: a J. M. Arnold, living in the Bonita Casitas condominiums; the other, a husband and wife, David and Michelle Arnold, 19832 Los Pueblos.

He tossed the sweatshirt on the passenger seat and gunned the cruiser down the dirt road until he hit the light at Junipero. The last of the sun cast saturated light against the shining cars, the street wet-black and ruler-straight, everyone speeding—he could tell by the way they zipped through the intersection to his one-two counts instead of threes or fours. When he turned the cruiser onto the road, everyone throttled down to speed limit—three rows of brake lights, nervous glances at intersections. His car was unmarked, but the silver spot-light above the sideview gave him away.

It took him ten minutes, mostly spent idling at timed stoplights, to reach the house, a ranch with a half-pipe in the driveway. The kid was blasting punk music, and his eyes bugged out when he saw Ben. He jumped to the boom box in the empty garage and flipped it off.

"Dude, what'd I do?" he said, his cool lost now.

"Nothing yet, I hope."

"What? No, man," he said, shaking his head. "Nothing. I mean, we've kissed, but that's all."

It was nearly 7:00, and there were no cars in the garage. The front door was wide open, the house dark and quiet inside.

"Where're your parents?"

"Mom's working," the kid said. "My dad?" He looked at his feet. "You got me."

He saw this all the time, kids alone at home for hours after school, cooking their meals, drinking their parents' whiskey, creating trouble where there didn't need to be any while parents worked their tails off to pay inflated mortgages.

"This is yours," Ben said, tossing the kid the sweatshirt.

"Yeah, man," he said. "I let Em wear—"

"Emma."

"—Emma wear it because she said she was cold."

"Chivalrous of you."

He shrugged. "I guess."

Ben turned to go back to his car.

"How'd you know where I lived?"

"I know a lot of things, kid. I got eyes and ears."

A BIRD WITH A HOOD OVER ITS HEAD

What he had wanted to ask the nice lady in the yellow shirt was: Why didn't anyone come to get me?

His eleven-year-old self had gotten sick—this was a long time before social services and the nice lady in the yellow shirt—his insides turning to water, the basement floor wet with it, and his father had taken him to the doctor. The ladies in the candy-colored clothes had weighed him. They had stood him on a silver pedestal and marked the notch where the top of his head ended. They had stabbed a tube into his arm, and the blue vein sucked the warm liquid into his body. They had stared at him, shaken their heads, and whispered. They had given his father a slip of paper and let the two of them walk back out into the spotlight-sunny day. And they didn't come for him, not yet.

But later, after they did come for him, when the nice lady in the yellow shirt asked him why he didn't call out, asked him why he didn't tell the nurses and the doctor-man at the clinic, his twelve-year-old self had still been a bird with a hood over his head. And the twelve-year-old-self words in his brain didn't sound like the words coming out of her mouth, and a bubble of silence expanded between them. He wanted to tell her that the sun had been too bright that day, that his father's car, hurtling down the road, had felt like the world exploding, that the office noises—the rings and beeps and child cries, the TV box with the people locked inside—pounded like fists against his skull. And he had wanted to get out of there—to rest his eyes, to let the noises crawl out of his ears.

If he could see that nice lady in the yellow shirt now, he would tell her that he didn't know he could free himself. He didn't know that the words in his head could be arranged to say, "There's a deadbolt on a door that is always locked."

But after his father was locked behind a deadbolt in a prison, with a barbed-wire fence cutting the sky, he had sat at a dinner table with a foster family and learned to speak like them; he had gone to school and learned to think like them; he had ridden bikes and made forts and taken pictures that people put in scrapbooks; but he was never really there with them: In his mind he was still in a room with a deadbolt that was always locked. He played tag and dangled from monkey bars, but the old self watched this new self and whispered things in that other language that made him itch inside.

In foster care he discovered that doors could remain unlocked. Once he found them unlocked, the doors, he couldn't stop walking through them—their handles turning so easily, sweeping open as though he was invited inside. He walked through neighbors' unlocked doors—when they were gone away at the office or off at the shopping center, when they were praying at their church. Once a boy came home from school when he was inside, and his thirteen-year-old self had to hide in a closet until the boy turned on the hi-fi in his bedroom. The door to the boy's room was cracked, and for a few moments he stood at the top of the stairs, just two feet from the open door, and listened to the music. It was the first time he'd heard the song. It was loud and angry, the singer's voice like an animal growl, and he felt the electricity for the first time, too. He could see the boy's bare feet on his bed, crossed at the ankles, his toes keeping beat with the drums. He felt the electricity first in his fingertips, then up his arms. (Like now, like it was moving in his body now.) Then it went supernova in his chest, and his hands felt like metal clamps. Standing at the top of those steps, he felt his body grow, felt his spine elongate, the bones of his legs lengthen, the sinew of his muscles bulge to superhuman size. But then, through the open window, he heard his foster mother call him for dinner. He was thirteen and he had been hungry.

But the itch inside grew, like animal nails clawing the cavity of his chest, like teeth gnawing the ridges of his skull; it grew until he felt raw inside and the itch made him smash a lamp against his foster mother's head. Then they sent him to another place with deadbolts on the doors. Not like the basement, but with beds and painted walls and time in a courtyard with cooing doves in the trees. Here he learned to act like them, learned the right answers to the right questions, learned to smile and say things like "It's nice to see you" and "I feel fine" and "Please don't do that," and on the outside he seemed like them, but he wasn't. You are me, but I'm not you. He said this in his mind when talking to them. You are me, but I'm not you. There's a black hole in me; he could feel it, gravity turned inside out, an ever-expanding implosion.

Now he swerved into the sky, a huge cement half circle sweeping above the low-slung houses. The on-ramp slipped the Toyota into the stream of cars riding the Santa Ana Freeway, the red taillights like rushing capillaries of blood. For a quarter of a mile, the freeway was raised on cement columns, the basin twinkling below him, the sky so clear the L.A. high-rises shimmered in the distance. Sometimes he drove all night, listening to the music on the cassette player— "Find a little strip, find a little stranger"—the Santa Ana Freeway looping into the 110, the downtown skyscrapers like things earthquaked into the air. The 110 carving a tunnel through the broken-glass sparkle of the Carson refineries, the highway system like the arteries of a huge heart, the whole basin falling toward the ocean, gridded with streetlights and back-porch spotlights, millions of people sitting in their little homes, watching television. From here you could feel their insignificance, parasites on a larger organism.

He had slept in the car yesterday morning, curled up like a rabbit in the back of the Toyota, the car parked on the edge of a construction site, the skeletons of half-framed houses casting shadows across the ground. Someone had rapped his knuckles against his window. He had jumped and his heart beat like grenade explosions, his eleven-year-old-self heart again, curled in a corner, his chest thumping with fear. But it was a plainclothes policeman, his hand gesturing for him to roll down the window.

Girlfriend kicked him out, he'd told the cop.

He was a broad-shouldered Rancho Santa Elena detective with nothing to do, a coffee in his hand as though meeting a friend for breakfast.

"Well, you can't sleep here," the cop said. And then he gave him the coffee, fresh and warm in his hands, and let him go. "YMCA in Tustin," the cop said. "They'll take you in for a night or two if you've got nowhere to go."

He liked the cop. His niceness made him stupid, and his stupidity made him blind to the thing in front of him.

Then he had driven down Laguna Canyon and stood on the side of the road with the Mexicans and Hondurans and El Salvadorans, begging rich white men for daywork. He didn't need much, just enough money for gas and the boxes of latex gloves, just enough for donuts or a drive-through hamburger. He wasn't Mexican, but he was olive-skinned and small, like the half-starved illegals. And no one asked questions, no one wanted to know, especially the rich white men who were afraid of the fines for hiring illegals. A few hours' work, a palm full of cash, goodbye. Move on to the next corner in another town.

This morning he jumped into a Chevy pickup bed with a Nicaraguan and they huddled in the back together, clutching their chests as the truck hurtled down the freeway. The truck took the Magnolia exit, swung right, and drove into a gated community with a little fountain of reclaimed water and streets lined with palm trees. The man pushed the silver buttons and the gate slid open and the truck drove through, and he watched the gate lock behind them, a little castle wall to keep the world out. The houses had columns and cathedral windows and a greenbelt that snaked between the yards — kids dangling from monkey bars, a woman touching her toes before a jog. At the house, the rich man handed them shovels and he and the Nicaraguan dug a kidney-shaped hole in the ground, where they would pour cement for a pool. It was a hot day, and the earth was dry and pebbly until it gave way to hard-packed mud, tangled palm roots, knots of worms.

At noon a woman opened the sliding glass door to the kitchen and *brought them glasses of ice water and orange slices. He smiled at her and they talked. Yes, they wanted the pool dug before her husband was back from New York. Yes, thank you for working so hard. Later, he stood at the sliding glass door and waited as she rose from the couch, setting aside a magazine. She unhooked the lock on the door—a little click like a small bone breaking. Yes, she said, of course, and he walked down her cool hallway to find the bathroom with the white towels and the seashells in a glass bowl. He kept his eyes on the sink, watched the water swirl into the drain; still he caught glances of himself in the mirror—his dark hair slicked with sweat, his thin jaw, his foreshortened nose, his straight mouth like a slit across his face, his soft teeth the color of butter. If he looked up, he'd see his eleven-year-old self, the one he saw for the first time at the doctor's office, the boy self with saucer eyes and sores on his face. He hated his eleven-year-old self, the way it sat like a bird with a hood over its head, the way its heart exploded like grenades and burst flashes in its brain. But it followed him everywhere—he couldn't get rid of it.*

When he was finished, he asked for another glass of water and he stood in the doorway of her kitchen, complimenting her house, thanking her for the work; her little fingers drummed on the countertop, nervous to get him back outside. He liked her for that—it turned her beautiful, her body rigid in her own kitchen, the forced smile an unlocked door to her fear. He drank the glass to the bottom and thanked her again, and when he stepped outside he heard the latch click again in the sliding glass door. The wind blew palm fronds and electricity raised the hair on his neck and the buzz in his fingertips electrified the shovel and he dug and dug, deeper into the earth.

Now he was driving past the airport, the planes descending to the tarmac like giant insects. He took the Magnolia off-ramp, swinging around the cement berm, and merged into the stream of suburban traffic. At a stoplight, he turned to look at a man in his idling car, the dashboard light greening his face. He stared at the man until the man felt him and glanced across the lane, and when he met the man's eyes he kept staring until the stoplight turned green, and then the man was gone. But his eyes went with the man, crouched in the backseat of his car, riding with the man down the boulevard, staying with him until he was deadbolted inside his house.

He turned the car in to the driveway and idled at the gate. He punched in the five numbers on the silver box—he had watched the rich man earlier today, memorized the 6, 6, 9, 3, 6—and the gate that made them feel safe rattled open and he drove inside.

5

THE DECEASED WOMAN, EMILY, HAD NO FAMILY. NO CHILdren, a dead mother and father buried together in Forest Hills, a divorced husband living in Phoenix. The husband hadn't seen her in four years, he said when Natasha called him, but he was driving out to collect her body, to bury her in the empty plot to the right of her mother.

Mendenhall was done for the day, off to dinner and a movie with his wife at South Coast Plaza, and Natasha was left to prep Emily's body before the ex-husband's arrival. She had already incinerated the organs. Mendenhall avoided the incinerator, too. Maybe he didn't like the smell; maybe there was something too final about the architecture of the body being reduced to ash that he couldn't stomach before sitting down to steak and red wine. Maybe he just didn't care. Emily had had a heavy heart; her liver, too—a drinker.

After the incinerator, she sewed up Emily's body, trying to line up the imperfections of skin, reanimating a hollowed shell. When she was finished, she cleaned up and filled out paperwork until the husband arrived. Emily hadn't been sexually assaulted. Definitely not the serial's MO. She had a small tumor in her left lung, which would have become a problem soon. Otherwise, she had been mostly healthy.

The ex seemed like a nice man, tired from the drive, genuinely upset about his duty.

"She was strangled?" he said, his voice weak.

"Yes," she said gently.

She had pulled the sheet back for him to see Emily's pale face. She made sure to stop at the neck, made sure not to show him the baseball stitch running down the length of her torso.

"I feel guilty," he said. "Maybe if I hadn't left her."

She replaced the sheet.

"Death makes everyone feel guilty," she said, touching his elbow to guide him toward the papers he'd have to sign.

After the men from the funeral home wheeled the body out to the hearse, Natasha made copies of the two reports—one on Emily and one for the unidentified Mexican boy. She filed the originals away, placed the copies in two separate folders, one marked *Detective Rafferty (Mission Viejo)* and the other *Detective Wade (Santa Elena)*, and left to meet her friend Allison for a drink.

When Natasha got to Las Brisas, Allison was already into her second margarita. She was at the patio bar, sitting poised at a tall table overlooking the cliffs and the surf below, a forty-something man in khaki pants and a guayabera leaning into her, shadowing her from the late-evening sun.

"Tash!" Allison said when she saw her. "Ronald, this is my friend Natasha."

They shook hands, but the hawklike smile on his face collapsed into the frustrated squint of a man who's just had his plans ruined.

"We're going to have a private drink, Ronald," Allison said, touching the man's tanned forearm. "Tash and I need to catch up."

"No problemo, *cariño*," Ronald said, glancing a rebuke at Natasha. "Let me know if you need another one of those."

"*Cariño?*" Natasha said when he was gone.

"He's cute," she said.

"He's trying to get laid."

"Of course he is," she said. "He's lonely. Everyone here is lonely."

"The kids with David?"

Allison pouted for a moment and took a sip of her margarita.

"With my mom," she said. "David's in New York. Again."

Natasha had known Allison since they were seven. They had been the only two kids on a cul-de-sac of brand-new homes in the second housing development in Santa Elena. Most of the houses hadn't been purchased yet and sat empty. It was like living in a ghost town that first year, but they had each other. If they'd met today, though, Natasha doubted they'd make much of an impression on each other. Their lives were too different—Allison the bored (ignored, she would say) housewife to a traveling exec named David. She ferried her kids from soccer game to dance recital to karate training. Natasha was the career woman who worked 24/7, a decision Allison could never wrap her mind around. "It just seems so empty," Allison had said to her one night when too much alcohol dulled her sense of social etiquette. "I can't imagine life without kids." Yet here Allison was, poured into a dress the crimson of a ripened strawberry, accepting drinks from a half-drunk man hoping to get her in bed tonight.

Natasha ordered a whiskey and they talked for a while—the kids and their grades, little Donnie and his anger problems, the work on the kitchen that had been delayed because the Mexican tile they wanted was out of stock, David and his job, David and his bonus, David and his endless travels, David and . . .

Natasha lit a cigarette and found herself tuning out, nodding when appropriate. She wanted to say, *Hey, you know someone was murdered last night? Shut up and enjoy the big house and the big car and the spoiled kids and the absent husband. It's what you wanted.* She wanted to say this, but she knew it would sound like jealousy to her friend's ears. That was the nature of privilege, to assume any argument against it was jealousy. Natasha wasn't jealous. She couldn't live Allison's life, couldn't lock herself up in a faux Mediterranean house in the hills and drive a minivan back and forth to Lucky's. Natasha needed to define herself by something other than the man who took care of her and the children she took care of. Natasha's mother had been a housewife, a smart woman who wandered around that brand-new home like a ghost, disinfecting this and washing that, her brain atrophying. When Natasha discovered evidence that blew a case wide open, nailed some perp to the wall, the satisfaction was like a drug. And, Lord, she wouldn't know what to do with a man like David—he drank white wine, liked smoked Gouda, and dry-cleaned his jeans. Jesus, pressed creases in his Levi's denim! He talked down to Allison, too, as if she were some teenage girl in threat of getting out of line. Maybe she was being too hard on her friend. Maybe Allison was like Natasha's mother—bored out of her mind. Maybe that's why she was here, getting free drinks from middle-aged men who dressed like they thought Jimmy Buffett was high art.

"But enough about me," Allison finally said. "How are you?"

"I've been busy at work," Natasha said.

A waiter swooped in and set down two sweating margaritas in front of them.

"Compliments of the dudes over there," the kid said.

And before she knew it, Ronald was back, leaning into Allison's ear. His friend, Aiden, was sitting cross-legged in the seat next to her as if he owned the table.

"So what's your line of work?" Aiden asked. He was in his mid to late forties. His face was sunburned, his eyes watery and bloodshot, his sunglasses perched on the top of his head.

"She's a doctor," Allison chimed in.

"A doct—"

"A medical examiner," Natasha said.

Allison shot Natasha an annoyed glance. *Don't do it*, she was saying. *Don't bring it up*.

"Like a coroner?" Aiden said.

"Something like that." She called the waiter over and ordered a Dewar's. "I'm not crazy about drinks that need shade from umbrellas."

"So what's a beautiful girl like you doing in that line of work?"

Aiden's voice wheezed a little, as though he were having trouble breathing.

"I like to know what killed people," she said. "For instance, say you died suddenly, just dropped dead in the shower, went to bed and never woke up, whatever the case. If I cut into you, I'm pretty sure I'd find a liver in the early stages of cirrhosis."

"She's joking," Allison said. "She likes to play this little game."

Natasha lit another cigarette.

"Cardiomyopathy," she said. "You know what that is?"

"No," Aiden said. He was leaning back in his seat now.

"A weakened heart," she said. "Alcohol enlarges the muscle, thins the walls so the heart can't pump blood efficiently. That's why you're having a hard time breathing. It causes other problems, too. Blood can't get to the extremities, if you know what I mean."

"Excuse us," Allison said, grabbing Natasha's arm and pulling her away from the table.

"Why do you do that?" she said when they were in the foyer of the restaurant.

"I'm not in the mood for the dating game," Natasha said.

"You're never in the mood."

"You know," she said, "Ronald thinks you're going to give him something tonight. He doesn't know you're just using him to feel important for a few hours."

"So what?" she said. "He's using me, too."

Natasha let out a deep breath. "I'm going," she said. "I'm too tired for this."

She sped home in her 280Z; she liked a sports car, liked the feel of the road. At her apartment, she showered and almost called Tony. Something about Las Brisas, being together with all those lonely people throwing sexual Hail Marys, made her feel lonelier.

Tony was an adjunct communications professor at Long Beach State who had written a couple of screenplays, one of them optioned-but-never-produced by Jerry Bruckheimer. She'd met Tony at a Memorial Day barbecue thrown by Mendenhall and his wife, June. It

was a narcissistic evening, she could see that now—the writer fasci-
nated with the medical minutiae of the medical examiner. (He'd
probably already written her—or a medical examiner like her—into
another failed screenplay.) But she brought him home that night and
he jokingly kissed each part of her body, asking her to whisper the
medical terms: "orbital," "external auditory meatus," "labium superi-
oris." And then her shirt was on the floor—"manubrial notch,"
"costa," "areola," "umbilicus." Not to mention the metacarpals, the
malleoli, the pelvis, and the others for which words became unnec-
essary. It was fun, still was, when her body felt the need and he was
available and willing.

But she grabbed the phone and dialed Ben's number instead.

Tony was twenty-seven, almost a decade her junior, about as deep
as the Santa Ana River in summer, and for all the places he touched—
admittedly with an admirable flair—he was unable to reach her (she
smiled to herself) "myocardium." A shame, really. He was easy, un-
complicated, but that was another kind of loneliness—the body satis-
fied but the heart left hungry.

She got Ben's voicemail. "I'm buying if you're thirsty," she said.
"Call me."

There was some leftover Chinese in the refrigerator and two
Coors. She popped a can, warmed up the moo shu, and turned on
the television. The news, an Angels game, a sitcom about some perfect family and their perfect problems. She flipped the channels
again and found a Disney movie, Snow White. She had seen the
movie as a kid, her father driving her and her mother up to Grau-
man's Chinese in Hollywood to sit in one of the balconies and gape
at the huge screen. She turned down the lights now in her one-
bedroom apartment and watched Snow White asleep in her glass
coffin, her face like cold milk, beautiful in her false death. The
dwarves keeping vigil, the birds perched heavily on bare branches.
Snow White in her glass coffin, kissed and rising from the dead.

The phone rang. It wasn't Ben.

* * *

BEN WAS TOSSING IN BED at 1:03 A.M. He never slept well when he was on a case, and the winds made it impossible—the freight-train roar outside the window, the electricity tingeing the air, the way the rushing air put your whole body on edge.

After he paid a visit to Emma's boyfriend earlier, he drove across the city line into Tustin and ordered take-out tacos—lengua, al pastor, carnitas—from Taqueria Sanchez. He had been eating them alone in the barn, drawing penciled lines between crime scenes, checking mileage between them, when the phone rang.

It was Daniela Marsh, from the *Rancho Santa Elena World News*, a newspaper that didn't cover world news and rarely ventured beyond Conquistador Road. He had gone to school with Dani. Even at sixteen, she was in everyone's business, spreading any shred of gossip she could unearth. She had caused more than a few breakups then and alerted the principal to the part-time night janitor who was banging a JV cheerleader in the riding-lawnmower shed behind the practice fields. She'd written a couple of articles about Ben, too, in the high school paper, back when he was the star swimmer. She had called Ben three times earlier in the day at the station for comment about the boy in the field. He would only confirm or deny her questions. *Yes, it's a dead body. Yes, the body was shot. No, there's nothing, yet, to suggest that it was murder.*

"I'm at deadline for the morning paper," she said. "Anything from the autopsy? Murder? Suicide?"

"How'd you get my number? It's unlisted."

"I'm a reporter, Detective," she said. "Come on, Ben, we went to school together."

"You wanna talk?" he said. "You call me at the station."

He slammed the phone down and it immediately rang again and he let it go. She'd keep hunting around, he knew, until she got something to print, but he wasn't going to give her anything; she'd have to work for it.

Now he couldn't stop his mind from running—an endless loop of evidence and crime shots. He got out of bed at 1:06 and slogged through the windy darkness back to the barn. He left the lights off, only flipping on the scanner and the desk lamp. He pulled the Mexican kid's file from the desk drawer, found the slip of paper he'd taken off the body, and read it. *Q: How would she feel if she knew?* it read, in an elegant cursive. *A: You know exactly how s—* The paper hastily ripped.

The scanner squawked: 926. Tow truck needed.

Ben had learned over time that the best investigators were not the savant kids straight out of university armed with criminal-justice degrees and math theorems to connect the dots. They weren't the tough-guy cops with marksmanship skills and judo training. They weren't the forensics geeks, either, with all their scientific magic tricks. The best investigators knew that most things were simple, that usually there were straight lines to connect suspects to crimes. If a young woman was killed in an apartment, it was a boyfriend or an estranged lover. If a teenager got shot in the street, it was the rival gang. If a man was popped in a car, in a house in the hills, at some dramatic deserted location, it was probably drugs. If a convenience store was robbed, the perp lived around the corner.

If a mysterious note was found on a dead body, it probably led to the killer—or at least someone responsible for the death.

459-A: bank alarm, Security Pacific, Barranca.

But figuring out who did what to whom was the easy stuff. What was a bitch to sort out was why. And what was a bitch and a half was proving it beyond a reasonable doubt.

The rafters shuddered, and next door Annie Oakley huffed air through her snout.

"It's all right, girl," he said. "It's just the wind."

He fanned through the pictures of the boy, his glazed eyes staring at the cloudless Southern California sky, his left index finger still hooked in the .45. Ben looked at the slip of paper again.

Who is "she"? he wrote on his legal pad. *Girlfriend? Mother?* He ran his fingers over the letters, imagining he could feel the scar of the ink against the paper.

He underlined *girlfriend*, but then he heard Hernandez's voice in his head. *You've got nothing, Detective. She could be the Virgin Mary for all you know.* He erased the line and tossed the pencil on the desk.

"187," an out-of-breath voice scratched from the scanner. The cop's voice was tight, pumped with adrenaline. "19745 Buttonwood Street."

Ben turned up the dial.

"Received," the dispatcher said. "Be advised, possible 187 at 19745 Buttonwood Street. No word on suspect."

"DB still warm," the voice said now, his words quick, his voice pitching higher. Ben knew the feeling—your heart thumping in your ears, the fog at the corners of your vision, your whole body pinpricked with heat. Didn't matter how many times you came on scene, especially a fresh one, you felt it: death and fear, married to each other. "Need backup. Need a perimeter."

"One Adam 9 en route."

The speaker clicked on, nothing but static and quickened breaths for a moment, then clicked off. Another unit called in as responding. The speaker clicked again, and yelling could be heard in background. "Family member on scene," the uniform said. "Suspect fled. No visual."

"Be advised," dispatch said. "Suspect fled. No description."

Ben listened with his elbows on the table, his knees bouncing; dispatch was calling in a crime-scene unit. He stuck a red pin on the map of the address: 19745 Buttonwood Street, Westminster, a quarter mile from the 22 Freeway, off-ramps and on-ramps just two right turns from the victim's house. The killer was using the freeways, turning off when the urge hit. The house was just fifteen miles away from where he sat. In the hollowed-out silence of the night, he heard the rush of the 5 Freeway, the Santa Ana, slicing the length of the basin from Bakersfield to the Mexican border. It was a fifteen-minute drive if the highway was clear, and by the sound of it—a smooth-flowing river rush—it was wide open.

*   *   *

HE MADE IT THERE IN eighteen minutes, parked next to an Eyewitness News van, and pushed his way through the crowd. At the perimeter he flashed his badge at one of the uniforms.

"Wondering if I can take a look?" Ben said. "Got a body cooling in county. Might be related to this."

"It's out of control in there," the uniform said. He lit a cigarette, the wind blowing it back across his face. "Mackensie's the IO, and he's shutting it down. You're not in there right now, you're not getting in."

Ben walked the perimeter, watching the faces of the crowd. Some killers returned to the scene, got off watching the police work—crime porn, they used to call it up in L.A. No one stuck out here, though, just neighbors, their faces dumb with fear, a couple of teenagers stupid with excitement. *Shit, dude, she's dead. Like, someone killed her.*

There was an elementary school behind the house, a sweep of grass and handball courts, a greenbelt with a trail weaving beyond the playground. Ben drove the cruiser two blocks over, coming around the front of the school—a pair of classroom windows lit from within, papier-mâché art hanging on the sun-yellow walls. A couple of black-and-whites spun lights at either end of the property. Ben pulled up beside the first one and flashed his badge at the uniform.

"Mackensie wants me combing the school grounds," Ben said, and a few minutes later he was in the lightless field, a black square of grass surrounded by the glowing windows of Tuscan-style homes. There was a half fence, three feet high, separating the backyard from the school yard. From here, thirty yards away, Ben could see the detectives working the kitchen. He flashed his penlight across the ground—stomped-down grass that thinned to dried mud. Zigzag prints, kids' shoes. Handprint, Tonka truck tracks, a soccer-ball pentagon. He inched toward the fence that separated the yard from the playground and found it: Vans skate shoes—at least three footprints in the dirt, trailing toward the fence.

"Get Mackensie on the horn," Ben said when he got back to the uniform.

The cop did. Ten minutes later, investigators were in the field, snapping photos.

By the 6:30 Wednesday-morning newscasts, the L.A. and Orange County sheriffs' offices had declared the obvious. Before most people had finished their first cup of coffee, the L.A. news stations had christened the killer the Night Prowler. Goddamned news. And by 7:45 Ben was sitting in a briefing room with Lieutenant Hernandez and two other detectives, chewing NoDoz and gulping coffee.

"We've got a BOLO for a serial," Hernandez said, his coat still on, which meant business, the jacket still buttoned, which meant real-deal business. "LAPD and both counties made it official. Random strikes, all after eight p.m., all entering through open first-floor windows or doors. So far, no discernible motive."

"The joy of strangling people?" Marco Giraldi said. Marco had recently been promoted to detective, primarily on the merits of breaking up a teenage marijuana ring while working patrol. Barely twenty-eight, he looked like a teenager himself; above his top lip was a wispy line of peach fuzz he seemed to think was a mustache.

Lieutenant Hernandez nodded. "Most likely sociopath," he said, as he passed a stack of folders around the table. "None of the victims seem connected."

"Except by the killer," Marco said. The more a man shot off his mouth, the more vulnerable he was. In L.A., Ben knew a vice cop who always bitched about "faggots on the make," how they disgusted him, how they were disease magnets. He was busted three months later with a "faggot on the make" in a Santa Monica motel room. Then there was that homicide detective, twenty-year veteran, big tough guy always cracking jokes over dead bodies, broke down one night in the precinct after a murder/suicide, just turned to water at his desk and spent the next three months hardening up in a facility in the valley. Maybe it was rookie nerves, but Ben suspected the serial had Marco spooked.

"Multiple races," Hernandez said, ignoring Marco. "Multiple sexes. Likes to tip the cops after the deed is done."

"Jesus," Carolina McGrath said when she opened the file.

Ben took a file from Carolina, a shot of acid in his stomach when he saw the crime-scene photos. A woman's white knees, her torso twisted on the carpet, stacks of magazines spread across the floor, a broken vase, water soaking the carpet near her left foot.

"Sexual assault?" Carolina said, standing up with her file to pace the room. She was nearly six feet tall, a former University of California volleyball player who could never sit still. Some of the uniforms who didn't make detective resented her, thought her getting promoted three years ago was some affirmative action BS, but she was a good detective—a real eye for detail.

"No," the lieutenant said. "At least, no evidence to that effect."

"Suspect wears Vans skate shoes," Ben said, noticing it wasn't written down in the description of the perp. "Eight and a half? Nine?"

"Heard about your extracurricular activity, Detective," Hernandez said, his reading glasses slid down his nose to look at Ben.

"Couldn't sleep."

"Read a book," Hernandez said. "It works for me."

"Try a romance novel," Carolina said, raising an eyebrow at him. "They'll put you to sleep immediately."

"ID on that boy's body yet?" Hernandez said to Ben.

"Waiting on the science geeks," Ben said. "Bullet in ballistics. No fingerprint matches."

"Keep it quiet," Hernandez said. "The mayor's in my ear about this one."

"Too late for that," Ben said. "For keeping it quiet."

Ben slid the morning's paper across the table. HISPANIC FOUND SHOT IN STRAWBERRY FIELD. He'd picked it up at the Rancho Market on his way to the station early that morning, along with a cup of coffee and a microwaved breakfast burrito. He'd glanced through the article and found the line: *Detectives offered no comment on the connection between this killing and the Night Prowler.* When Reza Salehi, the owner of the market, rang Ben up, he set aside the paper.

"Was this boy killed by the Night Prowler?" He was frightened, and he wanted Ben to assure him that Santa Elena was still a safe little bubble.

"Not sure, Reza," he'd said. "Lock your doors."

Now Lieutenant Hernandez skimmed the article himself. "Dammit," he said. "Call this Miss Marsh and let her know the medical examiner suspects it's self-inflicted." He dropped the paper on the table, pulled his glasses off, and massaged the bridge of his nose. "Anonymous tip on this Mexican kid, right?"

"Yeah," Ben said. "Shooting, though. Nothing else fits this guy."

"You never know," Marco said, turning a page in the file to photos of another victim. "This serial may be branching out."

Ben flipped the page and saw what Marco saw. He had to glance away for a moment, out across the courtyard to the field beyond, where a man with a chain saw was quartering trunks of eucalyptus felled the week before. They were going to build a strip mall there, a Lucky grocery, a car wash, a wine store.

"Bludgeoned," Hernandez said.

"Got more than he expected with this one," Marco said, no joking in his voice.

"Used a Remington bronze," Hernandez said.

"Sculpture?" Carolina said, briefly stopping her pacing. "God."

Ben returned to the shot. The left side of the man's skull had been bashed in. Bruises again on the neck, but the killer had crushed the larynx—the picture showed the sinkhole in the neck. The victim had been a big man, and he must have fought and fought.

"He's not branching out," Carolina said. "This one was back in August. It's all women since then."

"ME says the killer's got small hands," Ben said. "Woman-sized hands."

"Doubtful it's a woman," Carolina said. "A woman would use a ligature, especially if she was going to overpower a man bigger than herself."

"He wasn't strong enough to strangle this one," Ben said.

"So he used the sculpture," Hernandez said.

"Then it's all women after that," Marco repeated, nodding.

The next shot was of a woman's face, her head yanked to the side, her neck mottled with bruises. Petechiae on the eyes and cheeks, a cluster of purple dots pinpricking the skin.

"The place last night was gated," Ben said. "A playground behind the house, a greenbelt leading out of the playground."

"Unlocked doors," Carolina said. "Playground deserted at night, so no witnesses."

Ben turned the pages to find more photos, this time an elderly man, back in July. The refrigerator door behind him was swung open; a gallon of orange juice and a forty-ounce bottle of malt liquor sat on the shelves. Bruises again on the body, finger-pad marks circling the throat. Strangled. The most intimate of crimes. Face-to-face, watching the terror and recognition there — either terribly personal or completely impersonal. A serial. Had to be impersonal.

"Rafferty's case in Mission Viejo wasn't gated," Ben said. "But it was master-planned. A greenbelt running behind it."

"The Palos Verdes place," Carolina said, "is master-planned, too. I dated a guy near there for a while."

"If he's got a thing for master-planned," Ben said, "Santa Elena's the place."

"All we got is in the file in front of you," Lieutenant Hernandez said. "Maybe an ID from last night in Westminster: Five six or five seven. Dark clothes. A woman was walking her dog in the park around one A.M. when she saw him come out from the backyard. She was halfway down the block, though, and that's all she's got."

"He stayed on foot?" Carolina asked.

"Turned the corner."

"Car parked on the next block probably," Ben said. "All killings are less than a half mile from a freeway."

"Narrows it down" — Marco smiled — "to about five million possible future victims."

Using the freeways. Master-planned communities. Vans shoes. Open windows.

"One more thing," Hernandez said. "They found something

scratched into the bedroom wall last night." He glanced through the file. "*Swear* something or other—it's jumbled and cut off. Westminster thinks the husband nearly stumbled in on the killer. Just back from a business trip in New York."

Ben flipped the pages and found the photocopy of the Polaroid. The image was grainy, and the words scratched into the plaster were clumsy and poorly drawn—letters backward, some of the lines squiggly and indistinct.

"It's like kid writing," Marco said.

"A cipher?" Carolina said.

"Something about *Swear you're going*," Ben said, trying to decipher it.

"*Swear you're going* what?" Carolina said.

"Pretty obvious, isn't it?" Marco said, holding up a shot of the last victim.

"CAN I SEE YOU A moment?" Lieutenant Hernandez said.

They stepped into Hernandez's office, a rectangle of floor-to-ceiling windows. "The hamster cage," the detectives called it, since you could watch every single thing the lieutenant did behind the glass. If the man picked his nose, the whole station knew. Once, when Hernandez had an argument with his wife, some of the guys thought it hilarious to tie a fake ball and chain to the front door.

"Moonlighting it, huh?" Hernandez said.

"Just trying to connect the dots," Ben said.

The glass office was supposed to reflect the new transparency of an organization built on trust and coordination. The windows, cleaned every night by a "rehabilitated" felon, were streakless; if you didn't know they were there, you'd think you were sitting out among the crowd of cubicles and metal desks.

"Did you sleep in the cruiser last night?"

Ben shrugged, not sure what to say. He got twenty minutes in the station parking lot before the meeting.

"Maybe you should talk to some—"

"No one's shrinking my head," Ben said.

"The first divorce is tough," Hernandez said. "I know." He smiled and slapped his big hand on Ben's shoulder. "The second one's a little easier."

Ben laughed sarcastically.

"You put me in a tough spot with Westminster, crashing their scene," Hernandez said, serious again.

"I know."

"It's not professional." Hernandez waited a moment. "Usually people offer an apology right about now."

"They wouldn't have found the print," Ben said.

Hernandez nodded. The lieutenant knew the cops had never found the driver of the Chevelle, the one that hit Ben's father that night years ago and killed him. He and Ben had talked about it one night over beers soon after he'd joined the force. Whoever hit-and-ran his dad was probably still out there, living his life. The cops had probably never even tried to find the driver; they had murders to deal with, robberies. Who cared about some old cowboy thrown from his horse? "Ghosts," Hernandez had said then. "The ones that get away." Hernandez meant that Ben had to let it go; some perps got away, that's just the harsh fact of the matter. Hernandez was right, but Ben couldn't stand shitty police work—or no police work—that let a criminal dissolve into thin air.

"What dots're you trying to connect?"

"Maybe I'm still looking for them."

"To my reading, the Mexican looks like a suicide, not this serial," Hernandez said, sitting down at his leather desk chair. "Depressed strawberry picker."

"Right-handed but gun in left?" Ben said. "Shot in the back of the head? That doesn't spell suicide to me."

Hernandez looked at him closely. Ben knew he wanted this neat and clean, wrapped up, filed away. Hernandez was good at the politics of the job, knew how to deliver the right message, giving the mayor and the town what they wanted: an illusion, not reality. That's why he got paid the big bucks. Ben was pretty sure the lieutenant had his eye on higher office—the first Hispanic mayor of Santa Elena, maybe.

"A kid, right? Teenager?"

"Yep."

"You haven't been to the high school yet?" Hernandez said. "Unless I missed something."

"He's most likely illegal," Ben said, a pitch of defensiveness coloring his voice.

"Doesn't keep them out of the schools."

"No, I guess not."

"I would've thought you'd already checked there," Hernandez said, crossing his arms over his chest. "I'm not used to telling you how to do your job, Ben."

THE HIGH SCHOOL COULD WAIT. Ben grabbed the Polaroid camera from his filing cabinet, then called Rafferty off an affidavit for a ring of car-stereo thieves and met him at the Mission Viejo scene that afternoon.

Police tape still ribboned the house. A memorial of flowers and half-burned candles littered the driveway gutter. The house had been shut up for two days, all the curtains drawn, the air still thick with the dank fetor of death. Investigation chalk hieroglyphed the kitchen linoleum, and a salted stain ringed the corner of the floor like a dried-up lake.

"Jesus, Raff," Ben said. "Get a crew to clean that up, huh?"

"Got orders not to touch it," he said. "Still an open investigation."

"Natasha's got what she needs from that."

"Would love to shut it down," Rafferty said. "I've got recitals and baseball games to get to. Didn't move down here for this kind of shit."

How he kept his marriage together after Delia found out about his screwing around was beyond Ben. Rachel wouldn't have stood for that crap. Put up with a lot else, but she wouldn't have any of that.

"Etched into the wall?"

"With a paper clip," Ben said. "Or an X-Acto knife. Something like that."

They searched the walls in the kitchen—grease stains, calendar pinned to a corkboard. They pulled back the curtains on the pantry windows to check the lime-green painted plaster, combed over the cabinets and wooden dining table.

They split up, Rafferty taking the family room and Ben searching the living room. He ran his palms over the green recliner, unfolded the quilt spread neatly over the headrest. He ran his fingers over the brick of the fireplace, checked the backs of the framed photos on the mantel, checked the silver face of the Pioneer hi-fi sitting on a shelf beneath the television. "You're going, you're going . . ." he whispered to himself. "Swear you're going to what?" He got down on his knees and brushed dust from the baseboards and swiped a hand underneath a couch, pulling out an old *Sunset* magazine and a green jelly bean.

"Ben," Rafferty called from the family room. "Think I got something."

Rafferty was holding back the curtain to a small window that overlooked the backyard.

"Jesus," Ben said. "How'd we miss it?"

"Looks like kindergarten writing," Rafferty said.

It was small, jaggedly etched into the wood of the windowpane. The letters were malformed, turned backward, the words misspelled and nearly indecipherable. It looked like the kind of writing a child would leave on his bedroom wall.

"What the hell is wrong with this guy?" Rafferty said.

Ben got down on his knees and rubbed his thumb across the rough edges. A backward S. Inverted N's.

"I mean, who writes like that?"

A lowercase g with the tail turned the wrong way. An upside-down A.

"Get the camera," Ben said.

Rafferty grabbed the Polaroid from the kitchen counter, and Ben snapped two pictures—one he slipped into an evidence bag, and the other he slid into his coat pocket.

A backward lowercase h, an upside-down A, an inverted N, a b. No, a backward lowercase d. *"Hand,"* Ben said, rubbing his fingers against the jagged wooden edges.

The first word was indecipherable, though there was a squiggle that could be an S, an M that could be a W, if you turned it right side up. *"Swear you're gonna . . ."* Ben said out loud as he read it. An F, a lowercase i, and a backward L. *"Feel,"* he said. *"You're gonna feel my hand."*

"Holy shit," Rafferty said.

"Swear you're gonna feel my hand," Ben said again, standing up now.

"Yeah," Rafferty said. "I guess so."

WHAT NATASHA COULDN'T GET OUT of her head from the Westminster scene, even three hours later at the morgue, was the woman's husband. She knew what she was going to get with the body—the bruises around the neck, the sclerotic eyes, the livor mortis—but she hadn't anticipated the husband, the way he lost it. Detectives had been with him, locked inside an upstairs bedroom, but his wails still echoed in the house. Bent over the woman—Karena Avery was her name— snapping shots of bloodied skin caught in the crescent beneath her fingernails, Natasha had thought, You're a lucky woman, to be mourned like that. If there was a half-world after death, a purgatorial membrane between this world and whatever was beyond it, where the dead could stand witness, this is what you wished to see: your loss tearing a hole out of someone.

Stop, she thought then. She actually stepped outside for a smoke, leaving Karena's body alone, while she tried to exhale the thought away. Natasha was shocked by her selfishness. Yet it was there, like a ticker-tape sign announcing her true self: She wanted to mean that much to another person. She wanted her death to hurt someone.

She left the morgue at dawn, a yolk-yellow crack in the eastern sky above the San Gabriels. She drove home through the empty morning streets, poured herself a finger of Dewar's, and stood in the shower until the water went cold. Before getting in bed, she called Allison, who was awake and rested-sounding, getting the kids ready for school, and told her to close and lock all the doors to the house.

"You're frightening me," Allison had said.

"He's looking for easy targets," Natasha said. "So don't be one."

Natasha slept until 10:17, when the garbage truck in the alley slammed loose the trash from the apartment cans. And in the silence of the retreating truck, there he was again, trapped in her mind, the husband and his guttural wails.

"Get a cup?" Natasha said into the phone, when Ben picked up.

"I'm on duty," he said.

"I'm sunbathing at Newport Beach," she said. "You martyr. It's a business coffee."

She met him at a table outside the Blowhole Café on Thursday morning, a half mile from the station, near the 5 Freeway. He stood when she got there, pulling out her chair.

"You look tired," he said.

"You look wrecked."

"Occupational hazard." He sat down and she placed the files on the table next to two cups of coffee.

"You on scene last night?" he said, picking up the file on the Mexican boy.

"Till three," she said, nodding.

She took a sip of the coffee he'd fixed, black, cut with hot water — tea, really, just as she liked it. She didn't know when they'd crossed this line into banal intimacy, but it *had* been crossed. It was a strange comfort, an illicit one in a way, tinged with guilt. (She knew Rachel; they'd all gone to school together, though Natasha was two years behind them and had been an anonymous geek with her nose always in a book.) Natasha had enjoyed this little attention when he was married, too, and she returned it: He liked his coffee sugared up, quarter full of half-and-half. The first time she'd made it for him — five years ago when he kept visiting her office, pressing her for forensic evidence on a gang-war shooting that had spilled over into Orange County from L.A. — she'd called him "sweetie." He'd quietly laughed then and said, "Yeah, don't tell anyone. They'll make me a meter maid." There was a generosity in Ben, the ability to laugh at himself, though she hadn't seen that spirit in him in a long time.

"Why haven't you called?" she said. God, she hated the way she sounded, like some needy, fragile woman, like her friend Allison. *Why haven't you called me? We had such a nice night together.* She wasn't going to ask it; she'd told herself she wouldn't bring it up. It was a simple question, though, and she wanted a simple answer. They'd had dinner. Sure, it was just In-N-Out Burger, but Emma was there, too. In her stupid groaning-woman mind, she thought that meant something.

"I thought this was a business cup-a-Joe?"

"It is," she said, sitting back in her chair, "of course."

"I've been busy," he said vaguely.

"I've been sipping champagne and nibbling caviar."

"I hate caviar," he said, a wry smile on his face.

Levity, deflection, ironic triviality, all Ben's specialty. He was an expert at it, the friendly banter that kept you at arm's length.

"Russian," she said. "It has to be Russian."

"Damn Communists."

He turned the file page. "What've we got?" he said, all business now.

"The bullet ripped through the frontal lobe, clipped the basal ganglia, and shredded the parietal lobe." She lit a cigarette and blew the smoke above her head. "You know how to read."

It was a cool morning, the wind pumping in high desert air, and they sat beneath a heat lamp near a planter blooming with bird-of-paradise. The wind swung the flowers' heavy heads back and forth. A half block away was an on-ramp to the freeway, and a steady stream of cars raced up the pavement to join the rush toward Los Angeles. From here, the freeway was a pleasant white noise, the rush of a river, the cascading of a waterfall.

She watched him read, his elbows on the table, his lips moving slightly as his eyes ran across the pages. The boy's height, 6'3". Weight, 185. The liver weighed 2,551 grams. Heart, 346 grams, slightly above average.

She and Ben had met a few more times after the gang case, even after the case was closed and Ben had gotten his man, Ben asking her about evidence on open cases, picking her brain about shooting angles, time-of-death indicators, stuff like that, as though he wanted an education. Then they didn't see each other for three years, until they were both on scene for a backyard pool drowning, after he and Rachel had moved back to Santa Elena. But it wasn't until after his separation from Rachel that they started meeting for drinks; she made sure of that. They talked open cases, tossed around evidence on cold cases, played out hypotheticals on suspects' motives. Sometimes the conversations turned serious. What is hate? What makes a criminal? Was it something physical, something she could pinpoint in the brain, in the size of the heart? He wanted to know if fear showed in the body, like physical scars in the tissue. It was chaste stuff, mostly, and she had almost resigned herself to her platonic role, when one drunken night five weeks ago he'd pushed the line.

"What is sex?" he had asked.

They had been clumsily dancing at the Reno Room, an old haunt of his from his Long Beach days, Ben plunking down quarters for old R&B tunes. The question caught her off guard, and she couldn't tell at first if he was serious or flirting.

"The body's reaction to physical stimuli," she said, the two of them swaying to Marvin Gaye.

"What is sexual attraction?" he countered.

"The body's reaction to an irrational feeling."

He smiled. "No," he said, his hand on the curve of her back. "No, it's more than that."

Then he bent down and kissed her, once, and the song ended and they stood there in the middle of the room, the sounds of the bar coming back to them.

"Any chance this was an execution?" Ben said now. "Any gang tats?"

"Would be a bad line in Vegas," she said, shaking her head. "The boy's prints are all over the gun; his thumb was bruised. He must have jammed it when the gun recoiled."

A .45 caliber bullet. Meninges penetrated at right temple. Perforation of skull behind left ear. The description of the brain damage ran in her head. Intracranial hematoma. Ischemic cascade. She was beginning to hate medical terms: A half dozen years before, they felt comfortingly precise. Now they were beginning to feel deceptive, inaccurate in their scope of things.

"There was sperm?"

"Traces of semen in the underwear."

"Any other signs of sexual activity?"

"No," she said. "No tears, no bruising, no vaginal secretions."

He was quiet for a moment, his index finger tapping the page in front of him, his lips tightening.

"Any signs," he said, hesitating, "of unusual sexual activity?"

Cops, she thought, the fraternity of delicate sensibilities.

"No," she said. "No signs of *unusual* sexual activity."

"You checked?"

"Of course I checked. It's not as unusual as some of us like to think."

He took a sip of his coffee. Ben's hand seemed to shake a bit. Maybe he was tired.

"A little in the underwear is not uncommon," she said, "especially with teenage boys, if you know what I mean."

He nodded and stared off at the cars in the parking lot.

"ID on the Colt?" she asked.

"Not yet. Slow as hell over there."

"It'll be faster," she said, "when they get the computer database running. They say they'll be able to analyze DNA."

"Sounds like sci-fi bullshit to me."

She took a drag of the cigarette as he read on. Musculoskeletal system. Urogenital system. When they left the Reno Room that night, she was determined not to go home alone. He strolled her the six blocks back to her place, the fireworks exploding above Disneyland, a police helicopter slashing a spotlight across Westminster streets, and when they got to the front door, she said, "I want you to come up."

Five minutes later, her jeans and shirt were off, and his fingers were on the lip of her panties when she touched him through his jeans. She could feel him alive there, and she wanted him inside her. She worked the button loose. Now, now, now, she thought, and then he pushed her hand away. Cute, she thought, feigning hard to get, but she wasn't in the mood for cute, for his ironic deflections. His fingers were hooked in her panties, and she raised her hips to help him slip them off. She touched him again, trying to get his zipper to peel apart, and he recoiled.

"I can't do this," he said. Then he was up from the bed, his back to her, his shirt already pulled over his shoulders. It happened so fast it took her a moment to register what was going on.

"You can," she said. "You can do whatever you want." She regretted that now, that willingness to give all of her body away.

"I can't," he said, his voice strangled in his mouth. "I'm sorry. It's not you."

"Oh, Jesus," she said. "Be more creative than that, at least."

"It's really not," he said. He touched her bare knee, though it seemed to pain him. "I can't explain." And then he was gone.

She took a shower after he left, sure it was the smell of her skin, all that death, all those opened corpses. She exfoliated, used a nail file to carve dirt from beneath her fingernails, washed her hair, and washed it again, and still when she got in bed she could feel the taint on her skin—the death, the rejection, the embarrassment of letting herself be so exposed. She almost called Tony, to satisfy her body, but her heart made its demands and she tossed in bed alone.

"He'd been drinking?" Ben said now.

"There was alcohol in his system. Difficult to say how much when he pulled the trigger."

"He'd had some drinks, though? Not just the beginnings of de-composition?"

A gust of wind blew the birds-of-paradise, the necks tangling around one another. Natasha leaned forward and unwrapped the stems carefully, setting them loose and swaying.

"Seems so." She lit another cigarette with the tip of the first and blew the smoke into the heat lamp.

"He must have been drinking with someone."

"I don't know," she said. "Some drink alone."

He glanced at her but went back to the file.

"Why'd you stay through the autopsy the other day?" Natasha asked. "I know you can't stand those things. Don't even like to see me afterward."

A woman leashed to a Labrador retriever sat at the table next to them. She tied the dog to the table leg and went inside the coffee-house.

"Didn't want to leave the kid alone."

"That's not it," she said, glancing at his tapping fingers. "You know something, don't you?"

He closed the report and went quiet. Together they watched the woman stride out of the coffeehouse. She unwrapped a chocolate muffin and set it on a paper plate in front of the dog. The Lab licked the sugar off the top and then huffed it down in one bite. Natasha rolled her eyes at him.

"No," he said finally, but he was a terrible liar. Ben Wade was a window, when he wanted to be a wall. You could see through him, but into what? An open window that led into a dark room.

"I was just thinking about Emma," he said. "How I wouldn't want her to be alone, if it was her. It's irrational, I know."

She wanted to hate him, but there was an honesty in his lies. Most men would have swallowed their disgust in the face of an easy lay and gone through with it. She'd met enough of those guys, my God. The prettiest spin she could put on it was that he knew it meant something to her, he knew it was unfair to her if he wasn't sure.

Maybe that was being too generous, but she wasn't prepared to hate him yet for the things he was unwilling to give.

"Excuse me?" the woman with the dog said to Natasha. "Can you smoke that somewhere else? The wind is blowing it right across my table."

Natasha spun around. The woman was windshield-wiping a skinny hand in front of her nose. She was one of those pretty Santa Elena women, plastic pretty and easy to hate.

"It's not your table, honey," Natasha said. "This is not your shopping center, this is not your courtyard, and this is not your outside air. And you're poisoning that poor dog feeding it chocolate. Theobromine. Destroys their organs."

The woman muttered something under her breath, gathered her stuff, and huffed away with the dog in tow.

"God," Natasha said. "I hate these people and their registered mutts."

"No match on fingerprint records, dental?" Ben said.

"*Nada.*" She stubbed out the cigarette and lit another. "Some poor mother in Chiapas or Oaxaca thinks he's sending her money this month."

"I think the mother's here," he said.

She sat up. "You do know something."

"I saw a woman the other day in the camp," Ben said. "She was upset. She wouldn't talk to me. No one would talk about the boy at all."

"They never talk to anyone. You know that."

"There's an older man, a picker, protecting her." He wrote something across the top of the report. "I think he's the one who called it in."

"The serial's tipping, I know," she said. "But I've been on three scenes now, and nothing about this one adds up that way."

"A body hasn't turned up in a dozen years in this town, and one just appears while this serial is running around? It's all a coincidence?"

"This kid was outside," she said, counting it off with her fingers. "Shot in the head, no marks on his neck, no crazy saying carved anywhere near the body."

"So why doesn't a mother claim her son?"

"She's afraid of getting sent back," she said.

"It's something else," he said. "A mother wouldn't leave her son in a morgue."

"It's not her son anymore, and—"

"No." He looked at her. "It's always, forever, your son."

She sat back in her chair, silenced by his glare. She couldn't stand that, the way parents threw their sentiment in your face, the way they thought they understood more about the human heart because they brought children into this world.

"I meant," she said, taking a deep breath, "that maybe there's something else she needs to protect. Maybe she's got no other choice."

"Maybe," he said. "Let me have a pull."

She handed him the cigarette and he took a long drag on it. He left the filter wet, like all novices, and when she took her own drag she let her tongue press against that wetness.

"Oh, chlorine," she said. "Chlorine in his hair follicles, some pool water in his lungs."

"Saw that," he said.

"He's a swimmer."

"Seems plausible."

Seems obvious, she thought. Swimming was a big deal in Santa Elena. "Teenager, illegal," she said. "Doubt he had access to a community pool. Maybe on the high school team."

Ben nodded. "You seem pretty comfortable doing my job."

"You get the shiny badge and the hot wheels."

"Dime-store tin and a Chevy."

"You want to get a bite tonight?" she said. "I know a great quiche place."

He laughed; he got the stupid joke. "And you know how I like quiche."

"The body needs sustenance."

He looked at his watch. "I gotta get some paperwork done at the station."

She crushed the cigarette against the leg of the metal table. "Yeah, all right."

He leaned forward, put his hands on the table between them. "It's not that I haven't wanted to call," he said, his voice quiet. "It's just . . ."

She touched his right hand, stroked the edge of it with her thumb. She could feel the heat rise in his palms. "Forget about it, Ben," she said. "I'm not losing any sleep over it."

6

At 6:17 THE NEXT MORNING, BEN WAS CLIMBING OUT OF THE drainage ditch that moated the strawberry field. He'd changed into jeans and a sweatshirt—no khakis, no button-down, no necktie. He wanted to blend in. The western half of the field was empty, yellow police tape fluttering in the wind, a black-and-white parked on the street, keeping an eye on things. Beyond the black-and-white, a front-loader toppled an avocado tree, the gnashing of its mechanics carried in the wind. There were at least two dozen pickers working the eastern half of the field. From this distance they looked like foraging animals, backs bowed in the sun, stripping the plants clean of fruit.

As soon as he stepped into the field, a picker shoved two fingers between his lips and whistled. Two women bolted, dropped their buckets and fists of strawberries, and stumbled down the rows. Others shuffled away, glancing to see if Ben was in pursuit, but three others simply ignored him and bent again to the fruit. Ben recognized one of them.

"Right back at it, huh?" Ben said, when he got to him.

The Mexican stripped three strawberries from a plant, looked at them closely, and tossed the fruit into a bucket that was slung over his shoulder.

"You all need to eat, right?" the picker said.

"I hate strawberries."

"Me, too."

Ben watched the other pickers scurry into the cardboard houses, a woman snatching a half-naked boy who was pissing in the street. Suddenly the camp seemed deserted, a jumble of discarded boxes bleached by the sun.

"You're legal, right?" Ben said. "That's why you didn't run?"

"I've got papers," he said, "if you need to see them. They usually don't ask until later, though."

"Yeah, well, I'm not those guys," Ben said. "I don't give a damn, really. There's a demand, you fill it."

Ben plucked a strawberry off the vine and held it in his palm. It was bruised, and a splotch of pulp smudged his fingers.

"The whole field is infested," the man said. "Black rot."

Ben dropped the berry and wiped his fingers on his pants leg.

"Foreman wants us out here anyway," the man said. "They'll still sell it."

The man shuffled down the row and started working on the next shrub. The hunch of his back suggested a warped spine, muscles broken down from years of labor, but his hands moved with a gentle dexterity and the fruit seemed to leap off the stem into his fingers.

"You know the boy, right?" Ben said. "*El muchacho*. You knew him?"

Ben watched the man's jaw go hard, grinding his teeth. A shadow swept across the plants. Ben looked up, hawk wings passing in front of the white sun.

"The woman in the corner of the room yesterday," Ben said. "The one crying. Is she the mother?"

"*No se*," the man said.

"You don't know?" he said. "Or you won't say?"

The man stood and grimaced. Nose-to-nose with him, Ben saw that they were close in age. In the darkness of the cardboard house the other morning he had looked older, but in the early-morning light Ben saw that they could have gone to school together.

"Look. You people either *don't give a damn*," the man said, mimicking Ben's inflection, "or you give a damn. But no one cares, *me entiende?*"

Yeah, he got it.

"Shit happens out here and you all just stay over there"—he looked toward the houses lining the field—"where it's all nice and clean."

"I care what happened to this kid," Ben said. "If I didn't, I'd be at home, feet up, drinking a *cerveza*."

The man thumbed the brim of his hat off his brow; a line of paler skin creased his forehead.

"You know," he said, "busting out a Spanish word here and there don't mean nothing. You're still a gringo cop, *cerveza* or no *cerveza*."

"Where were you Tuesday night, two A.M.?" Ben asked.

"I was faceup on my cot, watching the wind shake the walls."

"Anybody vouch for you?"

"You gonna play this TV-cop bullshit with me?"

"I think I want to see those papers now."

The man broke his stare and looked off toward the mountains in the east, hunks of thrust-up land hovering above the band of smog.

"I knew the boy," the Mexican finally said. "I liked him." The man wouldn't look at Ben, just stared at the suspended peaks. A man doesn't look you in the face, he's being honest, embarrassed by his feelings. One of those general truths Ben had learned over the years. "He was a good boy. Gave us hope."

"Hope?"

"Yeah," the man said. "Hope, you know? That thing you come to this shitty place for?" He kept staring at the mountains, a crust of snow on the tip of Mount San Antonio. "You been there?" the man said, nodding toward the peaks.

"Yeah," Ben said.

"What's it like?" he said. "What's snow like?"

"Cold," Ben said.

The man laughed cynically and bent to the strawberries again.

"The mother the one who can vouch for you?"

"No," the Mexican said. "My wife, but we got kids, and you'll have to arrest me before I let you near them." The man weeded a clump of dandelion, garnishing the muck in the bucket. "Now I gotta get to work. They're weighing at four-thirty."

Ben nodded, watching the front-loader flatten the avocado grove. Maybe the man had papers but his wife was illegal. Talk to the police, you get sent back. It was the law, when certain men wanted to use it. The gangs in East L.A. had exploited this, used the law as another form of terror. *No snitching or we'll call immigration, and they'll dump your pinche ass on the other side of the fence.*

"Your back isn't good," Ben said to the man. "You seen a doctor?"

The man shot Ben a who-you-kidding look and inched down the row. Ben joined him. The Mexican kept an eye on Ben for a few moments and then ignored him. If the gringo wanted to pick strawberries, he seemed to think, let him. The man was right: Most of the berries were rotten, bruised and bleeding juice, but a few remained on each bush. Ben plucked them from the stems and placed them in plastic cases fitted together inside the wheelbarrow. When they were five plants down, Ben returned to the wheelbarrow and rolled it down the line. The man said nothing, just looked Ben in the eye.

"Name's Ben Wade," he said, lifting a strawberry from the stem. It was a good one, shining red in the sun. "My grandfather used to work the fields. When he first got here in '34." Ben pressed his knees into the sun-bleached dirt, the heat of it burning through his jeans. "He came here when the windstorms hit Kansas and destroyed everything." He found another good fruit and placed it in the plastic container. The man glanced at the berry, pulled it out.

"No," the man said, pointing to a tiny mark hidden beneath the green leaves. "This'll make people sick."

They went down the row together, five minutes in silence, picking the fruit, tossing the rotten, packaging the few worth selling. Ben barely remembered his grandfather, but he knew the story. The southern Kansas farm. The "black snow" of '34. Winds billowing dry soil into a two-thousand-foot undulating wall that peppered the clapboard house with pebbles. The family huddled together in the pitch-black living room, the sand scouring their teeth, the dust sucked into their lungs. A milky blind spot in Ben's father's eye had attested to the day: The dirt had sandpapered his iris. When the storm finally passed the next morning, the west side of the house was buried to the eaves. The barn leaned east, the whole thing swaying toward collapse. Inside the barn, the chickens clayed still, their beaks open in frozen gasps. The land was drifted with soil; great heaves of it duned the cornfields and sludged the well. Who knew about the horses and the sheep lost out there on the land? And before the month passed, a man in a suit with a police escort stood on the porch with papers saying the bank owned the property.

Ben wondered what it must have been like for his grandfather, a man who held property once, a man with a Model A, a man with chickens and livestock and his own garden, bent in a field like a tenant farmer. Then even that job was taken away by the waves of Mexican immigrants. The anger he must have felt, the rage Ben felt now radiating from this man—rage that breaks down the body, wilting it toward the soil. That's why Ben didn't like the raids; he was barely a generation removed from this world.

"Something's wrong about this boy's death," Ben finally said. "Murder or suicide, neither add up."

"The whole pinche world don't add up." The man leaned back on his haunches. "I was awake," he said, wiping sweat from his forehead. "The wind had me up all night. I had to tie the corner of the ceiling down with packing twine. I didn't hear anything. Replayed the whole night in my head, wondering if I missed something, wondering if I could have done something, you know, but all I remember is the wind."

Ben pulled the slip of paper he'd taken from the boy out of his back pocket and showed it to the man.

"You recognize this handwriting?"

The man looked at it, glanced at the mountains, then stared too hard at Ben when he said, "No."

"Nothing?" Ben said.

"No, man," he said, his voice aggravated. "Just some writing."

"I need to talk to his mother," Ben said, standing up now.

The man said nothing, just kept his face to the ground, his hands working the fruit.

"*Entiendes?*" Ben said.

The Mexican looked up at Ben. "She's got other kids," he said. "Do *you* understand?"

"Yeah, I get it," he said. Natasha was right yesterday: something else to protect.

Ben stood there, watching the man shuffle down the row, the wind whipping bulldozer dust across the fields. The yellow machine tipped an avocado tree, the roots clinging to the soil, the front-loader and tree locked in stasis before the roots ripped loose and the trunk fell.

"They'll keep the body for a few weeks," Ben said. "After that they'll donate it to UC Med School." Ben pulled his card from his wallet and handed it to the man. "You think of something," Ben said, "there's that phone over at the Texaco station."

The man blinked, found out: Just as Ben thought, this man had made the call about the kid's body. The Mexican slipped the card into the chest pocket of his sweat-wet shirt.

"There was another boy," the man said.

"Another?" Ben said. The Mexican wasn't going to give up the mother, her other children. Ben respected him for it.

"Someone he knew from the school."

"He went to school?"

"We got him a fake address," he said. "From someone sympathetic to us."

"This sympathetic person's name?"

"You think I'm going to tell you that?"

"I'll find out."

"Then find out," he said. "You can explain to the other kids why they can't go to school. Kids are allowed, but not without an address."

"This person is letting others use the address?"

The man glanced at the San Gabriels again. He stayed silent.

"The boy wanted to go to the mountains," the man said in answer to the question. "I said I'd take him one day." He shook his head.

"What about this other boy, the one from school?" Ben pressed.

The man glanced at Ben. "I found them together in the orange groves one day," he said, hesitating. "The boy's mother's a good Catholic, *tu comprendes*?"

"Yeah, I understand."

"I told him I wouldn't tell her," he said. "I promised him."

"You feel guilty now?"

The man nodded. "Promises," the man said. "Maybe some aren't worth keeping." He tossed a disintegrated strawberry into the bucket. "He was a good boy. Confused, but good."

"You got a name for this school friend?" Ben said.

"Neil."

"Last name?"

"No," he said. "Just Neil."

THERE WERE FIVE NEILS REGISTERED at the high school: Neil Cleffi, Neil Kowolski, Neil Peck, Neil Roth, Neil Wolfe.

As soon as the students were hunkered down in their first-period classes, Ben was in the attendance office, going through the class lists with Helen Galloway, a fifty-something widow who still wore her wedding ring.

"What do you know about these kids?" Ben said. "Any gossip?"

"All business?" she said, arching her eyebrows. "How about a hello? A hug?"

She tugged Ben's shoulders toward her and forced her affection on him, her hand swiping up and down his back. Behind her, hanging on the wall above the typewriter, was a picture of her dead son, Paul, a Marine dressed in his black formals, his white cap pulled low over his brow; he was killed in the barracks bombing in Beirut in '83.

Helen was the eyes and ears of the school. Most of the stuff that flew under the radar of the rest of the administration, Helen knew about. If you knew kids were absent, it wasn't difficult to find out why. Years ago, Helen was the one who finally called Ben's mother when he stopped going to school, spending his days down at the beach, riding waves. She was the only one who called—not the assistant principal of discipline, not his teachers, not the swim coach. He'd hated her for it then.

"I heard about you and Rachel," she said, her hands on his shoulders and looking up at him. "I'm sorry."

"I appreciate it," he said.

"Married too young," Helen said. "I told you."

"You did." When he was missing class and showing up with forged excuses, she always told him: *Nice girl, but don't be in any hurry. Marriage doesn't come with a get-your-life-back guarantee.* "But what can you tell a kid?" Ben said.

"You can tell them the world," she said. "But their ear canals haven't made it to their brains yet."

She glanced at the picture on the wall, just for a second, something habitual, as though to check that her son's face was still there. Helen kept other kids out of trouble, but she couldn't help her son. In high school, Paul hung out in the smoking section and spent his senior year stoned in a black van in the student parking lot, listening to Mötley Crüe with the metalheads. He was arrested three times, once by Ben. The boy missed graduation, earned his GED over the summer, and then signed up for the Few and the Proud and got blown to bits in his sleep in a cinder-block room in a foreign country.

"It's too bad," she said. "I like Rachel."

"Yeah, me, too."

"How's Emma handling it?" she said.

"With sarcasm and disdain."

"Be patient with her," Helen said. "Some kids feel like it's their fault."

"I've told her it's not," he said.

"Tell her again," she said. "She crossing over from the junior high school next year?"

"Yep, unless I can afford sending her to Mater Dei."

He and Rachel had been saving money to send Emma to the private school before the divorce, a fund the legal fees cut into. Rachel had never been sold on the idea anyway, pointing out that people moved to Santa Elena because of the good public schools. Why shouldn't they, he'd argued at the time, give her the best if they could? They were giving her the best, Rachel countered, by moving back to Santa Elena. Regardless, he'd prefer his daughter getting her reading, writing, and arithmetic elsewhere over the next three years, and he added to the savings account each month to that end.

"I'll keep an eye on her," Helen said. "She's got a boyfriend, I've noticed."

"Yep."

"He's a mess," she said. "But a nice kid."

"Be great if he wasn't a mess *and* was a nice kid."

"Would be, wouldn't it?" she said, patting his hand. "Kids are a mess. That's the only way to explain them."

"Neil Cleffi?" she said now, settling onto her swivel chair and sliding it across the floor to get a file. Helen was overweight and rarely lifted her body from her chair, but she could race the wheels across the concrete floor with a single push of her left foot. "Freshman. Hasn't hit puberty yet. Runs around rabbit-earing girls. Neil Peck. Junior. The perfect kid. Associated Student Body. Calculus Club. Long-distance track." She started spinning her hand in the air. "Wears Top-Siders and pastel polo shirts. Never misses a day. Blah, blah, blah. He'll probably be president one day."

There was a knock on the door and Assistant Principal Bryce Rutledge stumbled in. "How many kids we have on this field trip to the tar p—" He stopped. "Ben, I didn't know you were here. Someone park their bike illegally?" he said, with an I'm-a-funny-guy grin straining his face.

"Just visiting with Helen," Ben said. He had never liked Rutledge, didn't now.

"Catching up," Helen said.

A half hour earlier, Ben had sat in his cruiser outside the admin office, listening to the dispatch scanner. A Mercedes keyed in the parking lot of an office complex. Expired registration on a landscaping truck. Then silence, the empty static of the perfect job. He knew teachers were looking out their windows while jotting formulas on chalkboards, watching his car with one eye while they read Shakespeare to sleeping kids. Why was he here? Who was he coming for? Had they paid their parking tickets? He saw his former teachers and friends around town—at the grocery, sitting in the waiting room at the car wash, throwing Frisbees in La Bonita Park. He could cite them for sipping beer in the park or for their illegally tinted side windows. He could pull over Brian Cappecci, a famous stoner in school and now a chemistry teacher, and search his glove compartment for a clip and some shake in a plastic bag. Ben knew it was there; people changed but not that much. He could set up a raid of the massage parlor Mr. Powers visited, but he was a lonely old man, had been a lonely middle-aged man when he taught Ben calculus, and that would only make him lonelier—and disgraced. Ben knew these things, and others, and people in town suspected he knew, too, and the fear that he knew their secrets earned Ben a disdainful respect. People's guilt kept them in line. The fear of being exposed made them play it safe in other areas of their lives. In a way, a safe town owed its calm to the small immorality; it offered a taste of passion in a world that feared it.

"How's your better half?" Ben said to Rutledge.

For instance, Ben knew Rutledge was cheating on his wife, Carol; had been for at least three years. Ben stumbled upon Rutledge and his mistress fogging up the windows of his six-year-old Mercedes, parked on a newly paved cul-de-sac of recently framed tract homes. A blonde, of course, radiating the forced sexual brightness of plastic surgery and makeup.

"Carol's wonderful," Rutledge said, patting Ben on the shoulder. "I'm a lucky man."

"Nice to know happy marriages still exist."

"Put a little weight on?" Rutledge said, gesturing toward Ben's belt. "You still swimming?"

Rutledge had been the water polo coach when Ben was on the swim team and had since risen to AP by being a lousy political science teacher and a suck-up to the superintendent.

"I'm allergic to chlorine."

Rutledge laughed, lines fissuring his tanned face.

"Sixty-two," Helen said.

"What?"

"The field trip," she said. "Sixty-two." She handed Rutledge a printed list.

"Great," he said. "Couldn't survive without you, Helen."

When Rutledge was gone, Helen laughed. "That man is proof cream doesn't rise to the top."

Rutledge was smarter than she gave him credit for. He knew when to ignore things that would cause trouble, especially trouble for him. Ignoring things was half the battle in this world, three-quarters of the battle when you rose to positions of power.

"Any of these kids have boyfriends?" Ben said.

"Of course not," she said, smiling. "We don't have those here."

"Let's pretend we're in the real world."

"Oh," she said, turning the sheet around to him. "That place." She put her finger on the paper.

"Neil Wolfe. I don't know about a boyfriend, but it would be him if it was anyone. He's polite, stares at the ground a lot, dyed his hair to match his shoes once. Tries to disappear but wants to be seen, too."

"A lot of six-period absences," Ben said, noticing the A's dotted beneath the dates.

"He doesn't seem to like shop."

Ben wrote the kid's name down on his legal pad, jotted down the time and the number of absences: seven in the last five weeks.

"I need one more thing," he said to Helen. "Is there a Mexican kid on the swim team?"

"Two of them," she said.

"The best one?"

"Lucero Vega," she said.

For a moment, the name brought the kid to life in Ben's mind—sewed up his chest cavity, blew air into his collapsed lungs, stood him six foot three from toe to crown. Ben remembered holding his daughter for the first time in the hospital fourteen years ago, when he first whispered her name and she became Emma Eunice Wade. Those five syllables animated her with the beginnings of her personality. The dead boy's mother had had the same moment seventeen years before, when the promise of a new life seemed endless.

"They talk about Lucero," Helen said, "like they talked about you. State, nationals, who knows what else."

"I've got to show you something, Helen," he said. "It's not pretty, but I need you to look at it, all right?"

He felt terrible asking this of her. When Helen's son was killed, there was nothing to identify, just his dog tags, one edge of the metal melted and cooled like scarred skin. She wore the tags around her neck, tucked beneath her peach blouse. She had picked up a bag of pieces and ash at El Toro Marine Base and buried that.

"We found a kid the other morning, in a strawberry field."

"Oh, no," she said. "That serial killer?"

"We don't know," he said. "Looks like he could have shot himself."

Her eyes fluttered and filled with tears.

"One of ours?" she said, grabbing a package of tissues.

"That's why I need you to look," he said. "No one's identified him yet. His parents are illegal. They're scared to come forward."

From his wallet pocket he pulled the autopsy photo, pilfered from the evidence file at the station, and held it out to her. When she saw it, she sucked air through her teeth.

"Is that Lucero?" he asked.

"Yes," she said, pushing the picture away, looking at Ben now. "There wasn't someone else to ask?" she said, the tone in her voice changing. "I'm the only one here who could do that?"

"I'm sorry," he said. "I trust you."

She cracked a teary smile.

"Something's wrong about this kid's death," he said.

"He's seventeen years old. Of course there's something wrong."

"I mean, there's something else behind it."

"Gangs?" she said. "Rutledge and Mr. Perry keep talking about Hispanic gangs."

"No," he said. "Love, I think. Or something like it."

He asked for Lucero's address and Helen pulled the file. "Fourteen seventy-six El Ranchero Road, number four."

A condo complex off Margarita Avenue.

"Someone's going to call here, asking about this," Ben said. He would have liked to keep this under wraps until he sorted it all out, but another day or two of the boy's absence and people would start putting two and two together. "Daniela Marsh, from the *World News*. I want you to tell her his name, okay, but keep me out of it."

She nodded. "Now get out of here," she said, anger still in her voice. "I've got things to do."

He touched her shoulder. "I'm sorry about Paul," he said. "Your son was a good kid. Always polite, never pulled anything with me."

"They're all good kids," she said. "Just confused."

HE FOUND NEIL WOLFE LEANING against the metal fence of the swim complex, a cigarette dangling from his fingers. The fence jutted from the top of a landscaped hillside that overlooked the pool, and people often stopped here to watch the tournaments when they were out walking their dogs or finishing a jog around the man-made lake in the adjacent park. Through the fence, Ben watched the lines of swimmers slice through the water. The pool was packed. Swimming was more popular than football at the high school, infinitely more popular than basketball. On meet days, for the last two decades, people turned out and filled the bleachers to watch.

The kid glanced his way, took a drag of the cigarette, and then blew the smoke above his head.

"You a truant officer or something?"

"Nope."

"Only truant if I miss the whole day," he said. "I'm only cutting class now."

"Truant if you're off campus, missing any of your classes."

Diamonds of sunlight danced off the surface of the pool. The wind carried the droplets kicked up by the swimmers, a haze of chlorinated water darkening the cement deck on the west side of the pool. The coach was sitting down at the lifeguard bench, a bullhorn resting on his lap, his back to the fence.

"Well, I'm on campus," the kid said. "So I'm simply late to class."

"Very late," Ben said. "It's an issue for the assistant principal."

The kid looked at him for a moment, taking Ben in. Neil's hair was peroxide white, the tips dyed green.

"I know you," Neil said. "There're pictures of you all over the walls in the men's locker room. Hall of Fame–type stuff. Medals with your name on them, trophies with your name on them, race caps with your number."

"I won a few races when I was your age," Ben said.

The coach called out something on the bullhorn, the wind carrying the words west, away from them. The swimmers lined up on the wall, their heads bobbing up and down, their mouths wide open as if they were fish gasping at the air.

"I can't stand that asshole," the boy said. "Any city statute against cursing?"

"Not yet," Ben said. "But I'd have a few things to say if I was your father."

"Come on over," the kid said. "And the two of you can have a scolding party."

"Someone told me you're polite."

He laughed. "Keep quiet, get left alone."

The kid took a drag. He had small hands.

"There *is* a statute against underage smoking," Ben said. "Got a fake ID, or do you go to the Taiwanese place on University Ave.?"

"The cabinet above my mother's Crock-Pot," he said.

"Convenient."

The coach called out on the bullhorn again, and the swimmers dove beneath the water, dolphin-kicking into the butterfly.

"What's your beef with the coach?" Ben asked.

"He likes to be in people's business," the kid said. "Thinks he's cool shit, you know, because he's coached a couple Olympians. Thinks he's down with the common student and all that."

"What business is that?"

"Forget it," Neil said. "I like watching boys in Speedos. That's what you're going to say, right?"

"Nope," Ben said, looking at him now. In high school, Ben remembered, he'd broken a kid's nose for calling him a fag. He was sixteen, about the same age as Neil. "Wasn't even thinking it."

It happened on the sidewalk off campus after school, and the kid and his buddies were coming toward him, hogging the cement. When Ben passed, they bumped shoulders and the kid spit the word at him, and Ben spun and clocked him square in the face. "How's that for a fag?" he said to the kid, whose blood was dribbling onto the pavement. The kid and his friends never said anything to him again. Fags didn't crush people's faces, everyone knew that.

"Thanks for that, then," Neil said, flicking the cigarette butt on the ground and heeling it dead with a ratty two-tone skate shoe. Vans, Ben noticed.

Three kids had fallen back in the butterfly, one of them simply bobbing his head in the water, his nose and mouth just barely above the surface. The coach climbed around the edge of the pool, got down on his knees, and started laying into him.

"Your friend's not there," Ben said.

Neil straightened his back. "What friend?"

"Lucero."

The boy stared at Ben, sizing him up.

"I know," he said, letting his shoulders drop. "He hasn't been around for a few days." He lit another cigarette. "Are you immigration, then? You sent him back?"

"No," Ben said. God, he hated this part of the job. "Kid, I'm sorry. He's dead."

Neil's face fell apart, just collapsed. "Oh, Jesus," he said. "Oh, Jesus, oh, Jesus, oh, Jesus."

"GET ME OUT OF HERE," Neil had said. "Please, just get me out of here."

And Ben did, the kid in the back of the cruiser, curled against the doorframe, crying all the way down to the beach. Ben had parked the cruiser on a bluff overlooking Crystal Cove, and that's where they stood now, Neil grasping the wire fence between barbs, sucking in the salted air, trying to calm down. If this kid was involved in Lucero's death, he was earning an Academy Award for this performance.

"He did it himself, right?" Neil asked.

"That's what I'm trying to figure out," Ben said.

The surfers were out, black wet-suited bodies on white arrows carving the face of hollowed-out waves. Ben leaned against the hood of the car, the heat of the engine burning through his pants. It was hot as hell this afternoon, the basin sky like a magnifying glass for the sun. Out beyond the beach, a band of smog, pushed offshore by the wind, hovered like an approaching dust storm.

"How?" Neil asked.

Ben didn't say anything.

"Please tell me how."

"He was shot."

"Did it hurt?" Neil said. "I mean, would it hurt?"

"No," Ben said. It must have hurt, at least for a moment, at least for that flashing second. Maybe it hurt for a few minutes, in the twilight of the heart winding down. But that's not what this kid needed to hear. "I don't think so."

"How do you know?"

"I don't, really," Ben said. "I've seen men shot, though." The armed man running out of the 7-Eleven on Wilshire. The laid-off middle manager holding the vice president and his secretary hostage in Century City. The dealer at the party in North Hollywood. "In the right place, it seems to be over immediately."

"Was he shot in the right place?"

"Yeah," Ben said.

The boy nodded and turned away to face the ocean and smog. "Can I see him?"

"You don't want to."

"Don't tell me what I want," he said, his frail profile framed by the ocean. "People are always telling me what I want and don't want, and they don't have a fucking clue." He turned to look at Ben, his face all kid—pimpled, flushed red cheeks. "I want to see him."

"I'm sorry," Ben said, "but I won't do that."

Two military jets swooped down the coast, afterburners shooting blue flame. Probably back from target practice, bombing the hell out of San Clemente Island. They banked left over Laguna and thundered low into the canyon toward the base.

"Were you in love with him?" Ben said, as gently as he could.

"I don't know." Neil finished one cigarette and lit another. "I just liked him. He had a cowlick on the back of his head. It always stuck up, even after he got out of the pool. That made me smile."

"Were you sleeping with him?"

"What the hell kind of question is that?"

"A common one when death is involved, especially a violent one."

Neil hesitated, looking down the coast where the swells stacked up. Ben gave him a few moments and watched two surfers catch the same wave. When the first one cut back across the face, he shoved the other off his board. The second one went backward into the maw of the tube, sucked down below. The first one rode the wave to the rocks and flipped out the backside. There was about to be a fight. Stupid kids.

"He was Catholic, you know," Neil said. "He hated himself for it, said it was a sin, said it was disgusting. I asked him if that meant he thought I was disgusting. He said no, but I didn't believe him. He was disgusted by me and by himself, but we were still us, you know, didn't matter how much we hated it."

"I have to ask again," Ben said. "I'm sorry. Were you sleeping together?"

"We kissed," he said quietly. "We were too scared to do anything else. You get told your whole life something's wrong with you, you start believing it." He laughed bitterly. "I mean, that's what they want, right? To make you hate yourself out of being this way? Shit, I get it, I get what they do, but it's still working on me."

"You and Lucero were fighting, then?"

"No," Neil said. "We were supposed to go to the movies tomorrow night, *Aliens*. I was going to pay because he didn't have any money. His parents pick strawberries and tomatoes."

"I know."

"Have you told them yet?" the boy said, turning to look at him.

"They know."

"Jesus," he said, turning back to the ocean. "I hate his mom, but I still feel bad for her."

"You've met her?"

"No," Neil said. "Lucero wouldn't let me. He said she would be ashamed of him, of us."

Neil drew on the cigarette. Below him, in the water, the second surfer threw a punch from his perch straddling his board. The first surfer threw one back, but he fell into the water, and the second surfer pressed the man's head into the water. He let him up, though, and the first surfer, spitting something at the second surfer, turned and paddled his board to shore.

"He used to bring me strawberries," Neil said. "He'd stuff them into a pocket in his backpack and give them to me between classes."

Through the cruiser's open window the radio called out a robbery, a gas-station holdup, out near John Wayne Airport.

"She found out, didn't she?" Neil said.

"His mother?"

"Yeah," he said. "She found out about us, that's why he did this."

"There was that man who found you two together in the orange
grove. You think he said something to Lucero's mother?"

"You talked to that guy?" Neil said. "He said he wouldn't tell
anyone."

"He didn't know someone was going to get killed."

Neil thought about it for a moment. "No," Neil said. "He didn't
tell her. That guy was cool. He'd warn us if someone was coming,
and we'd hide."

"You know his name?"

"No one ever tells you their name over there." The kid stubbed
out the cigarette against the guardrail. "It was that fucking swim
coach. He told her."

"Lucero's coach knew about you two?"

"We screwed up," he said. "The coach keeps this condo near the
school. Supposedly rents it out, but it's still full of his stuff, and nobody's been renting it since I've known about it. Lucero mowed the
lawn for him, cleaned the windows, kept it up, you know. He had a
key, and sometimes we'd meet up there, pretend it was ours." His
voice cracked. "It was stupid fantasy bullshit."

"Doesn't sound stupid to me."

"What's with you, man?" the boy said. "I mean, like anyone else
in this town would laugh at that, call me a faggot."

"Well, this place isn't always as nice as it looks," Ben said.

Neil nodded. The tide flowed in, the froth snagging the tops of
the rocks, the waves crumbling the base of the cliff point at Corona
Del Mar.

"So he found you guys?" Ben asked. "The coach? He walked in
on you or something?"

"Yeah, like nine at night. On Monday. We weren't doing anything,
just sitting on the carpet together, drinking a couple beers left in the

fridge, but he knew." The kid laughed bitterly. "Lucero would have told him anyway. Lucero was too honest. He was scared of the coach."

"He had a few things to be scared of, right? He was illegal, didn't want to be kicked off the team, kicked out of school, didn't want to be sent back, didn't want his parents to know he was gay and had a boyfriend."

Neil shrugged. "He talked about the coach like, I don't know, like he was his father. Like it freaked him out to disappoint him. Like it was a really big deal."

"This condo," Ben said. "Where is it?"

"Over on El Ranchero. Fourteen seventy-six."

The surfers were coming in now, the waves crashing high up on the beach, eating away at the cliffs. Soon the beach would be gone, submerged until morning.

"You ever think about doing it?" Neil said. "Suicide?" He was pressing the point of a barb against the meat of his thumb.

Ben had once, a long time ago.

"Why are you so sure it's suicide?"

"I've thought about it myself," Neil said, his finger pressing the barb harder.

"Stop that."

The kid ignored him. "I tried with a razor once, but I couldn't make my hand do it." He lifted his thumb and looked at it. It was bloodless, though there was a little pink point in the center. "I decided I wasn't going to let them kill me. That's what it's like, you know, like they want to kill you. I'm not letting them have that." He was quiet a moment, and the sound of the waves rushed up the bluff. "Lucero wasn't like that, though. He wanted to make everyone happy. I told him it was impossible. Someone has to be the enemy and you have to hate them back."

"What happened after you left the apartment?" Ben said. "After the coach caught you?"

"I ran off," Neil said. "Through the greenbelt behind the house. I was freaked. My dad would kill me if he knew."

"What about Lucero?"

"Him and the coach were arguing when I left," he said. "I could hear their voices."

"Where'd you go?"

He hesitated and lit another cigarette.

"There's this, like, old building in the hills behind the orange groves near the camp," he said. "Lucero said it used to be a cowboy camp or something."

Loma Canyon. It was another camp, like the one up in Bommer Canyon he and Emma had ridden past the other day. There were a half dozen or more of them dotting the hillsides surrounding town.

"We used to meet up there," he said. "I thought he'd come find me afterward."

"Did you see him again?"

Neil put the back of his hand to his eyes, cigarette smoke curling around his face.

"No," he said. "After a while, I went over to the camp and waited in the field, thought I'd catch him before he went home, but he never showed." He took a drag. "I went back up to the cowboy camp and there was some other dude there. I was already late to get home, so I ran back."

"There was someone at the camp?"

"Yeah," Neil said.

"What'd he look like?"

"I don't know," he said. "I didn't go in. I thought it was one of the ranch's security dudes. You know, one of those guys who patrol with their salt-pellet guns? I didn't feel like being shot in the ass with one of those, so I got out of there."

"If Lucero did kill himself," Ben said, "you know where he got the gun?"

"No," Neil said. "You going to arrest me?"

Ben looked at him, trying to weigh the advantages of arrest against letting him go.

Second to the last to see the dead boy alive. Possible motive. Arrest the kid, shit hits the fan. He wanted to keep this quiet for now. Besides, he believed Neil's story.

"Not today," Ben said.

"I swear I'm telling you the truth."

"If I need to talk to you again," Ben said, "where do I find you?"

"The lake, sixth period. I'm not into hammering and drilling in shop. I like to hang out with the ducks."

Ben nodded. "You got anyone to talk to?"

"Who am I going to talk to about this?"

"Your mother," Ben said, though he already knew the answer. "Your father."

The kid laughed. "Jesus," he said. "I'm going to walk through my front door all smiles and full of bullshit about chemistry class. Then I'm going to lock myself in my room."

Ben pulled a card from his wallet and handed it to the kid. "You call me if you need to talk," he said. "Don't do anything stupid. Call."

AFTER HE DROPPED NEIL BACK at the school and made sure the kid walked through the front doors, he called Natasha.

"Got an ID on the kid," he said. "Write this down."

"Hold on," Natasha said. There was the muffled sound of the phone being fumbled from hand to hand. "Starting at the clavicle," she said to someone.

"Teaching a class?" he said.

"Lost one to the toilets already," she said. "Go ahead."

"Lucero Vega."

"No." The phone was muffled for a moment. "Right here." The high-pitched zing of the saw. "Sorry. Vega? Anyone claiming it?"

"Not yet," he said. "But don't let it leave the morgue. I don't want him sent off to the med school."

"I'll see what I can do," she said. "But I don't make the rules around here."

On the drive out to Loma Canyon, he put in a call to Daniela Marsh, the reporter at the newspaper.

"Are you calling," she said, "so you can have the pleasure of hanging up on me again?"

"Helen Galloway at the high school is expecting a call from you." The police generally didn't release the names of the deceased before next of kin were notified, particularly when the deceased were minors, but Ben wanted this out, wanted to see what it would shake up. "You say you heard it from me, though, and I'll deny it. And I'll never tip you again."

"Never tipped me before."

"First and last time for everything."

"Why are you telling me?"

"Public service," he said, and hung up, and, yes, he took a certain pleasure in it.

He drove Junipero Road, past the strawberry fields and the pickers bent in the sun, past the rows of orange trees blowing in the wind. The pavement ended where the hills began, and he eased the cruiser onto the rutted dirt road, snaking a low hill of needle grass clumped with cactus. The road ended at a chained gate with a NO TRESPASSING sign bolted to the metal. Ben parked the cruiser and scanned for ranch security, men with 12-gauge shotguns loaded with salt pellets who tended to shoot first and ask questions later, especially since the preservationists had gotten worked up over their bulldozing of the land. Ben scaled the fence and hoofed it through fifty yards of orange grove to an open field and the Loma Canyon hut.

It was nothing, really, a twenty-by-twenty square, the windows broken out, the front door long knocked from its hinges, an old cowboy camp neglected and falling apart, just like the Bommer Canyon place. When Ben was a teenager ditching classes in high school, sometimes he would hike up here and sit alone in the dark, enjoying the silence, soaking up the sweet stink of the leather cots and the dank musk of the adobe walls. The southwest corner roof was sagging now, the foundation badger-holed. He came up on the east side of the hut, the wind blowing swirls of dust into the grove, the early-afternoon sun slanting into his eyes. When he stepped through the door, something jumped in the corner.

For a moment, everything was confused—his pupils adjusting to the darkness, his sudden flinch and grasping for his revolver. The thing growled, a low guttural sound that blurred Ben with panic. When he got his vision back, the cat's yellow eyes were zeroed in on him, his ears peeled back, teeth bared. It was a bobcat, manged and wiry, a gutted rabbit caught in the claws of its right paw. It growled at him again and lurched forward. Ben leveled the muzzle of the pistol between its eyes. The animal pressed itself into the corner, its back arched, its ears speared backward, the tang of fear on its skin.

Ben small-stepped it outside, knelt on the edge of the orange grove, and listened to the low growls from inside the hut. Five minutes, and the bobcat swung its body through the front door, eyeing Ben until it loped into the brush and manzanita of the hillside. Inside, Ben found the rabbit, clumps of sinew and viscera staining the cement foundation. He grabbed the animal by its hind legs, the dead weight of it swinging from his fist, and flung it to the edge of the hillside. The cat was there, he knew it, hunched in the needle grass, waiting for Ben to leave, waiting to claim its kill.

Back inside, Ben found little to go on—a mash and jumble of shoe prints, an empty Michelob 40-ouncer, Dulces Vero candy wrappers, X-rated graffiti on the walls, an ancient used condom folded and cracked in the corner.

And when he left the camp, the rabbit carcass was gone, just a few tufts of white fur snagged in the mustard weed.

IT WAS 3:23 AND BEN was back at the high school. He hoofed it past the football team running sprints on the field, the cheerleaders stacking themselves into pyramids on the sidelines. The marching band ran drills on the baseball diamond, dressed like military officers who had never seen the battlefield. The whole thing, this Norman Rockwell crap, was hard to take after the morgue, after Neil. He wanted to tell these Santa Elena kids that safety was only an illusion, but who the hell would listen to him? How could you feel anything but safe with a tuba strapped to your body?

He stopped at the east fence of the swim complex and watched the lines of swimmers, five or more in each lane, cut through the water. Swimming, in Rancho Santa Elena, was a tradition. The school had produced three Olympians already. Two national-team water-polo players. Regular scholarships to big-name universities. Pictures of the complex were in the glossy brochures the new city had made up to advertise the town as the Shangri-La of Southern California. The pool complex had even hosted the pentathlon for the '84 Los Angeles Olympics.

A kid hung his elbows on the edge of the pool, gasping air, and the coach—Lewis Wakeland was his name—got down on his knees in front of him. Ben was too far away to hear what he said to the kid, but he heard the coach's voice in this head. *I know, son. Your lungs are shredding, your arms feel like lead. It's just your body, not your mind. Your mind is stronger than your body. Get out there and prove it.* The kid spit a glob of mucus onto the pool top, slipped into the water, and pushed off.

The school bell rang and he left the pool to find Emma. No Lance the stoner today, just Emma's dart eyes, her angry strut to the cruiser.

"You hid his sweatshirt, didn't you?" she said, strapping herself into the passenger seat.

"Listen," he said.

"You went to his house, Dad?"

"Listen, Em," he said again, putting his hand on her shoulder. "You can scream at me later."

She looked at him now—his face must have given it away.

"What's wrong? You're acting weird."

He was. The last few days had turned him inside out. He wanted to tell her how dangerous the world was, how dangerous it was to be a teenager. He'd tried to hide the ugliness of the world from her, but it seemed the wrong tactic now, sheltering her like that. How could she keep herself safe if she didn't know what she needed to be kept safe from?

"No matter what it is," he said, "no matter how terrible it is, you can tell me, okay?"

"I haven't done anything."

"Just listen, please," he said, squeezing her shoulder. He'd frighten her, though, telling her those things. And he didn't want her frightened. Life would be full enough of fear; she didn't need it now. "Anything, anything at all, you can come to me, all right? No sitting in your room alone, depressed. No cutting yourself in the bathroom. No overdosing on drugs. None of it, all right?"

"All right, Dad, okay. You're freaking me out."

7

It was Chocolate Friday, and on Chocolate Friday—the second and last Fridays of the month—they visited Margaret, Ben's mother, out at Leisure World, armed with a box of See's Candies, her favorite. This afternoon they were bringing two boxes, the second one compliments of Rachel. Ben knew he'd screwed it up with the sweatshirt stunt, so for atonement he let Emma tune the radio to KROQ, the "Roq of the '80s," on the way out from school. When they pulled up to the house, the DJ was playing some obnoxious crap by a pretentiously named British band. Guitar scratches and squeals and something about Bela Lugosi being dead. Jesus.

"Where have you been?" his mother said when she opened the door. "You said you'd be right back."

Emma kissed her grandmother on the cheek, handed her the boxes of candies, and squeezed past her to turn on the television.

"I said I'd be back next week, Mom," Ben said. "It's been a week."

"A week?" she said, her face stricken with terror.

"I'm sorry, Mom," he said. "I should've come right back."

"Darn right," she said, her eyes going dull again. She stabbed the edge of a box with a fingernail, her hands shaking. "You better not have eaten the ones with the cherries in them."

He opened the package and pulled one out to show her. She smiled and opened her mouth like a baby bird waiting to be fed. This was a new one. Two weeks ago, she opened the door naked. A few weeks before that, she lay cocooned in bed and made Emma sing her "You Are My Sunshine," a song Ben used to sing to Emma when she was a child, the same song his father sang to Ben when he was a little boy. After a moment, Ben came to his senses and set the candy on her waiting tongue.

"Mmm," she said, eyes closed, savoring it.

"It's on, Grandma," Emma called, and the two of them retired to the couch to watch *Magnum, P.I.*

Ben checked the pantry and the refrigerator, scribbled a grocery list while sitting at the kitchen counter. He'd hired an aide for Monday through Thursday and saved a little money by taking care of things himself Friday through Sunday.

"He reminds me of Warren," his mother said, when Thomas Magnum stepped out of the Ferrari.

A gust of wind burst through the window and ruffled the edge of the paper. He stood to close the window, hooking the latch down tight.

"Mom," Ben said. "I want you to keep this window closed, all right?"

His mother stared at the window, as though trying to remember what that rectangular hole in the wall was called, before turning back to Emma, a childlike excitement erasing the dullness in her eyes. "Have I told you about Warren?"

Emma glanced at Ben and then smiled at her grandmother.

"No," Emma said, shaking her head. "Please tell me."

"I was pretty then," his mother began, leaning into Emma, "and Warren had good eyes."

Ben retreated to his mother's bedroom to strip the bed. In the last few months, she had been telling this story every time they visited, a memory loop snatched from her blankening mind. Margaret had been sixteen, on a family outing to Laguna Beach, posed on a cotton blanket, trying to look like Ava Gardner in her pinup red-and-white polka-dot bathing suit, when Warren clomped by on a horse, hoofing up sand.

"Get that goddamned horse away from my daughter," Margaret's father had said.

Warren stopped the horse directly in front of Margaret, casting a cool shadow across her body. As far as Warren was concerned, these people had no business burning themselves on the beach, sitting on blankets and eating sun-heated watermelon. This stretch of beach was part of the old ranch, though the company had sold it years before and the town of Laguna had built hotels along the "California Riviera" for the hordes of people who wanted to gaze at the endless blue.

"Your daughter?" Warren had said, staring at her, not even bothering to hide it from her father, taking in her painted nails and her sand-speckled legs, the polka dots cut in half at the fold of her waist, her green eyes watching him watching her. "Seems she got her looks from her mother."

Margaret's mother, who had been pinching a cherry tomato between forefinger and thumb, blushed bright pink in the sun.

That did it for Margaret. She never asked for her father's permission to take the diesel bus from the traffic circle in Orange down the coast highway to sit on a blanket on the beach and wait for the cowboy to return. She never asked his permission to meet Warren in the rock cave where the tide pools were alive with sea anemone and starfish. She never asked his permission to meet Warren's family and she never asked his permission to marry, which sent her father into such a rage that he broke a wooden chair against the kitchen doorframe, but still he couldn't stop her.

"It's hot in here," Ben heard his mother say now. Then the scrape of the window sliding open in its frame.

"It's a good story, Grandma," Emma said when Ben came back into the room.

He closed the window again, this time closing the blinds, too. Out of sight, out of mind.

"My funny valentine," Margaret said.

"Mom, I need you to keep this window shut."

She glanced at Ben, her eyes wet and lost-looking, then turned back to Emma. "That's what he calls me when we're in bed. My funny valentine."

Emma raised her eyebrows at Ben.

For years his mother rarely mentioned Ben's father, just brief recollections guiltily offered when Will Voorhees, his stepfather, wasn't around. Then it had made Ben feel as though he was part of some shameful past, like some bastard son born of a mistaken affair. Now, though, his mother's voice quickened with excitement, and it was comforting to Ben to know that when all else was erased from the mind, there was still the memory of love.

Magnum, P.I. was back, and Ben assembled the bowl of vitamins he had to make his mother take with a glass of water. He had to wait until a commercial break to give her the pills, though, and he stood behind the couch, watching his daughter and his mother gape at Magnum hopping into a helicopter that zoomed him down an impossibly green coastline.

"Where's that woman you married?" his mother said, when the commercial break came and he handed her the first pill.

"Rachel," he said, dabbing a drop of water from her chin with a paper towel.

"That's what I said. That woman you married."

"She's moved out, Mom," he said. "We divorced. You know this."

Two more pills and a slurp of water, his mother's clouded eyes staring at him. The vitamins were supposed to enrich the brain, open up the vascular walls and flood the synapses with oxygen.

"I know what I know," she said. "How did you mess that up? You always mess things up."

Emma glanced at him—a look of sympathy, he thought.

"I didn't buy her enough chocolate," he said.

Emma laughed, and his mother studied the two of them, trying to figure out if the joke was on her.

"Oh," Margaret said finally, sighing, "you were always a difficult child."

But then Thomas Magnum was back, diving from the hovering helicopter into the water to swim down a murderer, whom he dragged back to shore. Thomas Magnum had unraveled a murder with a connection to a drug ring run by an old Vietnam buddy, who was bringing the stuff in from Southeast Asia. He had fallen in love (again) with a beautiful, vulnerable woman, raced around Oahu in a red Ferrari, and tossed off a moral soliloquy at the end with his wet shirt clinging to his carpeted chest.

"Eye candy," his mother said, popping another chocolate into her mouth.

"Got a nice car," Ben said. "I'll give him that."

A half hour later Ben was backing his truck into the street, while Emma was fastening her seatbelt. The blinds flashed open on his mother's living room window. There she was, the wispy shadow of her body backlit through her nightgown, her thin hands yanking the window open to the wind again.

THEY TOOK A LATE-EVENING RIDE, Emma up ahead of him, her shadow and the horse's undulating across the blowing grass. The visit to her grandmother and the ride had taken the edge off Emma's anger, and she deigned to point things out to him—a mule deer's ears flicking above the brush line, a kestrel hovering in the wind, a clump of flowering bladderpod.

They were picking their way down Quail Hill when someone stepped out of the Bommer camp and hiked into the canyon. The man seemed to speed up when he saw the two of them, but then he reached down to retrieve something—an errant golf ball from Bommer Canyon Links, just on the other side of the ridge. The club sent caddies up to collect lost balls, but his presence broke the illusion of wilderness, of Ben and Emma alone in their own golden-lit bubble.

Back at the house, they had ¡Fiesta! Night, complete with a wrinkling construction-paper sign Emma had made two years before, pre-divorce but imminent separation and forced family "fun" together. He let Emma play her radio station again—the whining pleas of some group he didn't care to know the name of—while they worked together at the stove. He asked her about her classes, about her friend Heather, whose father had suffered a mild heart attack and had just been released from the hospital. "Fine" was all she'd give him, as she diced jalapeño, scooped the bits onto the knife blade, and slid them into a glass bowl.

He waited a few moments, letting them work in the echo of the music, the singer moaning about reeling around a fountain and being slapped on a patio.

"What is this stuff?" he said.

"The Smiths," she said. "They're from England. Manchester, to be precise."

"Fifteen minutes with you?" he said, repeating the lyrics. "I wouldn't say no?"

Emma just shrugged.

He wasn't crazy about the lyrics, but she was growing up and he didn't need to tick her off any more than he already had.

"You know," Emma said, "it's pretty crappy that you went to his house. You scared him."

Good, Ben thought. You follow the rules when you're scared. "It's kind of crappy," he said, "that I don't know what's going on with my own daughter."

"I don't tell you because you go all Big Brother on me." She cut into a tomato, seed and juice wetting the board. "I swear, it's like you'll arrest me if I don't floss."

"Did you?" he said in an official voice. "This morning?"

Eyes rolling.

"I don't like secrets," he said, pouring oil into the frying pan. "They lead to bad things."

"Is that what happened with you and Mom? You kept secrets from each other?"

He reached for the top cabinet, but pain shot through his shoulder. Emma stood on her toes and grabbed the packet of taco sauce for him.

"You should put stuff in the lower cabinets," she said.

"Thanks," he said, tossing the ground beef in the frying pan. "I don't know what happened with me and your mother."

When they told Emma they were getting a divorce, Ben and Rachel had settled on the easiest explanation: They had fallen out of love. "It happens sometimes," Rachel had said, hugging Emma. Since the divorce, Emma and Rachel seemed to have grown closer, while Emma had dug a moat around herself with Ben, and he'd wanted to tell Emma the real reason for the split: Your sweet, sweet mother couldn't keep her hands off the fucking history teacher down the hall. She and Mr. Timeline had worked together on a grant to get Macintosh computers for the library at the crappy, underfunded North Hollywood high school. The history teacher listened to her, Rachel had said at the time. Clearly a rebuke of Ben, whom Rachel had called "abstracted" and "distant." Ears, the gateway to love! In the year since the divorce, Ben had wanted to tell his daughter the truth; he wanted her sympathy, her loyalty, especially since she and Rachel both seemed to blame him for the death of the marriage. Fallen out of love? Jesus. As though he and Rachel had sighed together one morning in mutual realization that Love had slipped out the back door and was never coming back. *Oh, well. We'd better tell Emma.*

"Mom says you guys grew apart," Emma said, "whatever that means."

He sprayed the raw meat with lime, the citrus stinging a hangnail on his thumb.

"Is that a quote?" he said.

"Paraphrasing," she said.

He flipped the meat, browned side up, and watched the place on his ring finger where the band had been, the fat still indented. He'd tossed it in the trash one drunken night but then retrieved it immediately and hid it in a box in the rifle cabinet.

"I guess that's one way to think about it," he said.

He had been completely broadsided by the affair. "I wanted you to know," Rachel had said late on a Friday night, while they sat watching a Dodgers game and ate Vietnamese takeout. "I *needed* you to know." One moment he'd been sitting on the couch, Rachel's warm shoulder leaning against his, watching Fernando Valenzuela strike out the side, and, whiplash, the next he was some idiot who'd been T-boned by a cheating wife. He'd first met the history teacher, Dennis Jackson, a couple years earlier at a school fundraising BBQ, shook Mr. Timeline's hand, talked with him for a few minutes about Skylab falling back to earth. "Hope it falls west of Alameda and east of Wilmington," Ben remembered saying. "We have to educate the kids," Mr. Timeline had said, "not arrest them." Rachel swore it hadn't started back then, swore it'd only been a few months, but she could have kept on sleeping with the man, and Ben, the goddamned veteran detective breaking open drug cases, wouldn't have been the wiser to what his wife was doing in her afternoons after classes. Grading papers, my ass!

Rachel wanted to explain *why* to him that night. She needed him to understand, she said, but he wasn't sticking around to listen to what she *needed*.

"Stay," she said, following him to the front door, tugging on the edge of the windbreaker he was yanking over his shoulders. "Ben, I told you because I love you."

He imagined slapping her then, when she said that, a vivid, satisfying smack of skin against skin, and he knew he had to get out of there before he did something stupid.

"Let's talk," she said, still holding on to the zipper of his coat. "We need to talk, please."

"Let go," he whispered through clenched teeth.

He got trashed that night in a seedy bar on Venice Boulevard. When the bar closed, he got a motel room overlooking the stream of cars on the 405 Freeway and stayed through the weekend, and when he finally stumbled back to the house on Monday after Emma had gone off to school, prepared to kick Rachel out, she was sitting on the steps to the front porch, looking like hell. He sat down next to her and watched with her in silence as a trash truck made its way down the street.

"Let me explain," she finally said. "I need you to understand."

"No," he said. "I don't want to know why."

"We have to talk about this, Ben. There's a reason why—"

"I just want it to stop."

She nodded—giving up a little too easily, he thought—and ran her fingers along the edge of his hand. He didn't pull away, and she finally clasped his pinkie between her thumb and forefinger and they sat like that for five minutes, the trash truck stopping and starting, the compactor crushing what the neighborhood tossed away.

Maybe that's why he got shot three weeks later. He was distracted in the street: Moments when he should have been watching a suspect's right hand for sudden movement, moments when he should have been tuned to the bullshit some perp was feeding him, he imagined Rachel, her hand on his coat, pleading for him to stay and him not knowing how he could or how he couldn't.

"You know, sweetheart," Ben said now. "It's hard to explain what happens to husbands and wives."

"You mean you think I'm too young to understand, right?"

"No," Ben said. "I mean it's difficult to explain."

"Give me some credit," she said. "I'm fourteen, not some little girl." She sliced a red onion in half and then pointed at his arm with the tip of the knife. "I know what that scar on your arm is. I've always known. You don't think I believed that stupid story about being in a car accident?"

Yeah, he did think she bought that stupid story. Rachel thought she bought it, too. Ben remembered Emma, a nine-year-old in ponytails, peeking around the corner into their bedroom, her face white with fear, while he unwrapped the bandage and drained the fluid from the hole. He yelled at her to go away, and a few moments later he listened to her crying in the kitchen while Rachel tried to calm her down.

"We were just trying to protect you."

"Well, it made it scarier, not knowing the truth."

After he came home from the hospital, Rachel babied him. She wanted to bring him dinners in bed, wanted to swab the wound with alcohol, wanted to drain the pus and blood herself and wrap the blue-yellow flesh back into the gauze and tape. She tried once. He was groggy-headed and looped with painkillers, and when she touched his arm he slapped it away. No way could he let her touch him. She took his punishment, which just pissed him off more, made him feel like an absolute jerk. When she went back to teaching after a week's leave to care for him, Ben put in a call to Dan Garrett, the resource officer at the high school, and had him keep an eye on Rachel and the history teacher. Dan said he never saw them together, not even a glance in the hallways, and Ben, sitting on his ass in the house in Marina del Rey, unwrapped the wound and dabbed it with the stinging alcohol twice a day until it healed into a molten scar of flesh.

"I'm sorry it scared you," he said.

"Well, you can't take it back," she said, halving an avocado now. "I just wish you and mom would stop BS'ing me."

"We're not BS'ing you," he said. "Sometimes I don't really know what happened. You know, I'm not all that great with emotional stuff."

"No kidding," she said. "Maybe it's because you were always out in the barn, listening to the scanner." She hacked the pit with the knife and twisted it out of the avocado meat. "I mean, Mom would sometimes stand in the kitchen, staring out the window at the barn. It was kind of depressing."

"Maybe," he said. Ben remembered Helen Galloway this afternoon, saying kids sometimes blamed themselves, thought they caused their parents to split. He knew Emma wanted a clear answer, some one thing to blame that would acquit her of any responsibility. Maybe he did spend too many nights alone after they returned to Santa Elena. Maybe he did ignore Rachel. But coming back here had been more difficult than he imagined, a sort of desperate retreat, an admission of failure. The big bad world was too big and too bad for Benjamin and Rachel Wade.

"Look, whatever happened with me and your mom," he said, touching the back of his daughter's head, her hair fine and soft like her mother's, "has nothing to do with you, okay?"

She stopped cutting into the avocado, her eyes welling with tears.

"I love you and your mother loves you, period. You got it?"

"Yeah," she said, nodding. "It's rotten." She showed him the blackened half of the avocado.

"It's a tragedy," he said. "We'll have to suffer through."

Ben threw the tortillas in the pan now to fry them up, and Emma started setting the table. The radio went to commercial, some announcer screaming about a monster-truck jam. Ben reached into the refrigerator and popped the tab on a Coors, happy to have an evening off and glad to have that conversation out of the way. Then the commercial gave way to guitar and driving bass.

"Yeah you're gonna feel my hand." The voice a low growl from the hi-fi speakers. "Honey you're gonna feel my hand . . ."

He set the beer on the counter and ran across the room to turn up the music. "What is this?" he said to Emma.

Emma leaned her hands on the kitchen counter, cocked her hips, and smiled.

"The Stooges," she said, bobbing her head to the beat.

"Danger . . . little stranger . . ." There was a vulgar power in the voice, as though the singer would destroy everything and no one could stop him.

"What?" Ben said, turning down the noise.

"Iggy and the Stooges." Then she launched into a pop-music history lesson. Detroit. Godfather of punk. Something about David Bowie. Drugs. But Ben wasn't really listening; he was rifling through his coat in the hall closet, pulling out the Polaroid he'd snapped at Rafferty's scene.

"Iggy did crazy things onstage," Emma was saying. "Cut his chest open with shards of beer bottles, smeared himself with peanut butter."

Ben stared at the words in the picture. That was it, lyrics.

"He walked over a crowd once, with people in the audience hold-ing him up," Emma went on. "Said he was Jesus afterward."

"How do you know this stuff?" he said, looking up at her. He didn't like the excitement in her voice.

She shrugged. "I'm just cool, I guess," she said, smiling again. "Iggy was crazy. People walked out of his shows freaked out."

He wrote down the name on a slip of paper by the phone and stuffed it into his jeans pocket.

"What is that?" Emma asked, nodding to the picture in his hand.

"Nothing." Ben slipped it back into his coat.

"Ah, an investigation. But that's 'adult' stuff."

"Stop it," he said, his voice louder than he wanted.

"Geez," she said. "All right."

When the song was over, he switched off the radio and put Al Green on the turntable—sweet, sweet vinyl, with all the scratches and pops. They sat silent, bent over their tacos, Al Green preaching the "Love Sermon." But the killer's song had upset the air of the house, filled it with a darker tension. He only sat at this table when Emma was here, the empty third spot generally relieving him of his appetite. "I want to do everything for you," Al sang, "that ordinary men won't do." Yeah, man, preaching to the choir.

"So who is this guy your mother's seeing?"

"Come on," Emma said, tossing her taco on her plate. "Fiesta Night, Dad."

As a rule, while eating during Fiesta Night, they could only speak Spanish. Emma instituted this rule when he and Rachel started breaking their agreement not to argue in front of their daughter. "I hereby declare we shall only speak Spanish while eating tacos," Emma had said. They knew little Spanish, just the pleasantries and basic commands, and the dinners on Fiesta Night, at least, were all politeness and awkward phrasings.

"I don't care about Fiesta Night," he said. "I want to know what's happening in your lives. It's like covert ops between you two."

"I don't want to be your informant, Detective."

He exhaled a long line of air. *"Muy bien,"* he said now, bobbing his head from side to side in mock silliness. *"Salsa es muy caliente!"*

"Sí," she said. *"El carne asada es muy bien!"*

"Feliz Navidad," he said.

THE GARGANTUAN SELF

He'd watched her for two days while he and a couple of Hondurans laid PVC for a sprinkler system next door, his shovel digging deep into the clay soil. He'd gotten strong doing this kind of work, his shoulders rippled with muscle, his biceps and forearms wiry sinews. The old woman clipped dead heads from thornbushes, watered flower baskets that were like purple constellations.

She reminded him of someone, someone from a long time ago, but for the first day he couldn't say who. He kept watching her until he remembered the woman, the one who had lived next door to the house where he was kept in the basement. He saw her the day his father brought him home from the doctor. The woman had been in the side yard, near the painted-over window to his basement, watering flowers that were like pink explosions. His dad made them sit in the car and wait, the sunlight so bright that he had to squint to keep it from stabbing inside his head; they waited until she rolled up the hose and went inside her house. Down in the basement, there had always been a shadow cast across the painted-over window, something like smoke that rippled into arms and legs, a shadow he sometimes spoke to when he was in the darkness. It hadn't been smoke or a black angel, it had been this woman, just outside the painted-over window, watering flowers in the sun.

He cut the shovel into the dirt now and watched this new woman; she clipped wilted flowers from the bushes, her shoulders slumped as though Death were teasing her bones toward the peat earth at her feet.

Soon *after he was released from the state hospital with the doctors who tried to fix what was wrong in him, he tried to go back to that house, the one with the basement and the mattress and the lock on the door. He took a bus to the town and walked to the edge of the street, his eleven-year-old self thrashing around inside his adult body, but he couldn't make himself go, and he sat alone in a motel that night, cursing names at his face in the bathroom mirror.*

When this new woman was finished with the flowers, she drank tea on her porch and stared at the grass. Later in the afternoon, she sat in a recliner and watched people kiss on television—he could see her, her back to the windows. She was alone. A widow maybe, an old maid.

He had learned to avoid men. He'd had to shatter the skull of one with a statue, the brain like melon seed spilling out. It was brutal, beneath him. He wanted it to be calm, quiet, like an act of love. He didn't hate them; he simply needed what they gave him.

Tonight he sat in the car and listened to the song—the cutting guitar, the bludgeoning bass, the singer's voice devouring the eleven-year-old self—then listened to it again, his muscles electrified, his hands becoming clamps. Music had waves, and they pulsed in his body. When he slipped through the sliding glass door, she was asleep, breathing quietly on the couch—her nightgown loosely tied around her waist, her gray head lolled against the headrest. He had learned how to move quietly, like a cat, soft on the balls of his feet, his weight hovering in the air, wraithlike.

His thumbs pressed into the notch at the base of her neck even before she opened her eyes, her fish mouth gasping. Her irises were gray, with yellow starbursts exploding from the pupils. The dark holes dilated with shock. Is this really happening, her eyes seemed to ask, is this a nightmare? Yes, he said. It's really happening. Tonight I'm taking you with me. She kicked the footrest, scratched at his forearms, but soon her muscles slackened and her eyes gazed at him, milky and floating, her lids finally closing.

He let go of her then and watched her, her neck ringed red, her lips contorted but softening, her chest rising and dropping. Asleep. They were beautiful when they were sleeping. This is what his eleven-year-old self must have looked like to the man, his father, the man who locked him in the basement. He understood this about that man: They looked so innocent that you needed to own them, wanted them for yourself. He leaned over her, admiring the placid look on her face, watching the pulsing vein in her neck. Her face made him think of milk, for some reason. White and clean. He could do anything to her while she was asleep, anything at all. But he didn't want those things. He didn't want what that man, his father, had wanted from his eleven-year-old self. They were dirty things, animal things. He had been so small then. A bird with a hood over his eyes.

She started to move, her mouth gasping air as though she'd been held underwater. He sat on her lap and clasped his fingers over her throat again. He heard the singer's voice in his head, the urgent pummel of the music, and he felt his body grow, his gargantuan self filling the room. He could feel her pulse on the edge of his thumb — arrhythmic, out of time with the song, a thrumming persistence against his skin. Find a little strip, find a little stranger. He had been so small, but he was gargantuan now, and she lay there between his legs, asleep, a false mirror of her coming death, and he loved her. Loved what she would give him, loved that he could take it. It was like food, sustenance. That man had made him do things for food, disgusting things, and he was no longer hungry. Had to force himself to eat, the smell of each bite conjuring his father's body, billowing that man with ugly life.

Nothing in my dreams, just some ugly memories. Still her pulse, beating against his palm, her eyes erratic beneath the lids. The song looped in his head, the guitars, the bass, the singer's growl filling his body. Swear you're gonna feel my hand. The wind shuddered the windowpanes, a gust blowing papers from the kitchen table. A siren wailed in the distance, carried aloft on the wind and growing faint. The soul of the body was electricity. There was no heaven or hell. The soul became clouds, joined the thrum of power lines, dissipated in the desert air if you didn't catch it.

8

THE GROVE BEHIND THE HOUSE EXHALED A SHARP METHANE OF rotting oranges. Ben was in the backyard, kneeling over a footprint, shielding his eyes from the spotlight set on a tripod on the edge of the patio, while Jacob Pass, the forensics investigator, sprinkled talcum powder across the tread.

"Not a big guy, is he?" Jacob said, pouring out the dental cement now, the footprint turning white in the harsh light.

"Five foot five," Ben said, nodding his head in agreement. "Five six." A kid? A woman?

A flash burst through the sliding glass door and Ben glanced up to see Natasha snapping pictures, her knees on the edge of the carpet, where they had found the body lying next to the couch. Strangled. Broken hyoid bone. Crazy lyric scratched into the living room wall. Definitely the serial. April Howard, a widow. Alone, as usual. Natasha was whispering as she worked, her face close to the woman's stunned eyes. Ben could see her lips move—even from here, bent in the wet soil of the flower bed—talking to the woman as though easing the transition into another world.

A light flashed behind Ben.

"Detective," someone called.

Ben spun around.

"Detective, is it the serial?" A reporter and his cameraman were standing on the edge of the backyard fence, the orange grove looming dark behind them.

"Jesus Christ," Ben said, pointing to two uniforms standing watch on the edge of the patio. "Get these jerks out of here."

"Is it the Night Prowler?" the reporter said again, as the uniforms hopped the fence and pushed him backward into the grove. "Has he hit in Santa Elena?"

Yeah, Ben said to himself. Welcome to the world.

"Give it thirty," Jacob said, slapping his hands free of cement dust. "It's not a deep print. It's like he barely touched the ground. Can't guarantee it won't crack."

"It's the same as the others," Ben said. "Just need to make it official."

The whole house was lit up like a movie set—the backyard white with spotlight, every bulb in the house flipped on as if it were a party. It stank out here, the air humid with rot, the early fruit falling and browning months before the pickers came in. Maybe he was tired, but the stink of it tonight was too much, like the whole world was decomposing. He had some Vicks in his coat pocket, left over from the morgue, and he slicked the skin beneath his nose.

Inside, the house was broiling, all the windows shut to keep the wind from blowing dust across the scene. Two cops dusted the handles of the sliding glass door, but they weren't going to find his prints, Ben knew. Latex gloves. Lieutenant Hernandez was directing traffic: "You, print that door. You two, start gridding the place." Marco was in his cruiser, on the horn with the lead investigators of other crime scenes, running checks on the Stooges song, trying to piece together some message that would tip them off to the killer's next move. Natasha was on the floor, the camera pressed to her eye, snapping shots of the woman's fingernails.

"You made him bleed," she whispered to the body. "You hurt him."

Flash.

"Officers," Hernandez said. "Get out there and push back the perimeter." Hernandez was rarely on scene, but he was taking over this one, barking orders, seeming to enjoy being in charge, enjoying the show of it. Ben wondered what spin he'd put on this to keep the politicians happy. "Get these media people at least three houses down."

"We need a perimeter into the grove," Ben said.

"Walters and Beck"—Hernandez pointed—"go pick some oranges."

The light from the television crews cast an oblong reflection of the bay window against the far wall.

Hernandez ran a handkerchief across his wet forehead, sweating it out in the stifling heat.

"Come with me, Ben," he said. "We got a number of possible witnesses out at the van."

Then they were outside into the blinding glare of television-crew spots, forensics lanterns, black-and-white light-bar circulars. It was so bright that the cars and crime-scene vans, the people milling around, cast shadows across the pavement. Hernandez was out in front of him, striding between cruisers. The lieutenant got to the witnesses first, pulling two women aside before Ben realized who was in front of him: the high school swim coach, Lewis Wakeland.

"They said you might have seen something?" Ben said, his voice coiled in his throat.

Wakeland swallowed, his blue eyes darting back and forth.

"They said you might have seen something," Ben said again, his voice getting away from him. He glanced at Hernandez, who was taking the testimony of one of the women. Keep it cool, Ben thought. Keep it cool.

"Is she dead?" Wakeland said, scratching the meat of his left thumb with the nails of his right hand. "Is April dead?"

"She's dead."

Wakeland blinked. "She was a good neighbor," he said. "Kept to herself, never bothered anyone."

"Did you see something or not?"

Wakeland blinked again, water in his eyes as he stared at Ben. Ben thought he probably hadn't seen a damn thing.

"I live two doors down," Wakeland said.

Ben knew that. A rose-colored stucco. A Bayliner Bowrider sitting on a tow in the driveway. Wakeland was married, two kids: the good life.

"I was in the kitchen," Wakeland said. "And I saw something run along the fence line . . ."

Ben was scribbling on his legal pad, but he didn't know what he was writing. The lights were so bright, blinding almost, and he had the strange feeling that the wavelengths passed through his body, making his skin transparent.

". . . he was bent over, dressed in black . . ."

Ben's hand scratched across the page, his words a strange hiero-glyphics he couldn't make out. The light was hot on his face, the stupid reporters and their spots.

"It's nice to see you," Wakeland said.

"Did I ask you a goddamned question?" Ben said, startled by his own outburst.

Wakeland flinched and backed up against the police van.

"Did I?"

Hernandez turned away from his witness, eyed Ben.

"No," Wakeland said quietly.

Suddenly Hernandez was by his side. "Coach." He nodded at Wakeland. To Ben: "Detective, maybe you can check on forensics inside."

Then Ben was striding back to the house, the lights casting his shadow in front of him, Hernandez blabbering apologies behind his back, spewing some bullshit about professionalism and the stress of investigations.

"THIS GUY HIT THE WRONG house," Ben said.

He was balanced on his haunches in front of the body. He should have gone out back to get some air, to get his head back, to cool off, but something pulled him here to the center of things. Natasha's hand was under the woman's neck, lifting it an inch to get a picture of the red marks striated there. She pulled the camera viewfinder away from her eye and studied him.

"Serials never kill the right people," she said. "I'd let them run wild if they did."

The yellow pad was shaking in his hand, the chicken scratches on the page indecipherable. Natasha noticed before he could turn it facedown. She gently released the woman's neck and touched his hands, cupping them in hers, steadying them.

"You need a rest," she said, but he could see other questions in her eyes. She held his hands a moment, the latex cool and plastic-feeling. But her touch allowed him to breathe and he got his hands under control.

"Which house would be a good one?" she said, almost a rhetorical question.

"Not this one," he said.

She let go of his hands and got back down on the floor to take pictures.

"No," she agreed. "Not this one."

And then she was talking to the woman again, whispers he could barely make out. He thought he loved Natasha then—or at least he felt something urgent like love. It wasn't the first time he'd felt it, but the way the feeling hit him frightened him; it was pure need, utterly exposed.

"Why do you do that?" he said.

"Excuse me," he heard her whisper to the body.

"Why do you talk to them?"

Natasha set the camera down and offered him the kind of patient smile reserved for the ignorant.

"A little kindness to take with them," she said.

Part
Two

I T'S SATURDAY," BEN'S MOTHER SAID THROUGH THE PHONE RE-
ceiver. It was 7:46 A.M.

"Not today, Mom." He sat up, found the NoDoz on the bedside table. He'd left the scene at 1:45, finished the paperwork nearing
3:00, checked the windows and doors at Rachel's, and then sat in the
barn until 4:30, putting away three beers while listening to the scanner. It was hard to sleep when you knew someone was out there,
someone who would strike again. "We'll go tomorrow."

"It's Saturday the twenty-fifth," she said. "It's circled on the calendar."

There was no use arguing. If they didn't go, she'd be agitated all
day, even after she'd forgotten what she was agitated about. He took
a shower, grabbed his case notes from the barn office, and drove the
truck out to pick her up. By 8:45 they were parked in the lot beside
Pacific Crest Cemetery in Orange, which was neither near the ocean
nor situated on a crest but crammed between a strip mall dotted with
taquerias and a cement wall that separated the cemetery from the
rush of the Santa Ana Freeway.

"Yes," his mother said, nodding. "I remember this place."

Margaret was working at the seatbelt, her fingers searching
around for the button. He softly took her hand and pressed the re-

lease and the belt came loose. "Oh," she said, as though searching for words. "Oh." And then her hand was pressed against her nose and she was crying.

"It's all right, Mom. It gets stuck sometimes."

When she calmed, he walked her by the elbow to the wrought-iron gate but stopped there and let her go on alone.

"The disrespect," she muttered as she shuffled down the palm-lined path. He'd driven her out here the last Saturday of every month for the last six years, ever since Will Voorhees, Ben's stepfather, had died of colon cancer. He wouldn't join her at graveside, though, never had. "You better visit mine," she said.

Ben got a coffee at a taqueria across the street and then settled himself in the cab of the truck. She might be there ten minutes or two hours, he never knew, and there was no use rushing her; she'd thrown a fit once, bombarding him with insults while other mourners laid flowers at gravestones. So he sipped the coffee and watched her stand sloped-shouldered beneath the swaying palm trees, conversing with a stone.

There was no plot of land for Ben to visit, no spot of grass he could speak to. Ben's father had wanted to be cremated, his ashes sprinkled into the Pacific. He and his mother had walked the cheap plastic urn out to Abalone Point at Crystal Cove, just eight months before she met Voorhees, and poured the ashes in with the rockweed and gooseneck barnacles. But Ben wanted a monument, felt his father more deserving than Will Voorhees of something permanent.

Ben had never liked his stepfather, from the moment he met the man at New Life Mission Church's spring picnic—and these visits always got Ben chewing on things that were long over. The Rancho had kicked Ben and his mother out of their house—no more employee of the Rancho Santa Elena Corporation, no more house. His mother found a one-bedroom apartment surrounded by a sweltering cement parking lot, and from the living room window they could watch backhoes dredge Moro Creek—a prime watering spot for cattle—to build a fifty-yard-wide "greenbelt."

On the ranch, Margaret had always been up before Ben and his father, frying eggs and beans and wrapping orange wedges in napkins for the ride into the hills. On the ranch, she could rope a calf at full canter or reach inside a cow to deliver a breech calf. But she had no degree, not even a high school diploma, no skills that would serve this new California. She had been raised in Orange by a domineering man who worked in a glass-bottle factory, a man who taught his daughters to be quiet, to look pretty, to marry up in the world. A cowboy made little money; a cowboy had a tiny Social Security pension that barely covered the rent and left just enough to purchase butter and salt and thirty-nine-cent spaghetti from the new Lucky, with its piped-in music and bleached checkered floors.

So five months after being evicted from the ranch, five months of rejected job applications, five months of buttered pasta, Margaret took her pretty self to New Life Mission Church. Dresses she hadn't worn in years fit her again. She grew two inches in high heels. Her hair curled around her made-up face like the tendrils of a vine. On Sundays she and Ben walked the quarter mile to the church. Inside, skylights cast desert light across the wooden pews, light that lit up the curve of Margaret's calf at the crossed knee, light across the triangle of skin that fell into her blouse. They prayed and they sang and the minister spoke about sins of the flesh, sins of the mind, sins of the heart, sins of the appetite. You sneezed, it was a sin.

At the spring picnic, Ben and this girl Elizabeta had run off while the adults played a game of volleyball. Ben dreamed about Elizabeta — her coiled black hair, the question mark of her back, her accented English, which made his full name sound like something exotic. In the courtyard after church, they'd sip lemonade together and tell stupid stories about kids at school, but mostly they just sweltered in the heat of each other's gaze. They found a spot to be alone behind the plastic geodesic-dome gym on the edge of the duck pond. There Elizabeta agreed to show him her new bra. It was embroidered with tiny flowers, and through the blooming center of one he thought he could see the darker skin of Elizabeta's nipple. Fair is fair, so he unzipped his pants and showed her his penis—just a quick look, because she'd never seen one before and her older sister, back from college, had told her they were gross.

"What're you doing over here?"

The man came out of nowhere, and Ben didn't have time to zip. He stood there hyperventilating, his fingers clasping closed the waist of his only pair of churchgoing khakis.

"Go on," the man said to Elizabeta. "Get out of here." He leaned his bare forearm against the plastic orb of the geodesic dome, his hand hanging like a butcher's hook above Ben's head. "A little 'I'll show you mine if you show me yours'?"

Ben nodded.

"Button those pants." The man turned away. "And at a church picnic," he laughed. "I wonder what your mother would think."

"Sir, please don't tell her." Ben's stomach turned to water. "We weren't doing anything, just looking."

"Listen," the man said, "you introduce me to your mother and I'll keep this between you and me and God."

Ben's mother sat on the edge of a cement picnic bench, her face glowing in the sun, a plate of fruit salad balanced on the knob of her knee. When they got close, the man curled his fingers around Ben's elbow.

"Ms. Wade?"

"Yes," Ben's mother said, turning her face toward him, the left side lit up with sun.

"I thought you should know what your son's been up to," he said.

"Up to?" she said, standing up now.

"I'm sorry," the man said, shaking his head as though it killed him to have to tell her. "Maybe we should speak in private."

The three of them shuffled away from the table and stood in the heat of the midday sun. The man introduced himself. "Will Voorhees," he said, taking Ben's mother's fingers in the palm of his hand.

"Yes," she said. "I've seen you from a distance."

A crescent of white teeth lit up Voorhees's face.

"Boys will be boys, of course." Voorhees let out a long sigh and shook his head once. "But I found your son showing his"—he cleared his throat—"his private parts to this poor girl over here." He nodded in the direction of Elizabeta, who was sitting next to her father, her eyes saucers of fear.

His mother showered him with a scalding look. Ben wanted to object, wanted to tell his mother about the promise Voorhees had made. He still had a hard-on, though, and he figured that fact alone made whatever he'd say worthless. God knew he had a hard-on.

"I've upset you," Voorhees said. "I should have kept my mouth shut."

"No, Mr. Voorhees. Obviously, I need to keep a closer eye on my son."

"I can't imagine how difficult it is to raise a boy alone."

Sunlight sparkled on the tears in his mother's eyes. Will Voorhees touched the bare skin of her upper arm. "Let me get you something to drink," he said.

At home, his mother made Ben scrub his hands with pumice stone, made him wash his mouth out with soap. "I'm so embarrassed," she said. "Thank God for Mr. Voorhees."

A week later it was "Thank God for Mr. Voorhees" when he took them to Balboa Island for an ice cream and a walk among the wealthy. "Thank God for Mr. Voorhees" when he purchased them a new couch and coffee table and then sat on it and drank a sugared cup of coffee. "Thank God for William" when she forced Ben to play catch with him in the completed greenbelt behind the apartment complex. And "Thank God for Will" when, on the edge of eviction from the apartment, he paid their rent.

One night four months later, Ben woke after midnight to the sound of the wind rattling the aluminum windowpane. He needed to pee, so he tiptoed down the hall in his underwear and caught the faint strain of classical music humming from behind his mother's closed bedroom door. He stopped in the hallway to listen—the bowed tension of violins rising and swelling, the rhythmic sound of breathing, as though two swimmers were sucking oxygen out of the air between strokes. Despite the episode with Elizabeta, Ben knew almost nothing about sex, at least not the specifics of the act, but something in him divined the meaning of the sounds and he stood there listening, the breathing growing heavier, tears slicking his face, knowing that whatever was happening on the other side of that door finally severed him from his father.

It was a quick slide into marriage after that, and that summer they all were moved into Voorhees's three-bedroom townhouse overlooking the brand-new third hole of University Golf Club. Ben tried to get along with the man; he tried to sit at the dinner table and read passages from the New American Bible. He tried to let the man help him with his geometry homework. But Voorhees's voice grated Ben's ears, his aftershave twisted his gut; the man's fake smile couldn't camouflage his hostility toward Ben. So Ben pointed to a scalene triangle instead of an isosceles, solved for circumference instead of area, until the man gave up. Then Ben started running away. He escaped into the open fields, where he flushed out rabbits for a falconer and his Harris's hawk. He rode his bike out to the end of the El Toro runway and let jets swoop over him to a landing. He hiked it up to the ranch's stables in Bommer Canyon, where Billy James, one of the last cowboys, let him take Comet, retired and swaybacked, for trots into the finger canyons that led to Crystal Cove. There he'd tie up Comet and strip down to his underwear to dive through the kelp into the Coke bottle–green below, imagining the ash of his father floating cilia-like among the sea-palm algae. When his stepfather told him to be home at 5:00, Ben stumbled in at 6:00. When his stepfather told him to go up to his room, Ben went out the sliding glass door and ran through the rough and the sand traps of the golf course. When Voorhees kinked his arm to force him into the car to go to church, Ben ripped his elbow away and hid in the geodesic dome in La Bonita Park, thinking of the day he almost saw Elizabeta's breasts.

Then one night Voorhees slipped a folded pamphlet across the kitchen table to him—boys smiling on the edge of a pool, boys coiled on diving platforms ready to spring into the water. A boy hanging his head to have a medal hung over his neck. *We build character, we build discipline, we build CHAMPIONS!* read the caption.

"This will give you structure," Voorhees said. "Focus." And then they prayed on it, the three of them clasping hands around the dinner table, their heads bowed.

Seven hours every day, from 8:00 A.M. to 3:00 P.M., with a break for lunch.

There were twenty kids, none of them boys Ben knew, and each morning they ran laps around the track, then weight-trained in the high school gym. They swam in the afternoons to a rhythmic count Coach Wakeland called out, twenty boys synchronized to a 4/4 rhythm. They fist-swam to work on body positioning, ran long-axis drills, sprinted freestyle 25s and 100-meter butterflies and 200-meter individual medleys. Swimming uncoupled Ben from his anger; there was only the celadon-blue water, the black line on the pool bottom, and the endless somersaulting at the wall. And the coach's voice that summer was the metronome to his life. Three strokes and a breath on four, Wakeland's four-beat striking Ben's ear as it broke the surface of the water, his body slipping down the lane, his voice in his head indistinguishable from the coach's. It happened without him recognizing it, his voice becoming Wakeland's, and one night when his stepfather berated him for not taking out the trash, Ben escaped to the upstairs bath and slipped his head beneath the scalding water, Wakeland counting to sixty-seven before Ben burst to the surface, his anger drowned in the tub.

Margaret was sitting now, her knees pressed to her chest. He was in for the long haul today. Over at the taqueria, he got a concha and another coffee. On a television bolted to the wall, *Eyewitness News* was showing a picture of the Santa Elena victim, April Howard, smiling in front of a Christmas tree.

"Freaky," the man said, handing Ben his pastry. "Complete loco."

"Lock your windows," Ben said.

"Got bars on the windows around here," the man said, laughing. "We already know what's up."

Right. This guy's not hitting poor neighborhoods.

Back at the truck, Ben made a note on his legal pad. *Opportunis-tic. Neighborhoods with low crime rates. You feel safe, you're dead. Santa Elena: bull's-eye.* He underlined it twice.

His mother was still sitting down, brushing her hand across the stone. He glanced over his notes, three pages of them from the Mission Viejo scene where Emily was killed, another two from last night's scene until his interview with Wakeland, where his notes became mostly indecipherable. He'd seen Coach Wakeland around in the last four years, sure—once in the Safeway near the school, when Ben left his basket of milk and eggs in the frozen section and walked out; a few times from afar when picking up Emma at school—but Ben lived on the other side of town and could mostly avoid the man. From a distance, Wakeland was abstract, someone from another life and time; standing right next to him, though, the man was as concrete as Ben's own flesh and bone. Flipping through the pages, Ben found the notes from his conversation with Neil Wolfe. *He talked about Wakeland like he was his father. Like he was scared to disappoint him.* Ben added to the notes: *Emotional leverage.*

That fall after summer camp, Ben had pulled a fire alarm during lunch. All the kids standing in lines on the baseball field, the teachers and staff streaming out through the front doors of the school, two fire trucks and three police cars spinning their lights on the blacktop. It was fantastic. All of that, all of that drama—he had caused it. But some seventh-grade goody-goody girl told the principal she saw Ben yank the lever, and before he could revel in the prank he was suspended for three days.

"You're a fraud," Ben yelled at Voorhees when he took Ben by the arm that night and dragged him upstairs. "A liar, a loser."

When Voorhees locked him in his room, Ben kicked through the particleboard door.

"Please"—his mother's small voice on the other side of the door—"please, Ben, calm down. We need this." He didn't realize then what she was saying to him: Ben was hurting their marriage, threatening to throw them back into poverty.

"You're a bitch," he said to his mom. "How could you marry that loser?"

Then he punched out the screen, jumped from the second-story window, and ran into the dark across the golf course. He ran to the high school swim complex; the lights were off, the gate locked. That didn't stop him: He scaled the fence, tore off his shirt and shoes, and dove into the water in his shorts. He freestyled it down the pool, spun, and freestyled it back, the water dark and stinging with chlorine. He didn't know how long he was out there, but his lungs burned, his muscles cramped. When he finally pulled up, Coach Wakeland was sitting on a plastic chair near the pool's edge.

"Give me a reason not to call the cops," he said.

"Call them," Ben said. "Let them arrest me." And then, hanging on the edge of the pool, his feet dangling in the dark water beneath him, he spilled it all to Wakeland. Leaving his dad in the ditch. The police never finding the Chevelle that killed his father. Pulling the fire alarm. His asshole stepfather. Calling his mom a bitch. All of it.

Wakeland watched Ben's face, a sad smile on his lips. "You've gotten faster," the coach finally said. "Get inside and dry off."

In the locker room, Ben toweled off. His legs were rubber, his arms Jell-O, his muscles shaking.

"You're hypoglycemic," Wakeland said. "You need to eat."

Wakeland found him a pair of shorts in the lost and found, and then they were in Wakeland's Mustang, blasting down Conquistador Road through the patchwork of fields separating Santa Elena from Tustin. They were silent in the car, Ben exhausted and feeling stupid about all the shit he'd said. When they crossed over into Tustin, Wakeland pulled into a strip mall, parked, and then steered Ben into a booth in a run-down taqueria with brightly colored sombreros hanging from the drop ceiling. Wakeland ordered in Spanish, which impressed the hell out of Ben. His father had spoken some Spanish, but Ben had never met another white man willing to utter a single *hola*. Five minutes later, a massive burrito was sitting in front of him, soaking in red sauce.

"Lengua," Wakeland said.

Ben glanced at the cutting board behind the counter, on it a slug of raw meat.

"Tongue?" Ben said. "I'm not eating that."

"When someone takes you to dinner, you eat."

Ben bit into it, and damn if it wasn't the tastiest thing he'd eaten, at least since the mule-deer steaks his father used to grill when he was a kid.

"First," Wakeland said, putting his palms on the table, "never call your mother that name again. She brought you into this world, and you respect that."

"Didn't ask to be born."

"You sound like a stupid thirteen-year-old kid."

He was a stupid thirteen-year-old kid, but he didn't want to sound like one.

"Second, what happened to your father was an accident," Wakeland said, his burrito sitting before him, untouched. "You were a child. You were in shock. People do strange things when they're in shock, things that can't be explained."

Ben set down the burrito and stared at a Spanish phrase scraped into the wooden table. *Chupa mi pito.*

"Forgive yourself," Wakeland said.

"That's stupid."

"Right now," the coach said. "At this table. Forgive yourself."

It was confusing. If it wasn't his fault, why did he have to forgive himself?

"Say it."

"I forgive myself."

"Say it again."

"I. Forgive. Myself."

Wakeland finally bit into his burrito, and Ben, getting his appetite back, joined him.

"I want you on the swim team next year," Wakeland said.

"Yeah, all right." He wanted to be on the swim team, but he wanted to sound cool about it.

Wakeland smiled. A boy, maybe Ben's age, started hacking away at the meat on the counter with a chopping knife.

"Third," Wakeland said, "when we're done here, I'm calling your mom and stepdad and taking you home."

"I'm not going."

"You'll go back, because there's nowhere else to go," Wakeland said.

The stark goddamned truth.

"Your stepfather might be a jerk," Wakeland said, "but see it through his eyes. Every time he looks at you, he sees the face of the man who loved his wife before him. That's not easy for a man. Besides, he's paying for that roof over your head, for the food you eat, for the clothes you wear, and it sounds to me like you're being a pain in the ass in return. Some people might call that ungrateful."

A man in the back called in Spanish to the boy behind the counter, waving a finger at him. The boy stopped chopping the meat and the man came over, taking the boy's hand in his so they sliced the meat together. Ben felt a lump in his throat watching it.

"They don't give a shit about me," Ben said.

"Part of being an adult," Wakeland said, "is dealing with things that make you uncomfortable. The only way you'll make anything of yourself is by learning to do that."

Wakeland took two more bites of his burrito and then said something in Spanish to the man behind the counter.

"Sí," the man said, and pointed to the phone on the wall.

"What's the number?" Wakeland said.

Ben glared at him but then rattled it off and watched Wakeland talk to his mother on the phone, reassuring her that everything was fine, that Ben was safe.

"She was in tears," Wakeland said. "I don't think you have any idea how your mother feels."

When they got back into town, Wakeland swung a left at Junipero. Ben told him he was going the wrong way.

"I want to show you something."

Two minutes later, they were idling in front of a condominium.

"This is my place," Wakeland said. "The next time you need to get out, you come here and cool off. You got it?"

The condo was painted off-white, the shrubs clipped into rectangles; a basketball hoop dangled over the driveway.

"Yeah," Ben said. "I got it."

And then Wakeland drove him across town, into the waiting arms of his mother. When Margaret took Ben inside, Wakeland and Voorhees stood outside in a pool of streetlight, talking. Ben had no clue what they said to each other, still didn't all these years later, but when Voorhees came back in he didn't lay into Ben, just looked at him and said, "Let's get you to bed. You must be exhausted." A minor miracle, and the beginning of a sort of truce between Ben and his stepfather.

Now waves of heat were rising from the hood of the truck, the sun rust orange in the smog. He watched his mother, on her knees in front of the grave. Man, he'd been a pain-in-the-ass kid—though knowing that didn't warm him to his stepfather's memory. Seven cholos, dressed in wifebeaters and inked with gang tats, jaywalked Katella Avenue, forcing cars to hit their brakes. Yeah, tough guys. He couldn't sit here anymore; serial murderers didn't take breaks on the weekends.

When he got to his mother, she was holding her right hand up to her ear. "What's that sound?" she said.

"The freeway, Mom."

"It's so loud."

Midmorning traffic, hordes daytripping to the beach. It'd take an hour to get her home.

AT 12:47 THAT AFTERNOON, BEN got a call from Rutledge, the high school AP. They met at the Orange Blossom coffee shop in the strip mall adjacent to the school complex. Inside, Rutledge had his face buried in the paper, a plate of chorizo and eggs in front of him, untouched. A firm handshake and Ben sat down.

"I took the liberty," Rutledge said, gesturing to a cup of coffee. "Figured you might have been out late last night."

Ben drank the coffee black.

"You figured right."

It would be his fifth cup of the day, plus the couple of NoDoz to get the morning rolling. He'd barely slept all week. It didn't help that he had been chasing ghosts since dropping his mother off at home— strange cars parked in the street, suspicious-looking men walking the sidewalk, unusual noises from the next door neighbor's, a Mexican orange picker napping in a greenbelt. Santa Elenans didn't bat an eyelash about a dead strawberry picker, but when they thought some- thing was coming for them, they banded together like a tribe fighting a common enemy. The television news cycled and recycled the im- ages of the Santa Elena house; they plotted the path the suspect must have taken on a freeway map of the basin. People woke to the news, coffee mugs in hand, their windows still slid open, the rush of the freeway in the near distance. The killer had stalked past them while they slept, when they were most vulnerable. It was only luck that separated them from the woman strangled last night.

"Scary stuff," Rutledge said. "My wife closed up the house this morning, shut all the windows, locked the doors. And we don't have air-conditioning."

Rutledge was in his early sixties. He wore a California Angels baseball cap that half-hid his rheumy eyes. Ben remembered his po- litical science class from junior year, the man skewing all of modern American history to prove that liberals were the downfall of civiliza- tion. It was total crap, but the class had been full of political fire and brimstone and it kept Ben awake, which was really all you could ask out of high school.

"Open an upstairs window," Ben said. "The serial's not climbing. Not yet anyway."

"Makes things feel fragile, you know?"

"That's not what's on your mind, though, is it?"

Rutledge hesitated before folding the paper over. There was Lucero, smiling in front of a crushed-blue studio backdrop. Ben hadn't seen the paper yet this morning. It looked like a yearbook photo. RANCHO SANTA ELENA STUDENT FOUND SHOT IN STRAWBERRY FIELD. The story was on page two, near the bottom of the page—the front page dominated by the bold headline about the Night Prowler—and nobody would pay attention to a dead Mexican kid.

"Did Lucero kill himself?" Rutledge asked.

"Could be," Ben said.

"Any chance this serial did it?" Rutledge said.

"The ME hasn't made a final determination."

Rutledge nodded, looking down at the paper. He was spooked.

"I knew another kid, years ago," he said finally. "He took an entire bottle of aspirin. His mother found him home midday, unconscious on his bed, and rushed him to Hoag emergency." Rutledge swallowed before continuing. "They pumped it out of him, thank God, but his parents pulled him out of school once he was healthy; had to finish at the alternative school with the losers and thugs. In the summer, the family moved away. I was his homeroom teacher. He was pretty popular, had good grades until junior year. Then he started failing classes, girlfriend broke up with him. His mother came to talk to me, asking me to keep an eye on him. I met with his teachers, his coaches, asked them to let me know if anything seemed out of sorts, you know? Just six hours before he ate those pills, I asked him how life was treating him, and he says, 'It's a long, strange trip, Rutledge.' It was our little joke."

He folded up the *Rancho Santa Elena World News* and turned the front page facedown on the tabletop. Ben could still see the headline in his head, though, the picture of Lucero, his electric smile.

"This kid who took the pills," Ben said. "Was he a swimmer?"

"Yeah." Rutledge nodded slowly, staring at his scrambled eggs.

Ben's stomach turned to water.

"This Lucero kid," Rutledge said. "He was a swimmer, too. I imagine you know that."

"Yep."

"Maybe as good as you," Rutledge said. "Maybe better."

"So I've heard." Ben sipped his coffee, though he had the caffeine shakes by now. "What're you trying to tell me, Bryce?"

"There's this one day six months or so ago," Rutledge said. "I had been working with our goalie late, twenty minutes, thirty maybe, after water-polo practice. So I send him home and come into the locker room. Everyone's gone, but I hear shuffling around the corner of the lockers and Lewis comes out, nervous, asking me all about my classes, about my family. Mr. Jovial, you know?" He paused. "I like Lewis. We go to the same church, United Methodist over on Universidad. His kids are great—polite, good in school. Known Lewis for twenty years. Before he met Diane. Going back to before you were in school."

"I know."

"I didn't think much of it then," Rutledge said. "He was always there after practice. You don't build a great program without putting in the extra time."

"But something's eatin' you."

Rutledge turned his neck and the bone cracked. Ben could actually hear it pop into place.

"I got to my office and saw the boy, this Lucero kid, come out of the corner of the locker room." Rutledge shook his head. "He didn't have his shirt on yet and he was holding the towel in front of him, but, you know, he just got out of the swimming pool, so that wasn't unusual. The boy glanced at me, though, and I could tell something wasn't right. There was just . . . there was a look in his eye."

"Like he was embarrassed?"

"No," he said. "Like . . . he was wondering what I was going to do."

"Well? What did you do?"

"I asked Lewis about it later and he said the boy's parents wanted him to quit the team; the kid was upset and Lewis was trying to talk him through it."

"And that sounded reasonable to you?"

"Yeah, it did," he said. "I mean, you line up all the students Lewis has helped get into good schools and it'd stretch from here to downtown L.A." He hesitated a moment. "This kid, Lucero, was up for a big scholarship. Wakeland was excited about it. USC, I think."

"Does it seem strange to you that the parents of an illegal would tell their kid to quit the team when he was up for a scholarship at USC?"

"Shit," Rutledge said, looking down at his cup of coffee. "I didn't know the boy was an illegal."

Rutledge said he needed to use the facilities. He got up and headed for the restroom and Ben sat in the café, his coffee going cold, his stomach roiling. He watched a group of water-polo players clear the table of tacos and baskets of tortilla chips. The kid nearest him was huge, his shoulders straining the trainer jacket, the white letters of the S and A stretching against his shoulder blades. "My dad's got a .45 under his bed," one of the boys facing him said. "Blow his fucking head off if he tries our place."

"Boom, man," the big one with his back to Ben said, gunning his finger in the air.

Even from here, Ben could smell the chlorine on their bodies, that chemical stink that bleached your hair, soaked into your pores, and dried your insides out. He remembered the August before his freshman year in high school, when he was invited to preseason training with the swim team. Maybe that's what Voorhees and Wakeland had talked about that night after Wakeland drove him home. His mom and stepdad were all gung ho for it, and by the end of the second week of training Ben was blowing by the frosh-soph kids and sticking close with the JV. By Wednesday of the third week, Ben was chasing down a junior, Russell Paxton, in his lane. Russell was a big kid, as Ben recalled, at least six foot three. Russell was fast, but no way in hell would Ben let him pull away. If he started to lose the kid's toes in the bubbles, Ben kicked harder, shoved more water out of the way.

"You should be with the frosh fags," Russell spat at Ben once while they hung from the pool edge between sets.

"Nah," Ben said. "I like it here with the junior pussies."

That afternoon, the university diving team was doing flips off the platform, chopping waves across the surface of the pool. Russell came off a turn and met one of the waves mouth first. He pulled up, gagging, and Ben slipped by him, not missing a stroke. Five strokes in, Russell grabbed his ankle, yanking him into the water mid-breath. Ben sucked a gallon down his throat, and when he kicked to get to the surface, Russell's chest was there, blocking his way. Ben thought he was going to drown, his lungs clogged, his limbs leaded weights, but then his head punctured the surface and he got air again and a surge of fury electrified his limbs. When Russell came off the wall, Ben punched down through the water, nailing him on the back of the head. Russell got Ben by the balls, the kid's fist clamping down, sending stars into his eyes, but Ben kept throwing punches until Wakeland and the assistant coach got their tentacles around them and yanked the two apart.

Inside the locker room, Wakeland let him have it.

"I'm not having any of that bullshit in my pool," he said. "You got it?"

Ben nodded, his balls throbbing in his stomach.

"I'm calling home," Coach said.

"No, don't," Ben said. Things had been relatively calm between Ben and his stepfather, and he didn't want to go back to the old days. "Please don't."

"You're better than Russell," Wakeland said, his face softening. "Faster. That's why he did it."

Ben smiled. Damn right he was better.

"You're off the pool today. Dress and get out of here."

The next day Wakeland called races: 100-meter freestyle, single elimination, two kids at a time. Wakeland shuffled the frosh and JV, and after three rounds Ben and Russell were the last two swimming. Wakeland smiled at them, sizing them up before opting for a 200-meter individual medley to finish things off—50 butterfly, 50 breast, 50 back, and 50 free. Brutal.

Ben had Russell on the butterfly, at least two strokes ahead and pulling away as he came off the first wall. Ben glared at the kid as he passed him. Take that, asshole. By the time he spun for the breast, Ben had gained a length, and he burst out into the calm water in front of him, surfacing into the hollers and whistles of the boys on the side of the pool and then back down into the thrumming water. The first wall off the breast, Russell closed the gap by a length. At the first wall off the back, Russell was at Ben's feet, and Ben's chest suddenly constricted, his lungs closing down. His left calf cramped, a knot of muscle curling his toes with pain, and Russell torpedoed ahead of him. Shit, shit, shit. Ben barely got his shoulders out of the water, his lead legs sinking into the deep, and then Russell was at the wall and that was it. When Ben hit the wall, he climbed out of the water and puked his guts out all over the green grass.

He sat there next to his own stinking insides and watched the boys retire to the locker room, until the pool went a flat reflective blue. It was at least ten minutes before he realized he had been digging a hole in his wrist with the nails on his right hand, and by the time he got back to the locker room and out of his suit, everyone was gone.

"You've got what counselors would call an anger-management problem."

Ben spun around: Coach Wakeland, his arms crossed in front of his chest.

"I'm rude, I'm ungrateful," Ben said. "Don't take responsibility for my actions, mean, thoughtless."

Wakeland grabbed Ben's wrist and turned it over. Four crescent nail marks, swelling with blood.

"No," Wakeland said. "You're just unhappy."

Wakeland hunted bandages and antiseptic out of a cabinet in his office while Ben slipped into his jeans and T-shirt and sat back down on the bench, suddenly feeling the life go out of his muscles.

"You know why you lost that race?" Wakeland said as he swabbed the cuts on Ben's wrist.

"'Cause I suck."

Wakeland laughed, a sad one.

"Because you don't know how to breathe." The coach taped the bandage to Ben's wrist. "Stand up and take a breath."

Ben did, a deep one.

"Keep your shoulders down; stop puffing out your chest." Wakeland put his hands on Ben's shoulders and shoved them down.

Breath. With the palms of his hands, Wakeland clamped Ben's ribs in place.

"You lost that race because you only got sixty percent of the air you needed," Wakeland said. "Your legs cramp up?"

"Double knots."

"Your chest feel crushed?"

"Like someone jabbed fists into them."

"That's because they were empty and your stomach muscles were pushing against them, constricting them. You panicked and you started breathing with your chest and shoulders, and you let Russell pull away from you."

Coach grabbed the waistband of Ben's jeans. "You breathe with your diaphragm," he said. "Here." Wakeland's fist pushed against Ben's stomach and he explained how the diaphragm worked, the way it contracted, opening up the thoracic cavity and allowing lung expansion, the way a man who is breathing right simultaneously takes in more air and uses less. "It's like singers," he said. "Opera singers. You ever listen to them?"

"My mom and stepfather love that crap."

"Next time sit down and listen with them," he said. "Pay attention to how long they hold notes. That's the diaphragm. Breathe," he said. Wakeland's fist knuckled Ben's stomach. "Push my hand away."

Ben tried, but the coach's fist was stabbing into his gut.

"What are you, some kind of wimp?" he said. "Push my fist."

Ben had to brace his feet against the floor, leaning his torso into Coach's fist. Ben took another breath, this one bigger than the last, and a new compartment opened in his lungs; he could feel it, cool air against the inner warmth of his lungs.

"Good," Wakeland said, letting go of his waistband. "Now you're breathing."

After dinner that night, Voorhees and Ben's mother retreated to the backyard patio while Ben finished the dishes. They liked to share a glass of white wine in the setting sun while they debriefed each other about their day and listened to the classical station on the radio. This was husband-and-wife time, and Ben wasn't invited. "There is no more important relationship than the one between husband and wife," Voorhees liked to say. He meant that the husband and wife were the glue to the family, that without that bond everything else would fall apart—the marriage, children's morals, western civilization—but Ben came to understand it as Voorhees's biblical justification to get his wife alone. And he wanted her alone a lot.

Finished with the dishes, Ben locked himself in the bathroom, stripped off his shirt, and stared at himself in the mirror. He was sinewy and lean, his shoulders broadening, a few wisps of hair creeping up his belly. He liked the bulge of his muscles, the planks of his chest; it was a body, he thought, that deserved to be admired. He pressed his fist into his lower stomach and breathed, trying to push against it with his rising diaphragm. Outside, he could hear the baritone's beefy notes rising and falling. He didn't know what the man was singing about—it was in Italian, or Spanish or something—but the music made him feel weird, sadly happy. On the bathtub edge, Ben tried to breathe with the singer, even voicing a few off-tune notes. He felt stupid doing it, but he was in the bathroom and who the hell cared? When the man hit the final note, holding it solid against the pulsing strings, Ben held the note with him. He sounded like an idiot but he held it, his diaphragm pushing against his jeans, his shoulders flat and square, the air vibrating his vocal cords with the singer's until the baritone cut out and Ben's unsteady voice went on for one beat more.

Wakeland called races the next day, too. Again it was Ben and Russell in the final round. It was another 200-meter IM, and nearing the first 100 it was a dead heat, the two of them crowding the line, their bodies surging forward with each stroke. At the turn for the first 25 breast, the fists knuckled the bags of Ben's lungs and fire seared his legs. Coming into the wall, Ben was staring at the white bottoms of Russell's feet, and following the turn those feet started to disappear into the bubbles and froth of his stroke. Ben was going down, worse than the day before, and in his distraction he sucked in water on the upstroke. He choked and then swallowed it down and shot his head above the water, spitting and huffing at air.

He felt it then, the oxygen bellowing his lungs. Screw the race. Just breathe. He dunked his head and stared at the black line beneath him. He imagined knuckles stabbing his gut. He tried to shove them away and the oxygen expanded his lungs. The power came back into his legs, the burn cooled by the oxygenated blood coursing through his veins. When he came into the wall, he flipped and caught the back of Russell's feet. When he came into the wall for the freestyle, he flipped and pumped his legs for ten seconds before surfacing, never taking his eyes off the line, his muscles exploding with power, obliterating some physical wall built by his mind. Breathe. Just breathe. On the other side of that wall was nothing but open water, and in the open was nothing but Ben's body torpedoing through the clear space. He closed his eyes and stretched it out, floating in that beautiful darkness, everything narrowing and opening up at the same time. Here, Ben hadn't left his father dead in a ditch for forty-five minutes. Here, he didn't feel unloved by his mother. Here, there was no lying stepfather. He didn't feel like smashing his hand through plywood doors or stabbing himself with his fingernails, and he rode that blackness into an oblivion of time and space until someone was tugging on his arm and he was rifled back into the light.

"Stop," Wakeland said, when Ben surfaced. "You can stop now." Ben blinked into the light and looked behind him to find Russell and the other kids staring at him from the other side of the pool, an awed confusion on their faces. He'd swum an extra lap.

"You found something there, didn't you?" Wakeland laughed, slapping Ben on the chest. "Yeah, you found something."

* * *

RUTLEDGE WAS BACK AT THE table, his face flushed, the edges of his hair wet.

"You all right?" Ben said.

"I'm fine," he said, but the man still seemed spooked. "About a month ago, I was down at Balboa Island with my grandkids. We were on the car ferry back. I saw Lewis and the boy sitting two cars up, in that little Corvette of his. I almost went over to say hello, but then I realized they were arguing—at least that's what it looked like. The boy got out of the car, and then Wakeland hopped out and grabbed his arm. When they reached the other side, the boy got back in the car and they drove off."

"You tell anyone about it?"

"No," Rutledge said. "I figured they were arguing about the scholarship, about coming back to the team."

"But . . . ?"

Rutledge stared at the untouched chorizo and eggs.

"It looked like a different kind of argument," he finally said—embarrassed, it seemed.

The kid's out for a joyride with a teacher in Newport Beach, Ben wanted to say, *and you don't say a thing to anyone?*

"Listen," Rutledge said, shooting Ben a look. "The man's married with kids, for Christ's sake." He rapped his knuckles once on the table-top, as though checking its solidness. "I've known him for twenty—"

"Years," Ben said, nodding. "I know." He leaned back and let out a breath. "I knew this cop in L.A., in narcotics. We weren't close, but we worked a couple cases here and there. Eighteen years on the force, and no one knew he was dealing in West L.A., from Santa Monica to Bel Air. Hooking up television stars and their kids, getting the stuff in South Central and jacking up the price ten miles north. Would have gotten away with it, too, if a washed-up movie star's kid hadn't OD'd on bad heroin. He was a nice guy. Had a wife and two sons, a Labrador retriever, let the guys use his condo in Mammoth for free."

Rutledge was staring at the table, nodding slightly. "There was a settlement with the other kid, the one who took the bottle of aspirin."

"What was his name?" Ben said.

"I can't tell you that," Rutledge said. "The settlement was confidential. But I think you should know he's out there."

"How long ago?"

"Enough years to make it feel like history—six or seven," Rutledge said, lifting his cap and rubbing his palm across his damp forehead. "After this kid was out of the hospital, he started talking, to the therapists at the alternative school. Started throwing accusations Lewis's way."

"How do you know this?"

"Like I said, I was the kid's old homeroom teacher. They called me to the district office to be grilled by the lawyers. Lewis talked to me about it, too. We went out one night, got some beers, and he spilled his guts to me. Said the boy was taking it out on him that he was kicked off the team because of bad grades. Said the boy had a lot of problems and needed someone to blame. I mean, why would he talk to me about it if he was trying to hide something?"

"You want me to answer that question?" Ben said.

Rutledge shook his head and looked away.

"What did the lawyers want to know?" Ben asked.

"If I'd seen a change in the boy's demeanor. If he had confided anything to me about a teacher—" He stopped and swallowed. "About a teacher doing things."

"Had he?"

"No," Rutledge said, a strength coming back into his voice. "No, never. I would have said something if he had."

Rutledge picked up his fork and stabbed it into the eggs but set it back down without taking a bite.

"What happened then?" Ben said.

"They settled out of court. The district paid up. Lewis never said another word about it."

"Confidentiality."

Rutledge nodded. "You think I'm a fool, right?"

Ben let that question hover between them for a moment. Most men could answer that question for themselves, if they were honest about it.

"Would you testify," Ben said, "to what you saw with Lucero—the incident in the locker room, the argument in Balboa? Give an official statement?"

"I didn't see anything."

"It's circumstantial," Ben said, "but it's something."

"Lewis is a friend."

"Is this friendship unconditional?"

Rutledge waited a minute to answer, had to think about it. "It's nothing and you know it," Rutledge said.

"Does Wakeland know about your girlfriend?" Ben said.

Rutledge's eyes flashed.

"Is that why you won't test—"

"My wife knows about Paula," Rutledge said firmly. "That's our business and it's not illegal." Rutledge put his elbows on the table and looked Ben straight in the eyes. "I don't want to ruin a man over nothing."

"You can't believe it's nothing."

"I believe that what I saw can be interpreted any number of ways."

He was right, but it didn't let him off the hook.

"It's the interpretation you choose that matters," Ben said.

"Don't give me that bullshit," Rutledge said. "I've got a son-in-law for a lawyer, and I know a little bit about how this all works. I've seen nothing."

Ben leaned back in his chair and stared at Rutledge. He was six feet tall, strapped with sinewy muscle that extended up his neck, his face the sort of chiseled mask of invincibility all men tried to wear sometime in their lives. His face was upset now, though, his brow furrowed, his lips pulled back, showing teeth. He'd just admitted he didn't have the guts to face up to what he knew was the truth.

"This other boy and his family," Ben said. "You know what happened to them?"

"They moved somewhere south," he said. "Dana Point, I think."

"Anyone else know about this settlement?"

"The higher-ups at the district office," Rutledge said. "There were a few rumors among the teachers."

Jesus. What was the law worth if it was used to keep people quiet about what they all knew? What was his job worth if that was the law?

"All right, Bryce," Ben said, nodding to the eggs and cold chorizo. "Enjoy your lunch."

Ben was three steps toward the door when Rutledge spoke up.

"You get anything solid," he said, "anything you can nail to the wall, I'll tell what I've seen."

Ben nodded and walked out into the heat and blowing dust.

WHEN BEN ARRIVED AT THE station on Monday morning, the parking lot was mobbed with news vans. Reporters slapped their palms against the cruiser windows, wanting a statement. Inside the station, the mayor, dressed in a linen suit and apricot button-down, was seated in Hernandez's office. Hernandez stood behind the desk, his hands in his pockets, his chin pushed against his neck—the demeanor of a man who didn't like what he was being told.

"Don Johnson's on site," Carolina said, nodding toward the mayor. "Doesn't look like good news."

"Politics is always shit," Ben said.

Ben checked his messages: The owner of the skate shop wanting to press charges against the boys who stole the boards. They'd scraped up the tails. Jesus. A reporter from *The Orange County Register* wanting information on the Night Prowler investigation.

When the mayor left, wafting cologne through the room, Hernandez called Ben and Carolina into his office.

"This came in the mail this morning," Hernandez said, handing Ben a plastic evidence bag. Inside was an unfolded piece of college-ruled paper, a note typed across the page.

Dear Detectives and Police Men,

You cant cach me. I'm evrywhere. I'm on the street corner, I'm in yor office, I'm in yor house. I'm the thing you cant get rid of. You cant cach me. I'm in the places you dont want to look.

"Postmark?" Ben said, handing the letter to Carolina.

"Santa Elena," Hernandez said. "Saturday."

"Sent the morning after the killing?"

"Appears that way," Hernandez said.

"He's still in town," Ben said.

"Got this, too." He handed each of them a cassette tape. "Marco picked it up at Viral Records. Made copies. L.A. County's got people trying to decipher it; think the lyrics might be some kind of code."

"This guy's not making a secret out of this, is he?" Carolina said.

"He wants us to know," Ben said. "It's a power move that way."

Carolina set the note on Hernandez's desk. "What does he mean? Where don't we want to look?"

"Someplace obvious," Ben said. He picked up the letter and re-read it.

"I don't know," Hernandez said. "But let's get on it."

When Carolina left, Ben stood and set the letter on the desk.

"Stick around a minute," Hernandez said. Ben sat back down.

"This is a suicide," Hernandez said, dropping Lucero's case file on the desk in front of him.

"That doesn't take care of the serial."

"The serial's random," Hernandez said. "But serial plus dead kid looks like a crime spree."

Ben nodded: The mayor was shutting the case down. "Investors," he said.

"ME's report will be in tonight," Hernandez said. "Besides, we need all our resources on the serial."

Ben opened the report and saw that the box had been marked *suicide.* All Hernandez needed was Ben's signature. Sign it, file it away. Some screwed-up kid kills himself. It happens. No one to blame but the kid. Sign it and it all goes away. The master-planned illusion intact.

"What was the deal with you and Coach Wakeland the other night?" Hernandez said.

Ben scanned Natasha's report—*bullet penetrated the meninges, causing traumatic damage to the cerebral cortex and corpus callosum, ischemic cascade resulted.*

"He asked too many questions," Ben said. "Had to remind him that I was the one doing the asking."

"Didn't you swim for him years ago?"

Ben nodded once, flipped the pages, and found a ballistics report. No one told him the report had come in.

"Had some kind of falling-out, right?"

"I blew states," Ben said. "He didn't like that."

Ben glanced at the report: .45 caliber. Purchased Chula Vista, down near the Mexican border, 1977.

"Unfinished business, huh?" Hernandez said.

"Just lost my patience, Chief."

Hernandez's secretary called him over: *L.A. Times* on the phone, wanting a quote about the investigation.

"Keep it professional, Ben, especially with pillars of our little society," Hernandez said. "And drop that file on my desk before heading out."

10

B EN STOOD ON THE EDGE OF THE FIELD AND WATCHED THE AF-
ternoon sun stretch the pickers' shadows, darkness that collapsed into the dirt when they bent to the fruit. The wind was
up, electricity sparking the air—it tingled his fingertips, tasted metal-
lic on his tongue. Ben saw his man hunched over his wheelbarrow,
pushing it down the row.

"Santiago," Ben said when he got to him.

Santiago Rodrigo Torres, DUI; picked up three years before for
driving a landscaping truck while under the influence, 0.11, barely
over the line. Santiago stood up, three strawberries in his gloved
hand, and looked at Ben for a moment before tossing the rotten fruit
in the wheelbarrow.

"You going to arrest me?"

"That depends on you."

"Depends on me?" he said sarcastically. "You'll find a reason if it
suits you."

"The gun was yours," Ben said. "You think we weren't going to
find that out?"

The color drained from his face. "The gun belongs to the foreman," Santiago said. "He just put it in my name."

"It would be easier to believe that," Ben said, "if you'd been straight up with me from the beginning."

Santiago glanced toward the mountains that hovered above the band of smog like the hulls of ships. "He likes to keep a low profile," Santiago said. "You know?"

The foreman was a runner, a coyote for the big man. Either he was smuggling people over—stuffed in car trunks, sardined in hidden compartments in vans—or he was working with the smugglers, buying illegals from them to work in the fields. If the shit went down with immigration, the foreman was safe, the owners of the fruit packaging company were safe, but men like Santiago took the fall.

"The foreman got me my papers," Santiago said. "I owed him."

"How'd the boy get ahold of it?"

"Some of these people around here aren't so nice," he said. "I was showing Lucero how to use the gun, just in case. Sometimes they take people, strong boys, to work in other places. I didn't want that to happen."

Ben nodded. Trails zigzagged through the Santa Ana Mountains, coyotes running folks through the night to drop-offs at the dimly lit edges of cities.

"You let him keep it?"

"No," Santiago said. "I don't like the gun. I only pull it out when I need it."

"He knew where you kept it, though."

"Sí."

"It's a good story, Santiago," Ben said. "And I believe it, but not everyone will."

Santiago glared at him. "I've got responsibilities," Santiago said. "People depend on me."

"I get it," Ben said, "but some people don't give a damn, especially about a Mexican with a prior. There's a dead kid, it's your gun—simple math." Ben hadn't signed the report yet. Left it on his desk at the station and headed over here. Maybe it was a suicide, probably was, but this wasn't just some depressed kid, his circuitry gone haywire. This kid was pushed to do it; Ben knew it. "This serial killer complicates things, too," Ben continued. "There's some pressure to haul someone in soon."

"I got kids," Santiago said, terrified now. The cops could do anything they wanted—Santiago knew that.

"I need to see Lucero's mother," Ben said. *"Entiende usted?"*

Santiago toed a rotted strawberry for a few moments and then finally nodded.

AT THE CAMP, SANTIAGO MADE him wait outside the door. He needed to talk to her first, Santiago said, to explain the situation, to assure her that Ben wasn't here to deport her or her daughters. Sidewinders of dust blew down the alleyway between plywood homes. A few stragglers waddled down the field rows, but the streets of the camp were empty. Doors were tied shut, blankets yanked across window openings. People were watching him from inside, their eyes flashing between wooden slats, blanket ends snapped aside to get a glance.

Ben's head throbbed now, his body hopped up with anxiousness. He watched the line of tiled rooftops of the housing complex on the other side of the field. New suburban homes—a whole other world. He followed the rooflines of the last street—one, two, three, five— and settled on the peak of what he knew was Wakeland's house. Four hundred yards away, a five-minute walk. Ben wondered if Wakeland had ever stood on this dusty street, enveloped in the sugary rot of oranges, and looked back, imagining how badly Lucero would want to run across those four hundred yards and get the hell out of this world.

Santiago scraped open the door to the house. "Please don't talk about the other boy," Santiago whispered. "She doesn't need to think bad of him in his death." The mother couldn't speak English, Santiago explained. He would have to translate. "She's frightened," he said, and Ben could see that Santiago would keep any pain from her, if he could. "She hasn't slept in five nights."

"I'll be soft about it," Ben said.

Lucero's mother sat in the corner of the room, on an upturned

plastic milk bin. A flickering veladora candle of the Virgin Mary illuminated the deep circles of her eye sockets. It was the same woman
from the other day, the one he thought he heard crying the morning
they found Lucero. There was a terror in her eyes that unsettled him.
It was shocking, even to him, the hostility of her world right next to
the placid order of the city.

"Where are the children?" Ben said. The little girls he saw the
other day weren't in the small room.

Santiago just shook his head. He had shuffled them out the back
while Ben waited, Ben guessed, taken them to one of the other plywood shacks to be safe. Even if she was going to be arrested, their
mother wanted them here, not in Mexico. That's how bad it was back
home.

"Where's her husband?" Ben said. She wore a simple silver ring
on her left hand.

"Back in Chiapas. He went home to see his sick mother and he
never came back. Almost three years ago."

"They heard anything?"

"*Nada.*"

"You've been taking care of them, right?"

Santiago nodded and looked at the ground, a gesture Ben took as
respect for the absent husband.

The mother's name was Esperanza. Ben smiled at the woman,
gesturing to another upturned milk bin, asking if he could sit. She
glanced at Santiago and then nodded.

"I'm sorry about your son," Ben said in awkward Spanish once he
was sitting. "*Lo siento.*"

She stared at the dirt floor.

He explained through Santiago why he needed her to identify
Lucero. The body had to be claimed by a family member, or it would
be used for medical purposes or buried in an anonymous grave. He
explained that she and her children would not be sent back to Mexico. She would be allowed to claim his body, bury him here, if she
wished, or send him back home to Chiapas.

"The state will pay for it," Ben said. "If they don't, I will."

Esperanza glanced again at Santiago and nodded. Ben pulled out the forensics photo of Lucero's empty face from his coat pocket, the one taken from the right side that didn't show the damage to his skull. What if he'd been asked to do this with Emma? God, he wouldn't survive it. She took the picture in her shaking hand, and Santiago put his hand on her shoulder. She looked at it for a long time, until a cry leapt from her throat.

"Sí," Esperanza said into her hand. "Sí."

Santiago took the photo from her, but she snatched it back. They waited in silence while she stared at the picture, as though she was trying to burn the shape of his face into her memory. Doubtful anyone had cameras here. Doubtful she had any pictures of the boy at all.

Finally she handed the photograph back. Ben gave her a handkerchief and she held it to her eyes. Esperanza said something to Santiago, and he said yes back to her.

"What was that?"

"She said he was a good boy." She spoke again, shaking her head with grief, and Santiago translated. "She hopes God will forgive him."

"Forgive him for what?"

"For killing himself."

Anger surged in Ben. Sin. Ben understood plenty about sin, but he didn't understand blaming the child. And no way could he believe in a God who would condemn a boy as young as Lucero.

"Was Lucero close to Coach Lewis Wakeland?" Ben asked.

Santiago glanced at him—afraid, Ben guessed, that he knew Wakeland was the one who gave the kids the address to go to school.

"Ask her, please," Ben said.

Santiago did, and Esperanza said yes.

Ben asked if he spent a lot of time alone with the man. Sí. He asked if he got gifts from Wakeland. Yes, clothes.

She showed him a makeshift drawer with new Levi's, a few polo shirts, an unopened package of underwear. The kind of clothes an illegal couldn't afford. Next to the drawer was a cot with a bunch of flowers on top of a pillow. Below the cot was a cardboard box.

"Can I look?"

She nodded once.

Ben thumbed through the box—math assignments from school, a marked-up essay on *Macbeth*, a swimming cap—while Esperanza talked on about the swim coach. Wakeland sometimes brought them food from the grocery. He bought Lucero his books for English class. When Esperanza was afraid to go to school conferences, Wakeland got a written report from each of Lucero's teachers. On Christmas, he gave everyone gifts. Ben found a piece of paper with neat cursive written in the margins, notes on a rough draft of an essay that Lucero was writing for history class. *Need a topic sentence here. You're not proving your thesis. This section makes no sense. Wrong word. Great point here.* Ben found another envelope with the same neat cursive on the front.

"Recognize this writing?" Ben said to Santiago pointedly, holding the envelope up to him.

Santiago looked at the ground.

Ben opened the envelope and found a birthday card. Inside, beneath the Hallmark platitudes, was written: *You're a wonderful young man, talented and thoughtful, special in every sense of the word. I'm happy to know you, coach you, guide you as you grow up. I hope our friendship will carry beyond your years here. Happy 16th!*

It was nothing. Paternal, genuine, the love of a mentor. But there was that *special. You're special. You're different from the rest.* Why did that word have so much power? There were no other letters in the box, just teenage-boy detritus—*Sports Illustrated*, a photograph of what Ben assumed was the boy's father, swim goggles, a few pens.

"Tell her," Ben said, "that I know Coach Wakeland let her use his condo address so the kids could go to school. I know Lucero cleaned it, mowed the lawn."

Esperanza listened and then she spoke for a while, gesturing with her hands, speaking rapidly and with passion. "She says that Mr.

Wakeland helped them a lot, that he is a saint. Without him, Lucero wouldn't have gone to school. Without him, Lucero wouldn't have had the opportunity to go to college and become an American. Without Wakeland, Lucero would have been working in the fields, picking diseased fruit for gringos to eat."

"Without him," Ben said, "your daughters won't be able to go to school, either."

She flashed her eyes at him when he said it.

"Wakeland came here one day to tell you what an amazing swimmer Lucero was, sí?"

"Sí," she said. Before they came here, she explained, when Lucero was seven, he used to go swimming in the river.

"In Chiapas?"

"Sí."

He could dive underwater and hold his breath for a minute, maybe more. She would stand on the banks of the river and watch it swallow him up and hold her breath with him until she couldn't hold it anymore, waiting for his head to break the surface. When they first got here, her husband took an address from a phone book at a pay phone and registered Lucero in elementary school. They were frightened every day that the false address would be found out. They did this for junior high school, too. Then one week during his first year in high school, Lucero went swimming in physical-education class. Lucero hadn't gone swimming for four years, and he came home bragging about it. About the big pool, about the diving board. He had never been in a swimming pool. Esperanza had never seen him smile the way he did that day, and he made his parents walk to the school in the dark to look at the water, lit up with floodlights.

Esperanza smiled when she described this. Then one day, she said, Lucero showed up at the house with this man. Her husband was angry. He told Lucero to get inside, and he stayed outside and talked to the man.

"Wakeland?"

"Sí."

When he came back inside, her husband told her that Mr. Wakeland wanted Lucero to join the swim team. He said that Lucero was very talented. Her husband told her that Wakeland had looked up their address so he could find them. He had driven to the house, and when an elderly white man opened the door, he understood their secret. He said he'd let them use the address of his condominium, which he rented out, for Lucero and the girls. It was sitting empty now and no one would check. They were frightened at first, but Mr. Wakeland did everything he said he would do, and, besides, what choice did they have? Lucero didn't need to be bent over rows of strawberries for the rest of his life. That's not why they came here.

"Did Lucero take any trips with Wakeland?"

"Yes," Santiago said. "To Los Angeles, to swim for some college coaches."

Esperanza said something to Santiago. "He was going to go to the university," Santiago said, translating as Esperanza talked. "She was very proud. The college was going to pay for it."

"Did he get a letter from the college?"

"Not yet," Santiago said. "It was being sent to Mr. Wakeland's office."

Of course.

Did Lucero ever come home upset? No. Did he ever lose his appetite, suddenly stop eating? No, he was always hungry. Did he ever have trouble sleeping? No. Did he ever yell at you? *Sí*, but he was a boy and life here is difficult. Did he ever tell you he was uncomfortable around Wakeland? No, he loved Mr. Wakeland. Ben took a deep breath before this question. Did he ever come home without some of his clothes?

Esperanza hesitated. Then she shook her head no.

"Why did she hesitate?" Ben said.

Santiago asked her, and she spoke to him for a few moments.

"She says sometimes when she washed his clothes he seemed to be missing underwear. But that happened a long time ago, and he was changing his clothes in the locker room at school, and he probably left them there. Sometimes he had a sensitive stomach. It embarrassed him."

Ben felt dizzy: the dryness of the air, the stench of the rotting oranges outside, something starchy and thick, cornmeal burning on a propane stove. He rubbed his palm across his forehead and wiped the sweat on the thigh of his pants.

"Has Wakeland visited since . . ." Ben hesitated. "Since it happened?"

She was quiet for a moment, then she shook her head no.

"If Wakeland loved Lucero and your family," Ben said, "why not let you all live at his empty apartment? If the school district wanted to confirm the address, they'd find you living there and everything would be safe."

"Because the man could go to jail for helping illegals," Santiago said without translating for Esperanza.

Ben let that go, but a frustration was taking hold of his tongue. All things could be explained away when you were frightened of the truth.

"I think I know what happened to your son."

Santiago narrowed his eyes at him.

"I think Coach Wakeland . . ." Ben hesitated again. He didn't want to do this, knew how painful it would be, but she must've known something, must've had some shred of evidence he could use to build a case—or at least to get a search warrant for the empty apartment. "I think he had an inappropriate relationship with Lucero. A physical one."

Santiago's eyes widened, a shocked few seconds of silence. "I'm not telling her that," he said. "It will only make it worse. The boy was sad and he shot himself. That's hard enough to deal with."

"Tell her," Ben said.

"No," she said, shaking her head when she heard what Santiago said.

"I think Wakeland threatened to take everything away if Lucero didn't let him . . . The scholarship, the swimming—"

"*Callate.*" Esperanza pressed her fingers against her eyes now.

"I know this is hard," Ben said. "But there are other boys out there. He's not the first, and I'm afraid he won't be the last."

Esperanza spoke sharply again. "She wants you out of this house," Santiago translated.

"Lucero was ashamed," Ben said, his voice lowering. "Your son didn't want to shame you."

"*Fuera de aquí!*" Esperanza was crying now, her face turned to the wall of her cardboard house. She knew something she didn't want to know. What child came home without his underwear? What child took overnight trips alone with his coach? She would hold on to that ignorance; she would fight to protect it. The alternative—that she hadn't, couldn't, protect her boy—was too much to bear. And Wakeland counted on this, knew how human nature dealt with shame.

"He was a good boy," Ben said to Santiago, knowing he'd pushed too hard. "Translate that."

He stood and Santiago went over to Esperanza, his hand on her back, whispering to calm her. When Ben stepped outside, the wind had ripped loose the cardboard walls of one of the houses. A woman cradled her son in a corner of the exposed room, and a man chased the tumbling cardboard into the strawberry field. Ben pushed his head into the wind and trudged across the field, a tightness in his chest blurring his vision. Suddenly there were footsteps behind him. Ben turned and Santiago was nearly to him, his face blanched with fear and fury.

"It'd be easier," he yelled to Ben over the roar of the wind. "It'd be easier if that serial killer had shot him."

Ben couldn't believe what he was hearing.

"*Lo entiendes?*" Santiago said, grabbing Ben's elbow. "You understand?"

BEN DROVE PAST THE ENTRANCE to the complex three times, spinning U-turns on Margarita Avenue, before finally pulling in. He passed the Los Flores cul-de-sac, looking to see if the Corvette was parked in the driveway. Empty. He parked on the main drag, a half block down from the street. It was 6:37 and the sun was low and orange, drowning in the band of smog pushed out over the ocean. On a balcony across the street, a woman sat in a bikini, her toes propped on the railing, a book resting on her thighs. She was smoking a cigarette, and Ben waited for her to finish, his stomach roiling, his head thudding with frustration. *It'd be easier if that serial killer had shot him.* Jesus.

Ben started to open the door, but a car rolled down the street, turned into a cul-de-sac, and U-turned back toward him. It was a black Toyota. Ben sat low in his seat as it passed again, the driver invisible behind the sunset-streaked glass. He waited a few minutes more, the street empty and silent, and snuck into the greenbelt behind the apartments.

No one seemed to be home in two of the apartments—a light lit on a side table in the window of one, a sure sign of an empty place, the next one darkened but with the front window wide open. Someone could punch open the screen and slip right in and wait in the darkness. A woman was in the third apartment, sitting at a kitchen table, her back to him, the phone cord wrapped around her waist.

At the fence, he slid in next to the Weber grill and a glass-topped patio table. The table had been cleaned recently, the glass shining in the shaded light. The grass around the patio had been mowed, the edges trimmed, a geometry of green. A stunted ponderosa pine rose above the patio, an extra measure of privacy and shade. On the right side of the patio was a sliding glass door that led to the kitchen. He ran his hand along the ledge above the window and found the key. Jesus, he didn't really think he'd find it sitting there after all these years. No way in hell, but here it was in his hand. He didn't have a warrant to search the apartment, and no judge would deign to grant him one with the meager evidence he had.

When he opened the door, he stood with his toes pressed against the aluminum guide rail, his stomach cramping. The kitchen was the same as he remembered it—a beige-and-white linoleum floor, a mustard-yellow countertop, the framed photographs of orange groves and grapevines. There would be beer in the fridge. Vodka in the freezer.

In exchange for his address, Lucero had become Wakeland's housekeeper, an arrangement his mother could understand. Her son wouldn't be mowing lawns for long, wouldn't be brushing the porcelain toilet bowls of wealthy whites for the rest of his life. Lucero got to go to school, got to get a college degree on scholarship. But you had to rely on the kindness of strangers who offered an address to use, who mentored your son into a better world you could never fully join.

A distant thwamping of helicopter blades shook the windowpanes. It was one of the Sea Stallions from the Marine base, riding low over the rooftops.

Beyond the kitchen was the living room. Past that was the office, and down the hall from there the bedroom. He knew he would find something in there, but he couldn't make himself move any farther.

The helicopter broke over the greenbelt trees, its blades shearing the air. Then a car engine rumbled to a stop in the driveway; a door slammed.

Shit. Ben backed out of the place, closed the glass door, placed the key on the sill, and slunk around the privacy fence to get skinny behind the ponderosa. A moment later, Wakeland came through the garage into the kitchen and pulled a vodka bottle from the freezer. The evening sun glanced light across the window. Ben could see in, but all Wakeland would see, if he looked out now, was a yellow orb of light blinding the edges of the patio.

Wakeland fumbled with the vodka bottle's screw cap, his hands shaking, his face distressed with furrowed lines. He disappeared for a moment, and then he was back, carrying a tumbler. He filled up the glass—no ice, no lime, just clear liquid to the top—and stood at the kitchen counter and sucked down the drink. After three gulps, he set the tumbler on the counter and stared out the window. The orange sunlight burnished his face and Ben could see he was upset. He'd seen the look before—knew it well, actually; the vulnerability in it had always surprised him, the depth of feeling surfacing in his eyes. He topped the glass off again and then sat at the kitchen table, rubbing his temples with his left hand.

This was it, this should have been the moment. Ben should have gone in through the unlocked door, flashed his badge, and started asking questions. He'd spent hours in interrogation trying to get a man to his breaking point; it's when they screwed up, revealed things they'd been concealing. It was when cases broke open. He should have gone into that apartment, done his goddamned job, but he escaped the backyard, feeling weak and stupid, and hightailed it through the greenbelt.

Back at the cruiser, Ben fired up the car and was about to punch the gas when it came out of nowhere, just jumped out of him, and he barely got the door open before the contents of his stomach sprayed across the pavement.

11

W ITHOUT CONSULTING HER, MENDENHALL HAD SIGNED
off on the boy's file: suicide.

"What about the inconsistencies?" Natasha said to
him in his office on Monday afternoon. "Gun in left hand, shot near
the back of the head?"

"He's ambidextrous. He was agitated," Mendenhall said, writing
something down on a clean white piece of paper that he folded in
half. "His hand shaking."

"His hand shaking?"

"Yes, *Deputy* Medical Examiner," Mendenhall said, his voice
lowering. "His hand shaking."

Natasha called Ben and told him she needed a drink. By the time
she got to the Reno Room in Long Beach—a Sigalert for an accident
on the 22 Freeway had everything backed up to the Crystal
Cathedral—Ben was propped on a stool at the end of the bar, a Viper
fins cap pulled low over his eyes, halfway into a vodka tonic.

"You sign off on Lucero?" she said, lifting herself up onto the
stool next to his.

"So this is a business drink?" he said, an edge in his voice. His
eyes were rimmed red, blurred in the blue light of the television
screen bolted to the wall.

"It's been a while since I've seen you on the hard stuff."

"Something in the wind," he said.

She could see why Rachel left him. He was a room with a locked door, and a wife wanted access. She lit a cigarette and waved the bartender over for a Dewar's. "One rock," she said, "and three fingers."

"So, did you sign off on Lucero?" she asked again.

"It's a suicide." He gulped the last of the vodka and crunched a cube between his teeth. Shook the glass toward the bartender to ask for another.

"That's what the suits are telling me," she said. "Shaky hands." She blew smoke. "But I'm asking you. Did. You. Sign off on it?" She was leaning into him, trying to get a look at his eyes. He looked at her then, the door in him opening a crack.

"Not yet," he said. "There'll be some shit to catch for it, though." The bartender, a woman with a shaved head and loose-fitting Minutemen shirt, slid Ben another drink. "Mayor made a visit today. Got investors in. He can't make the serial go away, but this one he can."

"Because the kid's illegal."

"Yep, wetback Juan Nadie," Ben said. He put away half the glass in one gulp.

He'd had a couple before she arrived; she could tell. After Rachel had left him, when Ben and Natasha started meeting for drinks, he was drinking heavily, putting away vodkas on ice, soaking himself in it. Sick of bearing witness to it, she finally told him one night that Rachel had left him because he was a drunk.

"No," he'd said then. "That's not why."

But he never elaborated, and she didn't give him a chance. "Well, that's why I'm leaving you." She'd said it just like that, as though they were already a thing, and then she walked out the door, leaving him ringing wet circles on the bar. He called her a couple of days later and apologized. He'd stayed mostly sober since then, at least in her presence. A Bohemia, a few Modelo Especiales, but not the hard stuff, not like tonight.

"You know it *is* a suicide, right?" Ben said.

"No," she said. "No, I don't know that. And there's a protocol to follow here."

"Lucero was seeing a boy," Ben said. "Helen Galloway over at the high school put me onto him."

"Sleeping with him?" she asked.

"I don't think so," Ben said. "But it was pushing that way. They were having some kind of fight."

His voice didn't sound right. She remembered his hands shaking the other day when he asked her about "unusual" sexual activity. She had thought it was just the late nights, the burden of two death investigations, but there was something else. He seemed rattled.

"Fighting about what?"

"I don't know," Ben said, his voice sharpening. "How am I supposed to know what two fags fight about?"

She jerked her head back. In all the years she'd known him, she'd never heard him speak like this. Cops could be a macho group, assholish to the tenth degree at their worst, but not Ben, not as she'd known him. After a raid, he'd found foster homes for Thai girls prostituted out in a massage parlor. When he had to tell a loved one about a death, he did it in person, not over the phone like most of the guys did.

"Probably the same things we all fight about," she said pointedly.

He glanced at her. "Sorry," he said. "My head hurts."

"Could we get a water over here?" Natasha said. "God, and I thought *I* was the one who was going to get drunk tonight."

The bartender plopped a glass of ice water in front of Ben. Natasha lit another cigarette and twirled the ash to a point in the tin ashtray. A guy playing pool slipped a quarter into the jukebox, and Tom Waits's "Shore Leave" came plinking out of the speaker.

"You ever thought about doing it?" Ben said.

"Suicide?"

He nodded, his chin bowed toward the bar, his eyes fixed to the glass. He looked old suddenly—double-chinned, dark circles rimming his eyes, unshaven with patches of gray coming in.

"Not really," she said cautiously. "I don't have the dramatic flair. You think about it?"

He was silent for a moment. "A long time ago."

"Why?"

"I was upset."

She gave him a sarcastic look, but he wasn't playing.

"What'd it feel like," Natasha said, "'a long time ago'?"

"Like hope."

"Hope?"

"For relief."

"Relief from what?"

He gulped the water. She hoped that meant he was going to pull himself together, that he wasn't going to go home and put his service revolver to his temple. It happened with some of the cops, the synapses gone haywire with the things they'd seen.

"Look, this kid killed himself," Ben said. "Prints on the gun are his, there's no bruising on the body, no evidence there was a fight, no strangulation, so it's not the serial's MO." He was counting the reasons off on each finger. "Everyone I talked to—Helen, Rutledge, Santiago the strawberry picker—said he was gay. Santiago said he found out and threatened to tell the kid's mother."

"Who would do that to a kid?" she said, shaking her head. Something was off. Ben was never this sure about a case. He always had doubts.

He looked at her, his eyes wet steel.

"Santiago said it would be easier if he'd been killed by the serial."

"What?" she said.

"They're ashamed," Ben said. "It's that shameful."

"Jesus Christ," she said. "The body wants what the body wants."

"No," Ben said, his voice sounding as if something was unfastening inside him. "The body confuses things, works against you."

"What're we talking about, Ben?"

He pressed the heels of his hands to his eyes. For a moment she thought he was going to swing open the door and let her in. "Suicide," he said. "We're talking about suicide."

A rack of balls cracked in the corner of the bar.

"This kid," Natasha said. "This Lucero kid was a swimmer, right?"

Ben emptied the vodka glass, let a piece of ice roll around in his mouth.

"Yeah," he said finally.

"Wakeland was one of the witnesses the other night."

Ben gestured to the bartender for another vodka tonic.

"You know what I want to know?" she said.

"What do you want to know?" Ben said, not looking at her, his voice low and strangled-sounding.

"I want to know why you haven't interviewed Wakeland."

"What is it you always say?" Ben said, turning to her. "You do your job and I'll do mine?"

"You're not doing your job," Natasha said. "Wakeland should have been at the top of your list. There's something else you're not telling me."

He stood up and slapped a twenty on the bar top.

"Ben," she said, placing her hand on his forearm.

"Don't touch me," he snapped.

"Okay," she said, lifting her hand. He wouldn't look at her, his eyes shifting in his head as if he couldn't focus.

"I thought you wanted to see me," he said. "I didn't think this was going to be some sort of interrogation. I thought we'd forget about all this stuff together for a little while."

"Ben."

"See ya," he said, and then he was out the front door, a shadow against the traffic headlights.

HE DIDN'T REALIZE HOW DRUNK he was until he was on the 405 Freeway, four lanes clogged with swerving taillights. He pulled the truck into the emergency lane and rested his head against the steering wheel. He tried to recall his argument with Natasha, but only snatches of phrases rose to the surface of his muddied consciousness. *It'd be easier if that serial killer had shot him.* That was there; he couldn't get that out of his head.

He rode the emergency lane to the Seal Beach exit and slow-laned it to the Pacific Coast Highway, the streetlights blurring off the ocean, the crashing waves like phosphorescent explosions. The moon was almost full, its light casting the beach a grainy white. He found the pair of board shorts and his fins tucked behind his seat, fumbled them on in the dark parking lot, and dove into the ocean. The moonlight spread a greenish glow across the surface of the water, but three inches down it was inky black and silent. The swells flowing and ebbing, his body carried through ropes of bladder kelp and winged rib. The swells lifted him closer to the moon, before crashing him to the sand. He let himself be taken and dropped, lifted and thrown, until he got his head back and the horizon attached itself to the sky again and he noticed, for the first time, bonfires on the beach like burning eyes cast in a strip of bone.

By the time he got home, at 10:46, the wind had torn loose the barn doors, the broken latches slapping the clapboard siding. He turned on the scanner in the barn—a robbery at a gas station, a drive-by in Little Saigon—and nailed the latch back onto the door. A dead frat kid at Cal State Fullerton choking on vomit in his sleep, but nothing about the serial.

Inside, Ben slipped the cassette of the killer's song into the boom box and listened to it three times while he transcribed the lyrics. There was power in the song—the sneer of the voice, the rawness of the guitar—and he sat there staring at the lyrics, his body pulsing. *There's nothing in my dreams, just some ugly memories.* Something had happened to this guy, something in his past. The power of the song, Ben realized, was in its anger. *Yeah you're gonna feel my hand.* This wasn't about getting off. This guy was angry, raging furious.

"273.5," the box squawked. "Fourteen thirty-eight East Almond Avenue, Orange." Some asshole beating his wife.

A copy of the *Rancho Santa Elena World News* sat on his desk, a picture of April, the most recent victim, smiling on the front page. She was so innocent-looking, much younger in the picture, her blond hair curling around her neck. Maybe she was a bitch in real life, maybe she'd hurt people, had affairs; maybe she drank too much or cheated on her taxes. But in this photograph she'd be forever innocent; the serial had transformed her into an angel beyond rebuke. Maybe the horror of her death had earned her that.

Ben turned the page to Lucero's face. His smile was crooked, but he was a handsome boy, too handsome to seem innocent. There was something guarded in his eyes, something dissembling in his look. Or maybe Ben was imagining it. He ripped the paper in half and set their pictures side by side. April and her sparkling eyes. April and her blond hair. April and the lacy collar around her neck, like some saintly churchgoer. And Lucero, his dark eyes that hid something, the wave of slicked black hair, as though oil dripped down the back of his neck. Both dead, but their deaths didn't seem equal; one seemed purer than the other.

That's what Santiago and Lucero's mother knew. If he'd been killed by the serial, Lucero would be transfigured into innocence, just like April. Ben knew how people thought about these things. A girl could be held down, overpowered. If it was a girl, it was a violent act, a rape. But a boy's body couldn't be so easily pressed into submission. Even if Ben could prove that Wakeland did to the boy what Ben suspected he did, people would forever look at Lucero's face and see a faggot who must have wanted it. Blowing his brains out just made it worse. A *selfish act*, people would say. *How could he do that to his poor mother?*

Ben unlocked the rifle cabinet and found the box hidden behind his father's bolt-action. It was dust-covered and unlabeled, sealed with duct tape. It hadn't been opened in a decade or more, yet he'd taken it with him to his apartment when he'd entered the police academy; he'd carried it with him to their place in Marina del Rey and stuffed it in the attic; he'd packed it up again, too, into the back of the U-Haul that brought them here.

Now he set the box on his desk. He knew what he would find inside, so why did he still doubt himself? As a cop, his doubt made him look professional, conservative, always dotting every i and crossing every t. But in civilian life, it was like constantly forgetting, a sort of denial of himself, of the simple facts of his life. He didn't know when that doubt crept in, but he knew there was an archaeology of that change in this box.

He cut open the tape with an X-Acto knife—releasing the smell of mold and yellowing paper—and pulled an envelope from the stack inside. The letter had been opened years ago but had resealed itself with the hardening of glue and saliva. He set the envelope on the desk, his name written on the front in neat script: the same neat cursive as on the slip of paper Ben had found on Lucero's body, the same writing—the elegant loops of the B, the aggressive sweep of the j—as on the papers Ben had found this afternoon at Esperanza's. Black marks against paper as identifiable as fingerprints, the geometric intersections of letters as damning as ballistics on a bullet.

A scream punctured the roar of the wind. Ben, startled, dropped the envelope back into the box and stepped out into the spark-dry air, the song still playing in his head. The eucalyptus were bent to the wind like penitents. Dust deviled across the gravel driveway, lifting clouds over the drainage and into the grass of Quail Hill. Say gotta give me danger, wild little stranger. The scream cut the air again. It sounded like a woman out there in the hills, crying in terror. There it was again—a fox. Something had it spooked—a coyote, a mountain lion. It was farther away now, and when he caught it a fourth time it was deeper into the canyons, where soon only the darkness would hear it.

Then Ben remembered something Neil said the other day: Someone had been at the camp that night, when Neil was waiting to see Lucero. Back in the barn, Ben locked up the box, found his ser-

vice revolver. Five minutes later he was driving down Junipero, heading east.

BEN CLIMBED THE ALUMINUM FENCE with the NO TRESPASSING sign
and passed through two rows of orange grove before the canyon
opened up, cliff-lined and shadowed where the hills blocked the
moonlight. He found the deer trail and followed it through the thigh-
high brush to the Loma Canyon cabin.

Inside, the cabin stank of piss and spilled beer, of animal hide
and dried blood. His flashlight scanned a snout moth caught in a
web, one wing shuddering loose of the threads. In the corner next to
him, six 40-ouncers were stacked in an unstable pyramid. Pushed up
against the west wall was an old mattress, one corner gnawed open to
the stuffing. He scanned the plaster walls—wood-rat holes tunneled
to the grass outside. Names were scratched into the walls, too—
Alejandra + Emilio; Dead Kennedys; an anarchy sign, crude drawings
of penises and mouths. On the east wall, the high school's mascot,
the Vaquero, was spray-painted into the plaster. Then, near the broken window frame, to the left of the torn-up mattress, he found it:
find a little strangr. He didn't know if it had been here the other day.
It was small, scratched faintly along the joist of a broken windowsill
like a whisper, surrounded by other indecipherable scratches and
symbols, but it was there.

Beneath the spot were twists of opened paper clips, a half dozen of
them. He was about to head out to the cruiser for an evidence bag
when he heard something crashing through the brush outside. He
flipped off the flashlight, drew his revolver, and slid alongside the broken window frame. The moon, above the cliff ridge now, lit the canyon white, bowling it out of the hillsides like a pelvic bone. A trio of
deer threw shadows across the ground as they leapt toward the underbrush on the other side of the canyon.

Ben holstered the revolver, but new footsteps crunched the peb-
bled dirt. He stepped back from the window, reaching for the gun

again before he saw the shadow of the man through the open doorway. The shadow stood there for a moment, cast spindly and elon-
gated in the moonlight. Then it stepped forward, one skeletal foot
easing its toes to the dirt. Ben took another step back, pressing himself against the wall to get a shot if he needed to, and then something
crashed behind him: the pyramid of beer bottles.

The shadow bolted. Through the broken window Ben glimpsed
the figure—small, like a kid—running along the deer path. Ben
stumbled through the door and down the white line of the deer path,
the man ahead kicking up clouds of dust. Then the man cut left,
through the underbrush and into the orange grove, the fog of his escape floating out across the canyon.

Shit. Ben ducked into the grove three rows down and pushed
through the hanging fruit.

"Santa Elena Police," Ben hollered. "You run, I shoot."

Ben heard a shuffling up ahead, and he dropped to his haunches
to peer beneath the limbs.

"Turn yourself in and we can talk," he said. Mottled moonlight
and darkness. He couldn't see a damn thing. "So far you're only trespassing."

Then he saw him—legs opening and closing like scissors as he
snuck through the grove. Ben dove through the trees, the branches
scratching at him, fruit falling at his feet. When he hit the row, the
moonlight illuminated the man sprinting ahead of him, his hands
stretched out, knocking branches out of the way. Ben was closing the
gap, the man raking his hands across the trees as he ran. The fruit
rolled and popped beneath Ben's feet, the tangy citrus flesh cracking
open. He could hear the man's breath now, wheezing with fear. Ben
could take a shot, but what if it was a panicked teenager? What if it
was one of the pickers looking for a place to throw back a 40 in private?

Ben was about to dive for an ankle when his foot twisted on the
fallen fruit and he face-planted. He pushed himself up, stumbled
back into a sprint, and tore into the open on the other side of the

grove. A black car peeled out, fanning gravel across the road. Ben ran into the road, trying to see the license plate: 6MV2— The car swerved around a corner before he could read the last numbers, and he was left alone, catching his breath, listening to the rev of the engine as it descended into the grid of the city.

12

NATASHA SPENT EARLY TUESDAY MORNING WITH LUCERO, sliding him out of the cooler and examining his body again, wondering if she'd missed anything. Adductor, pectineus, rectus femoris, the scrotum, the corona, the glans penis—so exposed, in some ways more vulnerable than a woman's body. There were no bruises, no lacerations, nothing to indicate anything other than a bullet to the brain.

It had been a week since Lucero's body was found in the field, a week of the boy lying here on this stainless-steel table. The boy was seventeen, had pool water in his lungs, chlorine in his hair follicles. Ben himself had said that Lucero was a swimmer. But Ben hadn't interviewed Coach Lewis Wakeland. She'd done her job, but Ben hadn't, not this time. Wakeland should have been at the top of his interview list. She couldn't get over that, had thought about it all last night and was still turning it over in her head this morning. Ben always followed protocol, always filled out the right paperwork, always tied up every loose end, and it pissed him off when other cops didn't do the same.

Twelve years ago, nearly two weeks after the boy took her up to Signal Hill for the "submarine races," she had gotten up the courage to go to the Long Beach Police. It was a rape. She had been raped. The first thing they asked her, two uniforms hovering over her in an interrogation room, was: "What were you wearing?" The second: "Had you been drinking?" They took her name and number, but she knew as soon as she left the station that they weren't going to do a damn thing about it.

After the police, Natasha spent three days in her dorm-room bed; Kris, her roommate, brought her soups from the cafeteria, thinking Natasha was sick. The police wouldn't do their job, the police wouldn't protect her; it had been terrifying, that realization. It was like a crack opened up in the façade of the civil world, and she had glimpsed the chaos behind it. She had grown up in Santa Elena, and she had naïvely believed the world to be as safe as its organized streets. On the fourth day, she finally got herself out of bed and immersed herself in her studies. She spent whole days in darkly lit alcoves in the School of Medicine, in a corner behind the biology stacks in the Darling Library—and snuck into bed after Kris was asleep or stayed away completely, resting her head on the open pages of her quantitative-chemical-analysis textbook.

For weeks her body had throbbed—the inner part of her thighs (the gracilis); her hip joints (the acetabula), even the back of her knees (the popliteal fossa) ached. And it hurt where the boy had pushed into her, burned like alcohol dabbed on a cut—though there was no blood, no obvious lacerations or bruises. It was a ghost pain, the body offering no physical evidence of its cause. She had never been so aware of her body, never so conscious of the foundation of the pelvis, the way its crescent arc fastened her frame into balance. She read every textbook at least twice and even read the recommended texts and the texts cited in those recommended texts. The body broken down to its forensic parts, their functions and the myriad ways those functions ceased to function, and she came to understand that she was imagining the pain. Her body didn't have a story to tell. That's what took her three months to figure out. The pain was in her mind, in the realization that her body could be so quickly stolen away from her. Once she understood that she had let him take her mind, too, once she identified the cause of the pain as something irrational, the pain went away and she got her body back.

She'd thought about this last night after Ben stormed out of the bar. "Don't touch me," he had said. In her experience, that wasn't something a man said to a woman. She thought about the night five weeks ago when they almost slept together. He had said it wasn't her, and it was clear to her now that he had meant it.

She covered Lucero's body now and slid him back into the cooler. The boy's body wasn't going to tell her anything she didn't already know. The evidence she thought she was looking for could be washed away; the evidence she thought she needed was rotting in the dead tissue of the hippocampus, in the memory that couldn't be accessed now. If family didn't claim him soon, the county would incinerate the body and bury him in El Toro Cemetery, whatever story the boy could have told lost forever.

Midmorning, she cleaned up and told Mendenhall she had a dentist appointment. It was bullshit, of course, and Mendenhall knew it was bullshit—she hated dentists, hated their fingers and instruments rooting around in her mouth—but she never took days off and the paperwork was finished and no new bodies had been ambulanced in overnight, so he let her go, muttering some crude joke about gingivitis.

She idled through the midday traffic on the 5 Freeway and was at Santa Elena High School by 12:30. There were three black-and-whites on site, one at each entrance and another parked in the handicapped spot near the front steps of the school. They had almost caught the serial last night, and the city had the jittery energy of a place under siege. Three patrol officers stood at the top of the steps, one resting his hand on the butt of his revolver, as though the killer was about to ambush the students in broad daylight.

She wanted to talk to Coach Wakeland. When she had decided at 2:00 A.M. that she was going to look into this on her own, that's what she wanted. She'd written down a series of questions at her kitchen table, but when she woke early this morning she was sure that was the wrong way to go. If Ben wouldn't question Wakeland, then the darkness of the thing she needed to expose would never be willingly dragged into the light. This was not science anymore, this was not forensics, the body could not be cut open and measured into quantifiable truths. She needed to come at this the way firefighters fought a brush fire: set a backfire and push it onto itself.

She hadn't seen Helen Galloway in nearly fourteen years, but the woman, at least twenty pounds heavier, psoriasis reddening the root edge of her gray hair, recognized her immediately.

"Sweetheart," she said, struggling up from her chair and embracing Natasha. "Oh, sweetheart, it's so good to see you."

Helen was one of those rare people who had love for everyone. From this little office, a plague of benevolence infected the school—Tootsie Rolls even when you were late, gentle reminders that you were not the kind of kid who forged notes for absences, bear hugs and tissues when a boyfriend dumped you—and Helen became the unofficial counselor/den mother to the two hundred or so students who walked through the doors of the school.

"I'm sorry about your son," Natasha said. She meant to call, to send a card, but she had—she was ashamed to admit it—let work get in the way of common decency. Teenagers, needy as they were, soaked up Helen's unsolicited love and took it with them after commencement, and Natasha had done the same.

"He was a good boy," Helen said, letting go of Natasha to perch back on her swivel chair. "I don't even know why we're over there. Why we send our boys." She glanced at her son's photo. "Sometimes it feels to me like I raised him only so rich old men in Washington could get him killed, like I'm a part of some sick farm system."

"I can't imagine," Natasha said.

"But you're not here to see me," Helen said, straightening. "You're here about the boy, Lucero."

"I am."

"I've been thinking about him a lot," Helen said. "Since Ben was here." Helen leaned back in her chair. "You're a medical examiner, right?" she said. "Seems a bit out of your job description to be here talking to me."

"My job's to find out what killed the boy," she said. "Ben's is to catch the person who did it."

"Sounds like he did it to himself," Helen said, "according to Benjamin."

"According to my boss, too."

Helen scrutinized her. Her willingness to give out love could sometimes make Helen seem stupid, but she wasn't. She'd always been good at reading people—that was true when Natasha was a student here, and it was true now. It was as though she was finding all your secrets and adding them up one by one.

"Helen," Natasha said, "I'm not a cop; I have no authority with this and you don't have to talk to me." Helen watched her closely. "I'm here for personal reasons. . . ." Natasha hesitated. "Between you and me, I think whatever happened to Lucero is connected to Ben."

"You always had something for Ben, didn't you?" Helen said. "Even way back then."

Natasha could feel her face go hot.

"Don't worry, sweetheart," Helen said, patting Natasha's knee and flashing a conspiratorial smile. "You weren't the only one. He was a gorgeous boy."

Helen turned and reached toward a shelf of yearbooks. She grabbed one marked 1973 and opened it up to a page with a yellow Post-it.

"I've been here for twenty-seven years," Helen said, nodding her head slowly. "Sometimes it seems like forever, but since I've been thinking about Lucero it feels very short—like no time at all, really."

"Memory is a strange thing," Natasha said. She'd been working as deputy medical examiner for six years now. Her first cadaver felt like a century ago, but his face was still with her, clear as his meltwater-blue eyes.

"You know, Lucero was one of Wakeland's boys."

Natasha nodded. "He was a swimmer."

"It's more than that," Helen said. "Coach Wakeland's always taking the swimming team out for pizza or having them over to his house for barbecues, that kind of thing, but Lucero was the boy he'd chosen to mentor. You'd sometimes see them driving around together in Wakeland's Corvette."

"Anyone question why a teacher was driving around with a student?"

"Well, it was so out in the open," Helen said. "If there was something to hide, you'd think they'd hide it."

"Did you question it?"

"I'm the attendance lady."

"And he's the big-time swim coach," Natasha said.

"The city's using the swimming program in its brochures to get families to move in."

Natasha nodded.

"Most of the time everything feels disconnected," Helen said, "especially over so many years, but then when you start thinking about it, really thinking about it, you can find threads of things, you know?"

"A pattern."

"Kind of." She turned the pages of the book and pointed to a boy, Ryan Bell. "He went to Stanford. If you remember, he was the butterfly leg of the Olympic relay team in '76. His grades were terrible, missed a ton of classes, especially senior year. So how does he get into Stanford, full scholarship?"

"Wakeland's got connections."

"If you were on the swim team," she said, "you wanted to be one of Wakeland's boys. You got special privileges—excuses from classes, rides in fancy cars, scholarships to the best schools."

She grabbed another yearbook from the shelf: 1979. She turned to a page marked by another Post-it.

"Tucker Preston," she said. "I hadn't thought about him in a long time, until Ben came in here the other day." She rubbed her finger across the boy's forehead. "He dropped out of school his junior year. After swallowing a bottle of aspirin. Parents sold their house and moved."

"One of Wakeland's?"

She nodded. "State record in the backstroke."

"Any rumors?"

"There was a meeting with the superintendent. Lawyers were involved. Some kind of confidentiality agreement."

"Hush money," Natasha said. "Anyone say why?"

"Everyone had a reason," Helen said, "but it depended on how you wanted to see things. Some people thought it couldn't be such a big deal if the family was so willing to shut up about it. Others thought the opposite."

"What about you?"

"I think anything that has to be shut up about is a bad thing," she said. "But police, lawyers, the superintendent, made the decision they made. People tend to think that counts for something."

"Maybe the people in charge don't deserve to be in charge."

"I might agree with that."

Helen grabbed another yearbook, from 1970. Ben. There he was, his beautiful seventeen-year-old face creased with a guarded smile.

"The world is full of open secrets," Helen said. "Kids like Lucero are being raised in cardboard boxes; the military tells children it'll give them a future."

She handed Natasha the yearbook, and she stared at Ben's picture. He was beautiful then, but there was something in his eyes, something you could still see today if you looked at him closely: something lost about them. Natasha remembered him from high school—six foot two, his swimmer's shoulders twice as wide as hers, his sinewy muscles that were literally carved by water. She'd see him around, sometimes with Wakeland—in the man's Mustang multiple times, now that she thought about it. She was a child, a little girl, and

Ben had looked like a man and she believed him to have a man's authority in the world. More than a few times in high school she had fantasized about him using that authority on her.

"Why'd no one say anything?" Natasha asked.

"That's what I've been wondering about," Helen said. She was quiet for a moment. "I don't know exactly, but I guess I can only speak for myself." She went quiet again, thinking. "Years ago, something like that was an embarrassing secret, something you didn't want to look at, something you didn't want to point out. It was so embarrassing you wanted to believe it wasn't true." The phone rang, but Helen let it go. "It's like being fat," she said when the ringing stopped. "Everyone can see it, but they don't come up to you and point it out to you. They talk to your forehead instead of looking in your eyes, anything to avoid the embarrassing fact of your size." She picked up a pencil and chewed on the eraser. "The boys didn't complain, as far as I know—except for Tucker, maybe—and after a while Wakeland and a boy in his car was just another part of Santa Elena—like the illegals in the fields, the coyotes in the backyard, the bulldozers knocking down people's homes to make new ones. Besides, it was hard to see how a boy like Ben—so big and strong—could be forced to do something like that if he didn't want to."

Natasha had to admit it was. If she'd been big enough, strong enough—if she had been six foot two, two hundred pounds, like Ben had been—she would have fought the boy off. She stared at Ben's face and wondered who he really was. She went into the sciences to find clarity and had found the opposite. She'd begun to realize in the last few years that most things were difficult to understand—from love, to murder, to the very muscle and tissue that held the body together. We gave them names, but identification was simply the illusion of understanding.

"And then Wakeland got married," Helen said, "and everyone sighed in relief."

"Where'd Tucker and his family move to?"

"Dana Point, I think."

Natasha closed the yearbook, sealing Ben's seventeen-year-old face inside, and handed it back to Helen.

"I don't know about these other boys," Helen said. "I'm not sure how to think of it, but Lucero was gay—or at least he had a boy-friend."

"Gay has nothing to do with it," Natasha said, shaking her head. "This, what Wakeland does, is something else."

"I don't know," Helen said. "But I don't understand it, I really don't. You should have to take an oath to become a teacher—the Hippocratic oath or something."

"An oath is just words," Natasha said. "They don't mean much."

"HE'S USING THE HILLS," BEN said at the Tuesday-morning investiga-tions meeting. "That's where we're not looking."

After calling in the scene last night, after cordoning it off and bagging the paper clips to send off to forensics, after taking pictures of the scrawled words, after fending off reporters pushed back beyond the NO TRESPASSING sign, Ben had stayed up late in the barn, looking at the map, trying to piece together a symbol that would reveal some-thing. He drew lines between scenes, erased them, and drew lines again. He tried to make pentagrams out of the points, letters that created a message, shapes that would reveal the killer's next move. It wasn't until sunrise, moted light slipping through the slats in the wall, that he saw it. The dark spaces of open territory—the hills of the coast joined to the Santa Ana Mountain foothills in the east by a tendon of undeveloped groves. He had remembered, suddenly, like pieces fitting into place, the man sleeping in his car a week ago. He had been small, Ben remembered, a teenager or early twenties. His eyes were rimmed bruise-blue, as though he hadn't slept in a long time. His girlfriend had kicked him out, the young man had said, and Ben had bought it, given the guy his fresh coffee even, but he didn't look like the kind of guy who had a girlfriend. He looked like the kind of guy who stood on corners and watched people, the kind of guy who called in bomb threats to schools, the kind of guy who was invisible until he exploded into visibility. Ben remembered the ride with Emma the other day, the man coming out of the Bommer Canyon camp and walking down to the golf course. He had been small, too, lean and wiry, his limbs awkward, as though parts of him were unhinged. Surrounding the horseshoe of open space, the developed basin was a grid of steel and lights, but that horseshoe was a dark zone, a shadow cast by city light, lined with foot trails and dotted with rotting cowboy camps.

"The hills are off the grid," Ben said now. "Old cowboy cabins in Bommer and Loma Canyons. Another up near the Sinks in Santiago Canyon."

"Just deer and coyote up there," Carolina said.

All of them had been on scene until after 2:00 A.M., and probably none of them had slept. Hernandez called them in at 8:30 this morning, after Westminster found a print on a water glass at their crime scene. Marco, working the night shift, cross-referenced the prints with the numbers and letters Ben had gotten off the plate, and they had their man: Ricardo Martinez, twenty-three years old. By 8:00 A.M. there was an inter-department BOLO for all of the Southern California basin; they'd sent out the killer's mug shot to the press, uniformed officers were canvassing neighborhoods—but the hills were it, the hills were ground zero.

"The Santa Ana Freeway," Marco said, running a finger up the map that covered the east wall, "and the 405 both run the edge of the hills. Six on-ramps. In and out, disappear."

"He was down in Chino," Lieutenant Hernandez said, passing out the folders. CIM. California Institute for Men.

"Something's off in his face," Carolina said.

"It's him," Ben said, looking at the mug shot. The killer's face seemed misaligned, not obviously so, but enough to throw off the eyes. "It's the guy I found sleeping in the Toyota last week."

"He spent time in Reception Center East for assaulting a prostitute."

Reception Center East was for inmates with mental-health problems. Ben had been there a few times, back when he was in L.A., questioning low-level drug pushers who worked the system to get time off for emotional instability. The place was unsecured; inmates started pickup games in the courtyard. Therapists were on hand to hold inmates' hands and help them talk out their problems. A place for coddling, if you asked him, though he had seen the genuine article there, too: Men breaking down like little girls, recalling traumatic events from childhood. Men smearing feces in "quiet room" pens, their eyes dense and occluded, the brain closed off to the present world.

"According to the prostitute's formal statement," Hernandez said, "he started choking her during sex."

"Erotic strangulation?" Carolina asked.

"No," Hernandez said. "Not according to her. Choked her until she passed out. She woke up and he was gone; the money in her purse was gone, too." Ben looked at the pictures of the woman's throat, the finger bruises, the scratches on her chin where her nails had dug into her skin. "Turned himself in," Hernandez said, "but then wouldn't admit to anything."

"He scared himself," Ben said. "But found it exciting, too. That's probably when he got hooked."

"Any priors?" Marco asked.

"No," Hernandez said, "but he's got a long case history."

Ben read the file: mother in and out of rehab before overdosing, father a junk dealer who locked the kid up in the basement, perhaps for as long as five to six years. Signs of sexual abuse, suffering severe malnutrition when found, stunted growth. The small hands, Ben thought. Three foster families. First assault at twelve, a desk lamp cracked over the head of a foster mother. Placed in a group home and school for troubled kids. Restrained for trying to stab a pencil into his own eye. Restrained for banging his head against a cement wall. Restrained for carving words into his arm with a paper clip. Back in another foster home at thirteen. Claims to a therapist that foster mother "touches" him at night when the other kids are asleep. Ben highlighted this in orange. Placed back in group home while investigation takes place. Second assault at group home, punches female teacher in the neck. Briefly incarcerated at the California Youth Authority after the incident, in with the teenage heavies. Who knew what happened to him there, a thirteen-year-old in with violent sixteen- and seventeen-year-olds biding their time for the big house. Sent back to foster care, with the same woman who touches him at night; there was an opening and no evidence to prove she'd done anything wrong. He highlighted this, too. Spent three years there, complaining three times about the foster mother to a therapist who wrote his complaints off as "a regressive behavior" brought on by traumatic family memories.

"Are any of the victims," Ben said, "this foster mother?"

"No," Hernandez said. "Long Beach checked that out. She's been dead for five years."

"Natural causes?"

"Stabbed in the liver with a kitchen knife."

"Another foster kid?" Ben said.

"You got it." Hernandez nodded.

"Man," Carolina said. "I hate the psychos with painful pasts."

Marco threw the file on the table. "Ugly memories," he said, referencing the killer's song. "No doubt."

Ben found the pictures of Ricardo as a twelve-year-old, when he was first put into foster care. His face looked swollen, the skin cracked at the edges of his lips. His hair was a strange red color, as though the red had been washed out of it and the stain remained. He tried to smile for the camera, his front teeth too big for his face, one canine stabbing sideways into his lip. No dental care in a basement. His eyes were yawned open, nocturnal, as though they were trying to suck in the light. Ben found the next shot, when he was thirteen and incarcerated at CYA. His jaw clenched so that the muscle showed, inverted triangles for cheekbones, a homemade tattoo scratched into his neck. His eyes hardened and black-looking, as though the pupils had swallowed the irises. The last photo was the adult Ricardo, twenty-one and booked for nearly strangling the prostitute. His face was all angles, his cheekbone knives ready to cut open the surface of the skin. He smirked in the picture, stared straight into the camera and gave it a crooked look of contempt. He was gone, completely gone.

"Last residence?" Marco said.

"Apple Valley," Hernandez said.

"The desert." Carolina closed the file.

"A year ago," Hernandez said. "No address since. Apple Valley's checking the place this morning. But it's been rented out for nine months."

"Make of car?" Ben asked.

"A 1980 Toyota Tercel."

Ben remembered the car from last night.

"The back taillight cover was smashed out," he said. "Just the naked bulb." He flashed on the car that had passed him when he sat outside Wakeland's apartment, too. A black Toyota Tercel. Shit, the killer had driven right past him.

"Not exactly a bat out of hell," Marco said.

"Practical." Carolina shrugged. "Gets good gas mileage."

"Get a few hours' rest," Hernandez said. "Then start hitting the coffee. Everyone's on tonight."

Chairs slid across the floor, cups were thrown in the trash, but Ben stayed in his seat, reading the file. Jesus, locked in a basement for six years. Created his own language. Ben couldn't move; he'd seen terrible things before, but nothing like this.

"Ben," Hernandez said.

"Lieutenant."

"Thought I'd lost you for a second."

"I remember this case," Ben said. "Kid locked in a basement. Made headlines for a few days, ten or so years ago."

"Yeah," Hernandez said. "The house was up in Norwalk, I think. Some old house with a basement."

"Jesus," Ben said. "There *are* monsters in the world."

"You're just now coming to that conclusion?"

"How can you do that to a kid?"

"Don't get sentimental on me. He's not a kid anymore," Hernandez said. "Listen, I've got a special assignment for you."

NATASHA WAS DRIVING DOWN THE Pacific Coast Highway, riding the cliffs of south Laguna, glimpses of turquoise coves between white high-rise hotels and squat bungalows with squares of manicured Bermuda grass. Salt Creek Beach curved below like bleached whalebone, the surfers carving hollowed-out swells, their wakes contrailing the water. The radio buzzed with Night Prowler coverage — a hotline had been set up, an award offered, *lock your doors and close your windows, no matter how hot it gets.* Ten minutes and the bay at Dana Point unfolded, the rock jetties and cement breakwater sheltering slips of white-hulled boats. Out in the open water, a tall ship, its muslin sails stretched triangular in the wind, leaned out to sea. And beyond the ship nothing but an opaque blue arcing slightly with the curve of the earth. It was beautiful, unbelievably so, but today it felt like a lie, this beauty, like something false and dissembling.

It had taken her only three hours to hunt down the Prestons, that was it. They were unlisted in the white and yellow pages, had severed ties with their former neighbors. She had called down to the Dana Point Police and asked if there were any arrest records — DUIs, outstanding parking tickets — if there were any filed complaints, any police reports. Nothing. She found them then by calling down to the Dana Point assessor's office: 20019 Bonita Agua Street, purchased June 1979. She simply couldn't believe Ben didn't know about them. He must know. He just didn't want to know.

The house was a split-level with dwarf palms swaying out front. It perched on the cliffs above the bay, the back patio propped on cement stilts stabbed into the crumbling hillside. Natasha could hear a pool-filter system humming from the side yard. It was 4:16, and the late-day sun radiated off the white plaster house.

Mrs. Preston opened the door, a fragile smile creasing her face, her frosted hair sprayed into a feathery nest. "What can I do for you?" she said, her voice frail and quiet.

Behind her, through the hallway and into the family room, a man was on the phone, pacing, his tie askew from an unbuttoned shirt.

Natasha introduced herself, her fingers pressed over the MEDI-CAL EXAMINER etched on her badge when she flashed it. The woman's smile collapsed and Natasha immediately doubted herself. Tucker had said something; Tucker had spoken up — three hours ago, she saw strength in that. Now, though, facing this wafer-thin woman, she saw someone on the edge of breaking. The woman, whose right hand had never left the door handle, started to push the door closed.

"Please," Natasha said. "It's about a suicide, a boy's."

It was stifling inside, all the windows shut, a fan in the corner of the room swirling stale air. The house was immaculate — white walls, white carpets, a smudgeless glass-topped coffee table, pastel-tinted paintings of the sea, and through the hallway that led into the open kitchen the windblown blue of the Pacific. Mr. Preston cursed into the phone. "Dammit, Jim," he said, leaning on the kitchen counter. "These assholes can't go under when they owe us fifty thousand." Mr. Preston held up an index finger to indicate he'd be with her in just a moment. "Don't talk to me about bankruptcy regs."

The white sofa in the living room was so perfectly symmetrical it seemed no one had ever sat on it, so Natasha was surprised when Mrs. Preston offered her a seat there. Mrs. Preston sat opposite her on a piano bench and placed a tanned hand on the fallboard of a black grand piano.

"Do you play?" Natasha said, nodding toward the piano.

"When I was young."

A framed photo of Tucker and a girl who must have been his

older sister sat on the fireplace mantel behind the piano. It was a studio shot, at least ten years old, Natasha thought, Tucker's elbow resting on his sister's knee, both of them forcing smiles for the camera.

"My father used to play," Natasha said. "We had a baby grand in the living room. I miss it."

Natasha glanced at the photo again. Something about Tucker looked like Ben—the green eyes, the tanned skin, the depth of the eye sockets.

"I like it quiet." Mrs. Preston lifted the hand from the fallboard and brushed back a strand of hair that had fallen across her forehead. "My husband won't like that you're here."

"I don't blame him."

The slam of the phone and the swish of Mr. Preston's suit slacks preceded his arrival in the living room.

"Mary Kay? Tupperware?" the man said, flashing the disingenuous smile of a man used to being in control. Sure, Natasha thought, I'm driving a pink Cadillac. She disliked him immediately. "You get me my fifty thousand back and I might buy what you're selling."

Natasha extended her hand.

"Sorry about the heat," he said, taking only her fingers in his. "Not taking any chances with that maniac running around. Always said we should get central air."

"Detective Betencourt," she lied, squeezing his hand as hard as she could.

"Did he hit around here?"

"No," Natasha said. "I'm down from Santa Elena."

Mr. Preston glanced at his wife, blame in his eyes. She studied a spot on the carpet.

"What do you want?" he said.

Natasha told him about Lucero's suicide, about the information she'd gotten from Helen at the high school. She started to ask about Wakeland, but Preston cut her off.

"Don't say that name in this house," he said.

"I understand," she said gently.

"Do you?" Preston said. Sweat that had beaded on his forehead ran down the edge of his nose. "You come here unannounced, barge into my house, and utter that man's name while standing in my living room."

"I'm sorry," she said, and she was. She had no right, no subpoena, no legal justification to be here. She was an intruder climbing unwanted into their lives. "It's just—I think what happened to your son happened to this boy."

Mrs. Preston turned her head and stared at the closed lid of the black piano. "It's what I was afraid of, Mark," she said. "We should have—"

Preston put his hand on his wife's shoulder and squeezed the bone there.

"I am sorry to hear that." He wiped the sweat from his nose with his free hand. "But it has nothing to do with us."

But it does, she wanted to say. *It does.*

"This man," Natasha said, "is still a teacher."

"Please," Mrs. Preston said, her palm turned upward as though begging for food. "It's taken years of therapy, years of medication. He's doing better—"

"Don't," Mr. Preston said.

"—now he has a job, he's in college, he's got a girlfriend."

"I know there was a confidentiality agreement," Natasha said. "But there are ways around—"

Mr. Preston hammered the top of the piano with the heel of his hand, knocking the strings into a discordant thrumming.

"We *cannot* talk about it," he said, glaring at his wife. He turned to Natasha, his eyes like rock. "Now get out of my house."

NATASHA HAD SLIPPED HER 280Z into gear when Mrs. Preston pushed open the gate to the yard and jogged across the street.

"How old was the boy?" Mrs. Preston said, when she sat down in the passenger seat.

"Seventeen."

She glanced at Natasha's cigarette curling smoke into the car. "Can you put that out, please?"

Natasha flicked it out the driver's side window, and Mrs. Preston sat there picking at a hangnail on her right thumb.

"Tucker has a class at five fifteen," she said.

The curtains were pulled aside in the front window of the Preston house and Mr. Preston stood there framed by the sill, his face exploded by a sunburst on the spotless glass. Mrs. Preston was watching him through the open window of the car.

"Men don't want to talk about these things," Mrs. Preston said. She put her hand on the handle and cracked the door. "Advanced Poetry Workshop," she said, before swinging her legs onto the street, "at Saddleback Community College."

HERNANDEZ HAD CALLED IN COPS from the Ventura County Sheriff's Mounted Enforcement Unit. The MEU guys rode the backcountry north of L.A., in the Santa Monica Mountains and the Los Padres, looking for plots of marijuana, busting kids with illegal campfires, occasionally tracking fugitives into the scrub pine higher elevations.

"You know the canyons around here as well as anybody," Hernandez had said to Ben. That was his special assignment: heading up the mounted team to flush out the killer. The horses were in trailers doing 55 down the 101 as they spoke. "You'll brief them tonight and then get up there."

After the morning briefing, Ben drove up to the Norwalk Police Department and asked to check the files on the decade-old case. The twelve-year-old Martinez had been found locked in the basement at 3562 Grayland Street. Father charged with sexual assault, sexual abuse, willful harming and endangering of a child, severe neglect. The father—if you could call him that—had been sent up to Folsom, twenty-five years to life. Didn't last long there, though: shanked in the liver with a filed-down toothbrush just two years into the sentence. In that respect, Ben appreciated the harsh law of the convict.

The house sat abandoned on a leafy street of 1930s bungalows, a desert grapevine devouring the left side wall, a chain-link fence cordoning it off. It wasn't a wealthy neighborhood, but the rest of the homes were well kept, green postage-stamp yards behind cinder-block fences, trimmed hedges. There was a faded FOR SALE sign out front, but apparently no one wanted to buy a house with that kind of history.

Ben grabbed a flashlight from the trunk and then bent through a hole in the fence. The front door was knocked off its hinges. Inside smelled of cat piss and mold. A torn-open couch was pushed up against one of the walls, littered with empty beer cans. Leaves bunched in the corner. He found the steps at the back of the kitchen, three of them missing, the others tilted and rotting. He flipped on the flashlight and went down into the darkness.

It wasn't a basement, really; more of a crawl space. A rusted combination lock was clasped to a hook on the wall. Weak light filtered through a painted-over window, beetle carapaces flittered in the wind funneling down the stairs. An old mattress leaned against the stairwell, and on the wall next to it strange symbols were scratched into the plaster, gibberish mostly, etchings with indecipherable patterns, a few vowels and consonants. The kid had created his own language, to talk with himself. Six years in a hole. Jesus. The killer's father had locked him down there soon after the mother overdosed, according to the report. Social Services was alerted after the father had taken the boy to the doctor for severe diarrhea. Vitamin D deficiency, anemia, rickets, and softened bones. Still, it took nearly nine months after the first report to Social Services to get the boy out of here.

Ben crouched under the stairwell and turned off the flashlight and sat there in the dark, listening, letting his eyes adjust to the lightless place. The cement smelled of mold, a fecund rotting in the corners of the room, and the murky gray light was like being submerged in muddied water. He tried to imagine what it was like for the child, huddled down here in the dark with the insects, while the rest of the world went on above. Ben had felt alone most of his life, pushed out onto the edge of normal existence, but this was a different kind of alone. What did this kind of powerlessness do to you? Lucero—and the others—hadn't been locked up; they could leave. But why didn't you? That was the question. That was always the question. Why didn't you? That question made you hate yourself. But this, being locked down here: There was no choice, no blame to level at yourself. The blame was put outside you—onto the world outside. Almost nine months after the doctor's visit. Nine goddamned months before Social Services and the police got him out.

A shadow flashed in the window.

Outside, he found an elderly woman next door, watering a rosebush. It had been her passing legs that disturbed the weak light seeping through the window.

"Are you going to buy that place?" she said, when she saw him emerge from the basement. "Tear it down?"

"No," he said. Water from the hose was trickling a path past his toes. Her yard was lush with flowers, vines climbing a trellis. "Police business." He showed her his badge.

She looked closely at him. "I already told them I never knew about the boy," she said.

"You knew the people who lived here?"

"They were neighbors," she said. "But I didn't *know* them."

Ben looked at the window and measured the distance in his mind. Ten feet, maybe twelve, to the spigot on the woman's hose. How was it possible? Six years in a hole and no one knew? She seemed to guess what he was thinking.

"We heard things occasionally," she said. "My husband and me. But those people never bothered us." She sprayed a fuchsia basket dangling from the trellis. "They really should tear it down."

* * *

"GOT TIME FOR AN EARLY dinner?" Rachel asked when he answered the Motorola in the cruiser later that afternoon. He'd been out in the barn, combing down Tin Man, filing the muck and horseshit from his hooves, when he ran out to answer it. He scraped clean his boots, dashed his neck with the Old Spice he kept in his desk drawer, and hit the road.

He indulged a fantasy on the drive over—the wedding china lifted out of the storage boxes, candlelight, Rachel slipped into the charcoal dress she liked to wear out to dinner. When he got there, she was wearing faded jeans and a V-neck with a wet stain on the belly. She wasn't wearing makeup—nothing that had ever bothered him, but the few times he'd crashed a date of hers she was painted up, some of the makeup fancy stuff he'd bought from Nordstrom's.

"Do me a favor," Rachel said, nodding at his boots, "and leave those outside."

He slipped them off, suddenly aware that he stank of horse sweat.

"I've got lasagna in the oven," she said, turning her back and going into the kitchen.

Lasagna: the meal of crisis. They had lasagna after her father died. They had lasagna after Emma broke her leg. They had lasagna the night she told him she wanted out.

"Where's Em?" he said, watching her pull the pan from the oven.

"Upstairs," she said.

"Mind if I go up?"

"Yes, I do mind," she said. "You and I need to talk."

Shit, she's marrying the computer guy. Wants more money. Whatever it was, it wasn't good.

"I'm not too crazy about the smoke and mirrors," he said. "It's been a long day."

"You know me, Ben," she said, holding her hot-mitted hands out to him. "I wouldn't waste your time, especially now. Just sit, please."

He did as he was told and took in the apartment—the painting of Catalina they had purchased together after taking a whale-watching cruise to Avalon, a photo of Emma in her softball uniform, a photo of her as a toddler kicking up wet sand at Laguna Beach. It was too hot in the apartment, made broiling by the oven, and he stood to open the two front windows, jostling loose the wooden rods Rachel had jammed between the aluminum frames.

"Close those," she said.

"He won't be out until dark," Ben said.

"I don't care," she said. "He's terrifying and he's out there some-where."

He shut the window and replaced the rod. She carried the pan of lasagna to the table and served him a hunk of it. It was watery, but he kept his mouth shut. She hadn't dished out any for herself, so he grabbed her plate and filled it.

"Thanks, but I'm not hungry," she said. "You look tired."

"You, too."

They watched each other, and for a moment he thought she was going to take his hand, but then she cut into the lasagna and that was that.

"Look, Ben," she said. "You and I were stupid kids once. Remember that day on the floor at my parents' house?"

He smiled. It had been their first time. "I still think about it some-times."

Her cheeks flushed. "What was I, sixteen?"

"Yes, you were."

"You were seventeen, just turned. I *was* in love with you," she said, glancing at him, a softness in her eyes he couldn't ignore. At that moment, he wanted her. Right now, in a way he hadn't in a very long time.

"That was one of the best days of my life," he said.

She leaned back in her chair and crossed her arms over her chest. "You're not going to like this."

"Then don't do it," he said. "We can give it another shot, Rach. I'll give you more attention, I'll work hard—"

She touched his wrist. "No," she said quietly. "This is about

Emma, Ben. About Emma and this boy. I came home from school the other day and walked in on them."

"What?" he said. "Sex?"

"No," she said. "Well, not then, but Emma told me some things when I started asking questions."

"Sex?"

"Lower your voice."

"Answer my question."

"Yes," Rachel said. "Yes, she's had sex. She told me. It was difficult for her to say it."

"What the hell, Rachel," he said. "You spending too much time with your boyfriend to be a mother?"

"Don't do that, Ben," she said, pointing at him. "You need to calm down."

It sickened him, the thought of someone—this stoner—touching his daughter.

"She's barely fourteen," Ben said. "He's three years older. He took advantage of her."

"It doesn't sound like that's the case."

"Who cares what it sounds like? She's too young to make that decision. He zeroed in on the up-and-coming high schooler and took advantage of her."

"She says they're in love."

"Love?" he practically shouted. "What does she know about love?"

"What did you and I know about it?" Rachel said.

Ben stood up from the table and faced the window.

"We can't change what's happened," Rachel said, her voice quieter now. "We have to be practical, realistic. We need to have a plan—one we're on the same page about. We need to get her to the gynecologist. Make sure she's using birth control. I mean, I've talked to her about it, but that was in the abstract. I didn't think it would happen this early."

"You're saying we should put her on the pill?" he said.

"You want to lock her in her room?"

"Yeah," he said. "Yeah, I do."

Rachel walked over to him and placed her hand on the small of his back. He melted for a moment. For a split second he would have done anything she said. "Ben." But then he pulled away and went for the stairs. He wanted to see Emma, his little girl; he wanted his little girl back.

"Don't," Rachel said. Somehow she beat him to the bottom of the stairs. "Don't go up there right now."

"Emma," he called up the stairs.

He could see Emma's closed bedroom door, a NO TRESPASSING sign hanging on a nail.

"Ben," Rachel said. "Look at me. Wait until you've thought it out. She's your daughter."

Why did it feel like she wasn't his anymore? Like she had been taken from him?

"Emma," he said. "I know you can hear me. Come out here right now."

"Look at me," Rachel said. He wouldn't. He was watching his daughter's door. "When you're upset you say stupid things. Things you can't take back. Don't do that to her."

Emma's door cracked open. He could see her darken the sliver of open space, watching him at the bottom of the stairs.

"Ben," Rachel said loudly, her hand pressed against his chest. "Go home and think about us."

He looked at Rachel; he hadn't heard her refer to them as "us" in a very long time.

"Think about us back then," she said. "Maybe that will help you understand."

NATASHA SAT DOWN AT A bench near the open classroom door. She could see the professor sitting on a table in front of the students, reading with mock anger from a text he had splayed on his lap.

"And what loved the shot-pellets
That dribbled from those strung-up mummifying crows?
What spoke the silence of lead?

Crow realized there were two Gods—

One of them much bigger than the other
Loving his enemies
And having all the weapons."

He let the words hang in the air for a moment before releasing the students, yelling over the din of their shufflings which poems to read for the next class. Natasha recognized Tucker immediately, though the young man's hair was long and he had grown a beard. He was bigger than she expected—six foot four, she guessed, broad shoulders, biceps straining his shirtsleeves. She followed him, weaving in and out of the students as they made their way to their classes. He had a backpack slung over his shoulder, a skateboard strapped to the bag with a bungee cord. The barrel of a gun was painted on the board, and band names, too, were drawn in Sharpie across the empty spaces—X, Black Flag, Social Distortion, Dead Kennedys. He sat down at a bench beneath a tree and opened the book he was carrying. He teethed the cap off the pen and began scrawling words across the page.

"You like poetry?" Natasha said.

"The good stuff," Tucker said, squinting up at her.

She asked him the poet. Tucker dog-eared the page, closed the book, and showed her the cover. Ted Hughes.

"Sounds like angry stuff."

"Cathartic, maybe," Tucker said. "Beautiful, if you ask me." He slipped the book into his backpack and pulled the hair out of his eyes. His body was all muscle, but his face was soft—a boy's face still. "I didn't see you in class. You an extension student?"

"I was listening outside," Natasha said. "The professor was putting on a show."

"Yeah," Tucker said, sly smile. "A wanna-be actor."

"He'd be a pretty bad one."

"Who are you?" Tucker said, a hardness coming into his voice.

"Natasha Betencourt." She showed him the badge, her thumb hiding the MEDICAL EXAMINER etched into the metal.

"Let me see that again," he said.

She showed him, not bothering to hide it this time.

He squinted up at her, fear bleaching his face. "Who's dead?"

TUCKER AGREED TO MEET AT a park set against the hills and the remnants of an avocado grove. Natasha said she'd give him a ride, but Tucker said he wasn't getting in any car with her unless she had the authority to arrest him. So Tucker skateboarded there and Natasha followed him in her Z, until he reached a patch of irrigated green shaded by young junipers.

They were sitting on a cement bench near a new playground, watching a city worker push trunks of avocado trees into a wood chipper, when she told him about Lucero.

"How old was he?"

"Seventeen."

Next to a field newly cleared of trees, men lowered an irrigation system into a hole in the ground.

"One of Wakeland's?"

"He was a swimmer."

"Jesus," Tucker said, biting nails already chewed to the quick, one thumb rimmed in dried blood. "How'd you find me?"

"Your mother."

He narrowed his eyes at her. "Was my father there?"

"Yes," Natasha said.

"And my mom told you where to find me?"

"She did."

He studied her—astonished, it seemed.

"You know I can't talk, right? I mean, you've already found that out."

"I know that seven years ago you said something."

He glanced away, at the men lowering the pipe into the ground.

"How'd he do it?"

"Shot himself in the head."

Tucker nodded and looked at the ground.

"I wanted to talk," he said. "Wanted it off my fucking back. I didn't give a shit if people thought I was some freak."

"But your father didn't want you to, right?"

"Let me tell you about my dad." He pulled down the waistband of his pants to reveal scars, striations of them white and welted on his upper hips. "Belt," he said, letting go of the pants. "He would pull it right out of the loops and go at it." He bit a slice of fingernail and spit. "I got this because I cried in front of my Little League teammates when we lost a playoff game. I was eight. He said I needed to toughen up, you know. Get a backbone. He called me a pussy."

"Your father's the frightened one," Natasha said. "Sounds to me like you might be braver than him."

Tucker finished chewing his left thumb and moved on to his index finger. After the men lowered the pipe, a bulldozer dropped earth on it.

"What did Wakeland do to you?"

"You know, no one's ever asked me that question," he said. "It was always 'What happened?' or 'the accuser alleges that' and shit like that. Not even my mother asked me that question: 'What did *he* do?'"

"Maybe she's frightened to know," she said. "Maybe she's afraid it's her fault."

"Just like my mom," he said, "to make it all about her."

"But your mother sent me here to find you."

He looked at her. His eyes clear green like the deep end of tide pools. They were intelligent eyes, but she could see an insecurity in them. He would have been the type of child who tried to keep his parents from fighting, the kind of kid who tiptoed around the house to keep his world calm. A man like Wakeland would notice that. For a man like Wakeland, that would be an invitation.

"The problem is," he said, "I wouldn't know how to answer that question. What did he do to me?" He watched a bulldozer push the torn-up trees into a pile near the chipper. "Freshman year I get busted," he said, "in the parking lot, toking up. Goddamned resource officer trolling the lot has nothing better to do. He hauls me through the courtyard with the handcuffs on, right in the middle of lunch, in front of everybody. Wakeland just happens to be walking by and follows us out to the patrol car, jawing at the cop. 'C'mon, Joe,' Wakeland says. 'He's fourteen years old; get the cuffs off him.' But the cop says he can't do it and he slips me into the patrol car, and at this point there's this throng of kids standing on the steps watching the scene.

"'Joe,'" Wakeland says. 'He's one of mine.'

"And then the cop closes the door and I'm stuck inside the hot car with the windows up, watching the two of them talk. All I can hear is the police-radio static, so I have no clue what they're saying, but a couple minutes later the cop opens the door, keys open the cuffs, and hands me over to Wakeland. 'Lucky I'm a nice guy,' the cop says. 'No second chances, though.'

"So Wakeland hauls me over to his office in the swim complex, says he's gotta call my parents. I beg him. I mean, I fucking break down and beg him not to tell my father. He's got the phone in his hand, his finger in the dial, and I'm crying like an idiot. He puts the phone back on the hook, gives me a tissue, and watches me for a minute.

"'All right,' he says. 'This is between you and me.'" Tucker laughed ironically. "Between you and me.

"So Wakeland makes me promise," Tucker continued, "to come to his office each day at lunch, to get my homework finished. 'If I find out,' he says, 'you're smoking that garbage again, I'm calling the police and your parents.'

"And I did. I went to his office every day, did my homework, stopped getting stoned, got a B-plus average the next semester. My parents couldn't believe it. My dad mostly stopped belting me—that's how happy they were. They invited Wakeland over for dinners. Sent him Christmas cards. Let me watch movies at his apartment. I couldn't believe it, either, to be honest. I mean, I didn't believe I could do *anything* good, and here I was getting A's on tests."

The man running the chipper fed a severed branch into its mouth. A cloud of wood chips flew out across the ground and another man raked them beneath the new monkey bars and swings, a soft landing for kids when they lost their grip.

"It was almost a year," he said, "before anything . . ." He ran his hand through his hair and blew out air. "The problem is," he said, "he was like a dad, you know? He was like the dad I wanted. He'd show me extra attention after swim practice, giving me tips no one else got. We'd go to Angels games. I'd hang at his house, drinking beer. He'd help me with my homework, made me study for tests. I borrowed a fucking tie from him for my junior prom. It's crazy," Tucker said. "This college stuff is easy for me now because of Wakeland. I owe him for that, I guess, in a weird way."

"You owe him nothing."

"He kept copies of *Playboy* in his guest bathroom. Sometimes we'd look at them together, and somehow that started to feel normal, like the kind of thing you were supposed to do with a dad."

"You were a child."

"I was a teenager."

"You were a child," she said. "I could tell you a little bit about the childish brains of teenagers."

He looked at her. "I never said no. That's the problem."

Natasha didn't know what to say about that; whatever she knew about the teenage brain couldn't help her understand it.

"Sometimes," he went on, "even now, when things are shitty, I think about calling him. Like he's just some old friend and the other stuff didn't happen." He let out a long breath. "Fucking strange. Gets you wrapped so tight around his finger."

"You did, though," she said. "You finally said no."

"Not to his face," he said. "I stopped eating. Couldn't make myself go to school. Took a bunch of pills. I finally told my mom and she

ran to the bathroom and puked. After that it was all lawyers and inter-
views in small rooms."

"Confidentiality."

"Why are you down here?" he said. "Why not a cop?"

"The detective assigned to the case is frightened to see you," she
said.

"Frightened to see me?"

"He knows," she said, "that if he'd said something a long time
ago, you and I wouldn't be having this conversation."

"Yeah," Tucker said, "just another asshole that doesn't want to get
on the wrong side of Wakeland."

"No." Natasha shook her head. "It's not that."

Tucker stared at her, confused for a moment. "It happened to
him? Wakeland?"

She nodded. "I think so."

"So now you want me to say something."

"Lucero, that was the kid's name," Natasha said. "He's not getting
any second chances. His mother won't talk, either. She's illegal and
afraid she'll be sent back."

"God," Tucker said. He put his palm to his forehead, as though
shielding his eyes from the sun. "Wakeland knows how to pick 'em."

"Let me get you with a detective," Natasha said.

"The statute of limitations is up," he said. "The law doesn't care
about what happened to me."

"I know," she said. "I know about the statutes. But not on Lucero."

"You think I'm stupid?" Tucker said, standing now. "You don't
get it. This money's putting me through college; I got plans for it. I
said what I needed to say and no one gave a shit. Everyone retreated
to their corners and protected themselves—Wakeland, my father, the
school district. You know how long it's taken me to stop thinking
about killing myself, to be able to sleep with my girlfriend? I'm
twenty-five years old. All my friends are graduated, starting careers or
going to grad school. Some of them are married, have kids. I'm tak-

ing a fucking poetry class at a community college." He stopped and
took a deep breath. "I feel bad about it. I mean, I feel bad about this
kid, I really do, but I can't do what you're asking."

"Imagine how different your life would be if this detective had
said something all those years ago."

But Tucker's eyes were closed now, his fingers pressed against his
temples. "It's hard enough to deal with my own shit," he said. "You
can't expect me to be a hero, too."

BEN WAS IDLING IN THE cruiser down the street from Emma's boyfriend's house, watching Lance and two of his friends pulling tricks
on the half-pipe in the driveway. When he left Rachel and Emma at
the condo, Ben tore off this way, not thinking, just raging to punch
the kid in the face. Thank God for suburban stoplights and late rush-
hour traffic. By the time he'd turned the corner onto the street, some
fifteen minutes later, his head had cooled a bit. *Think about us*, Rachel's voice said. *Maybe that will help you understand.*

The sun was going down, and the kids took turns rolling back and
forth on their skateboards, the evening light casting their shadows
across the wall of the house. There were no cars parked in the
garage—home alone again—and they were blasting punk rock from
a boom box. One of the kids, not Lance, dragged on a cigarette, blowing rings into the air as if he was sending up smoke signals. *Hey, look
at me. See how cool I am?* The kid on the pipe wiped out, trying to
flip the board around in the air. Lance helped the kid up and then
dropped off the lip of the pipe and demonstrated the right technique.
He leaned down and flew above the opposite lip, grabbing the edge
of the board and spinning in midair, before hitting the landing. It was
a nice move, Ben had to admit.

He heard Rachel's voice again. *You and I were stupid kids once.*

Their first time wasn't planned, it just happened, on the floor of
her bedroom while Rachel's parents were entertaining friends in the
backyard pool. The two of them taken over with the feeling after

hours of swimming together. Neither was prepared for it—no condom, no birth control, nothing. Yeah, stupid kids!

He remembered her sixteen-year-old body lying beneath him, her wet hair spread across the floor. Her skin was dotted with goose pimples, and when he kissed her breast she tasted of chlorine. What a relief, the passion he had for her that afternoon. He was submerged by the feeling with Rachel, and until that day he hadn't understood what it was to willingly give your body away, to be or not to be consensual. She had led him up to her room. She had closed the door behind them. She had put her hands on his hips. He had been frightened, but he'd wanted it, too. And damn if it didn't feel right, just like she had been made for him.

But the idea of this punk's hands on his daughter's skin! Lance was gliding back and forth on the half-pipe, spinning 360s as if he and the skateboard were one. It was as if the boy snuck into their lives and stole Emma away.

And then Lance wiped out, got only half the rotation and landed head and shoulder first on the driveway.

"Oh, shit," Ben heard one of the kids say. The friends rushed to Lance, who was lying still on the driveway, not moving at all.

"Ah, Jesus," Ben said to himself, unbuckling his seatbelt, about to call in an ambulance.

The kid with the cigarette bent down and put his hand on Lance's chest, and Lance bolted upright, throwing his hands out at his friends, who jumped and then collapsed on the cement, cracking up at the joke, rolling on the ground like giggling children. Children, home alone.

Ben got out of the cruiser and walked the fifty yards to the driveway.

"Oh, man," Lance said when he saw Ben. He brushed off his shirt.

"Dude, it's the fuzz," one of the boys said. The kid with the cigarette flicked it into the bushes.

"Man," Lance said, "I know you don't like me, but I think Emma is like totally amazing."

"You guys go home," Ben said to the other kids.

Ben took a step toward Lance and the kid backed up, his skateboard held to his chest.

"And you . . . you get inside and lock everything up." It was getting dark, the streetlights flickering alive. "Are you stupid or something? Don't you know there's a serial killer running around?"

THE LIMBS AND MUSCLES OF FEAR

He had once watched a bobcat kill a jackrabbit. The sun had dropped out of the sky, the canyon slicked with shadow. It happened directly in front of him, as though the animal world didn't see him at all. He was coming down the deer trail to the cabin when the rabbit zigzagged the open ground, its rear legs frantically kicking out behind it. The bobcat chased, swiping once with a broad paw to send the jackrabbit tumbling. The animal righted itself and then it sat there, frozen in the open country, its ears pinned backward, its stomach heaving. The bobcat didn't hurry. It slunk across the ground, its body like a shadow inking the earth, and hooked the rabbit into its claws. The rabbit didn't scream or kick, it simply fell limp into the cat's talons, as though it had accepted its death. Then the cat sunk its teeth into the neck and the rabbit's legs went electric with kicking, and then they stopped.

The cat carried the carcass into the cabin and he'd followed, heel to toe, heel to toe, making himself silent. The cat hissed at him—it could smell fear, he knew. But he wasn't scared. He wasn't the rabbit. He sat there in the doorway, watching the cat rip the wormlike intestines from the animal until it was too dark to see and there was only the crack and shred of a small body being torn apart.

Last night, when he was crouched in the orange grove, he could smell the fear on the policeman's skin. They were ten feet from each other, both of them on their haunches in the irrigation trenches. The policeman held the gun, but his skin breathed fear—the sparked burn of it. He sat there in the darkness beneath the orange-tree branches and

*he felt a tenderness toward the policeman. I can end your fear, he
thought. I can release it from you into the air. But he had to run; the
policeman would catch him, throw him in jail, and jail was like a
basement, and the basement was where he'd been the fearful one.*

He'd raced into the city after escaping the policeman, backed his
Toyota up against a wooden fence on the edge of an open lot in the old
city where truck drivers and RV cruisers slept overnight in their rigs. He
half-slept, hemmed in by eighteen-wheelers and Winnebagos, until
midmorning when the last of the RVs pulled back onto the highway.
He drove exactly twenty-five miles an hour down side streets to the
Lucky's shopping center, where the people walked in and out of the
store like ants swarming a nest. Inside the store, he bought a screw-
driver and then next door, at a Hallmark store, bought red cellophane
and clear tape. Two security guards walked the sidewalk outside and he
lingered inside for a few minutes, smelling the cinnamon-scented candles, touching the porcelain figurines with the sad eyes, talking with
the pretty woman behind the counter about the crazy man who was
climbing through people's windows at night.

"Terrifying," he said, agreeing with the woman.

"I moved here," she said, "because it was safe. Because I didn't have
to lock my doors at night."

"I know," he said.

"Nothing like this happens here," she said.

These people were new to fear. There was a virgin sweetness to the
smell of it here. As though they weren't sure what to do with it yet, like
the rabbit in shock, paralyzed by the new feeling. He had discovered
that he loved being what they feared. As long as he was Fear, he wasn't
afraid. Fear had form, Fear had substance, it took up space; it had
possessed him for so long in the basement—its weight pressing him,
crushing his lungs, and stealing his voice. He had tricked Fear, though,
slipped his body into Fear's and learned to occupy it as though it was
another skin, until he was the limbs and muscles of it.

In the parking lot, he crouched between cars and unscrewed the
license plate from a nearby Firebird. Then he unscrewed the license

plate from his black car and swapped them. He unspooled the red cellophane and stretched it across the broken light and taped it in place. Then he drove the speed limit down the wide, clean streets. The midday heat made everything stink — the char of the Carl's Jr. burgers, the rank of industrial trash bins, the rot of the tomatoes turning black in the fields. He pushed play on the cassette and listened to the song — the ripping guitars, the singer's growl. He made a right into a housing complex, the new stucco homes with their red-tile roofs, the palm trees bent in the wind, the blinds swiveled shut on the closed windows, as though if they didn't see him he couldn't get them. He loved that, their belief that if they didn't look at what frightened them it would go away. He knew he should leave. The policemen would have identified him by now, they would know who he was. Or they would know what he looked like and where he came from but not who he was; they couldn't understand what he was. But he wasn't scared, and how could he leave now? He'd just gotten here. No, he couldn't leave this place now.

13

B Y DUSK BEN WAS UP IN THE WILDERNESS, HE AND TIN MAN picking their way through the greasewood and coyote brush. The shadows fell in long angles across Loma Canyon, slicing to the edge of the city, which glowed orange in the last of the sunlight. But up into the finger canyon, where the limestone fell away in collapsed breaks, the land cut open to its guts, it was already dark.

Two hours before, he'd met with the MEU guys at a turnout at the end of Junipero Road. There they parked their vehicles and the horse trailers, and Ben talked them through the topo maps. Ten guys total, two teams of five—a day shift and a night. Five men and their horses for seventy-two square miles of land horseshoed from the coastal hills of Laguna all the way up into the Cleveland National Forest. The Ventura guys had Remington 788s with Leupold scopes. Ben had his father's old Browning bolt-action with a scratched-up Weaver K-4. The Remingtons, according to a cop named Keating, could pop the back off a skull at four hundred yards. It would have been nice, Ben said, if they'd brought him one of those Remingtons. And they all had a good laugh over that.

Hernandez had called for extra patrols that night; everyone from meter maid to sergeant detective was on coffee patrol, cruising town, looking for black Tercels and a crazy man climbing through windows. Ben and the MEU guys were supposed to ride horseback into the hills to flush out the killer—check abandoned cowboy camps, shine lights in caves—and run the perimeter of the city, where the wilderness met civilization. They split the land into sections, each tracking close to the edge of town. Ben got the east end, from Loma Canyon to the Santa Elena reservoir, from Whiting Ranch to the Sinks. The Ventura guys had brand-new Bearcat handheld radios that they clipped to their belts. They hooked Ben up with one, too, and for the first ten minutes the radio squawked with chatter. But now it was silent, just the sound of the wind in the coyote brush and Tin Man's hooves cutting semicircles in the sand.

He first checked the cowboy camp where he'd almost caught the killer last night and then picked his way along Trabuco Ridge, the city spread electric orange in the valley, the reflected light casting a rusted hue against the hillsides. In the distance, across town in the coastal hills near his place, an Orange County Sheriff Department's copter spotted swaths of light across the ridges.

A week after his father's death, Ben's mother had called the sheriff's office to see if they had any leads on the driver of the Chevelle. The sheriff had to look up the incident in the report files to remind himself of the case. He had murders to contend with, rapes, grand thefts; an accident that left a cowboy dead was far down the list of concerns. Ben's anger erupted after that. Someone out there had killed his father and was going to get away with it. Ben saddled up Comet and rode through the brand-new housing tracts, looking for the Chevelle. He would recognize that car in a second, but there were a hundred garages with a hundred closed doors and not one green Chevelle parked in a driveway or on the street. Soon he was walking the horse through the old town, scoping the gravel parking lots, inspecting the Esso gas station. Nothing. For three days he rode circles in town. The driver might live a half mile away in one of the new homes or he might be a soldier on the Marine base or he might live in Los Angeles; there was no way to know. Ben was an eleven-year-old child and he had no resources, no knowledge of how to hunt down such a person. The car was a ghost, something shot out of another world to forever change his. And he realized then that he was going to have to accept it, that he was going to have to live with the killers that go free. But Ben never really could accept it; for him, there was always a ghost out there, always a man racing down a dark road in a Chevelle that Ben would never catch.

Now he and Tin Man meandered down Trabuco Ridge into the flats of orange and avocado groves, down a firebreak that separated the wilderness from the landscaped green of the El Paraiso housing tract. He hadn't intended to ride here. Or maybe he had. But here he was, and he and the horse rode the break until he passed the crime scene and found himself parked on the edge of Wakeland's backyard.

All the windows were shut, light illuminating every pane of glass, two backyard floods spotlighting the patio and the small kidney-shaped pool. Ben sat in the darkness, cut off from the yard by a firebreak and an irrigation ditch, and watched Wakeland, looking small from this distance, sitting on the couch with his son and daughter, watching television. His daughter, who couldn't have been older than seven, sat between Wakeland's legs, leaning against his stomach. His son, who was nine or ten, sat Indian style on the couch, a few inches from Wakeland's knee. Wakeland's wife sat on a chair opposite, reading a magazine, its pages fluttering in the wind of the fan oscillating in the corner. She was a beautiful woman, long-limbed, her chestnut hair tucked behind her right ear. She had a ballerina neck, and even in the chair she sat gracefully rigid, as though she were about to plié. She was the kind of woman men were jealous to have, and Ben felt that envy like a hot coal pressed to the back of his throat. How did a man like Wakeland stay married, while Ben was out here alone?

Ben pulled his father's Browning from the saddle holster and put the scope to his eye. Suddenly Wakeland was close enough to touch, his forehead filling the scope sight. Ben watched him for a moment and then estimated the distance: sixty yards, seventy. There were times in life when you realized how truly vulnerable you were. Life into death could be crossed over in a half second. You lived so close to it; it was a like a shadow cast behind you. The walls of a house, the glass in the windows, were nothing. You lived or died because someone chose one way or the other. You considered that too long, you'd lose your mind. You considered that too long, you were paralyzed with fear or you came out on the other side of it—like the killer did—and realized you could be death.

NATASHA PULLED UP TO BEN'S house around 11:30 the next morning, two foam cups of coffee in her hands.

She had been up most of the night in her kitchen, thinking about Ben and Tucker, thinking about the dead child Lucero. She was hurt for them, of course, but she was angry with them, too—their silence, their sense of helplessness, as though this horrible thing had only happened to them. She was most angry with Ben, though. Women expected to live in a world where they could be overpowered. You didn't walk down a dark street alone late at night. You didn't leave the door to your apartment unlocked. You didn't agree to meet someone at their place on a first date. Just being alone with a man in an elevator could be enough to make you sweat. But Ben was a cop; Ben's job was to protect people—her, if she should be attacked; his daughter, Emma; and the Wakeland boys—and he had the power to do so, physically and by the authority of the law. How could he not use it? How could he live in this town, knowing what he knew about Wakeland, and do nothing?

By the time she made it to the porch, Ben was standing on his threshold, half hidden behind the cracked-open screen door.

"Can I come in?" Natasha said.

For a moment he didn't move, but then he pushed open the screen.

It was cool inside—all the windows slid open, the wind billowing the thin curtains across the wooden dining table—but you could feel the heat starting to come off the walls. Outside, framed in the window, the hills rose, browning in the white sun. She set the coffees on the table. He stood a moment longer, dressed in jeans and a Viper fins T-shirt, his hair ragged and mussed, before taking a seat.

"I hear we have a genuine posse up here in the hills," Natasha said.

"Something like that," he said. "Back on it tonight."

"You get any sleep?"

"A few hours," he said. "One eye open, you know?"

"Yeah."

"I was drunk the other night," he said.

"Is that an apology?"

"Yeah, I guess it is."

They sat together, watching the wind bow the eucalyptus, listening to the helicopters that were circling the wilderness, looking for the killer.

"This business or pleasure?" Ben said.

"Neither," she said. "I'm here because I want to tell you something."

And then she told him—about being a stupid nineteen-year-old girl, about the party, about being drunk, about Signal Hill and the submarine races, about the police who did nothing, about the months studying alone until she pulled herself together. She told him and watched a police helicopter outside the window turning elliptical arcs above the hills.

"I've never told you because there was never any reason to," she said. "There is now."

He studied her, his eyes pooled with some kind of emotion she couldn't quite read. He was like that—full of emotion you could never nail down. What did she expect? That he'd break down and let her in, that he'd tell her, too? *I showed you mine; you show me yours?*

"Why are you telling me now?" he said, his voice guarded.

"Because you don't really know me without knowing that," she said, hesitating. "And I want you to know me."

He stared at her for a long time, his green eyes confused, it seemed, and then he set his right hand on hers and they sat like that for a few moments at the table in front of the window overlooking the wilderness.

"I know what happened to you," she said quietly.

He let go of her hand.

"It's not your fault," she said. "You were a child."

He pushed the chair back from the table and stood at the window.

"Nothing happened to me," he said.

"You won't tell anyone because you're afraid it makes you look weak," she said. "I know how you all think. I've been around police and their macho bullshit long enough."

"You expecting me to make something up so you can feel better about yourself?"

She stood and grabbed his hand. "Don't do that," she said. "You won't push me away. I'm not that soft."

He wanted to tell her, she could see it in his eyes. He was six foot two, two hundred pounds, his arms and chest still strapped with muscle, but he was trapped inside his body with his childhood self and the man who'd taken advantage of him and he didn't know how to get out.

He yanked his hand away. "You should go," he said.

"Listen to me, Ben," she said. "This isn't just about you. That's what you don't seem to understand." She held on to his wrist, but he wouldn't look at her. "You always tell me you don't know what happened to your marriage, but you know."

"Jesus," he said. "Talk about ulterior motives."

"How many nights did you sleep alone?" she said. "How many nights did you stay out in that barn? That's because of Wakeland, right?"

He went to the refrigerator, pulled out a Coors, and popped open the can.

"You need to go," he said again.

"I'm not going until I'm finished," she said. "You're the most dangerous kind of man, because you're frightened, and you lie so you don't have to face the thing that terrifies you. You think it's silence, but it's lying. You think it's only yours, but it's others', too. Yours, mine, Rachel's—Emma's."

"Leave Emma out of it."

"It's hers, too," she said. "Don't you think it's not. No one knows where they stand with you. No one knows who you are, for God's sake. You've given your wife—your child—the worst kind of pain."

"She had the affair, not me," he snapped.

"Because she was looking for what you wouldn't give her," she said. "Because she knows there's somewhere in you she can't access. She feels you don't love her enough because of it."

"You talking about Rachel?" he said. "Or are you talking about you? I mean, let's keep things straight here."

"Let me tell you something," she said, furious at herself for blushing. "I think I might love you, Ben Wade, I just might, despite my better judgment. But that's not what this is about. I'm not trying to take something from you. I'm not trying to *have* you. I'm trying to give you something."

"You can give me something when I ask for it."

"You know what's funny?" she said.

"No idea."

"You haven't even asked me how I know. The investigator's got no questions."

She handed him a slip of paper. It had Tucker's name on it, an apartment address, a phone number.

"You know about him, right? I mean, you did that much of your job?"

Silence, the paper shaking in his hand.

"Let me frame this another way," she said. "I don't expect you to tell me. I don't expect you to care enough to do so. Fine. But I expect you to tell someone, I damn well do. You're a policeman. You know what happened to Lucero, you know what happened to this boy, and yet you still keep that man's secret. He's out there and you know exactly where he is and still you do nothing."

"Get out."

"You're the evidence, Ben. You."

"Get out," he shouted.

She started toward the screen door, threw it open, and stopped.

"I know what happened to you, Ben," she said, "whether you tell me or not. I expect you to be the man I know, not the frightened child you were. And if you're not going to do something about it, I damn well will."

Then she was out the door, the screen slamming so hard behind her she thought she broke the frame.

14

AN HOUR LATER, BEN WAS AT THE WEDGE. A SOUTH SWELL WAS pumping hard, the peaks hollowed out by steady Santa Ana gusts. Ten-, fifteen-foot crushers collapsing in two feet of frothy water. A few of the hardcore guys were out, the beach bums who lived in rotting wooden apartments and worked stocking grocery shelves so that they could ride the waves every day, but these were swells that seemed to carry the whole weight of the Pacific in their walls, and they exploded onto the beach like trucks dropped from the sky.

He was out into the break, diving beneath the grind of the first wave, only to be knocked backward by the next. A gasp of air and down again, deep below the crashing peak of the third wave, into the dark silence. His head shot above the water on the backside of the break, a line of swells stacking up again on the horizon, barreling toward him.

The first time it happened, Ben was fourteen and half drunk on Negra Modelos. Wakeland had thrown out his back lifting a lane-line reel, and they had sat on the patio in the sun, Wakeland gulping vodkas to take the edge off his spasmed muscles.

"I need your help," Wakeland said. "I need to lie down."

Wakeland leaned on Ben's shoulder all the way to the bedroom.
There he gingerly stripped to his underwear, lay on the bed, pointed
to a bottle of lotion on the bedside table, and told Ben what to do: a
dollop in the palms, and then start at the lower lumbar, down near
the base of his back where the slatted muscles butterflied away from
his spine.

"Not like that," Wakeland said. "You've never done this, have
you?"

Ben shook his head, embarrassed about all the things he'd never
done.

"Let me show you. You learn to do this and the girls will love
you."

And then Ben was shirtless, pressed into the warm space left vacant by Wakeland, the man's hands working down his back. The
problem was, it felt good—to be touched, to have your muscles, sore
from workouts, kneaded out. His mother didn't hug, and he wouldn't
have allowed it anyway. He'd never had a girlfriend. Boys, friends on
the swim team, punched one another, slapped backs, but no one
touched him. It felt good to be touched, it did. Then Wakeland's
fingers pressed the muscle and bone just beneath Ben's underwear
line, and a nervousness pricked Ben's body. He closed his eyes then
and imagined Rachel. He had only just met her in algebra class—at
least a year before she'd pay any attention to him—but he loved the
way her hair hooked her ear, the way she held her pencil and ignored
him while he watched her take notes. He tried to imagine, as he'd
done every day in class, her thin body beneath her blouse, and he
could almost do it, almost conjure the shadow of her shape beneath
the fabric.

"Take these off," Wakeland said, tugging on Ben's jeans.

Ben kicked into the first wave of the set, his body flung forward
on the crest, his feet pitching out above his head. He dug his hand
into the face, and his fins found the glass below the lip, his lateral
muscles slicing into the water, his left foot carving a wake into the
peak. For a moment he shot through the tube, the lip of the crest

spitting out above his torso, his world narrowing to a cylinder of churn and hollow rush. Then the sunlight turned green and the tube closed off, tossing him to the beach floor. He let the wave take him, the roil of it spinning him through the sand and seaweed.

No, Ben had thought then, but it seemed stupid not to; shit, the guys on the team spent half their lives walking around in Speedos. The whole team took yearbook pictures in their suits, busting out push-ups before the shots to look cut for the chicks who would later ask them to sign the page. Besides, Wakeland was the coach, and you did what your coach said; it was practically written into the Constitution.

Ben's bare legs upset his imagination. He couldn't conjure Rachel anymore. At first he stared at a framed picture hanging on the wall. It was a print of an oil painting of the Laguna Coast. A single tree clung to a rocky outcropping, while huge waves exploded onto the rocks. The whitewash slammed the exposed roots, and Ben tried to place his mind there, in the water, down below the rocks, where his father's ashes floated in the salt. But he couldn't ignore Wakeland's hands, the man's fingertips crawling up the side of his torso, and he shut his eyes to try to find Rachel again. She was there and then she was gone, and he felt sick for a moment before he found her again — her naked body as he imagined it would be, bird-boned and softly curved, smelling of soap. The hands were on the back of his thighs now, the fingers fanning toward the center of his teenage world, and he made those hands Rachel's — her fingers small and delicate, warm across his skin. But Wakeland's callused hands scratched Ben's skin, and before he knew what was happening, before he could get back to Rachel, he was sticky wet, and a wave of confusion ran through him. He ran to the bathroom and cleaned himself up, throwing his soiled underwear in the trash, hiding them beneath the tissues and a cardboard toilet roll.

"It's all right, Benjamin," Wakeland said on the other side of the closed door. "That happens sometimes. It's natural. Nothing to be ashamed of."

Ben unlocked the door and came out into the light of the hallway, and Wakeland hugged him like a father, tousled his hair, and
told him it was all right, everything was okay. He wouldn't tell anyone.

"Just between you and me."

The wave finally let Ben go and he lay there in the shallows, getting the feeling back in his body. His wrist ached, his neck and shoulder were kinked and bruised, yet he swam out again and let himself
be punished by the waves. He wasn't even trying to ride them anymore. He simply turned his body into the swells and let the crushers
throw him onto the shore. He wanted to break his neck, wanted to be
planted in the sand. He crashed onto his back, slammed headfirst,
cracked his knee, but he kept coming up sucking air, kept swimming
out to meet the waves, to get pummeled onto the shore, and his body
kept rising to the surface, his lungs expanding with the salted air.

HE CALLED RACHEL FROM A pay phone in the parking lot of an In-N-
Out Burger on Balboa Boulevard in Newport Beach.

"I want to see you and Emma," he said. "Before I'm on tonight."

"You frightened her yesterday," Rachel said.

"I know," he said. "I overreacted."

"You did," she said. "You frightened me, too."

"Oh, c'mon, Rach."

"If you'd seen the look on your face, you'd understand why."

"Rachel," he said. "Let me come over. Please."

The line was silent for a moment. Someone ordered Animal
Style at the drive-up window. Please, Rach. Please. A seagull snatched
a crushed French fry from the pavement.

"No, Ben," she said. "Not yet. We need a couple days."

SITTING IN HER Z IN the parking lot, Natasha watched the boys stream
out of the swim complex, their hair wet and slicked, their workout

bags slung over their shoulders. They looked impossibly young to her, newly formed, their bodies a fragile miracle.

Practice was over, but between the slats of the metal fence Natasha could see Coach Wakeland still walking the edge of the pool, and the arms of a single swimmer slashing through the water.

Two minutes later, she walked into the boys' locker room. The cement was still wet with footprints. The air stank of sweat and mildew, of body odor and cheap cologne. She was here on impulse, driven not by any rational search for evidence but simply by a need to see the man, to look him in the eye—to see if you could read such sickness in the face.

The office was empty, the door locked. On the wall across from the office was a line of framed photographs—a dozen or more pictures of boys with medals dangling from their necks. THE WALL OF FAME was stenciled in light blue above the photos. Ben's photograph hung on the wall directly opposite the window to Wakeland's office, his bare shoulders covered only by the ribbon of a county medal. Two down the line was Tucker, bare shouldered, too, holding up a gold trophy, much younger-looking than he looked now—no dark circles under the eyes, no worry lines crisscrossing his forehead. Then Lucero, in the last picture frame. The boy held a medal up to the camera so that the gold edge of it filled up the bottom corner of the shot. The picture couldn't have been more than a few months old, maybe regional or state finals from last spring. He was a beautiful child—a shock of hair, a wide smile, and deep black eyes, all of him electric, alive, caught forever in gelatin and paper, pinned there behind the glass for Wakeland to enjoy from his office chair. All of them, a whole wall full of boys, smiling back at Wakeland as though they had given their blessings to be hung on a hook. Natasha had the sickening feeling that this wall was a different kind of trophy case.

She heard a whistle echo from the pool and then a man's voice calling out a cadence: "One, two, three, breathe. One, two, three, breathe."

She found Wakeland pacing the side of the pool, stopwatch in hand, a single boy freestyling down the line. She stood in the shadows of the cement diving platform and watched. He wasn't a big man, but his body was wiry, and there was a vanity about his dress— the shirtsleeves rolled up to reveal his biceps, the shorts tight around his muscular thighs. The boy flipped at the wall and kicked it hard down the line.

"Push it," Wakeland yelled. "Push through the pain. Pain is nothing. It doesn't exist."

The boy hit the wall and Wakeland clicked the watch.

"Fifty-nine point two," Wakeland said. "Needs to be fifty-eight, at least. We'll keep working at it."

Wakeland helped the boy out of the pool and flipped him a towel. The boy started drying off, his muscles long and lean, as though they'd just been formed. He couldn't have been older than fourteen.

"Is this the next one?" Natasha said, coming out of the shadows.

Wakeland spun around, caught off guard. "What?"

"You grooming him?" she said.

"This is a closed practice," Wakeland said.

"What's your name?" she said to the boy.

"Phillip."

"Phillip," she said. "Go home."

The boy looked at Wakeland, confused. "Go ahead," Wakeland said, and the boy flopped it across the pool top to the locker room.

"Let me guess," she said. "His parents are divorced, he's been having trouble in school, you're turning his life around, going to make him a swimming star."

"Who are you?"

She stared at him, letting him know she wasn't frightened. He was nothing—a leather-faced middle-aged man, his cheeks dotted with discolored spots that could be the beginning of melanoma, if there was any justice in the world. He was nothing, just blood and bone, viscera and sinew; he was the thing rotting by Thursday if killed on Monday.

"I'm the person who knows what you are," she said.

His face went white. "You're trespassing," he said. "You need to go or I'll call the police."

"I'll dial the number for you."

THE PROBLEM WAS, EVERYONE KNEW he was Wakeland's. He drove around town with the man in his Mustang. When Wakeland had the team over for barbecues, Ben was the one who stayed late, drinking beer on the patio. Ben was the star, the one with two county records—one in freestyle and one in butterfly—the one who would get scholarships to college, and Wakeland was the man who would make it happen. All the guys on the team were jealous of him, and Ben liked their jealousy. He needed it then; it was like food for his ill-formed teenage soul. Once, in L.A., Ben had helped internal affairs nail one of their own, a narco cop skimming off the top of the drug-raid stash and selling on the side. When they brought him in, he told them he'd gotten so turned around that everything seemed straight again. His kid needed to go to college. His wife needed a new car. His house was falling down and needed repairs. So what if he took a little dope that would grow mold in a precinct basement to make his family's life a little better? Maybe that's how it was for Ben, everything so crooked it turned straight again. By the time things started happening with Wakeland, he needed the man—felt love for him, maybe, the kind you felt for an authoritarian father—and when he didn't need him anymore, he was so far in he didn't know how to get himself out. He never should have gone back to Wakeland's apartment after that day. But he did; God damn, he did, and still, all these years later, Ben couldn't say exactly why.

After Rachel refused to see him, he drove to his mother's place. He needed an answer to something, needed it today.

"You haven't been here in a month," she said from the couch when he came through the door.

"We just went to the cemetery. I was here four days ago with Emma."

"Emma?"

"Your granddaughter."

"Oh," she said, her voice wavering, her hand pressed up against the side of her head, trying to grasp a fading memory. "How can I forget my granddaughter?"

"You're sick, Mom."

"This man is too hairy," she said to the television, as Tom Selleck climbed out of the water after a swim. "Why have you been away for a month?"

Ben turned off the television and knelt in front of his mother, pushed his face close so she would focus on him.

"You look tired," she said, putting her hand on his cheek. "Have Rachel make a nice dinner for you and put your feet up."

"Mom," he said. "I need to ask you about Lewis Wakeland."

"The coach?" she said. "Oh, he's a nice man."

"No, Mom," he said. "He isn't."

"Oh, he looks out for you."

"Why did you let me run around with him?"

"There were ants in the kitchen today," she said, waving her hand at the linoleum floor, shuddering. "Get rid of them for me."

He found a line of ants running along the edge of the floor from the laundry room to the cabinet beneath the kitchen sink. His mother had turned the television back on. "Don't you dare," Margaret huffed at the screen. He got down on his knees and sprayed the ants with glass cleaner, their black bodies wrinkling up with the chemical, and remembered the night he woke up soaking wet in his bed.

He was fifteen, for God's sake, and he'd dreamed he was standing on the edge of the school pool during a tournament. Everyone was up on the blocks, waiting for the starting pistol, but Ben had to piss. He was bursting with it, and in the dream he pulled his dick out of his suit and let a stream go into the pool, standing on the damn blocks, the whole world watching from the bleachers. The gun sounded and he dove into the water and that's when he woke up to find himself soaking wet, the smell of his own piss wafting from the sheets.

He panicked, stripped off the bedsheets, and carried them down in the dark to the laundry room. He closed the door and shoved the wet sheets into the washer and fiddled around with the dial, the stupid thing clicking loudly as he tried to figure out how to run the damn thing.

Then his mother was there, pushing open the door, her eyes squinting in the brightness of the room.

"What's wrong?" she said.

"Nothing."

How did you tell your mother you'd pissed yourself? How could you explain that? He turned the dial and tried to get the goddamned thing to work, but the machine was broken or something. Then she put her hand on his and held it there on the cycle dial, and he burst out crying. He was so embarrassed—about pissing the bed, about the new things that had started happening at Wakeland's apartment.

"I don't feel good," he'd said.

She touched his forehead. "No fever."

"No, Mom, I don't feel right," he said. "I feel messed up."

She ran her eyes over his face, trying to piece together his riddle. He wanted her to figure it out without him having to say it, wanted her to work some mother magic and suddenly understand everything.

"You're tired," she said finally. "Rest and you'll feel better in the morning."

The next morning out on the patio, Voorhees tried a man-to-man about the birds and the bees, while his mother fried up some eggs.

"It's normal," Voorhees said, misreading the situation entirely. "It happens to all boys."

And then he told Ben that he knew he wanted to do things with girls, about how God says you shouldn't do those things until you're married, how it was sinful and dirty, and all Ben could do was bite his tongue and think about what idiots adults were, goddamned fools. They sat down together and ate their eggs and then Ben's mother walked him into the laundry room and showed him how to use the machine. Yeah, he'd clean up his messes. In the dark, alone in the middle of the night, he'd fuckin' do that.

Now Ben finished with the ants and threw the towel in the trash. A commercial was on the TV, and he got down in front of his mother again to block out the screen.

"How could you not know what Wakeland was?" he said.

"The show is back on."

He hit the television knob and shut off the screen.

"You were always so much trouble," she said, her watery eyes glaring at him. "Always yelling, always running away."

"Why did you let me travel alone with him?"

"He's getting you a scholarship."

"No, he's not."

"I need to send him a thank-you card," she said, and started rummaging in the drawer on the side table, pulling out a pen, pushing around the papers and paper clips and coupons. "You hurt William," she said, her hand still shuffling things in the drawer—a bottle of aspirin, throat lozenges, a few playing cards. "Always fighting him, always pushing him away. I know he isn't your father, but he tries. We both try."

The pitch of his voice rose. "He's dead, Mom." He wasn't going to get any answers, and he wasn't allowed the relief of forgetting. "Both of your husbands are."

She blinked.

"Look at me," he said, taking her face in his hands. "I know I was a pain-in-the-ass kid, but didn't you know what Coach Wakeland was?" She tried to wiggle her head away, but he held it between his palms. "I was just a kid. I was scared."

She stared at his eyes, confusion and recognition swimming across them. She was there for a moment, her pupils registering the starkness of the question, but then she was gone again, clouds across the irises.

"You're hurting my ears," she said, brushing aside his hands. "And take a shower; you stink."

*   *   *

BEN WAS ON THE SANTA Ana Freeway, on his way back from his mother's, idling in late-afternoon traffic, when Ken Brady, the desk sergeant, called him on the Motorola.

"Some guy called in, asking for you," Ken said. "Said he had some information about a case."

"He leave a name and number?"

"No," Ken said. "Said he'd leave a voicemail."

"Another anonymous tip?"

"You got me," Ken said. "But he sounded freaked out. Like he was coming undone, you know? Figured with this freak running around, I shouldn't let it sit."

Ben pulled the cruiser to the emergency lane, the traffic limping by, and dialed the voicemail number.

"I NEED YOU TO LOOK up a student," Natasha said to Helen.

She had left Wakeland twenty minutes before, watched him struggle with his key to open the door to his Corvette and drive off.

"Current or past?" Helen asked.

"Current," Natasha said.

Helen pulled the 1985–'86 attendance binder from the shelf.

"I keep seeing boys' faces," Helen said, her voice shaking. "I was up all night thinking about them."

"It's not your fault, Helen," Natasha said.

"I knew something wasn't right," she said. "But I didn't want to believe it."

"Things like this aren't supposed to happen here," Natasha said. "That's what we want to believe."

Helen opened the binder. "Name?"

"Only got a first name," Natasha said. "Freshman, I think."

*   *   *

BEN WAS BACK AT THE barn by 4:17. He oiled the bolt action on his father's Browning and disassembled the .45. He bore-brushed the barrel and oiled the firing pin and hammer spring, then reassembled it and locked a full magazine inside. He set both of the firearms on the table, next to the killer's police file and the pictures of Lucero, and stared at them.

The voicemail had been from Wakeland.

"Benjamin," he'd said, his voice out of breath on the recording. "We need to talk. Please."

Ben had hung up immediately and sat on the side of the freeway for ten minutes, until a Caltrans truck came riding up his tail, trying to get to a stall a mile up the road.

Outside the window of the barn now, an owl swooped across the grass and lighted in the eucalyptus on the far side of the drive. Ben watched the bird in the afternoon light, a thumb smudge bending the tree branch, Wakeland's voice playing in his head. "Please," Wakeland had said. The man was frightened. Something had happened, something had shaken him up.

Ben unlocked the gun cabinet, pulled out the box, and set it on his desk. He sliced open the first envelope with his penknife and found three photos. He and Wakeland sitting in his Mustang, mugging for the camera with their sunglasses on. Ben's mother had taken the shot, just before the two of them drove up to L.A. to have Ben swim for the university coaches. There was one shot at regionals, Wakeland grinning while yanking on the three medals hanging from Ben's neck. Ben stuck his tongue out, pretending to be choked. Then there was another, a Polaroid taken by Wakeland at Laguna Beach. Ben had just climbed out of the surf, salt water dripping down his body. He remembered Wakeland taking the picture, the camera lens pointed at him in front of the sunbathing summer day-trippers. Three teenage girls watched Wakeland take the picture, one of them giggling at Ben, and Ben told himself they thought Wakeland was his father, though he was sure then that they could see the truth. In the shot, his bathing suit hung low on his hips, the wet fabric clinging to his body, the plates of his chest stretching across his swimmer's shoulders. He hadn't seen these pictures in nearly two decades. The sixteen-year-old in the shot looked younger than Emma. It was shocking, really, the child that he was. He'd remembered himself as an adult; he'd imagined himself to be one when he was sixteen. But here was the child Ben, newly shaving, his face plump with baby fat, his eyes stupid with miscomprehension.

He turned his attention to the file, flipping pages until he found the picture of the twelve-year-old Martinez, newly pulled from the basement cell and years before killing. There was hope still in the face, in the first picture; he wasn't gone yet. Order could still be restored; the kid believed the police could do it, believed they could still hurt him or hurt the people who hurt him. There were laws, the police enforced them, and you could be folded back into the order of things in a way that made everything clear and safe. For most people, the threat of the law worked. It kept them in line; it gave them a sense of relief to be ticketed or arrested—it let them know that you could only push things so far into chaos before someone said no.

Ben was the one who was supposed to say no; it was his job to keep things from spinning into chaos. Natasha was right. The day he got his badge, he stood in front of a judge with forty-three shiny new officers and swore never to betray his badge, never to betray his integrity, never to betray the public trust. He swore to have the courage to hold himself and others accountable for their actions, and he meant every goddamned bit of it. He knew what it was to have trust violated. He understood the corrosive effect of a lack of accountability. That was his job—to protect and to serve—even if others hadn't done it for him. That was his identity, the one he chose; it was how he left the child behind and became a man.

Ben reached into the box and pulled out an envelope with his name scrawled on the front. He opened the letter inside and spread it on the desk in front of him.

You're a coward. You've silenced me, X'd me out. You couldn't do a more terrible thing. Is this how you treat the people who love you?

*I'm still prepared to forgive you. That's what friends do—they for-
give, they forget.*

The letter was from the end of Ben's senior year, after he'd lost at
the state swim tournament, when he stopped being able to sleep,
when he stopped going to swim practice, when he started ditching
classes and spending his days alone up in the hills, doing anything he
could to stay away from Wakeland. He had lost ten pounds, he'd become distant—from Rachel, from his mom and stepfather, from
everyone—and Rachel had started asking questions. "Tell me what's
wrong," she said. "Talk to me."

*I've kept your secrets, Benjamin. I could have told your mother ev-
erything that's happened with Rachel. But I haven't. I don't want to
violate our trust, and I don't want to hurt your mother.*

Three weeks after he and Rachel slept together, Rachel missed
her period. Ben had tried to confide in his buddies David Ross and
Nick Distasio, both virgins, but as soon as he said, "We did it," they
couldn't get past the fact of the event itself to listen to his panic about
being a father. "What did it feel like, man?" "Dude, did you make her
come, too?" (As though any of them understood what that meant.)
Finally, exhausted and terrified, Ben had told Wakeland.

"When did this happen?" Wakeland asked.

Ben had promised the man, when he was fourteen and they'd
started talking about sex, that he'd tell him when he "lost his cherry,"
as Wakeland liked to say. But Ben hadn't wanted Wakeland to know
about him and Rachel; he didn't want to lay out the play-by-play for
the man who would use it as a pretense for other things. He *knew*
Rachel was pregnant, though, and, God, he needed help.

"A month ago," Ben said.

"I thought you'd tell me." A look of betrayal flashed across Wakeland's face. "Thought we'd drink some beers and celebrate."

"I was scared," Ben said. "I mean, I can't have a kid."

"All these years, all I've done for you, the attention I've given you, the hours I've worked with you on your stroke, on your homework, getting scouts from SC, from Berkeley, Stanford even. As if you could get into Stanford on your own." He let that hang in the air for a moment. "I've let you into my home like it's yours, like you're my son, given you space to get away from your stepfather; all the money and time I've spent on you, and you don't keep your word. You lie to me."

It hadn't been his word. At the time Wakeland had said, "You'll tell me when it happens," and Ben had simply nodded, unable to imagine at fourteen that he'd ever get laid and thankful for the tacit permission to do so.

"You're too young to be sleeping with this girl," Wakeland said. "You're too stupid to even put a condom on. Your mother needs to know."

"No! You can't tell her."

Wakeland retreated into the kitchen, clinked ice cubes into two glasses, and filled them with vodka. He came back, handed Ben a glass, and sat beside him on the couch.

"Listen," Wakeland said, his voice quiet now. "Sometimes periods come late. She's probably frightened, too. Stress can make it come later than normal. Chances are it'll happen soon. If it doesn't, then we can talk about what to do next. One thing at a time."

Three days later, Rachel got her period, almost as if Wakeland had planned it, and Ben was locked into a new kind of confidence game.

You're a good young man, Benjamin, but you get confused. You can't see things clearly. I know you think you're in love, but has Rachel given you more than I have? After all these years, after all I've done for you, how can you just push me aside? This is a stressful time, I know. Let's talk, please. Let me, your closest friend, help you. We can work through it together.

He never answered that letter—though it took all his energy not to. The only person Ben could talk to about the things that were breaking him down was Wakeland. Wakeland would tell him it was all right, he would make it all seem okay, and the cycle would keep feeding on him. He couldn't do that anymore; his body wouldn't allow it. All Ben had was himself, and he retreated into silence, into the hills that surrounded the town, staying away from school as long as he could, knowing Wakeland was trying to find him. Three days later, Ben got another unsigned note, slipped into his school locker.

If compassion will not reach you, think about this:
Q: How do you think Rachel would feel if she knew you were a little faggot?
A: You know exactly how she'd feel, Benjamin, exactly.

It was clear to Ben now how terrified Wakeland had been of being exposed: so terrified that he'd put his fear into writing, into one last attempt to shut Ben up. For all Wakeland knew, Ben had already said something—or was about to. But the seventeen-year-old Ben had been far too frightened of his own exposure to recognize Wakeland's fear, too much of a child to think rationally about it. He could have walked right into the counselor's office and laid the two notes on the table, but Wakeland had bet on Ben's cowardice and won.

Ben pulled out the slip of paper he'd taken from Lucero's body and set it side by side with his own letter.

Q: How would she feel if she knew?

Some keep your secrets out of kindness, Ben thought, and some store them up as weapons to be used later.

A: You know exactly how s—

*   *   *

THE COUNTY SHERIFF'S BELL WAS spinning circles overhead, spot-lighting ridges, exploding finger canyons with light, and Ben was in the dark zone between the grid of the city and the false daylight above. He was out in the wilderness with Tin Man, standing on the rise above Wakeland's house, watching the warm light radiate from the backyard windows. From here he could see the pickers' camp and the greenbelt that ran across town to the apartment near the school, a leafy causeway that joined one world to the other. The streets of town were mostly empty, a few black-and-whites spinning their lights down the straight avenues, the stoplights switching from green to red to green again. From here, Ben could see the crescent of dark land scything Santa Elena into the western hills, a negative space in the electric basin. It was nearing 9:00 P.M., and the scanner was unusually quiet—an occasional 10-code, a chattering of loca-tions called out, a few killer false alarms. The hills were silent, too, the animals hiding from the Nightsun spotlight that swiped back and forth across the ridges.

On the drive out to Trabuco to saddle up with the mounted unit, Ben had listened to the serial's song on the cassette player. Now the song played a loop in his head—the singer's voice like the voice of the killer himself. The serial was out here somewhere—hiding in the wilderness, cruising the streets, crouched in a backyard beneath an open window, ready to strike—and there was little anyone, including the police, could do about it. This town had never felt this kind of fear. It was in the air, hovering over the city, as palpable as the charge in the Santa Ana winds.

People who moved to Rancho Santa Elena were afraid of the world; that's why they moved here, to escape it. They believed master-planned order—straight streets, identical houses, brightly lit shop-ping centers—would keep them safe from the outside world, as though Rancho Santa Elena were a walled-off city, a fortress against the ugliness elsewhere. When they watched the news—the L.A. an-chormen recounting murders and gang wars—people here sat on their couches, smug with the self-satisfaction that their home was thirty-eight miles on the right side of paradise. The wolves lived in Los Angeles, and if wolves existed, someone had to be thrown to them—but not these people, not here.

That's what the killer knew. Locked in a basement, the whole world just a few feet away, no one asking where the little boy had gone. He knew people didn't give a shit until they thought the shit was coming for them. If you were the one thrown to the wolves, though, you understood fear, lived with it every day until it didn't feel like fear anymore, and once that happened you were alone, pushed outside the boundaries of civilization where most people lived, forced into a wilderness with its own rules.

Ben was used to being out here, off the grid, out on the perimeter of most people's existences. He could never really be one of these Santa Elena people, because there was a wolf inside the walls and he had been thrown to him—he and Tucker and Lucero. People knew what was happening, some of them knew who Wakeland was; they just didn't want to know: It ruined the illusion of their safety. If the predators were here, what did this place mean anymore? Ben had been made alone at thirteen years old, the day Wakeland taught him how to breathe. He had accepted it, made a destructive alliance with it, and, just like a good Santa Elenan, pretended the wolf didn't exist.

Ben and Tin Man switchbacked down the hill, rode the fence along Wakeland's backyard, followed the firebreak until they came to the turnout of Junipero Road. There Ben trailered Tin Man, shut himself inside the cruiser, and called the number.

"Hello," Wakeland's wife said, her voice soft, friendly, until Ben's hesitation frightened her. "Who is this?"

He almost felt bad for her, for her and her kids being dragged into this, but he didn't mind letting her think he was the killer on the other side of the silent connection for a moment.

"I'd like to speak with Lewis," Ben said finally.

"Who's calling?"

"An old friend."

"Can I tell him your name?"

"Lucero Vega," he said.

The phone went silent for a moment, some kind of music playing in the background, a child's voice.

"What the hell is this?" Wakeland said in a low voice.

"You said you had some information about a case."

"Benjamin?"

"Fifteen minutes," Ben said. "At the apartment."

HE WAS THERE IN FIVE minutes, walking the shadows of the green-belt, the wind shearing leaves from the trees. On the patio, he found the key, slid open the glass door, stepped inside, and pocketed the key. The living room was as he remembered it—the beige couch pushed against a gray-blue wall. A glass-topped coffee table, spotless except for a single tumbler, half empty and staining a ring onto the glass. The oakwood television console, the white curtains hanging open against the sliding glass door, the conch-shell table lamp: all of it the same, a fucking museum to the past. Only the pictures hanging on the wall had been updated: candy-apple-red Ferraris and artsy black-and-whites of female torsos. A Nagel print. Nothing pornographic, all within respectable bachelor-pad boundaries. Exactly the kind of pictures that appealed to teenage boys. The carpet had been changed, a lighter cream color, as if a sheen of ash had fallen over the room. There were footprints on the carpet—size ten and a half, Ben knew.

The guest bathroom had new brass faucets and white porcelain countertops. Next to the toilet was a basket of magazines, just as he remembered. Ben thumbed the stack—*Car and Driver, Outside*, a *Penthouse* with Vanessa Williams on the cover. There was a different desk in the office, a new swivel chair, the wall color changed to burgundy, the bookshelves gone. The same metal filing cabinets, though, stacked on top of one another near the closet door. He scraped one open: empty. Maybe he'd find a letter, a picture, anything solid to link Wakeland to Lucero. The next one empty, too. Of course. He checked the desk drawers, the side-table drawers near the living room couch, the cabinets in the kitchen: nothing.

The hallway was the toughest, his heart thumping his ribs, a vertigo at the edge of his vision. In his mind the room had become a sort of pale cell, hot and airless. He stood in the doorway and forced himself to look at it—the double bed, the quilt embroidered with sailboats, the throw pillows propped against the oak headboard. The sea-green walls. Was this room the same? He had no idea, had no recollection at all of the comforter, the sheets, the color of the wall, only of what happened here. Suddenly he smelled the man—his Drakkar Noir cologne, the chlorine in his pores, the tinge of vodka, and he spun around to find the hallway empty. Wakeland was with him in the room now, though, Ben could feel him, a tingling disgust on his skin. He remembered being pressed into the bed, his face crushed into the detergent-scented sheets. And then there it was, the painting; he found it on the wall. It was smaller than he remembered, the print faded and yellowed, the lone tree clinging to the rock against the crashing ocean, and he put himself there in the water, beneath the roiling surf, down into the deep cold of ebbing tides.

Ben understood the impulse to obliterate yourself, to destroy the body. He'd almost jumped from the Vincent Thomas Bridge when he was seventeen. He wanted out, out of Wakeland, out of his body, out of everything. It was his senior year, a couple of months after sleeping with Rachel, and he and Wakeland drove up to L.A. to meet with the coaches at UCLA, USC, Pepperdine, to swim for them in their Olympic-sized pools, to have them weigh him, measure his arm span, gauge the strength of his muscles, the capacity of his lungs. The first night there, Ben had woken next to Wakeland in a hotel room sweltering with forced-air heat, the sweat on Wakeland's skin pungent. Since Rachel, Ben had realized what his body wanted, realized that everything that happened with Wakeland fought against his desire. It was as if she had knocked everything into alignment—his head, his heart, his body—and the thought of the man's skin curdled his stomach. He slipped out of bed, lifted Wakeland's car keys, and snuck out of the room. He tore off in the Mustang, pulling onto the 405 Freeway, veering west onto the 110 toward the ocean and down into the harbor until suddenly there was the bridge, brightly lit and arcing green over the inlet. It wasn't until he rode over the bridge the first time that he knew what he wanted: He wanted to go into the darkness below the bridge, into that cold oblivion. He U-turned it six times over the span, each time his body telling him to pull to the side and leap over the rail, but each time the thought of Rachel stopped him. He couldn't do that to her, no way in the world. The next day he swam for the coaches at USC, shattering his personal record.

"You talked to someone." The voice snapped Ben out of himself. Wakeland was there now, standing in the hallway. "I thought we had an agreement."

"We never had any agreement," Ben said.

"My silence for yours."

"That was a threat," Ben said. A sixteen-year-old threat that bought sixteen years of mutual silence. "Not an agreement."

"Who'd you talk to?" Wakeland said sharply. "A woman came to the pool today."

"What woman?"

"She didn't tell me her name," Wakeland said. "I've left you alone, never bothered you after you came home. I've lived up to my end of the deal."

"There was no deal," Ben said, his voice rising.

"Then who was this woman?"

Natasha, Ben knew. It was Natasha.

"I haven't said anything," Ben said.

"Good," Wakeland said, relief in his voice. He leaned against the hallway wall, cutting Ben off from the rest of the apartment. "I didn't think you would. Not you."

"Get the hell out of the way," Ben said.

Wakeland stared at Ben for a few moments, stretching out time, and then elbowed himself off the wall and walked the other way.

When Ben made it to the living room, Wakeland was sitting in the recliner, his legs crossed, his hands clasped over his knees as if he were tied in a knot. Ben stood next to the couch, the glass coffee table separating them. Age had taken hold of Wakeland's face. Now that he was close, Ben could see it. The man's eyes were rheumy, the skin rimming them puffy and bluish. In the soft-white light of the side-table lamp, Ben could make out the bones beneath his skin. There was a time when the thinness of Wakeland's face made him look fit, handsome even, but now he looked underfed and ill.

"You want a drink?" Wakeland said. "We can catch up."

"No."

"I knew we'd sit down with each other again," Wakeland said. "Knew it as soon as you came back to town."

"Coming back to town had nothing to do with you."

"You sure about that?"

No, he wasn't sure about that. Maybe he had come back because of Wakeland, some sort of gravitational pull, a lot of unfinished business. Maybe he thought being here would keep Wakeland in check, as though Ben had been hired as a security guard instead of an investigative detective. Maybe—and this, Ben thought, was the most likely—he had come back because he had the two panicked notes, the one mistake Wakeland had made, the one thing Ben possessed that made the man vulnerable. Ben came back because he had the power, and he knew that every time Wakeland saw his cruiser parked outside in the high school lot, each time Ben made the newspapers for an arrest, each and every time he rolled past Wakeland's house in his patrol car, Coach Lewis Wakeland trembled a little.

"I know what happened to Lucero." Ben unfolded the slip of paper he'd taken from Lucero's body and set it on the coffee table. Wakeland glanced at it but he didn't move, just kept one leg over the other, one hand on his knee, the other on the arm of the chair.

"Maybe you misunderstand things," Wakeland said. "Maybe you're not seeing them clearly."

"I know what happened to Tucker, too."

"You have been talking," Wakeland said. He stood up, went into the kitchen, and made himself a drink.

"He took a bottle of aspirin because of what you did to him," Ben said.

"What I did to him?" Wakeland spun around in the kitchen, drink in hand. "His father beat him with a leather belt. He was failing out of school, was about to be sent to the alternative school, not to mention juvie for possession, before I met him." He huffed disdain. "What I did to him!"

He took a sip of the drink and topped it off with more vodka from the bottle that was sitting on the kitchen counter. "You boys," Wakeland went on, shaking his head. "You're so selfish. Every one of you. I give you so much, so much of my time, my energy." Another sip. "I didn't hurt you. You never said no, you never told me to stop."

That was the problem; that had always been the problem.

"Who is the *she* in that note?" Ben said, pointing at the paper on the table. "She's Lucero's mother, right?" Ben said.

"You seemed to enjoy the attention, if I remember correctly."

"You were jealous," Ben said. "Jealous that Lucero had a boyfriend. You threatened to tell his mother about him being gay."

Silence.

"Or maybe *you* shot Lucero," Ben said. "Maybe you were jealous enough to do that."

Wakeland took a seat in the recliner again.

"Maybe Lucero called your bluff," Ben said. "Maybe he was smart enough—brave enough—to do that. Maybe you figured he was illegal and no one would care."

Wakeland stared at him, his eyes narrowed. "No, you know that's not it, Benjamin. You—or someone," Wakeland said, shaking his head, "would have arrested me already if you had that kind of evidence."

"Evidence can be made to prove a lot of things," Ben said. "A witness says you were the last to see Lucero alive. This witness says you two were having an argument. Says there was someone up at the camp at Loma Canyon just before Lucero was shot."

There were beads of sweat now on Wakeland's forehead. "That boy," Wakeland finally said. "Neil, yes?"

Ben just looked at him.

"You think I'm a monster," Wakeland said. It was not a question, not a plea for understanding. He said it disdainfully, a declaration of Ben's naïveté. "I've changed. I have a family now. Family changes things."

"Sure," Ben said. "A personal enlightenment."

"I never did anything to Lucero," Wakeland said. "Understand? What you think I did . . ." He shook his head. "After Tucker, I almost lost my job. I started drinking heavily. I started hating myself. There was something ugly in me." He tapped his hand against his chest. "I started seeing a therapist. I met Diane. My life changed."

"But you couldn't help yourself with Lucero—"

"I loved Lucero like a son," Wakeland said, strength back in his voice.

"You treat your son like the other boys? Like Tucker, like me?"

"I loved him too much to bring him into that ugliness," Wakeland said, his fingers pressing against his temples now. "I did everything I could to keep him from that."

Wakeland stood suddenly and went into the kitchen, dropping cubes into two glasses.

What did that mean? He loved Lucero enough not to hurt him? What did it mean for Ben? He had been hated? He had been nothing? Ben had convinced himself, many years ago, that some part of Wakeland had loved him. That's what had made it bearable—that it hadn't simply been some sort of violence.

"I did everything I could to keep him from that." The interrogator in Ben couldn't believe he hadn't hit on that immediately. How could he miss that *everything I could*?

"No, you haven't changed," Ben said, shaking his head.

Wakeland had taught him to look past people's flaws, to see around the ugliness in them. Shaking down drug dealers in L.A., Ben could see past the murderous bravado, the threat in the language and the gun, to find the child raised by the junkie mother, the child who witnessed his father's murder. It made him a good cop; he knew when to arrest a kid and when to ride him home to his family. With Wakeland, Ben had found the father he needed, buried in the predator. Wakeland recognized that need and fed it, while the boy pretended that what happened to his body didn't matter. Ben hadn't known how to measure one pain against the alleviation of another. He didn't know that his gratitude could have limits.

"I think you did everything you could not to hurt Lucero," Ben said, "but you still couldn't help yourself."

It took a few moments, but Wakeland returned to the room with two glasses of vodka, his face bleached and drawn. He clinked a sweating glass on the coffee table for Ben and then fell into his chair and gulped down half the tumbler.

"You know the greatest joy in my life?" Wakeland said. "Watching my son in bed while he's sleeping." He took another gulp. "I do it often, sneaking up after he's fallen asleep, sitting in the chair in the corner. I've never once had that feeling with him. The feeling I had with you. Never. I know what I'd do to a man who touched him. I can imagine exactly what I'd do to such a man."

Wakeland lifted the drink to his lips, his hand shaking.

"I often think that if I can stay there, in my son's room, if I can just keep that feeling about him, the other feelings will go away, forever."

"But they don't."

"I remember you as a boy," Wakeland said. "Probably better than you do yourself. I can see the boy's body in yours right now. There are shadows of it, hints." He ran his fingers across his own neck. "The ring of your clavicle, the bony shoulders, the length of your torso." He was silent for a moment. "Yes," he said. "I still have the feeling toward the boy you were."

It took everything in Ben's power to not reach for the drink. He had to remind himself that he was not that boy, not anymore.

"And Lucero?" Ben said now. "You had those feeling toward him."

"You try to be good," Wakeland said. "You tell God you'll be good, ask him to help you . . ."

"But you can't stop the feeling."

"It won't go away," Wakeland said. "The feeling. It won't leave me alone." He put the heels of his hands to his eyes. "I never wanted to hurt him," he said. "I didn't like that boy Neil. His dyed hair, his pierced ears. He was a bad student, no ambition. Lucero had nothing, but he wanted out of that shack and he knew he had to work harder than anyone else to get out. He was tougher than any Santa Elena kid I've ever coached. That kid Neil wasn't good enough for Lucero."

"Tell me what happened, or I can easily make this a murder investigation."

Wakeland leaned back in the chair. "Yes, I threatened to tell Esperanza about Lucero and Neil," Wakeland said. "He told me he didn't care—said go ahead. I didn't expect that from him. He was such a good boy, never argued." He hesitated, took a deep breath. "The address. I was letting them use the address to this place, to go to school. I told him I wouldn't let him use it anymore."

"There's more than one way to kill someone," Ben said.

"I thought he'd come back," Wakeland said, pounding the arm of the chair once. "I didn't think he'd do this. I loved him. I loved all of you boys."

"That's not love."

"I know things about you nobody knows, Benjamin. I know who you truly are, and I never judged you. Other people would, but not me. We all need that—a place not to be judged."

Wakeland stood, picked up the drink on the coffee table, and brought it over to Ben. He held the drink in front of Ben, the ice clinking against the glass.

"I was a child," Ben said.

"You were a teenager, a young man," Wakeland said.

"I hated myself and you knew it."

"You were so sad," Wakeland said, nodding. "Your stepfather wanted your mother but not you. I practically raised you."

Wakeland smiled at Ben, and Ben felt almost like the child again. The child running his hands along the man's back, kneading out the knots in the muscles; the child who closed his eyes and let the man do things to him; the child who couldn't say no and had to kill himself by drowning in a tiny picture hanging on a bedroom wall.

"Lucero could have been killed by the serial," Wakeland said. "I have a family, kids now. You don't want to hurt them; they haven't done anything. Everything with us is in the past. If you arrested me, it would all get dragged up; I'd have no reason not to tell it all. Think of everything you'd have to explain. How would you explain, a veteran detective like you, not doing anything all these years?"

The wind gusted outside, rattling the window frames.

"You can make it go away," Wakeland said. "You could make that happen, couldn't you?" Wakeland put his hand on Ben's shoulder. "It could go away, and Rachel and Emma would never have to know."

Ben grabbed Wakeland by the throat. It was the man's touch, his hand on him again, that set him loose. They fell together onto the couch, Ben's thumbs digging into Wakeland's jugular notch. Ben could feel Wakeland's heart beating against his palms, erratic, terrified. He slapped Ben's wrists, dug his nails into Ben's forearm, but Ben was stronger, his limbs electrified with his strength. He buried Wakeland's head in the cushions of the couch, and a memory flashed in his mind, the night he and Wakeland ate lengua in the Mexican restaurant, Wakeland forcing him to forgive himself for leaving his father in the ditch. When Ben said it then, he felt the relief of the words, but the relief didn't last. He'd have to say it out loud over and over again, a thousand times and a thousand times more for that feeling to stick. "I forgive myself," Ben remembered his thirteen-year-old self saying under the bright fluorescent lights of the restaurant. "Say it again."

HE DIDN'T REMEMBER STUMBLING OUT into the greenbelt. He didn't remember firing up the cruiser. He came to himself when he nearly ran a red light on Margarita Avenue, skidding to a stop at the last second. His hands, already sore, gripped the steering wheel, the flexor muscle that connected his thumb and forefinger cramping up. Shit, what have I done?

Ben U-turned it at the next intersection and gunned the car back toward the hills. He needed to get back up into the darkness, into the wilderness on patrol. He was nearly to the turnout when the call came through on the radio. "Possible 921, 19786 Corazon. Man seen climbing through open window. White male, approximately five foot six, wearing dark pants and dark shirt." Corazon was Rachel's street in the Puente Madera apartment complex.

Ben hit the lights, spun the cruiser around again, and gunned it across town, riding the emergency lane before finally four-wheeling it through the dust and mud of a construction zone. At the complex, he jolted to a stop, threw open the door, and slid along the side of the apartment walls, pistol drawn. Three apartments down, curtains blew through an open window. He crept through shrubs and barrel cactus to the edge of the window frame. When the curtains billowed, he glimpsed a woman's legs kicking the tile floor. The wind caught the curtain again, and he saw the man bent over her, one hand on her throat and the other slapping at her pedaling legs. He was no bigger than a twelve-year-old, his face contorted, a malformed thing.

Ben couldn't shoot. It was too risky; the curtains sagged, the pantry door was swung open and blocked a straight shot. The curtains sailed again: The woman was scratching at the killer's face. The killer ripped his hand from her throat, a hoarse roar leaping from her larynx, and crushed her nose with his fist. Ben could hear sirens wailing, the rev of cruiser engines racing down the street. The killer heard them, too, and he sprang to his feet, running for the sliding glass door at the back of the apartment.

Ben hoisted himself through the window and popped off a shot at the killer, who kept running. Blood streaming from her broken nose, the woman grabbed Ben, swung her arms at him, pounded her fists against his shoulders, pummeled his chest.

"I'm a cop," Ben said. "He's gone." She threw up then, blood and mucus slicking the tile floor.

The uniforms burst through the front door.

"Call in an ambulance," Ben said.

Then he was burning the cruiser down Corazon, the light bar spinning circles; miraculously, he hit a green light at Mirador Road. Ben buzzed into dispatch. "10-80, Puente Madera, heading toward Laguna Canyon on Mirador." Dispatch squawked out his location. "Black Tercel," Ben said, clicking back in. "Registered to Ricardo Martinez." Two units were already in pursuit. "Suspect's turned south on East Arroyo," one of the patrols called out over the scanner. Ben floored the cruiser down Mirador, the traffic in front of him clearing to the side with the sound of his siren. He got on the Motorola. Rachel's phone rang and rang until the machine picked up.

Shit. He called it into dispatch.

"Get someone over to my wife's place," he said, "306 Corazon."

Ben slipped the cruiser down the bike lane, his hubcaps riding the curb. He was about to skid left onto Alta—he'd cut the killer off at Arroyo—but as he hit the intersection, a Mercedes spun through the box, popped the curb, and folded around the stoplight pole. Then, just behind the Mercedes, the black Tercel barreled through the intersection, two black-and-whites riding his ass. Ben cut the wheel across three lanes and spun into the intersection, flooring the V-8, closing the gap between them. They were pushing 65 when the intersection light turned red. The Tercel swung across the lanes, hopping the curb and gunning down the bike lane that ran along the cement drainage. The patrols, too close to react, slammed their brakes to avoid taking out the line of idling cars, but Ben, still twenty yards behind them, stomped the brakes and fishtailed it over the curb.

The Tercel was thirty yards ahead of him, the driving lights off now, a shadow riding the edge of the drainage. The bike path ended at Serrano Canyon Road. At the end of the path the killer would find a metal pole cemented into the ground to keep cars out and a closed emergency-vehicle access gate. Without headlights the killer would slam into the pole, likely pushing the engine block into his lap.

But the Tercel swerved and took out the access fence, sparks crackling in the undercarriage as the car bounced onto Serrano Canyon. Ben floored the cruiser, sped through the busted gate, and jerked the car onto Serrano Canyon, too, heading toward the Santa Ana Freeway. Shit. He could see the cars from here, backed up, a parking lot of taillights.

The killer sped the Tercel onto the shoulder, passed the line of cars stopped at the light, lurched into the intersection and up the on-ramp to the Santa Ana. Ben redlined the cruiser's V-8, rocketing up the left side of the Tercel. He leveled his revolver through the open passenger-side window and popped off a shot. The killer's window exploded, sending shards across the cruiser's passenger seat. The Tercel swerved, clipping the cruiser's nose, and both cars slid along the guardrail, metal screeching metal, until the Tercel righted itself and flew down the emergency lane, spitting rocks and shreds of tire onto Ben's windshield. Flashing lights filled the rearview, and on Santa Elena Road, just off the freeway, a line of cruisers converged on the next on-ramp. The Tercel veered erratically, clipping the guardrail and then shearing off a Volvo's side-view mirror. Ben was pressing the nose of the cruiser against the Tercel bumper, the speedometer pushing 70, when a BMW swerved into the emergency lane. The Tercel's brakes lit up and Ben stomped the floorboard and then a fender smashed the windshield and his head slammed into the collapsed steering column.

The brake lights outside went blurry, dashboard-indicator green bleeding down the edge of his vision. The Tercel was twisted in front of him, a puff of steam curling above the hood. And then the door opened and the killer's legs slid out. Ben was pinned between the steering column and the door, but the killer unfolded himself from the collapsed Tercel, a line of blood running down his left shoulder. The killer stood there for a moment, looking at Ben just a few feet away. Ben heard the swirling pitch of sirens behind him somewhere, but the killer didn't move. In Ben's blurred vision, the killer's face, Ricardo Martinez's, was twisted and off-kilter, his eyes dark, nocturnal-looking, and he watched Ben as though waiting for him to die. And then he was gone, stumbling through the parking lot of cars driven by people trying to get home through traffic.

Part
Three

15

N ATASHA WATCHED THEM THROUGH THE WINDOW IN THE DOOR
to his hospital room. Ben was unconscious—the left side of
his face bandaged, an IV tube stuck in his forearm. Rachel's
forehead rested on the edge of the bed, and Emma rubbed her palm
across her mother's back.

The accident had been on the late-night news—the videotape of
the cruiser accordioned on the side of the road, the slick of blood
across the dashboard, Ben's body being slid into the back of an
ambulance—and she'd rushed down to Hoag Hospital, passing the
site of the accident, panicked for lack of information. All she could
think about was Ben laid out on one of her tables, Mendenhall
charging her with performing the autopsy, knowing his body in that
terrible way.

Ben's chart was slipped into a plastic pocket next to the door. She
snatched it from the wall and read it, her hands shaking. Hyphema,
eye spasmed but intact. Inferior orbital blowout fracture. Split lacerations. Grade 2 concussion. She closed the file, breathed a sigh of
relief. Not good, but it could be a whole lot worse. She stayed on the
other side of the door, watching Rachel and Emma huddled at Ben's
bed. The bare toes on Ben's right foot were exposed to the cold room,

and Emma lifted the blanket to cover them. Rachel finally raised her head, eyes swollen and red, and Emma handed her a tissue. If Natasha had ever doubted Rachel's feelings for Ben, it was out of her own hope and not for the evidence, she could see that now.

"You can go in," a nurse said.

"No, it's all right."

She retreated to the waiting room and watched the breaking news on the television that hung anchored to the wall—a shot of the collapsed cruiser and Ben's police portrait, a grainy mug of the killer, and a helicopter shot of miles of freeway, the pictures cycled over and over again—until, an hour and a half later, she watched Rachel and Emma walk arm in arm out through the revolving door.

WHEN HE WOKE, HIS VISION starred and syrupy, a blurry Natasha sat curled into the visitor's chair, watching him. She leaned forward and took his hand.

"Have I died and gone to the coroner?" he asked.

She smiled. "I bet you feel like a million bucks."

He laughed, but it pounded his head. "Feel like I crashed into a steering column."

"I should tell you that Rachel and Emma were here before," she said. "Not trying to be an impostor or anything."

"No, no," he said. "It's good to see you. There're two of you, but they're looking good."

"Well, you look like you crashed into a steering column."

"Don't make me laugh," he said.

She told him what the chart said, about the concussion, about the blood in his eye, about the fracture to the orbital bone, about how he was lucky he wouldn't need surgery. Then they sat for a while, her fingers running up and down the outside of his palm. He had hoped to wake to Rachel, but he wasn't disappointed to find Natasha here, and it didn't feel so terrible to have her fingers on his skin, either.

"Did they get him? The serial?"

"No," she said. "He dragged a woman out of her Beemer and raced the emergency lane. All points bulletin, but they lost him on the 91."

"Helicopters couldn't keep up?"

"They got grounded because of the wind," she said. "He's bleeding, though."

He remembered getting the shot off, the driver's side glass exploding.

"They're already calling you a hero on the news. You got there in time to save that woman."

"What about the highway patrol?" Ben said. "I mean, how could he get away?"

"I don't know, Ben," she said, squeezing his hand. "Hasn't been my first concern for the last few hours."

Then the rest of the night came to him in a flood of disjointed memories. Maybe it was his broken-down body, his head ballooned with pain, or maybe it was the medicine they had him doped up on, but something cracked open and he couldn't hold it back. He told her everything she'd already guessed about Wakeland and about the things she didn't know yet—the things he'd never told anyone, the things he thought he'd take to his grave. "It's not your fault, Ben," he heard her say.

"I don't know why I let him," he said.

Maybe he was telling it because Natasha already knew, and despite that knowledge she was here, holding his hand. He had wanted it to be known for so long, wanted it released from his body, and here she was taking it from him.

"It's not your fault," she said again. And he kept talking, expelling it, and she kept whispering to him, *"It's not your fault, it's not your fault,"* with every disgusting detail he plopped in her lap.

"I choked him," he said, finally.

"What?"

"I met him tonight," he said. "At the apartment. And I lost it."

"Ben, is he dead?"

"I don't know," he said. "I really don't know."

THE APARTMENT KEY WAS STILL in the pocket of Ben's jeans, which were folded on a shelf in the corner of the hospital room. She drove across town, past an investigative unit measuring the skid marks of a Mercedes wrapped around a light pole, past the flashing lights of patrol cars guarding the entrance to the attempted-murder scene at the Puente Madera apartment complex.

She parked at the entrance to Wakeland's cul-de-sac, took a pair of investigation gloves from the hatchback, and walked the darkened greenbelt path, her body charged with adrenaline. It wouldn't bother her if the coach was dead, honestly, but it would eat her up if Ben had done it. She squeezed between the shrubs and the west wall of the apartment, glancing in the windows; a thin light emanated from a distant room. At the patio, she slipped the gloves on, pushed the key into the lock, and slid the door open, very slowly.

It was quiet inside, reeking of bleach, nothing but the hum of a refrigerator motor rattling from the kitchen. In the living room, she found a knocked-over cocktail tumbler and a dark spill on the carpeted floor. The light was coming from the bathroom, the door half closed, just an incandescent sliver cast against the hallway wall. She pushed open the door, holding her breath, and found a towel on the floor and a spit of blood in the sink but no body, no Wakeland sprawled out on the linoleum.

She checked the bedroom, the master bath—nothing, thank God.

She stood in the hallway, thinking. She wanted to get in here, go forensic on the place. She found empty filing cabinets in the office, a drawer of matchboxes and screwdrivers in the kitchen. She ran her hands between the novels on the bookshelf in the living room and found copies of *Penthouse* in the guest-bathroom magazine rack. She went back to the bedroom, her heart pounding in her ears with the memory of all Ben had told her. She rifled through the bureau—a few articles of clothing, a watch, cuff links, a couple of birthday cards, a Dulces Vero candy wrapper. She slid her hands inside the heels of leather shoes in the master-bath closet, fingered the chest pockets of two sports coats, and got down on the floor and ran her hand into the dark space in the back of the closet behind the shoe rack. Then her fingers grazed something: the edge of a small cardboard box. It was wrapped in rubber bands, a half dozen of them crisscrossing one another. When she pulled them off and opened the top, she only had to glance at the Polaroids to know what they were, and when she set them aside, feeling dizzy, her back against the wall, she suddenly broke down and let it all spill out of her.

FROM WHERE BEN WAS LAID up in Hoag Hospital, he could see the crush of news crews gathered outside in the parking lot. He'd watched the reports from his bed, his photo hovering behind the L.A. newscast anchors on the evening reports; he even made the national networks. Two days after the accident, Emma had read out loud Daniela Marsh's article about him in the *Rancho Santa Elena World News*. He had grown up in Rancho Santa Elena before the town had incorporated, when it was still a ranch. He had been a star swimmer in high school. He had been a decorated L.A. detective but returned home to "serve the community." He had saved a woman from the grips of the Night Prowler, and even though Daniela's story was full of stock platitudes about the selfless actions of "our men in black," he enjoyed listening to his daughter pronouncing him a hero. When she said it, he almost believed it.

But the serial was still out there, hero or no hero. Ben remembered the killer staring down at him when he was crushed against the steering column. *You can't get me,* the killer seemed to be thinking. *This close and you can't get me.* How the killer walked away from the crash, Ben didn't know. He was like a ghost, slipping through twisted metal untouched. All of the basin was looking for him, from the Colorado River to the Pacific, from Bakersfield to the Mexican border, and all Ben could do was sit here, his hyphemaed eye dilated with atropine drops, his skull feeling like two jagged pieces of a misaligned puzzle.

On Sunday, Rachel came to collect him from the hospital. She parked in the back to avoid the camera crews angling for an interview with the wounded hero, and Ben was forced to sit in the wheelchair like some invalid while Rachel rolled him into the late-afternoon sun. The wind was down now, but the scoured air was an explosion of brightness; even with the sunglasses on, halos of light attacked his vision. On the ride home, the sunlight glanced off windshields and freshly washed hoods, sending bolts of pain through his eye. The socket throbbed, too. They'd doped up the area with steroids to keep the swelling down and prevent the eye from being pushed into the broken socket.

It was strange, this nominal blindness, this helplessness he was forced to endure with Rachel. It was strange to see her next to him, as though in the foggy image of a dream, and when they rolled up the driveway, beneath the still branches of the eucalyptus, among the familiar smells of sun-heated leaves, of dried hay and horse manure, he felt, for a moment, that the past had been erased. There was a kind of hope in being injured, in letting go of pride enough to allow yourself to be cared for. Maybe he should have let it happen years ago; maybe that's what was missing with them. He never let Rachel take care of him, never allowed her to give that kind of love.

He let her take his elbow as he climbed out of her car, let her press her hand against the small of his back as she led him into his house, and when he got inside, Emma was already in the kitchen, dicing onions and tomatoes, meat sizzling and popping in the pan.

"Fiesta Night," Ben said when he saw it.

"*Sí*," Emma said.

Ben joined her at the cutting board, slicing into a bunch of ci-

lantro, relieved that the rules of Fiesta Night would keep them
from talking about the serial, about the boyfriend situation, about
himself. He had frightened Emma, Ben remembered Rachel saying last week, enough so that Rachel hadn't let him see his own
daughter. He didn't want to do that again, didn't want to be that
kind of father.

Emma spooned the beef into a bowl and Ben charred the tortillas. When all three of them sat down together, Ben playing an AM
station out of L.A. that broadcast Baja *norteño* music, he took a bite
of his taco and said, *"Ay, caramba! Este taco es muy picante."*

AFTER DINNER, EMMA WENT OUT to the barn to tend to the horses.
Ben grabbed a couple of beers and put on his sunglasses to save his
dilated eye, and he and Rachel settled outside on the porch, sitting
on metal chairs beneath the sign that declared the house CASA DE LA
WADE. Together they watched Emma, brightly lit and beautiful in the
exposed light of the barn, comb out Gus's flanks.

"I blinked and she grew up," Ben said.

"She's not grown up yet," Rachel said. "Her body's calling the
shots, and her mind's following."

Emma stood on her tiptoes now to comb down Gus's withers.
Ben remembered her child's body, the lean, wiry muscles she exposed without embarrassment. "Still in the Garden of Eden" was
how he and Rachel described it. The body just the body and not an
object of desire or possession. He hadn't seen her body in five years,
knew almost nothing about it now, a normal loss of intimacy that
hadn't bothered him until recently, until this boy. It was a trouble-
some thought, he knew, and he didn't really know what it meant to
be having it. Maybe all men thought this about their daughters, felt
the loss of that particular closeness. He didn't know.

"Sorry about the way I reacted the other night," he said, "when
you told me." He thought about it a second. "I felt robbed, like she
was just stolen from me."

"You can't keep her," Rachel said. "But you don't have to lose her. Ben, this is one of those moments when you have to get it right."

"I look at her and I see all the ways she can be hurt," he said.

"That's called being a parent. It's a permanent condition."

When Rachel had told him she was pregnant with Emma, almost fifteen years ago now, he was frightened that he might turn into a monster himself and hurt his own child. He knew the abused sometimes became the abuser, like some sickness gestating in the child. He was so frightened, he wouldn't change a diaper at first, wouldn't give Emma a bath. Rachel thought it was simply the stupid limitations of men, and she told him so. But he was terrified. Later he realized that he wasn't capable of doing such a thing, that his feelings toward his daughter were normal; the love, a love like nothing he had ever felt, was completely and wonderfully paternal, and he knew then he would do anything, any necessary thing, to protect her.

"This professor—this programmer," Ben said. "Do you trust him? I mean, do you trust him with Emma?"

"Do I trust him?" Rachel said. "Like do I leave him alone with Emma while I go get my nails done?"

"Is he safe?"

"Ben, you have to have a little faith in me."

"There's a lot of bad people out there, people you'd never expect."

"There're more good than bad."

He glanced at her. She was right, of course she was right, but it didn't feel like it.

"You have to have a little faith in your daughter, too," Rachel said. "That first night at the hospital, I was falling apart. I mean, I couldn't think straight seeing you like that. It was Emma who calmed me down. She's tougher than you think."

Emma had ridden over to the hospital on her bike every day after school. He hadn't asked her to. She just did it. She had stayed with him, read to him, hunted down nurses when the painkillers wore off.

"So this boy, Lance," Ben said. "Is he a nice kid?"

"He's not the brightest bulb," Rachel said. "But he seems sweet enough. I talked to his parents. They know the situation. I think we've got things under control—at least as much as we can."

"So you took her to the gynecologist?"

"Yes."

"Got a prescription?"

"Yes."

Ben nodded, letting that one settle in his chest.

"Ben, you can be upset, but you—we—don't have much of a choice about this. She's not ours. We just get to love her."

"GUS IS ITCHING TO GO riding," Emma said when Ben came into the barn.

"He misses you when you're not around," he said.

She glanced at Ben and then finished the liniment on the back legs, Gus lifting his foot with each touch.

"I'm sorry about the other day," Ben said. "I wasn't ready for that. I kind of lost it."

Her hand stopped on Gus's knee for a moment, and then she worked the liniment down to the fetlocks.

"Can we just skip talking about it, Dad?" she said. "It's kind of embarrassing, you know?"

"Yeah, it's not a topic I'm so comfortable with, either."

He watched her in silence as she started working a currycomb down Gus's hindquarters. The horse blew air in appreciation.

"Listen, when I was thirteen," Ben said, "I met someone. I thought they loved me." He didn't know where he was going with this, but somehow he wanted to reach her. He wasn't sure, though, what it was he wanted her to understand. "This person, they bought me things, took me places, and, because I needed the attention, I thought I"—he started to say "loved" but changed his mind—"cared about this person, too."

Emma stopped combing the horse, her ear turned toward him, listening.

"I would do anything for this person," he said, "because I didn't like myself very much and this person seemed to think I was worth something." He hesitated, looked out the barn window, and watched a hawk circle on an updraft. "I understood later that it wasn't love. But not then, not for a long time."

"So you were in love before Mom?"

"No."

"Did she dump you?"

He stared at her. "The point is, Em, I want to make sure this boy isn't using you."

"He's not." She straightened up now and looked at him across Gus's swayed back.

"I don't want you to get hurt," he said.

"You know what hurts me, Dad?" she said. "This." She pointed in the vague direction of the house. "You up here and me and Mom down there, in that little shitty condo. You know what hurt me? Listening to you two fight at two in the morning, having to speak the few dozen words we know in Spanish at dinner so I don't have to listen to you scream at each other."

There were tears in her eyes and she wiped them away with the back of her hand.

"You think I'm stupid?" she said. "You think I can't make my own decisions?"

"No, I don't think you're stupid."

"You think I *don't like myself very much*?"

"I was talking about me."

"He didn't pressure me or take advantage of me, you get it?" She looked him straight in the eyes. "I mean, *I* had to ask him out." She sighed. "I didn't tell you," she said, "because I knew you'd pull all this 'my little girl' crap on me and it'd make me feel like Hester Prynne or something. And it does. It makes me feel terrible. Like I'm a slut or something."

A punch in the gut. "I don't want you to feel like that."

"I really like him, Dad."

"You're moving a little too fast for me, sweetheart."

"He's really nice," she said. "You'd get along. I mean, you both like waves."

"I'm trying, Em. I'm trying."

HUNTING THE HUNTER

He saw the woman in her open garage, unloading groceries from the trunk of her sedan. He was parked across the street, two houses down, sitting low in the leather seat, sweating in the shade of a eucalyptus tree. He could smell himself, blood and sweat—his insides had leaked down his forearms and dried sticky-wet in the webs of his fingers, his shirt so soaked it felt like molted skin. She hoisted a paper bag to her hip and carried it through the little door at the back of the garage that led to the inside of the house. The door was propped open as though she were asking him inside.

It was late afternoon, the white light beyond the shade of the car setting off starbursts in his eyes. He thought it was the third day since the policeman shot him, but he wasn't sure. Day and night . . . night and day were blurred in his head. He remembered the bright lights of the highway patrol cruisers spread across the freeway, the traffic rolling to a stop in front of him. He remembered the way he slipped the car into the stream of other cars riding the emergency lane to the roundabout exit off the freeway to this new town. He remembered finding the raincoat in the trunk of the car, slipping into it to hide the bleeding hole in his arm, buttoning up its skin to become another person, and walking into the drugstore to buy medical gauze and tape. He had smiled at the teenage boy behind the counter, thanked him for the coupon he had slipped into his bag. Back at the car, he'd wrapped the shoulder with the gauze, the blood blooming on the fabric, and taped the edges so tight his arm went numb. He had to keep himself inside himself.

That night, the first one, he'd slept curled up in the driver's seat of the car, parked in the lot of a twenty-four-hour grocery, people coming and going, buying their milk and eggs, their carts rattling across the cement. Not one person peered inside his window, not one policeman shone his flashlight across the license plate. The second night, he'd parked in a used-car lot, exchanged license plates with one of the cars with a FOR SALE *sign in the window, and listened to the sirens of the police cars in other parts of the city. That's what he'd learned about these people in these safe places: They believed that what was dangerous hid in darkness, lurked down at the railroad tracks, stalked the alleyways between buildings. If he stayed in the open, in the light, where everything was neat and organized, he became invisible to them. He was a shadow man who made his own darkness and hid in it.*

She was back now, coming through the door toward the car. She was draped in a sundress, as though she'd just come from the beach. She was younger than he liked, but this town, this new town, was becoming like a room with a lock on it. He had to get out.

Last night when he slept in the used-car lot, he dreamed his father was digging his fingers inside his wound, pushing the bullet deeper into the muscle, shoving it beneath his shoulder bone and between the cage of his ribs and into the pumping muscle of his heart. He had startled awake when a police helicopter burst over the tops of the trees, slashing its light across the cement drainage of the dried-up riverbed below. This morning, he'd tried to get back to the freeway, but a patrol car sat in the grassy circle of the on-ramp. A second patrol car lurked in the circle of the opposite ramp, so he drove the other way, up into the hills, up into the curving roads of the residential streets. That's how he found her, the woman carrying in her groceries.

He'd used up all the medical gauze, and the bandage was soaked through and he could feel his inside-self emptying into the air. He also needed another car, one that looked nothing like the car he'd stolen. He'd watched her hang the car keys on the hook next to the open garage door.

When she hoisted another grocery bag to her hip, he eased open the driver's side door, his head spinning a little when he stood. She stopped, the heel of her left foot lifted in mid-step, and turned to glance over her shoulder. He knelt and froze—he was good at being still, good at becoming invisible—and let her feel him. This is what he truly loved, he knew that now—that moment he charged their little world with fear. If he could freeze time, he'd freeze it here and forever feel that charge of fear pass between them. But it didn't work without becoming death, too. Death the creator and the destroyer of fear.

She turned and started across the garage, toward the open door and the steps into the house. He slipped across the street, silently coming up the driveway as she stepped inside. When he reached the very same steps, he pressed the button to put the garage door down, and the mechanical wheels and chains came to life, rattling the wooden door down the guide rails until it snapped closed.

16

ALL SUNDAY EVENING THE HOUSE PHONE RANG OFF THE HOOK. He answered none of the calls, just let it go to the answering machine. *The Orange County Register* wanted an interview. A representative for the *Today* show was trying to fly him out to New York.

The fog was rolling in tonight, wisps of it coming off the ocean and tendriling down the ridges of the hills. He sat and watched it come in, drowning the land, and listened to the scanner. 904-G: Brush fire in Eagle Rock. 390-F: Under the influence of narcotics. 10-59: Funeral detail.

At 8:33 P.M., a truck came up the road. A Ford Bronco, Lieutenant Hernandez's truck.

"Thought I'd check in on the hero," he said, standing in the doorway of the barn. He had a six-pack of Coors dangling from his left hand.

Hernandez had visited the hospital two days before along with Marco and Carolina. They'd dropped off a vase of flowers and a *Playboy* magazine, ironically wrapped in a bow. "Since you'll have time on your hands," Carolina had said, and they all laughed about that, and then they left him alone to rest and read the articles. Hernandez had been up to Ben's place three times before, all invited.

"I'm on medical leave," Ben said.

"Yeah, I signed the paperwork."

Hernandez tossed him a can and took a seat on a metal chair across from Ben's desk.

"Mayor's talking about giving you keys to the city," Hernandez said.

"What the hell does that mean?"

"Means you're the story he wants to tell," Hernandez said. "It's good marketing."

Ben nodded and took a sip of the beer.

"Looking a little heavyweight, but not too bad," Hernandez said, raising the beer at Ben's eye. "You seeing straight yet?"

"It's all holy-light shit right now."

"Yeah," he said. "You look like a stoner."

The scanner squawked. 901: Accident—unknown injuries.

"Jonesing, huh?" Hernandez said, nodding toward the scanner.

"Thinking maybe tonight will be the night we catch him."

"The whole goddamned world's looking for him."

"I went up to the house," Ben said. "You know, the one in Norwalk where he was locked up as a kid?"

Hernandez nodded once.

"There was this woman there, a neighbor," Ben said. "I'm pretty sure she knew about the kid. People knew what was happening to that boy."

"It's a hard thing to believe," Hernandez said, hearing the question in Ben's voice, "that a man would do that to a boy. That's the kind of thing, I guess, that most people don't want to believe happens. You believe that, you have to believe a whole lot of other things about people."

415-F: Civil disturbance.

"To be honest," Hernandez continued, "after years of this job, I wish I knew a little less about people."

"I drive around this town," Ben said, "and think about all the shitty things that are happening inside those tidy little houses."

"That's the price of knowing," Hernandez said. "That's the price of this job." They were silent a moment. "Doesn't matter, anymore, what happened to the serial as a kid. Feel sorry for that kid, sure, but that kid's gone now. He no longer exists."

Ben nodded and watched the fog erase Quail Hill. He knew it, yes. He'd seen the bodies left behind, seen him choking that woman, and the look in his eyes on the freeway the other night. The serial had taken the evil done to him and turned it into a greater evil. It didn't matter anymore that once he was a kid and that kid was delivered into the hands of a person who would destroy him.

"Any leads?" Ben said.

"Thousands of them," Hernandez said. "The serial's everywhere, if you believe the tips. Everyone's bogeyman." Hernandez took a sip of the beer. "Last confirmed was an hour after you played demolition derby with him. OC sheriff's helicopter had visual of him on the 91 before being called off because of the wind. Highway patrol got a roadblock up out near Anaheim Hills, but . . ." He held up his open palms.

"Disappeared?"

"Disappeared."

Hernandez finished the can and opened another. Tossed a second to Ben. "He'll bleed to death, probably, if one of us doesn't catch up to him first. You got a good shot off."

390: Drunk and disorderly. Hernandez turned the dial down on the scanner.

"Really," Hernandez said. "Your dad would be proud."

"My dad would be pissed I'm getting the keys to this city."

Hernandez laughed and shook his head. "You're probably right. He was a good man, your dad. No bullshit from him."

"Nope."

"You know," Hernandez said, "I've been wondering about some things. Been thinking that since you've got some time to mull things over, you might be able to help me out."

"I'll do my best," Ben said, taking a sip of the beer, trying to play it cool.

"I've been wondering how you came to be first one on scene at

Puente Madera when you were supposed to be cowboying it up in Loma Canyon."

"Hunch."

"A hunch?"

"That the killer wasn't wasting his time up there in the hills," Ben said. "That he'd know we were hunting for him there."

"When you didn't sign off on this Mexican kid's suicide," Hernandez said, "I looked into a couple of things. Found out that Coach Wakeland keeps a rental property near the crime scene."

Ben remembered Hernandez watching him at the crime scene, when he blew up on Wakeland. Hernandez could piece things together; you didn't make lieutenant by being stupid.

"About a quarter mile away."

Hernandez nodded and sipped his beer.

The morning after the accident, Natasha called Ben to let him know that Wakeland wasn't strangled dead in the apartment. She called him that afternoon, too, to tell him she'd checked in with dispatch at the department and no assault claims had been filed, at least not yet.

"You were on that scene pretty fast."

"It was near Rachel's place," he said. "Freaked me out."

"Want another?" Hernandez said.

"No," Ben said. "I'm good."

Hernandez looked hard at him.

"You hungry?" Ben said. "I've got some tacos left over. My daughter makes some mean pico de gallo."

"No thanks," Hernandez said, slapping his knees and standing up. "Just wanted to check in on you, see how you're doing."

"I appreciate that."

"Get that head of yours healed up," Hernandez said. "Then let's talk when you sign off on that suicide."

THE FEAR BASIN

When it was done, when he had become not fear but death, he looked up and saw that the television was on. He hadn't noticed the flashing screen when he had followed her into the room; when he grabbed her, the pain in his arm had exploded and the inside of his mind had gone white. His head had felt distant from his body, a mile away from his hands, which clamped down until she stopped struggling and death had taken over fear.

He heard them call his name, Night Prowler, and when his vision puzzled back together, he was staring at his own face on the screen. It was him, but it was another him, the him when he'd first been arrested long ago and he'd only begun to understand what he had become. The face of the almost-him filled up the screen, and even he was moved by it — the dark, hollow eyes, the mangled teeth, the worm-brown skin. His face on the screen made him look bigger than real life, as though he were six feet tall, a fully formed monster. His face was being transmitted into every living room in Southern California. They saw him. They would see him now.

He covered her with a quilt he found on the couch — his blood had marred her face and made her ugly — and turned up the volume on the television. He found a bathroom at the end of a hallway, opened the medicine cabinet, and knocked aside lipstick and medicine vials until he found the gauze and the metal clips. The television said the police were looking for him, said people were terrified. It said all of the L.A. basin was on alert, a basin full of fear. A fear basin, he thought. He liked the sound of that, said it out loud to himself just to hear it. He rolled out the gauze and ripped a section off with his teeth. The television talked about the policeman who shot him and the woman the policeman had stopped him from killing. He unwrapped the old gauze, wet and pulpy with his insides. He wrapped the new gauze around his arm, the blood still leaking down his elbow and dripping onto the floor. The television read the names of the people he'd killed, and he smiled; they were a part of him now, and he a part of them, too. Other people wouldn't remember their lives; they'd remember their deaths; they'd remember the one who killed them. Even when he was gone, his name would send a shudder down their bodies. They saw him now and they'd remember him. Basin of fear.

When the gauze was wrapped, he pressed the metal clip into the fabric to hold it in place. But the blood kept coming, in little pumps, as though the policeman's bullet had tapped the muscle of his heart. In the garage, he found duct tape and he wrapped the gauze until the blood stopped running down his elbow. He found a crowbar and sledgehammer hanging from hooks on the wall, and he threw those on the passenger seat of the car. On a pegboard, he found the keys to the car—a Rabbit, the car was called a Rabbit—climbed into the driver's seat, and fired up the engine. Music blared from the radio, Wake me up before you go go!, and he slammed the dial off with the heel of his hand.

It was nearly dark now, a ribbon of pink in the western sky. Across the freeway, he could see the police helicopter spotlighting the rooftops dotting the hills. He drove down the road, out of the hills to the main street that led to the freeway. The police were still there in the on-ramp circles. He could see their lights spinning blues and reds. The traffic slowed and he watched two policemen walking between cars, showing the drivers pieces of paper. His picture was on those papers, he knew it. He edged the car to the left, into a turn lane that led to the twenty-four-hour grocery store. There he drove slowly across the parking lot and back out the other side, where he climbed the road back into the neighborhood and followed it as it curved up into the hills, past the neat little homes, past the backyard pools and parks with the tire swings, past the greenbelts and their electric lights coming to life. He drove until he came to the top of the hill where the pavement turned to rutted dirt, and he drove that road until it dead-ended at a metal gate. He had found the gate the second night he was here, but it was chained and locked and his crowbar was still in the trunk of his Toyota. Beyond the gate, the dirt road climbed a ridge into the hills and disappeared in darkness. One of the helicopters floated across the freeway now, its spotlight exploding across the rooftops below, the rotors chopping the air. Grabbing the crowbar, he wedged the metal between the gate and lock. It took three times, the helicopter floating closer, his head spinning with pain, but it finally snapped, and he drove the Rabbit through the gate and into the deep darkness of the hills.

THE CALL CAME IN OVER THE SCANNER AT 9:37 P.M.

Ben had been in the barn since Hernandez left, sitting in the dark to save his eye, putting away the rest of the Coors, trying to figure out how much Hernandez knew—and what to do about it. The lieutenant had made some connections, sure, but had he added them up? Whom had he spoken to? Had Natasha given him away? Regardless, Hernandez was putting him on alert; that was for sure. "Let's talk when you sign off on that suicide."

The call was out of Anaheim, East Station. "Possible 187. 14667 Sky Line Drive."

Ben flipped on the desk lamp to check the address, his vision blurring with the light. He turned it to spotlight the topographic map he'd tacked to the wall. He ran his finger down the map, following the 55 Freeway out to the 91, the exact route the serial had taken the night Ben had shot him.

The scanner squawked again. They'd found a black BMW parked across the street from the victim's house. Plates didn't match, but the steering wheel was covered in blood.

The night the serial escaped, the CHP had shut down the 91 Freeway for three hours, checking each car before letting them drive on: nothing. Just disappeared. Ben found the spot on the map where they had set up the roadblock. Just two exit ramps between the 55 junction and the CHP roadblock: Imperial Highway and Weir Canyon. Just two ways in and two ways out.

Scanner: The Anaheim police were shutting down the on-ramps to the freeway.

Ben found the victim's house and pinned it. It was in the hills, hemmed in between the freeway on one side and the open land of the Santa Ana Mountains on the other. Unless he slipped through before they closed the on-ramps, the serial was cornered.

No, that was too easy. He'd have a way out, if he was going to kill again. Ben ran his finger over the serpentine roads as they climbed through the residential streets. The roads curved back onto one another, a labyrinth of expensive homes pushing the edge of the wilderness.

There, he found it, the route that could get him out: Black Star Canyon Road. Ben knew the road, a graded dirt path that snaked the backbone ridge of the mountains down into Limestone Canyon and beyond. Ben followed the road with his fingers, tracing the ridgeline — three miles, four back into the wilderness, five miles, six, and the serial could go out the other side, right back into Rancho Santa Elena.

He called Hernandez at home.

"This better be good."

"We gotta get Anaheim on the horn," Ben said. "I think I know where he is."

NATASHA DROVE UP TO THE house midmorning and found Ben in the barn. She hadn't told him about the photos yet. She had covered them in tissue paper and placed them in a file folder and let them sit on her kitchen table, vibrating something ugly. She had decided to give him a few days to heal. This wasn't the kind of thing you hit a man with when his guard was down.

"You been out here all night?" she said when she saw him, sitting, elbows up on the makeshift desk.

He gave her a guilty glance. His left eye socket was still mean-looking, purple with yellow splotches on the edges, a little dried blood around the stitches of a zigzagging laceration.

"You on scene last night?"

"No," she said. "Mendenhall took this one."

"Thought he didn't like the field."

"He doesn't. But there's a lot of press on it now. He sees it as good exposure."

"Bastard," Ben said, half-joking.

"Political animal," she said. "I needed a break anyway."

A helicopter flew low over the barn. Outside the window, they both watched it head east toward the Santa Ana Mountains.

"I almost had him," Ben said. "If I had gotten him, that girl would be alive." She had been a college student, the one killed last night, a twenty-year-old back at her parents' place for a visit. "Now all I can do is sit on my ass doing nothing."

She looked at him, wondering if he heard his own words.

"Take a ride with me," she said.

THEY GOT IN HER Z and rode across town in silence. Cruisers were out everywhere, the city like a police state. Cops in grocery store parking lots. Cops guarding the dirt roads that led out of the hills. The yellow tape was still up at Puente Madera, and police cruisers were there, too, blocking the entrance to the complex. Everything else was back in order, though—the stoplight replaced, the skid marks and oil slick cleaned up.

"Hernandez paid me a visit," Ben said. "He seemed to know a lot about my recent activities."

She glanced at him, hearing the implication in his voice.

"I haven't said a word to him," she said. A light turned red; she hit the brakes and glared at him. "You know me better than that."

He stared at her for a moment, his eyes hidden behind dark sunglasses, and then nodded and turned away. It took five minutes and two cigarettes to reach the high school, all three hundred seconds ticking off in silence.

"You know this is the last place I want to be," he said, when he saw where they were headed.

"Yeah," she said, pulling into the parking lot. "I know."

She passed two more police cruisers at the entrance to the high school, parked her car in the lot in front of the swim complex, and cut the engine. They could see the lines of boys through the fence, freestyling down the pool lanes, Wakeland pacing the edge of the water with them, stopwatch in hand. She watched Ben as he stared through the fence, his jaw hard, his eyes narrowed.

"I want you to think about something," she said. "What if Emma were a boy? Would you be sending her here next year?"

He looked at her, his face darkening.

"Would you?"

"What's your point?"

"You know my point."

She reached into the backseat, grabbed the file folder, and tossed it on his lap.

"You need to see something," she said.

He opened it, glanced at the first shot, and his face collapsed. It was painful to see, painful to be the cause of it. He turned his face away and stared out the passenger-side window, hiding himself for a few seconds, and then looked back down at the Polaroids in his hands.

"There're more," she said. "Back at the apartment. In the master bedroom closet."

"I knew there was something there," Ben said. "I just couldn't—"

"Some things can't be done alone."

He turned the photos facedown in his lap, the black square of film paper betraying nothing of the ugliness on the other side.

"Any of me?" he said.

"No," she said. "Only Lucero."

Wakeland blew the whistle. They both looked up, watched the boys climb out of the water and strut across the pool deck to grab their towels.

"You know why I let go of him the other night?" he said.

"You're not a killer, that's why."

"No," he said. "I could have killed him." He turned his face away from her. "Somehow I still cared for the man. I don't know how, but the feeling was still there."

She let that sink in for a second, trying to find a place in her mind where it could be understood.

"Four or five years ago," she said, "this seventeen-year-old girl was rolled into the examination room. She had been kicked to death by her boyfriend—broken ribs, fractured skull, internal bleeding."

He wasn't looking at her, his face turned away still, staring into some middle distance of his mind.

"One of the detectives on the case kept coming back, two or three times. First he made a pretense of gathering evidence, but later he just seemed to come by to look at her. It was a pretty straight-forward case—I'd already sent my report over to the department—so I asked him about it. He said she had been put in the hospital five times by this man, a dealer in his late twenties. He'd tried to get her to press charges, but she wouldn't. She fell down the stairs, she'd say, or she got hit in the eye with a ball, stuff like that. She wouldn't leave him. And then she ended up on an examination table in my office."

"I'm supposed to be the seventeen-year-old girl?"

"The point is," she said, "there comes a time when the reasons don't matter anymore. I can't explain it and neither can you. It just needs to stop."

She handed him a photocopy of Phillip's picture, the one she got from Helen.

"Phillip Lambert," she said. "Fourteen years old. Wakeland had him alone in the pool the other day."

Ben stared at the picture, his hands shaking a little.

"Any pictures of him in that box?"

"Not yet," Natasha said.

The boy had big hazel eyes, a smattering of freckles across the bridge of his nose.

"What happened to you, Ben, isn't about your body. It wouldn't show up in an autopsy; there'd be no evidence. What happened to you is in your head. He's in your head—that's it. He can't hurt *you* anymore." She nodded to the school picture of Phillip. "That was you," she said. "That's how young you were."

She took the photos from Ben's hands, slid all of them into the file folder, and handed it back to him. The boys were streaming into the locker room now, a couple stragglers pulling on T-shirts, but Wakeland had stopped Phillip on the pool deck.

"That's him," she said, nodding toward the pool.

Ben looked up and stared hard at the pool.

Wakeland was pressing down on the boy's shoulders, saying something to him that they were too far away to hear. Ben shifted uncomfortably in the passenger seat.

"I can't do nothing, knowing what I know," she said, looking at Ben now. "The man you need to catch is right there." She pointed toward the pool. "So is the boy you need to save. People knew what was happening to you, Ben. Right?"

Water threatened his eyes, and she could see him grind his teeth to hold it back.

"They never said anything," she said. "Are you going to be one of those people?"

Nothing.

She glanced back at the pool. Phillip was walking toward the locker room, and Wakeland had turned, looking out at the parking lot toward Natasha's car. He recognized it from the other day, she was sure of it. Yes, she thought. We're watching you.

"No one's looking for Wakeland," Natasha said. "No one's hunting him down. I'll give you a couple days, but after that I am going to go talk to Hernandez."

He looked at her then, his face misshapen with swelling.

"I've covered for you," she said very quietly, "but I can't do it again." She took his hand then and he let her, and neither could look at the other. They just watched their fingers intertwined. "I don't know what we are, Ben. But if you make me do this, I don't think I can be anything to you anymore. It's yours to do."

*   *   *

AFTER NATASHA DROPPED HIM OFF at the house, Ben sat at the kitchen counter next to the phone, holding the number in his hands. Wakeland's hands had been on Phillip's shoulders. "Are you going to be one of those people?" He heard Natasha's voice ring in his head. Then Wakeland had touched Phillip's chest, just once, but Ben felt his body leap with panic. He was teaching the boy to breathe. That's how it started, that was the beginning. Even after all that had happened, even after Ben's attack, the man was laying the foundation for another boy.

It took Ben the better part of an hour—thinking about the evidence he already had against Wakeland, thinking about all the evidence he didn't have—before he finally dialed the number.

"Tucker Preston?"

"Who wants to know?"

"Ben Wade," he said. "I swam for Coach Wakeland."

The line hissed with silence.

"Can I buy you a beer?" Ben said.

"No," he said. "You can't." Silence. "Meet me at Cordova Park."

THE KID WAS SITTING ON a bench, smoking a cigarette, when Ben found him, his feet rolling his skateboard deck back and forth.

"I told the medical examiner I wasn't going to say anything," Tucker said.

Ben sat on the farthest edge of the bench, a square of orange trees before them, surrounded by a wooden fence. PRESERVING OUR HERITAGE read a brass plaque.

"But you gave her your number."

"Yeah," he said, turning to look at Ben. "I did. Wanted to see what you looked like, I guess." Tucker's gaze unnerved him. "You're the cop that shot the Night Prowler, right?"

"I am."

"But he got away."

"For now."

"Shit, man," Tucker said, shaking his head. "Wakeland loved you. Talked about you all the time, about how special you were, about how you understood things. When I pissed him off, he always compared me to you. I was so jealous." Tucker laughed ironically. "I could never live up."

"I could never live up, either," Ben said.

"There was someone before you?"

"I don't know," he said. "I wasn't good enough, then I was special, and then I wasn't good enough again. That was part of his deal."

Tucker nodded and blew smoke, and they both watched three crows attack the fallen oranges in the grove. "We had a peach tree in our backyard," Tucker said. "At the Santa Elena house. When the fruit was ripe, my mom would give them to the neighbors. She baked a pie once with the last of the fruit and gave it to Wakeland after state finals. He and I ate it together, the whole damn thing in one sitting. I think my mother had a crush on him."

"He's a con man," Ben said. "The best kind make you believe anything."

"I want to blame you," Tucker said.

"I know."

"Let me finish," he said, narrowing his eyes at Ben. "I want to blame you, but then—then I guess that makes me responsible for this kid, Lucero, too."

"I can't help you with that," Ben said. "I haven't sorted that out myself."

Tucker looked away. "What do you want from me?"

What he wanted was to find a kid in better shape than this one, one who wasn't screwed up and jittery with nicotine shakes, a kid who didn't have deep sleepless circles under his eyes, a kid who wasn't bitter with anger and blame, someone who had come out the other side of this unscathed.

"There's another kid," Ben said.

"Jesus."

"A freshman."

"How do you know?"

"Wakeland's getting him alone in the pool," Ben said. "After practice."

Tucker looked at the ground.

"That's how it started for you too, right?" Ben said.

Tucker nodded slowly, less an answer to the question than the unspoken recognition that Ben was right. This new kid, Phillip, was in trouble.

"People like this don't stop," Ben said. "If it's not this kid, it'll be another. I can't tell you if I'm responsible for what happened to you. But I can't let this happen again. We can't let this happen again."

"You're just going to drag me into this, aren't you?" Tucker said. "That's what you're here to tell me, right?"

"You almost stopped him once," Ben said. "You spoke up. You did more than I could do at the time."

"I don't know, man," Tucker said, shaking his head. "The statute—"

"Is up, I know." He did know. Six years. Penal code, section 800. He'd used the law as an excuse for years to pretend he was fine about the past. "We come forward, maybe others will. One accusation sounds like a personal grudge, two—or more—starts to sound like the truth. Even if he can't be prosecuted, people will know what he is."

"I don't think I can go there with you."

"That fear you feel," Ben said. "That panic you have right now . . . that's Wakeland. Wakeland's still got you. Don't let him."

"It's not just Wakeland," Tucker said, disdain in his voice. "It's my mom, my dad, it's my girlfriend. I mean, she doesn't even know and I don't want her to. The fear . . . it's everyone, you know?"

Ben nodded. "Yeah, I know."

"It's everyone."

Silence.

"Look, this is just about out of the bag," Ben said, "and I can't put it back in, even if I want to." Ben stood and watched a crow struggle into the air. "I won't expose you. I won't do that to you. But I don't know what others are going to do. I think you should be ready."

Tucker squinted up at him and then looked back out over the orange grove, shaking his head.

"You know the best thing about this serial killer?" Tucker said.

Ben just looked at him.

"Seeing everyone else scared. It's been kind of nice for a change."

HE WAS HOME BY SIX, alone in the barn, reading and rereading Wakeland's letters from all those years ago. *You're a coward*, Wakeland had written, and, damn, he'd been right. He was a coward, had been for years. Even choking Wakeland was the act of a coward, the desperate act of a man who still felt powerless. Why would Wakeland stop then, if Ben wouldn't arrest him, wouldn't use the power he did have?

He struggled through the photographs of Lucero, stared at the picture Natasha had given him of this new boy, Phillip, thinking about the evidence again—the birthday card to Lucero back at his mother's makeshift home, Neil's story about being caught holding hands in the apartment, the photographs Natasha said were hiding in the master bedroom closet of that apartment—trying to piece together some half measure he could live with to fix all this. *It's everyone, you know?* Tucker had said. Yeah, and everyone would know about him, if he did this. Everyone. Rachel. Emma.

Ben pulled the photos of him and Wakeland from the box he kept in his rifle cabinet, glanced through them again, him smiling, him showing off his county freestyle championship medal. He won regionals a few weeks later, and then it was states.

He was the favorite to win the 200 free, nearly seventeen years ago. He'd been ahead of the pack, his body torpedoing down the lane, the silence of the water and then the roar of the crowd when he turned for a breath of air. Rachel was there, in the stands; his mother and Voorhees, too. Scouts were on the side of the pool—UCLA,

USC, Stanford, UC San Diego. Coach Dixon, the USC coach who had timed, weighed, and measured him up in L.A. a few weeks before, was ready, Ben knew (or at least Wakeland had said), to offer him a scholarship. Before the race, Dixon and Wakeland shook hands, a fraternal swagger between them. Ben wondered then if Dixon knew about Wakeland, if this was a secret that handshakes secured; the two swam together back in the old days, bound forever by their triumph over bodily pain. If Ben took the scholarship, Wakeland would be there with him, too, in his friendship with the USC coach, in the reason Ben was at USC at all, in every breath Ben took above the flat surface of the chlorinated water.

Ben was coming into his last turn and it hit him: He could simply stop kicking and let it all go. He made the turn and dolphin-kicked off the wall. There was nothing but open water in front of him; everyone in the stands was on their feet. He could stop, blow it all up, but he kept pulling through the water, just thirty meters from winning it all. Stroke and a breath, just twenty-five meters from the wall, where Wakeland stood on the pool deck with a stopwatch in hand. It was his body, the power in his muscles, the strength of his mind, but the line on the bottom of the pool led straight to Wakeland. And he didn't want that anymore. Not anymore.

Then he did it: He let his muscles ease off, let his body sink into the water. He couldn't believe the relief; the tension seeped out of his body, and his head seemed to fill with clear light. He let the next three swimmers pass him, their wakes lifting him into his next stroke before he kicked into the wall, a disappointing fourth. The end of the scholarship. The end, he thought then, of Wakeland's hold over him. When he got out of the pool—his shocked teammates murmuring, Wakeland yelling, "What the hell just happened?"—he cocooned himself in a towel and sat on the cement wall. Then Rachel was there, her arms around him, whispering to him that it was all right. "It's just a race. It's all right."

* * *

Ben stayed out in the barn until nearly 1:00 a.m., the distant sound of helicopters hovering over the mountains, the contents of the box spread before him on the desk. *It's yours to do*, he remembered Natasha saying. For years this box had sat duct-taped closed in a dark corner of the attic or in the back of the garage. Wakeland had been stuffed inside the box, too. Reading Wakeland's letters again, Ben realized they were a form of interrogation—the expressions of care and concern followed by threats and chastisement, the twisting of the facts to get your man to feel guilty, to get him to say what you wanted him to say, to make him do what you wanted him to do, to make him believe what you wanted him to believe. He had fallen for it for years, when he was a six-foot-two child. When he grew up, he believed the man could do nothing more to him, and he was stuck for half of his life between his childhood self and his adulthood. These letters were the proof of that manipulation, of that half-life.

Here was the evidence.

The next morning, Ben met Hernandez in his office.

"You supposed to be driving yet?" Hernandez said.

"I gotta talk with you," Ben said.

"They found the killer's car," Hernandez said, flipping through the pages of a report. "You were right. He busted it up just outside of Limestone Canyon."

"He's in the Sinks then."

"What?"

"The Sinks," Ben said. "That's what the cowboys called it. It's got steep cliffs, like the earth just fell away. It was easy to lose cattle in there. My dad hated the place."

"The sheriff and the Ventura Mounted Enforcement Unit are up there," Hernandez said. "Thanks for the tip. Sorry, I know you want to be up there, too."

"I'm not here about the serial."

"All right," Hernandez said, setting the report on his desk.

The precinct was filled with cops, filing reports, making phone calls. Ben wanted to close the blinds, but that would only arouse suspicion, so he sat there with his back to the station desks, the murmur of the policemen sounding like whispers behind his back.

Ben handed Hernandez the file folder with the pictures of Lucero inside. When he opened it, Hernandez looked away and shifted in his seat.

"The Mexican kid?" he said, finally. "The suicide?"

"Yeah," Ben said.

"He was one of Wakeland's swimmers, right?"

"He was," Ben said.

Hernandez fanned the pictures out, studying them carefully, and then turned them facedown on the desk. He got up and closed the door and sat back down and stared at the desk, his chin pushed close to his chest. He didn't look at Ben for a while, something Ben was thankful for. Ben knew, though, that Hernandez was putting the pieces together. Ben's swimming, accosting Wakeland at the scene, refusing to close Lucero's case, defying orders the other night when he left his patrol in the hills and almost caught the killer. He could have interrogated Ben, could have asked him all the ugly questions, but Hernandez understood that some things shouldn't be said between men.

"The case is still open, right?" Hernandez said, looking at him now. "You didn't sign off on it this morning?"

"No."

Hernandez nodded slowly. "How'd you get these?"

Ben told him, and Hernandez just kept nodding, his mind chewing on the problem.

"There're more?"

"That's what Natasha says," Ben said. "She thinks he's grooming another kid, too, a freshman." He pulled Phillip's school picture out of his coat pocket—he didn't want the boy's picture in the same file that held the ugly ones of Lucero—and slid it across the desk. "Phillip Lambert."

Hernandez looked at the photo, and then let out a long breath.

"We can't use these to get a warrant," he said, putting his hand on top of the Polaroids. "They're gotten illegally."

"I know."

Hernandez tapped his fingers against the back of the pictures. "You got enough on this for a warrant?" he asked. "Without these?"

Ben told him what he had—Wakeland letting Lucero's family use his apartment address, the apartment itself and all that might be hidden there, the testimony of a half dozen people at the school and in the picker's camp, but he left Tucker out of it—and Hernandez jotted down notes on a legal pad.

Then Ben handed Hernandez the two letters Wakeland had sent to him years ago, and the note he got off Lucero's body. Blood thrummed in his ears while Hernandez read them.

Ben had sent his own letter soon after Wakeland's threatening one. He had written it nine days after states, in the middle of the night, at his desk in his room as his mother and Voorhees slept, just one sentence that he remembered as clearly as if he'd written it down yesterday: *If you say anything to Rachel, if you even go near her, I'll tell everything—to the school, to the cops—EVERYTHING.* The next morning, he rode his bike over to the post office. He dropped the letter in the slot and then rode down to the beach and spent the school day there. He never went back to the pool, never spoke to Wakeland again, even as his mother and Voorhees begged him not to let his embarrassment at states ruin his relationship with the coach.

Now Hernandez set Wakeland's letters on top of the Polaroids of Lucero and the picture of Phillip, and ran his hand through his hair. "We can get him another way," he said, gesturing toward the letters.

Ben thought of Natasha, of her final declaration to him. He wanted to be the kind of man she expected him to be, the man she believed existed in him. Like he said to Tucker, the fear he felt now was Wakeland. Hiding it, living in shame, meant Wakeland still had a grip on him. Unless Ben stopped letting him.

"No," Ben said. "This other kid, Phillip, is out there. It can't be about me anymore."

Hernandez nodded. "This will break wide open," he said, "especially now that you've had your fifteen minutes. You ready for that?"

"I don't know."

"You won't have a choice, if we move forward."

"That's probably a good thing."

Hernandez looked at him a few moments.

"All right," Hernandez said. "I'm going to get a couple patrols to keep an eye on that apartment. The coach walks in there with that kid, we're going in. It's my case. I'll take care of it."

Ben nodded, stood to walk out, but paused at the door.

"The Sinks," he said, "Limestone Canyon, it runs north to south. If they've pushed the serial into the canyon, there're basically only two ways out. There're a lot of places to hide, but if you block up the north and south ends of the canyon, you've got him locked in."

HE GOT HOME FIFTEEN MINUTES before Rachel and Emma pulled into the driveway. When the wheels crunched on the gravel, Ben was there to meet them, and when Rachel stopped the car, he leaned his elbows on the door.

"Come take a walk with me," he said to Rachel.

Emma was standing by the open door of the passenger side, watching the two of them.

"Em," Rachel said, "go get started on your homework."

Emma closed the door and walked up to the house, glancing backward twice before pushing through the front door.

Rachel waited until Emma was safely inside. "I've got *Crucible* essays to grade."

"Rach," he said. "Come on, I have to talk to you."

"Talk to me here."

"No," he said. "Just, please, take a walk with me to the top of the hill." He wanted to ride, wanted to get out on the horses, but he wasn't going to leave Em here alone until they caught the serial. "It'll be easier up there. I can't explain."

She stared at him and finally nodded.

They walked up the trail to Quail Hill in silence, an awkward five minutes that assailed him with doubt. Fog was pushing in from the ocean, and the sun turned to shadow and back again. At the top, they could see down into Bommer Canyon, where a front-loader was tipping over the last wall of the cowboy camp he and his dad used to rest at. They'd build a gated community here, homes with backyard pools, three-car garages.

"Come on, Ben. What is this?"

He turned to her and smiled nervously. He had almost told her, years ago. They had been married barely six months, and had just moved into the Marina Del Rey apartment. Ben was working on a criminal justice degree from Long Beach State—the only four-year college that would take him with his grades, without a scholarship, without swimming—and Rachel was up at UCLA working on an English bachelor's. They'd just discovered that Rachel was pregnant, six weeks along, and they'd spent the evening looking through catalogs full of cribs, her face shining with excitement. He couldn't sleep that night, and through their bedroom window he watched a police helicopter circling on the other side of the freeway, its spotlight flashing back and forth through the dark sky. Twenty minutes or more it kept circling, its rotors incessantly humming, the Nightsun flooding the ugly streets with white light.

"I have to tell you something," he had said, finally.

"What?" she had said with a dreamy late-night smile, her hand on her belly as though she could already feel the baby there. He wanted the relief of sharing it, of having her take some of the burden of it from him. But in that split second he realized there was no relief in telling her. He would have to explain everything, tell her all the ugly details, explain how it happened, explain how he could have let it happen, and he didn't have answers to those questions. She was carrying his child, and all he had to offer her was grief with the admission.

"God, I love you," he said, the back of his throat swelling, threatening tears. "I don't deserve you."

"It's because you know that," she said, a wry smile on her face, "that I love you."

They both burst out laughing, and then he was inside her, his head buried in her neck, her lips kissing the top of his head, the helicopter circling outside in the dark.

"Sit down," he said now.

She gave him a skeptical glance.

"Please."

They sat together on a jumble of rock, looking down over what was once *their* house. The city, still glowing in late-afternoon sun, spread toward the mountains in the east.

"A case is being built," he said, "that implicates Lewis Wakeland in the abuse of boys."

"What? Coach Wakeland?" She shook her head in disbelief. "What's the evidence?"

He took a deep breath. "Me. I am."

She jerked her head back to get a clearer look at him. The sun disappeared behind a ribbon of fog, reappeared, and then disappeared again. She stared at him, her hand on her lips.

"You?"

Then he told her—not everything, but enough; some things were meant to go with you to the grave. For ten minutes or more—he didn't know how long, really—he watched the surfacing emotions upset her face until he couldn't stand it anymore, and then he watched the fog thicken along the ridges, blurring the sloping lines between hills.

"My God, Ben," she said, water in her eyes. "I can't believe it."

"I know."

"Why now?" she said.

"There're others," he said. "It happened to others. If I had said something before, maybe—"

"Other kids?"

"Yes."

"That man needs to be taken out of that school," she said, standing up. "Right now."

"We need a warrant first," he said. "The statute of limitations is up on me. We need evidence about the others before an arrest."

"How can there be limitations on such things?" she said, pacing.

"You'd have to ask the lawyers about that," Ben said.

"We've known each other for almost twenty years," she said after a long silence. "Shared the same bed fifteen of those years. What did you think I'd do if you told me?"

"It's not what you would have done," he said, looking at her now. "It's what you would have seen."

She shook her head. "What did you think I would see?"

"It was like I won the lottery with you," he said, trying to explain. "Like I was an idiot, some disgusting fool who got lucky."

"What did you think I would see, Ben?"

A weak, frightened man. "I don't know. I would just always wonder, what you saw."

She gazed out over the fogged-in valley with a look of shock on her face.

"God," she said. "How many people know? I mean, a case is being built."

"A couple."

"Natasha?"

"Yeah. She's one of them."

"I wish you'd told me," she said. "I could've helped. I was your wife; it was my job to help. I would have *wanted* to help."

"I didn't know how to."

"You know what it was like living with you?" Rachel said. "You know what it was like to be ignored? Not to be touched? Then to move here and have it get worse . . . You sitting out there in the barn, every night. Do you know what that was like?"

How could he tell her, even now, that sometimes when she had rolled over to touch him, Wakeland's face had flashed across the dark screen of his mind? Moving back here was like having Wakeland move in with them. He hadn't expected that, didn't know his mind was still so weak to allow that to happen.

"I thought I'd lose you, if I told you."

She laughed bitterly at the irony, tears in her eyes. "Ben," she said, "you don't understand people at all."

SHE WALKED DOWN THE HILL in front of him, keeping her distance, the fog socking in and turning everything to cloud.

"I don't want Emma to see me like this," Rachel said when they got to the house. "Make an excuse for me. I need a little time." Then she was in the car, driving down the road.

Inside the house, Emma had the table set with a couple of steaming Hungry-Man Salisbury steaks.

"What's the breaking news with you guys?" Emma said, cutting into her meat. "Mom didn't even say goodbye."

"We had a discussion."

"An argument."

"No," he said.

She squinted her eyes at him, chewing.

"The subject matter?" she said. "*Yo?*"

"No," he said. "Not you." He took a bite of the steak, but it tasted like shit, freezer-burned and syrupy with congealed sauce. "*Comida es muy bien!*"

"Who're you kidding?" she said.

LATER THAT NIGHT, NEARING TEN, Rachel called. "I've been trying to catch you for an hour," she said.

"I can't get your daughter off the phone."

"Set a time limit, Ben," she said.

He was watching a cop show, *Hill Street Blues*. Somehow it got his mind off things, and he enjoyed, to his surprise, making fun of it.

"You called to offer constructive criticism?"

"I'm sorry about taking off like that," she said. "I just"—a big intake of air—"I needed to think. You caught me off guard."

"Yeah," he said. "Couldn't figure how to set the table for that one."

"I'm sorry, Ben," she said. He could hear her tearing up. "I'm so sorry."

"I know." Sympathy was fine, but the sound of it was tough on the ears.

"It explains some things for me, though, you know?" she said. "It wasn't me. What happened to us."

"No," he said. "It wasn't you."

"I always thought it was me. All that time you spent in the barn. The nights you slept on the couch. I felt so guilty. I always felt guilty."

"It was never you. Even after the history teacher."

She let out a long breath.

"I drove by the pool after I left you tonight," Rachel said, trailing off. "You know, I was jealous of that man when we were in school, all that time you spent with him. I should have known."

"No," he said. "You were a kid. Others should have known, but not you."

Silence on the line.

"You know," she said, "you've got to tell Emma, right?"

He knew, yes, he knew, but . . .

"Tonight, Ben," she said. "Before this gets out. I'll come over if it helps, all right? I'm coming over."

And she did. She was there in fifteen minutes and they sat around the dinner table together, a situation that would have otherwise caused him joy, and the three of them had a long talk.

RACHEL STAYED THAT NIGHT, SLEEPING with Emma in her bed. When he told Emma—God. When he looked in his daughter's eyes and said, "This is what happened to me," she took his shaking hands in hers and kissed his knuckles. Emma touched him, without hesitation, without a moment to think about the disgusting things he'd done. Now she and Rachel were asleep in Emma's room and Ben lay awake, replaying the moment in his mind: the grace of his daughter, the grace of their child. He lay awake, staring at the ceiling, unwilling to go out to the barn tonight. He and Rachel weren't sharing a bed, and he knew they never would again, but tonight he wanted to be under the same roof with his daughter and the woman that bore her into his life.

INTO THE WILDERNESS

They had followed him into the canyon—the helicopters floating back and forth like metal wasps, the policemen on horses trotting a line down the canyon floor trail. The bandages had bled through, leaving trickles of his blood in the bleached dirt so they could track him. He took off his shirt, ripped it into shreds, and tied it around his arm just above the hole to make it stop. But ten minutes later, the knot came loose and he had to stop to retie it with his good hand and his teeth, his inside-self dripping rust-colored spots onto the dirt until the fabric was cinched tightly enough.

He heard the horses then, close this time, and he had to leave the trail, disappear into the underbrush with the snakes and jackrabbits and mule deer resting in the afternoon shade. The men on the horses stuck to the thin trail—their rifles strapped across their chests, their binoculars glinting in the sunlight—but he slipped along the edges of the canyon, where the cliff walls rose white in the desert sun. For a while, he stalked them stalking him, the need to take one of them blooming in his chest. The men's bodies floated above the chaparral like brutal ghosts, the air around them tinged with sweat and leather, and he imagined what it would be to clench a fist around one of their necks, imagined the smell of their fear. But they had rifles, they had shotguns, they had clubs and snub-nosed revolvers, and his right hand wouldn't work anymore, wouldn't close into a fist without sending dizzying pain up his neck to explode in his head. So he snuck away, leaving them to the trail, crawling on his hands and knees through tunnels in the underbrush, dozing for a few moments among boulders when the clomp and scrape of the hooves receded down the canyon, his head whirling with cold sweat.

Two nights ago, he'd spun off the road, the car bottoming out in a rutted drainage. The engine rattled to silence, and he sat there in the dark, blood thrumming in his ears. He unwrapped the wet bandages from his arm and rewrapped it with the last of the fresh bandages and tape, keeping himself inside himself again. He lay down in the front seat then and watched the stars pulse the sky and talked to himself in his eleven-year-old language until his head spun into sleep.

He woke to hot breath outside the window, the stink of mangy hair, something clawing at the metal door. The sky was ribboned red-orange, and when he looked outside, he saw the coyote sniffing at his blood. Dark shapes moved in the brush beyond and then stilled to shadow again. He opened the car door and the coyote leapt backward. He placed one foot and then the other on the dry ground, and the coyote retreated, growling, its teeth bared in fear. He stumbled toward the animal—his head a balloon on a string floating high above his shoulders—and followed it into the brush until he was in the cold breath of the wilderness and the coyote became air. He would become a coyote, he decided then, a hunter disappearing into the night, and he would walk out the other side of the canyon, back into the town, back among them.

Now it was dark, the sky above him bruise blue. He listened for the men, listened for their horses, the rattling of the bits, the pounding of hooves, but he heard nothing, just the thumping sound of a distant helicopter. He slunk along the edge of the canyon wall, his body shadowless in the moonless night. Then the helicopter came thundering down the canyon, its spotlight exploding the brush and trees and rocks with overexposed light. He was caught in the open, between the canyon wall and a row of manzanita, and when he started to run, three mule deer burst out of the underbrush and he ran with them, the helicopter hurling light behind them, the deer darting and kicking in front of him. Up ahead he saw them, the policemen's flashlights like little lightning strikes against the sagebrush. The deer veering and cutting, careening through chaparral, and then a shot punched the air and one of the deer dropped and he could see the policemen's flashlights slashing across the shuddering animal.

"Shit," he heard one of them say.

There was another shot and he heard the policemen arguing, their walkie-talkies sending static into the air. He crouched then in a clump of cactus with the needles poking into his skin, and the helicopter's light burned across his body until it floated above the men and the dead deer. He crouched there for ten minutes, just outside the circle of light, the cactus thorns puncturing his arms, stabbing into his thighs, until he watched the legs of the horses pass him by on the trail.

"Fucking deer hunter here," he heard one of them say, a couple others laughing.

"Wonder how that's going to look in the report."

"Shut the hell up, Gonzalez. You practically jumped out of the saddle."

Then they were gone, following the trail north, back up to the entrance to the canyon, back where the stolen car lay broken in a ditch. He crouched there for five more minutes, watching the helicopter splash the canyon with light. The spotlight slashed across the canyon wall once, and he saw the fold in the land, a thin chute of rock rising to the ridge above. He knew then he couldn't stay on the canyon floor.

18

B EN SPED HIS TRUCK DOWN THE WASHBOARD RUTS OF BLACK Star Canyon Road toward the sunrise over Limestone Canyon.

He'd slept until three in the morning when he startled awake, remembering something from his senior year. He checked in on the sleeping Emma and Rachel, and then went out to the barn and studied the topographic map of the canyon, listening to scanner chatter of the manhunt, watching the helicopter spotlights circling above the distant hills. By dawn, it was clear to Ben they'd lost the serial. The mounted units had ridden up and down the canyon all night, foot patrols were searching under every bush; they'd shot a deer, for God's sake, startled up by the helicopters. There were a couple rangers from the park service up there, too, but they'd imported them from Alpine, down near San Diego, and they didn't really know the land. They had the north and south ends of the canyon bottled up, just like Ben had said, but the killer wasn't down in the canyon. Ben was sure of it.

When he got to the command post—a folding picnic table and a nylon canopy to keep the sun off—Hernandez and the county sheriff were bent over a national forest map.

"Don't believe you've got medical clearance yet," Hernandez said as a greeting.

"I don't believe you know where the hell the killer is," Ben said.

Ben was laying out his topo map over the national forest map, setting a walkie-talkie on each corner to keep the ends down.

"Well," Hernandez said, glancing at Ben's truck, "at least you didn't use city resources to get up here."

Hernandez explained to the sheriff, Barrow, that Ben used to ride these hills with his father, back when it was a cattle ranch. Barrow, a gaunt older man as tall as a basketball center, blew smoke from his cigarette and eyed Ben.

"You're the officer that shot him, right?"

"Yeah," Ben said.

"You're bleeding, son," Barrow said, and handed him a handkerchief.

"Thanks." Ben touched the cloth to his eye. Just a little blood, a stitch shaken loose from the rough ride up, maybe.

The sheriff explained the situation: patrols on the south end of the canyon, cruisers blocking all dirt roads leading out of the hills, Ventura and Riverside mounted units picking the canyon trails.

"Got a couple footprints," the sheriff said, pointing at the map. "Here and here."

Ben marked the spots in blue pen.

"Blood on the trail here," the sheriff pointed, "and a smeared handprint here, on the trunk of an oak tree. But that's it, as of an hour ago."

"He knows how to disappear," Hernandez said.

Ben glanced out along the ridge to where the land fell away in limestone folds.

"We need some foot patrols up on those bluffs," Ben said. "I think he's climbing."

"Up there?" Barrow said. "That's steep as hell. The guy's bleeding like a son of a bitch."

"There're coyote trails," Ben said. "Mule deer trails up and down the canyon walls. If he was down on the canyon floor, you'd have found him by now."

These were city police, used to alleyways and strip malls and neat rows of suburban homes. The sheriff blew smoke and then called to a captain, who sent a half dozen grudging officers hiking up the ridge-line. Ben watched them pick a deer trail through the scrub brush on the lip of the canyon wall.

"I need to get down in there," Ben said.

"Looks to me," the sheriff said, "like you should be feet up on a couch."

"There're a couple small caves," Ben said. "Here, and here." He stabbed his index finger into the map. "Anybody up here know that?"

The sheriff glanced at Hernandez.

"When an injured animal is being hunted," Ben said, "what does he do?"

"He hides," Hernandez said.

"Or attacks," Ben said. "If these guys were anywhere near him, he would've attacked already. He's in one of those fucking caves."

"Did you read your own medical report?"

"I can't just sit around on this, Lieutenant," Ben said, looking Hernandez in the eyes. "You understand?" He thought Hernandez would get it, thought he'd understand all that Ben felt he had to make up for. "Let me do my job. I'm going into the canyon," Ben said, turning to walk away from Hernandez. "You'd have to arrest me to stop me. You going to do that?"

DOWN INTO THE SINKS, LIKE a hole in the earth swallowing the land. The horse was skittish on the way down, balking at Ben's tugs on the bit, dancing around snakes sunning themselves in the sun-bleached dirt. Five minutes earlier, Ben had grabbed his service revolver, hand-cuffs, and his Viper fins cap out of the truck. He snagged a walkie-talkie from the command post while Barrow's men set him up with one of the sheriff department's horses. Hernandez railed about insubordination, threatened him with a desk job. The lieutenant could be a tough bastard, but he was smart, too. Arrest your own officer, the hero, and lose the serial? No.

Ben was supposed to meet up with the MEU riders at the bottom of the canyon, some two hundred feet down a switchback cattle trail that cut through manzanita groves and ears of prickly pear cactus. High above him, a sheriff's Bell and an Anaheim Police Defender floated circles around each other. It was hot now, the midmorning sun radiating off the exposed earth. The air stank of coyote mint and sagebrush, and even with the hat he had to squint through the brightness, watching the shadows beneath the trees, scanning the needle grass for any movement.

Nothing.

He found the Ventura guys clustered together in the shade of an oak grove, a couple of them smoking cigarettes, all of them looking strung out for lack of sleep. The horses were tied to tree trunks, their heads hung low with exhaustion. The sergeant in charge, Powell, and another MEU were consulting a map spread out across a boulder. When Ben trotted into the grove, Powell turned to watch him come, looking like a man who has just been told he's doing a shitty job.

"Barrow says you got some theory," he said.

SOMEONE IS COMING FOR YOU

By the time the sun was up he was high above the policemen, crawling among truck-sized boulders, his left hand smudging rust red prints on the rocks as he climbed. The sun was a hole cut out of the sky, sucking him into its white heat. The land tilted off-balance and was teetering in the sky. The canyon spread below him, the earth's guts exposed in limestone breaks as though the land were sinking into the ground. The men on the horses with the rifles were getting closer to the steep trail that took him up to the cliffs. He could hear them now, down in the valley, the snorting horses, the electric radio voices echoing off the canyon walls.

The boulders were like things dropped from the sky, shaken loose from the stars—bulbous and sharp, specks in the rock sparkling in the sun. The string holding his head above his shoulders had spun out into the white air, and he could see a cave above him, a dark mouth between rocks. He wedged his toes into the canyon wall, pulled himself up by the fingertips of his good arm, and crawled inside the mouth of the cave, dust on his tongue, an animal piss sour that tasted yellow in his mind. He curled into the corner of the cave where it was cold and lay in the dust and breathed the earth inside of himself, and for some reason he remembered the boy.

He had been hidden in the camp late at night, half asleep on the old mattress, when the boy came through the door. It was one of the boys from the pickers' camp, Mexican or Honduran, his dark skin and brown eyes. He'd watched this boy with another one in the orange groves. He'd been sleeping there once, hidden behind a picker's cart when he heard them, and he watched them kiss in the circle of shade beneath a tree. He liked to watch them, liked the way they touched each other. It reminded him of someone, the person who had said she was his mother; the one with the little holes in her arm who sometimes came into the basement and stroked the back of his head; the one who pressed her lips to his forehead; the one who stopped coming.

When the boy saw him in the camp the other night, he'd stumbled back toward the door.

"I thought you were someone else," the boy said.

"I know," he said. No one ever expected him.

The boy stared at him, trying to piece his face together. He knew he was strange-looking to them, knew his face was something that frightened people.

"Did someone else come here," the boy said, "looking for me?"

He noticed the gun then, hanging from the boy's right hand.

"No."

"No one?" the boy said, starting to shake. He was tall, his shoulders broad and straining his shirt with muscle. If he'd wanted to choke the boy, he wouldn't have been strong enough. "He said he'd be here."

"No," he said. "No one came. No one comes when you need them."

The wind shook the cabin, dust skittering across the floor.

"I need to talk to him," the boy said. He was crying now, running his fingers through his hair.

He had stood up and stepped toward the boy, felt something strange for him, something soft. He wanted to touch the boy, to feel the heat of his skin. He knew what it was to be left alone. Then the boy pointed the gun at him. The gun was shaking in the boy's hand, but the boy wasn't going to shoot him. The muzzle jumped around in the air and the boy was crying. When he put his hand on the boy's shoulder the boy shoved him against the wall. Then the boy stumbled out the door of the cabin into the roaring wind. He followed the boy through the orange grove shadows and down the moonlit white path, angry now that he'd been shoved, wanting to choke him.

He tracked the boy to the edge of the strawberry field and then crouched down in the needle grass near the irrigation ditch. The boy stumbled into the field, a tall shadow cut against the electric light of the city. In the middle of the field, among the dead strawberries, he sat down. He could see the boy, a blotch of black upsetting the rows of fruit, rocking back and forth, hugging his knees. Then the boy stood suddenly and paced up and down the row, the gun swinging from his hand. Twice he raised the gun to his head, before dropping it to his side. He paced in the row like an animal stuck in a cage, shifting the gun to his left hand, back into his right, and then into his left, and then suddenly, mid-step, he jerked the gun to his head and a pop of spark exploded, the sound carried away on the wind.

He sat there on the edge of the field, the wind blowing the needle grass against his arms, the city lights shimmering in the hot night, the clump of dark where the boy had fallen between the strawberry rows. Most people wanted to live; they fought him, dug their nails into his arms, kicked at his back, their whole body writhing to take another breath. He didn't know how to think about this boy, didn't know what it meant that he'd killed himself, and he sat there until morning thinking—the boy alone in the field for hours, the yellow light bleeding into the sky, the silent pickers going down the rows until one of them screamed.

Now they were coming for him, the men with their guns. They hadn't come for his eleven-year-old self, but now he'd done things that made him worthy of being found. They had sounded closer, but now, from inside the cave, their voices began to grow faint. He smiled to himself; they hadn't found him. But his head hurt and his vision was tunneled and he was in a hole in the ground again, deep in the cold mouth of the earth, and he could still just barely hear them—their radios, the horse snorts, a chain rattling from a saddle, all of it going the other way, fading down the length of the canyon floor. They were coming for him finally, but he crouched in the dark, sure they would not know where to look.

19

POWELL SHOWED HIM THE HANDPRINT PRESSED INTO THE TRUNK of one of the oak trees. Then they all were up in the saddle, single-filing it down the old cattle trail. It was hot as hell now, even in the mottled shade of trees, and the dust kicked up by hooves tasted like singed chalk. In the bright midday light, the vision in Ben's dilated eye was overexposed and washed out. Still his good eye kept the world in focus, and he found himself closing his injured eye to ease the ache in his head. A second handprint smeared against a boulder was fifty yards down the trail. From there, they followed a smattering of blood, like paint dripped from a brush, until they came to a small puddle, still wet in the dirt. Ben hopped off the horse and knelt on the trail, squinting through the manzanita. There were no other signs, nothing—no blood on the leaves, no broken branches, no footprints in the underbrush to indicate where he'd gone.

"Nothing for another five to six hundred yards," Powell said. "And then it starts up again. Like he lifted off the ground and flew there."

Ben glanced up at the cliffs, rising white in the sun. He hadn't been in this canyon for years, but he didn't think they were near the first cave yet. That's what had startled him awake this morning: the caves. His senior year when everything in his life was blowing up and he didn't want to be found—by Wakeland, by his mother, even by Rachel—he hiked up here alone. They'd find him at the beach, if they bothered to look, but not up here. A couple days after blowing states, when he thought he was going to lose his mind if he set foot on school property again, he hiked up here and climbed a coyote path up the steep cliffs. It was dangerous and he might have fallen, but that just made it better. He found one of the caves that afternoon and sat in the shade of it, trying to figure out what he was going to do next.

"Think he's got some kind of tourniquet working," Ben said now. "Probably had to retie it here."

"You must've tore a pretty big hole into him."

"Not big enough," Ben said. "You say six hundred yards up?"

"About," Powell said. "Same thing. Trickle of blood, but more up there. Like the spigot opened up and then closed. Tourniquet makes sense."

They passed the dead deer on the edge of the trail, a few jokes thrown around. In ten minutes they came upon another puddle of the serial's blood, congealed now, with flies swarming the edges. Ben scanned the cliffs. Two of the MEU guys did, too, using their rifle scopes. This was it, Ben was sure of it. He remembered the steep cliffs, the way the limestone breaks folded together like pleats.

"You can't see it from here," Ben said, "but there's a cave up there."

"Up there?" Powell said.

"Nothing real big," Ben said. "Bobcat den, shade for coyote in the afternoon."

"You think he climbed up there, with one good arm?"

"I think he'd use his teeth if he had to, with us on his heels."

BLOOD SMEARED AGAINST AN IRONWOOD tree. Snapped manzanita branch. A couple of faint footprints: Vans, eight and a half. They had him.

They were on foot now, four of them—Powell and two MEUs, one named Davis and the other Rutter—hacking through brush and cactus clumps, ironwood branches and tangles of sagebrush. Their guns drawn, safeties off. The trail was faint, but it was there—a deer trail leading to the base of the cliffs.

When they reached the cliff, a thin white line threaded up the wall of the canyon. A bobcat trail, coyote maybe. There they found a third handprint, like a petroglyph against the rock.

"Jesus," Rutter said. "Who is this guy?"

The limestone was soft. You could dig your fingers into it, carve the edge of your boot into the rock. But it could crumble underfoot, give way with the grip of your hand. Ben remembered this climb as he wedged his toe into a foothold, fifty feet above the canyon floor now, the way little landslides gave way underfoot, the way dust and rock fell from handholds and scoured your eyes. Davis was fifteen feet below him and Rutter ten below Davis, both of them staggered along the cliffside to keep out of the slush of sand and rock falling with each push up the wall.

The trail was steep, rock climbing the first seventy-five feet, but after that it leveled until it was like hiking a steep staircase. Still, when he looked back to see where Davis and Rutter were, the effect was dizzying—the land below felt tilted off-balance, the horizon out on the edge of the blue sky seemed to slide toward the ocean. Ben's head pounded now, his heart thumped his injured eye. But his body felt strong. His lungs were conditioned from holding his breath. His arms and shoulders, muscled from body surfing, lifted him upward, even as Davis and Rutter fell behind.

The sheriff's Bell came shuddering up the canyon, hovering below the lip of the ridge. An officer leaned out the open side door, one booted foot on the landing skid, his sniper rifle strapped across his chest. They were following them up the cliffside, ready to shoot the killer if Ben flushed him out.

Two hundred feet up, it walled out again, and Ben had to carve out toeholds, scratch away little crescents for finger pulls. If he lost a foothold here, it was a long, body-beating slide to the bottom. He was close, though; he could see the dark smudge in the limestone where the cave was carved into the rock. He found a lip to rest on, and watched the cave entrance, hoping light penetrated deeply enough to see inside. But the sun was already pushing west, and shadows fell across the opening. Blind. He'd have to go in blind.

The helicopter spun a circle above the canyon, its rotor wash spraying dust across the cliff wall.

"Get the chopper out of here," Ben called into his walkie-talkie.

In the noise of the rotors, Ben could just make out Powell's voice. Then the copter tilted its nose and spun high above the canyon, ready to dive down if necessary.

Ben edged along the wall toward the cave entrance.

"Wait for backup." Powell's voice scratched through the walkie-talkie.

He snapped the walkie-talkie off, not wanting the killer to hear it, and glanced down to see Davis and Rutter pulling themselves up the cliffside, still sixty feet or more below. Then he was on the threshold of the opening just to the left. His revolver drawn, he watched for movement. Nothing, an unnerving stillness—no birds, no buzzing insects. Nausea roiled his stomach, but he swallowed it down. He slid his back up against the wall and hoisted himself into the darkness of the cave.

Something lunged at him—a flash of movement, a slap of hands against his chest, a clenched wet grip on his neck. Ben stumbled backward, digging his heels into the dirt to keep from pitching over the edge of the cliffside. He ripped a hand from his throat and flung the thing off him—pointing the muzzle of his gun blindly into the darkness until his eyes adjusted and he saw him, the killer, cornered at the back wall of the cave, balancing on his haunches.

He was a shocking sight—shirtless and covered in his own blood, as small as a child but malformed. Crouched as it was, his body—all ribs and wiry muscles—looked like a coiled spring. The killer watched him, but his eyes seemed unfocused, as though he were staring out blindly. He spoke a gibberish, a ramble of inarticulate vowels and consonants.

"There's nowhere to go," Ben said, the gun shaking in his hand.

The killer's eyes seemed to adjust then, locking on Ben. "You knew where to look." His voice sounded almost pleased, an air of relief in it, Ben thought.

"Come with me, no bullshit," Ben said, "and we'll get you to a hospital."

Maybe it was Ben's beat-up head or the adrenaline still pumping from the attack, but the gun wouldn't stop shaking.

"Then you'll lock me up."

"Yes," Ben said.

The killer spoke gibberish again, turning his face away from Ben. There was something almost intimate about the voice, as though he were talking to another person inside of himself. "Throw away the key," he said suddenly in English.

"I know what happened to you," Ben said. "I saw the basement."

"Everyone knows what happened to me," he said, a sharpness in the voice now.

"Those people," Ben said. "The ones you killed were innocent."

The killer smiled disdainfully. "Innocent," he said. "Innocent, innocent . . ." spinning his good hand in the air now, "innocent, innocent, innocent . . ." until the word broke down into meaningless sounds.

"They weren't the ones that knew what was happening to you. They didn't do anything to you."

"Innocent, innocent, innocent . . . No one's innocent." He ran a bloodied hand through his hair. "I wanted the woman next door," he said. He was panting with exhaustion now. "She saw me when he brought me home from the doctor." He paused, his breath growing shallower. "But I couldn't go back to that place."

Ben remembered the elderly woman watering the fuchsias next door to the Norwalk house. "Those people never bothered us," he remembered her saying.

"To punish her?" Ben said. Killing her would have made sense: a clear motive, revenge for letting it happen to him. But not the others. "The last girl was twenty. She didn't do anything to deserve your punishment."

"I needed them," he said. He let out a long breath. "You know what it feels like? To take them?"

A rush of feeling overcame Ben; he remembered his fingers around Wakeland's windpipe, the incredible adrenaline high he felt knowing he could kill the man.

"No," Ben said.

In the days since, when he remembered the terror in Wakeland's eyes, Ben had buzzed with the feeling, like the aftereffects of a powerful drug.

"You do," the killer said. "You know what it is to take someone. To make them nothing."

He shuffled forward.

"Stay where you are," Ben said, the gun pointed straight at the killer's chest, his finger hooked on the trigger. Ben was terrified of the feeling, terrified that some part of him understood this killer.

"You're the one who shot me," the killer said.

"Yes," Ben said, "and I'll do it again if you move another inch."

"Wade," a voice called just below the cave. "You up there?"

"You're me then," the killer said, sitting down in the dust.

He'd come up to finish the job—to arrest the killer, to find him dead, maybe. But what he really wanted was the satisfaction of blasting a final hole into him, that was true; that was why he'd driven up here this morning, that was why he'd climbed up this canyon wall. And he had maybe a few seconds to do it, to pull that trigger, before Davis was witness to it. He had been attacked; no one would question him.

"You're my me," the killer said. Then he leaned back against the cave wall and spoke to himself with the incoherent syllables, as though trying to calm himself.

No. Ben wasn't this malformed thing, this murderer. He wasn't.

"Wade?" The voice closer this time.

The killer looked toward the sound, watched the entrance, his eyes blinking slowly.

"You can walk out of here with me," Ben said. "Or we can put another bullet into you right now."

"See," the killer said, "you do know what it feels like, to take someone." He let out a long breath, as though clearing the air from his body. "I can see it in your eyes."

Then the killer bit into the bloodied shirt wrapped around his arm, unraveling the knot with his teeth and good hand. When he did, the blood pumped out of the hole, slicking his arm. Ben should have held him down, cuffed him, and retied the tourniquet.

"There was a boy," the killer said, his voice growing quiet. "In the field."

"What?"

A shuffle of feet kicked up dust at the entrance to the cave. "Wade," Davis said, out of breath. "Got anything?"

"Stay there," Ben said to Davis. "A boy?" he stepped toward the serial. "Did you kill him?"

The killer smiled and shook his head slowly, watching his blood run down his arm, puddling useless around his hip.

"Fight or flight," he said.

"Did you kill him?" Ben said, kneeling in front of him now. He should have retied the tourniquet, but it was too late now. The killer's breath was strained and smelled like congealed syrup—the sweet stink of coming death.

"Jesus," Davis said, kneeling now at the opening of the cave, his gun drawn. "That's him? That's the guy?"

"Did you kill him?"

"There was a boy . . ." the killer said, his body slumped in the dirt, his voice fading now. He gazed up at Ben, but his eyes were unfocused and lost, veiled by what was closing between them. Ben leaned in to hear, trying to make out the words, but he heard only a withering of confused syllables that revealed nothing.

20

THREE DAYS AFTER THEY'D HELICOPTERED THE SERIAL'S BODY
out of the Sinks, bled out from Ben's gunshot wound, Hernandez called and asked if Ben wanted to ride along. They'd
gotten the warrant, they'd searched Wakeland's apartment, they'd
found the box in the back of the closet, even in the chaos of press
conferences following the capture of the killer. Ben was surprised.
He thought he had more time—thought it would sit on the back
burner with so many resources on the serial. He had spent the better
part of the past two days speaking to the media, fielding questions
about how he got the shot off that would eventually kill the serial. It'd
only been in the dark hours of the morning he'd been able to think
about Wakeland, about Lucero and Phillip.

"You've been keeping busy," Ben said. He was riding shotgun in
Hernandez's unmarked cruiser, following Marco's patrol car down
Serrano Canyon, where Ben had chased the serial's Tercel just last
week.

Hernandez nodded. "We can't sit on this one, not with that other
kid out there."

It was late afternoon, and Ben thought they'd pick Wakeland up
at his house or at the apartment, somewhere quiet and discreet, but

Marco's cruiser turned left onto Conquistador Road and he realized
they were headed toward the high school. When they pulled into the
parking lot, there were three black-and-whites parked in front of the
swim complex and two news vans parked along the curb.

"Making a show of this, huh?" Ben said, hearing the accusation
in his own voice.

Hernandez glanced at him, barely contained frustration in his
eyes, as he pulled into a parking spot. "Right now all we can charge
him with are dirty pictures," Hernandez said, slamming the gear shift
into park. "Helen Huntsman's talked to us; we're working on the AP,
Rutledge, but it's not enough yet. We can put him away for the pictures, but I want to get him on everything. You get it?"

Ben nodded.

"I want whoever else is out there to see this," Hernandez said.
"Maybe someone will come forward. I want everyone looking at him
when we walk him out of here, want everyone to know exactly what
he is."

From the cruiser, Ben watched Hernandez and Marco huddle
with the officers at the front door of the complex before they streamed
inside. Through the fence, Ben could see the boys swimming the
lanes, Wakeland stalking the opposite pool deck, calling out ca-
dences.

It didn't matter, Ben had finally decided yesterday, whether or
not the serial killed Lucero. Ben would never know for sure anyway;
the evidence was the evidence and it told an incomplete story—
which, to be honest, was almost always the way it was with evidence.
Beyond a shadow of a doubt? There was always doubt, even when
you—or at least Ben—knew you were right. Lucero had been threatened by Wakeland, Lucero had been upset, Lucero had found the
gun. Whatever did or did not happen after that, there were still those
pictures Natasha discovered in the closet, still the documented fact
of that ugliness. It didn't matter if there was actual blood on Wakeland's hands; there were other ways of draining the life out of someone. Regardless, Ben thought he was right about this. If there was a

God up there, or someone alive who knew exactly what happened the night Lucero died, he'd let them decide, let them judge him.

Now the officers were on the pool deck, Marco spinning Wakeland around, cuffing the man's hands behind his back, Hernandez flanked by three uniforms while he read Wakeland his Miranda rights.

They disappeared a few moments inside the complex before the doors opened and Hernandez and Marco emerged with Wakeland between them, his head bowed. Two reporters converged on Wakeland, shoving microphones in his face. Boys had jumped out of the pool, towels wrapped around their waists, and stood at the fence, watching. Phillip was there, too, his fists clutching the metal fence, his face awash in shock. Ben got out of the car then and stood in the parking lot, watching Wakeland, wanting the man to see him at this moment. Marco and one of the uniforms glanced at Ben, but the coach would not raise his bowed head. At Marco's cruiser, Hernandez spun Wakeland around and lifted the man's head by the chin and made him look at Ben. Ben stared at the coach, but Wakeland averted his eyes, watching the bars of the fence that separated the parking lot from the pool complex. Then Hernandez pushed Wakeland's head into the backseat of Marco's cruiser and they were gone—no lights, no sirens, the championship banners waving quietly in the ocean breeze.

Twenty-seven hundred dollars. That's what it cost to get the coffin and the shipping crate, the plane ticket on United to Mexico City, and the hearse to carry it to the cargo bay at LAX. Ten minutes to drain his savings account. Ben promised he'd drive Esperanza and Santiago to the coroner's office to claim the body, promised them no immigration police would be there, promised them that it would only be them, Ben, and his good friend who was the medical examiner.

When he arrived at the camp the morning after Wakeland's arrest, Esperanza and Santiago were standing on the edge of the field, dressed in what could only be described as their Sunday best. Ben got out of the truck and opened the door for Esperanza, who just stood there on the edge of the field, eyes fixed on him.

"Please," he said, gesturing toward the passenger door, lightly touching the small of her back.

A stinging slap clapped the healing bone around his eye. When Ben got his vision back, Esperanza was facing him, her right hand still raised in the air. She glared at him, her eyes watering now, and whispered something to Santiago.

"For your silence," Santiago translated.

Ben nodded. If that's all she was going to give him, he was getting off easy.

"Please," he said, gesturing again toward the seat. "Please, let's go get your son."

She crossed in front of him to take her seat but then paused, turned to him again, and touched her palm to his cheek, a small blessing before slipping into the car.

SANTIAGO LEFT THE COPY OF the *Rancho Santa Elena World News* on the bench seat of the truck. He'd walked into town this morning to get a gallon of water, he had told Ben on the ride to the coroner, when he saw Wakeland's face on the front page of the paper. LEGEND-ARY LOCAL COACH CHARGED WITH SEXUAL EXPLOITATION OF MINORS screamed the headline. Ben's name was mentioned in the paper, Santiago had said. That's how they knew.

After claiming Lucero's body and dropping off Santiago and Esperanza back at the camp, Ben pulled over in the bike lane and read the article. He was mentioned as one of two men who had accused Wakeland of sexual abuse. The other accuser was said to be anonymous.

He drove then, over to the Texaco station, and called Hernandez from the pay phone. He wasn't ready to walk into the station, not today at least.

"Who's anonymous?" he asked.

"You know how this works, Ben," Hernandez said. "I can't tell you. That's why it's anonymous."

"It's Tucker Preston, right?" Ben said. He hoped it was Tucker. Wanted to believe he could do it.

"We interviewed that freshman kid, Phillip," Hernandez said, changing the subject.

Ben's heart jumped into his throat.

"Looks like we got it in time," Hernandez said. "I'll keep you in the loop when I can, but you don't get any police privilege on this, no inside information. I don't want to compromise anything on this one. So keep the hell out."

THAT AFTERNOON, BEN DROVE OUT to the Wedge to ride some waves. Body surfing wasn't medically approved, he was sure of that, but the cut around his eye was nearly healed and he needed to swim, needed to be submerged in the cold silence of the water. He listened to News Radio 1070 on the way down, a special report about the serial. The reporter interviewed people on the street, and they recounted their terror with an excitement that verged on pleasure. Their relief was so absolute, you thought nothing terrible could ever happen again. It was finished. No sensational trial, no dramatic testimony—just a three-month burst of violence that would soon become a fearful memory. But there would be more, Ben knew; there were always more. There were a lot of malformed people out there to fear. Some of them lived down the street, some of them right next door. They seemed like you, except for that ugly thing they tried to hide.

The swell was small, two to three feet, coming out of the north, and its insignificance kept the surfers away. Before the sun dove toward the horizon, Ben was alone swimming toward the break, the water glassy and clean, turning into the tiny peaks and riding quiet lefts toward the beach.

When he was finished, he called her from a pay phone at the beach. She had been smart enough to wait and let him make the call, and when he came up the drive just after sunset Natasha was sitting on the porch, waiting for him. She took his hand when he got to her, held it a moment, and then let go. He sat down next to her a few inches away, not sure where the lines of demarcation existed now in this part of his life. Puffs of black bulldozer exhaust rose above the ridge of Quail Hill. He could hear the clangs of the machines erasing the hard evidence of a past that would soon exist only in memory. Maybe he'd forget some of it, maybe it would always be there, but he was here now, in this present, and he needed to live in it.

She took him inside and dabbed the cut on his eye with alcohol. It burned and she blew on it to cool it down. Then she kissed him and he kissed her, his mouth willing, his body, too. She pulled his coat from his right and then left shoulder and ran her hands down the sides of his back, and he shuddered.

She smiled at him and guided him toward bed. Her fingers found the top button of his shirt and he lay there, still, as she worked at the next button and then the next. When she neared the final button, the familiar tension came into his body, a sort of haunting inside, and he softly squeezed her hand and pulled it away.

"There's no one here," she said. "It's just you and me."

He nodded and unhooked the last button then and let her pull him free of the shirt. He shook once and something caught in the back of his throat. She kissed him there, on the soft indentation of his neck, her hand working down his chest.

"Just you and me," she said. "You and me."

Acknowledgments

Writing may be a solitary act, but no author finishes a book without a community of people who offer support, encouragement, honest criticism, patience, and sometimes stiff drinks.

I'm indebted to all my colleagues at Villanova University for their professional support, but also for their friendship. I'm particularly thankful to Evan Radcliffe, who could not have been a more caring and thoughtful department chair. Thanks to Joseph Lennon for his editorial insight, and for saying this to me one cold winter night over dinner: "You'll get this book done, because you have to get it done." To Jean Lutes for her friendship, her wise counsel, and her shared love of gin martinis. Gracias to my fellow Southern California expats who helped me keep one foot on the "best coast" while writing in the east: Lisa Sewell, Kamran Javadizadeh, and Alice Dailey.

All my gratitude goes out to my editor, Kate Medina, who waited all of the Obama administration for this novel. Thanks, too, to Gina Centrello for her enthusiastic support of this book. I'm indebted to everyone at Random House who helped shepherd this story through all its various forms: Derrill Hagood, Anna Pitoniak, Erica Gonzalez, Janet Wygal, Avideh Bashirrad, Sally Marvin, Jennifer Garza, Samantha Leach, Sanyu Dillon, Leigh Marchant, and everyone else in-house whose fingerprints are stamped on these pages.

Thank you to my wonderful agent, Dorian Karchmar, whose patience, intelligent criticism, and unwavering support kept me going when I was ready to give up writing and take up the ukulele.

I'm lucky to count good readers among my friends and family whose insight and cheerleading helped me keep the faith: Robert Rosenberg, Janet Baker, Adam Davis, Meg Cannon, Craig Rutter, Beth Frede, Dawn Roth, and Kara Cleffi.

And to my dear friend Caren Streb, to whom this book is indebted in immeasurable ways.

Love to my three families, Drew, Larson, and Frede, who endured numerous family visits in which I locked myself in a room and ignored them while working on this book.

All my heart and soul goes to my children, Nathaniel and Adeline, who may one day read this book and wonder, What the heck is wrong with Dad? You both are the greatest things I've helped create.

And big, big love to my wife, Miriam Drew, always my first and toughest reader! Without you, there is no book. Without you, I'm sitting on an iron-stained carpet in a San Francisco apartment, writing terrible poetry about a woman I might one day fall in love with. Thanks for letting me fall in love with you, and for getting me out of the poetry business.

About the Author

ALAN DREW's critically acclaimed debut novel, *Gardens of Water*, has been translated into ten languages and published in nearly two dozen countries. He is a graduate of the Iowa Writers' Workshop, where he was awarded a teaching/writing fellowship. An associate professor of English at Villanova University, where he directs the creative writing program, he lives near Philadelphia with his wife and two children. Learn more about his books at alan-drew.com.